D0449345

A Time to Surrender

Safe Harbor Book Three

SALLY JOHN &
GARY SMALLEY

THOMAS NELSON
Since 1798

NASHVILLE DALLAS MEXICO CITY RIO DE JANEIRO BEIJING

Published in association with Alive Communications, 7680 Goddard Street, Suite 200, Colorado Springs, CO, 80920, www.alivecommunications.com.

Published in Nashville, Tennessee, by Thomas Nelson. Thomas Nelson is a trademark of Thomas Nelson, Inc.

Thomas Nelson, Inc., titles may be purchased in bulk for educational, business, fund-raising, or sales promotional use. For information, please e-mail SpecialMarkets@ThomasNelson.com.

Scripture taken from the HOLY BIBLE, NEW INTERNATIONAL VERSION®, © 1973, 1978, 1984 by International Bible Society. Used by permission of Zondervan Publishing House. All rights reserved.

Publisher's Note: This novel is a work of fiction. Names, characters, places, and incidents are either products of the author's imagination or used fictitiously. All characters are fictional, and any similarity to people living or dead is purely coincidental.

Library of Congress Cataloging-in-Publication Data

John, Sally, 1951–
 A time to surrender / Sally John and Gary Smalley.
  p. cm.—(Safe harbors ; bk. 3)
 ISBN 978-1-59554-430-8 (softcover)
 I. Smalley, Gary. II. Title.
 PS3560.O323T57 2009
813'.54—dc22

2009014752

Printed in the United States of America

09 10 11 12 13 RRD 6 5 4 3 2 1

For our troops and their families

You were taught . . . to put off your old self . . .
to be made new . . . to put on the new self.
—Ephesians 4:22–24

Beaumont Family Tree

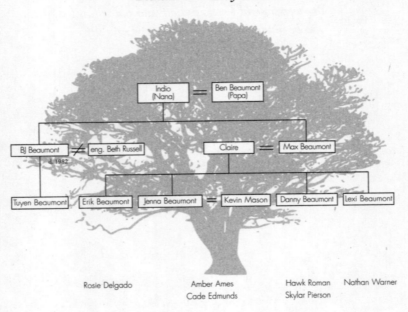

Indio (Nana) = Ben Beaumont (Papa)

BJ Beaumont (d. 1982) ≠ eng. Beth Russell

Claire = Max Beaumont

Tuyen Beaumont | Erik Beaumont | Jenna Beaumont = Kevin Mason | Danny Beaumont | Lexi Beaumont

Rosie Delgado   Amber Ames   Hawk Roman   Nathan Warner
                       Cade Edmunds   Skylar Pierson

The Beaumont family

Ben and Indio—Parents and grandparents.
BJ—Older son, MIA for thirty-five years.
Max and Claire—Younger son and daughter-in-law. Manage the Hacienda Hideaway, a retreat center near San Diego, California.

Max and Claire's four grown children

Erik—Former television news anchor, now a freelance film producer.
Jenna—High-school English teacher. Married to *Kevin Mason*.
Danny—Lexi's twin. Software guru and surfer.
Lexi (Alexis)—Danny's twin. Gardener. Artist.

Others

Kevin Mason—Jenna's husband. A Marine, assigned overseas.
Rosie Delgado—San Diego police officer. Erik's girlfriend.
Tuyen Beaumont—Ben and Indio's granddaughter.
Nathan Warner—Lexi's friend. Journalist.
Skylar Pierson—A newcomer to Hacienda Hideaway.
Amber Ames—Jenna's friend and coworker.
Cade Edmunds—Jenna's principal.
Hawk Roman—Danny's coworker and roommate.

One

Few things unhinged Jenna Beaumont Mason. She could do cool, calm, and collected. She could do serene. She could go with the flow. She could chill.

Honestly, she taught grammar and John Donne's poetry to sixteen-year-olds!

"Jenna Mason."

A rushing noise whistled through her head again. Her ears burned. The base of her throat pulsated in sync with a wildly erratic heartbeat. She flicked her straight black hair off a shoulder.

"Jenna?" Behind the podium onstage, the high school principal, Cade Edmunds, smiled in a gentle, expectant way.

Which was totally out of character for him.

Which totally defined the insanity of the moment.

Jenna sat with ninety-nine other abnormally subdued faculty members in the high school auditorium. Ten of those people, including herself, were related to military personnel, all currently deployed overseas. Ten teachers who had an infinite number of other things to do before the first day of school *tomorrow*. Ten teachers who had countless *better* things to do than sit around while their principal singled them out for a salute to the armed forces—aka *pity party*.

Cade extended his hand, palm up, waiting.

Beside her, the sophomore lit teacher touched Jenna's arm. The woman's eyes looked like overfilled bathtubs.

Evidently Jenna's fairy godmother had taken a hike. There would *poof*ing her from this wretched scene. Jenna rose to her full five- height, careful not to slouch, and stood rigidly next to her seat.

"As most of you know," Cade said, "Jenna's husband is Kevin ason, last year's winning varsity football coach and PE teacher here at Sundance High. He's a Marine, serving in . . ."

Jenna tuned out her boss and glanced around. Two others stood with her. That left seven to go. Seven more loved ones to name along with their branch, rank, unit, platoon, or whatnot numbers. Seven more foreign, unpronounceable locations to reference.

John Donne had it all wrong. "No man is an island"? Yeah, right. She disagreed. She was totally an island, hemmed in by huge swells of dread. The warm fuzzies directed her way at that moment could not build bridges over such waves. Applause could not warm her bed or explain why he left or fill the lonely dinner hour night after night.

Jenna blinked rapidly, focused on Cade Edmunds, and blinked some more.

The principal was a good guy. Great with the students, respected by his staff, liked by most parents. His tearing her inside out in public, however, was the most idiotic thing he'd ever done.

She remained deadpan throughout his presentation and imagined chiding him. The mental exercise worked. She made it through seven more intros, ears still aflame but serenity intact. Yes, Jenna Beaumont Mason could do cool.

And then the applause evolved into a standing ovation.

Okay. So her mascara was getting smudged. Not a problem. Jenna Beaumont Mason could do damage control, no sweat.

The scolding and makeup repair were both put on hold. As soon as Cade ended the meeting, several teachers surrounded Jenna, offering hugs and words of gratitude and concern. Finally the last one stepped front and center.

"Jenna! Oh!"

The woman was vaguely familiar. She had short, bouncy blonde curls and a perky demeanor to match. Wasn't she a cheerleader coach?

"Jenna, I am so, so sorry I didn't get with you last spring when Kevin left, but Joey shipped about the same time."

Joey?

"You know how crazy life is when that's all happening. I mean, to tell your husband good-bye for a year—" She mashed her lips together, shook her head, and then gave her shoulders a quick shrug. "So anyway. You made it through the summer, too, and here we are. Trust me, work is a godsend. At least it always has been for me."

"Mm." Jenna hummed a noncommittal reply that got lost in the woman's monologue.

"Put me in a lab with a bunch of kids and I'm content as a gecko with a cricket in its gullet."

Science department. Biology. Ann, Angie, Abby, Alison?

"Of course when we cover explosives, the kids are all over it. They say 'Mrs. Ames, why can't we build just a little bomb?' Then I've got Joey right there in the room with me. It's his specialty. Bombs, explosives. Not that I tell them that, but you know what I mean. I can't help but imagine what he's up to over there."

Amber Ames. Chemistry.

"Jenna, did you notice that out of the ten of us introduced, you and I were the only ones with spouses in the military? Everyone else had an in-law or a cousin. I bet this is your first, huh?"

"First?"

"Deployment." She pointed at one of her own eyes. "I gave up mascara the second time Joey went."

"*Second?*"

"This is his third. That I know about, anyway." She leaned toward Jenna and lowered her voice. "He's a Navy SEAL. What am I going to do?"

Jenna felt an arm brush hers and turned to see Cade.

He said, "Amber, you could join up."

"Ha! No disrespect, Mr. Edmunds, but those guys are certifiable. Stop laughing."

"Well, you are married to one."

"Which makes me only half-certifiable." Amber grinned. "Besides, I could never do the chin-ups. Jenna, let's get together and compare notes sometime, 'kay? Maybe over dinner. That's always the worst time of day for me. Gotta go!" She hurried off, waving a hand backward over her shoulder.

Cade chuckled. "No disrespect, but talking to her is like taking a drink from a fire hydrant."

Jenna shrugged. Fire hydrant or whatever, the chat with Amber had flushed the desire to lambaste Cade right out of her.

She grabbed her shoulder bag from the seat. "I better get to work."

"Jen." Cade touched her elbow, lightly, briefly.

She turned to face him.

"I know you're ticked at me."

Lowering her head, she unzipped her bag and rummaged through it—for what exactly, she had no clue. "I'm just generally ticked at life these days."

"You've taught in my building for six years. I know when you're ticked at me in particular."

She jerked the zipper shut and met his gaze.

It was rumored that Cade Edmunds bled ice water. Hence the nickname Mr. Ice Guy. His aggressive demeanor supported the bad-guy rep. Unwavering steel-gray eyes and biceps that even her husband admired did not exactly mitigate the image. His naturally balding head—already, at thirty-nine—only added a layer of toughness. Not to mention the stories of his off-campus encounters with gang members and gun-toting parents.

"And," he went on, "I know you hate the sort of attention I just directed your way."

"Is there a point to this conversation?"

"The point is you and Kevin are making a huge sacrifice. Your personal life went down the tubes when he shipped out."

She begged to differ. It happened the day her husband reenlisted. Yes, she had married a Marine. He wore his dress uniform in the wedding—gorgeous as all get out, but within weeks it was packed away, put away for good. Or so she thought. Then along came a war—and a husband compelled to serve his country.

"Jenna, you're on my team. When you're injured, I call for reinforcements. That's what this salute to the military was all about. We are here for you. The attention was necessary to drive the message home, to you and everyone else."

Rah, rah. "Got it, coach." She gave a thumbs-up.

He closed his eyes and exhaled audibly. "Okay." His tone hushed, he looked at her. "Just promise me one thing."

The tough guy vanished. Jenna felt her control slip again.

"Promise you will tell me when things get unbearable. When you want to pitch an unabridged Webster's at some kid's head, talk to me first."

She shifted her weight to the other foot and glanced around. The auditorium had emptied.

"Can you promise?"

"Okay."

He waited.

"Okay, okay! I promise."

"And I promise I won't hassle you if you want extra time off. Or if you need to leave spur of the moment. Hey, in a pinch, I'll even sub."

"Cade! I'm fine!"

"Yeah." He paused. "Don't they make waterproof eye stuff?"

"Oh, go take a hike."

"Good idea." He gave her a brief smile, spun on his heel, and walked across the front of the auditorium. "I think," he said without turning, "Amber will be a good friend for you."

Now he was choosing her friends?

Still without a backward glance, he called out, "Stop rolling your eyes, Mrs. Mason!" The door swished shut behind him.

So the rumor was true: Edmunds had eyes in the back of his head. And they were watching over her. Jenna felt the tug of a smile.

TWO

Skylar Pierson poised her finger at the doorbell, inhaled deeply, and blew out through pooched lips.

"Okay, Skylar," she spoke aloud to herself. "Here we"—she pressed the bell—"go."

The electronic device struck her as an anachronism on the obviously old, patched-up adobe wall. But then the whole place seemed to have hit a time warp. The hacienda and Wild West setting were straight out of a Zorro flick, pre-Antonio era.

The door opened. A middle-aged woman flashed a smile, full-on Diane Keaton–esque. "Hi." She glanced beyond Skylar's shoulder toward the driveway, a frazzled expression chasing away the smile. "You're not the delivery man . . . person."

"Uh, no. I'm here about the ad."

"I really, really wish he'd show up." Sunlight glinted off the woman's silver-rimmed glasses as she went up on tiptoe and peered sideways at the road. "You said ad? What ad?"

"For cook." Skylar slid her thumbs under the shoulder straps of her backpack and shifted its weight.

"Cook?" Now Diane swung her full attention onto Skylar. "*Cook?*"

"Uh, is this the Hacienda Hideaway Retreat Center? The sign out front says—"

"Yeah, that's us, but I didn't know we placed an ad for a cook. Where did you read it?"

"In *The West Coast Retreat Gazette*."

"Really?"

Uh-oh. Twenty-Questions Diane was leading them nowhere fast.

The woman chuckled. "Well, obviously, *really*. You found us, didn't you? I'm new at this. So then, I assume you cook and you're looking for a job."

"Do you need a cook? Or housekeeper?"

Again the quick smile beamed. "I'm Claire Beaumont." She put out her hand.

Skylar shook it, wishing the woman would just answer the question. "I'm Skylar Pierson. Skylar with an *a*."

"Welcome to the Hacienda Hideaway, Skylar. Come on inside. My mother-in-law will want to meet you."

Skylar followed Claire Beaumont across a narrow mudroom, its walls lined with coat hooks. A half-open door revealed a laundry room. They passed through another doorway and entered a huge, open space. A kitchen filled one side, family room and dining trappings the other.

Curious. All the appliances and furniture looked brand-new: shiny stainless steel, crisply bright upholstery, and wood that reflected like a mirror.

"Indio," Claire said.

On the other side of a stone fireplace, a woman in a padded rocker looked up from the book on her lap. She resembled every Native American grandma squaw portrayed in a western, complete with round face and a single thick braid of hair.

As they approached her, Claire said, "Do you know anything about an ad for a cook in some gazette?"

A tiny smile played at the woman's mouth. "I might."

"Mm-hmm. This is Skylar with an *a*. Skylar, this is my mother-in-law, Indio Beaumont."

"Hello, Skylar." Indio held out her left hand, tilting her head at the right one resting atop the book. It was wrapped to the wrist in a cast. "Tripped over a rock."

Skylar grasped the offered hand. "Hello."

"I placed that ad two years ago."

"I found the gazette in a stack of old papers, in a coffeehouse in Seattle. It was torn, the date was missing. Uh, I guess you don't—do you still even need a cook?"

Without responding, Indio released her hand. Her eyes were bottomless black pools, communicating the sense of an old soul, of an ancient wisdom. They held no threat. Skylar understood she could speak her mind and was probably expected to do so.

At last the old woman said, "You didn't call first."

"No, I didn't call. I prefer to feel the energy of a place before I even consider asking for an interview. So"—she shrugged—"I just stopped by."

"And decided to stay a bit." Indio's eyes twinkled; the crow's feet bunched. "The energy is more yang than yin, then?"

Skylar couldn't help but grin. "I'd say that's a fair assumption."

"Take off that heavy pack and have a seat."

"Thank you." She hefted her bag to the hardwood floor. Sitting in a low swivel chair, she glanced around.

Despite its size and upscale touch, the room delivered a snug ambience. A warm cinnamon scent lingered. The rich *ticktock* of a big, old-fashioned wall clock added a rhythm. There were braided rugs, plaid upholstery, and afghans. A sofa and loveseat formed an L in front of the fireplace. Her chair and the woman's rocker flanked a tall window that overlooked the front yard, parking lot, and distant hills. Sunlight flooded through its southern exposure.

Claire set a glass of iced tea on the end table between the chairs. "I thought you might be thirsty. It's chamomile ginger."

Herbal, no less. *Trippy.* "Thanks."

She looked more closely at the wall behind Indio. Again she was struck with the collision of time periods. There in the middle of an

Ethan Allen showroom and Wolfgang Puck's kitchen was an exposed adobe wall. Literally covered with religious artifacts, it might have been transported up the hill from one of the historical California missions.

Indio caught her eye. "Some of the things on this wall are from the original chapel that was part of this hacienda. My husband's great-great-grandmother hung several of the crucifixes. Her husband built the hacienda in the 1850s, after he found gold here." She smiled. "So tell me, Skylar, do you like to cook?"

Skylar nodded. "I like to cook. Actually, I love to cook. And I'm drooling over your Sub-Zero fridge and Decor ovens."

Indio laughed softly. "You noticed."

Claire carried a stool from the island and joined them. Sitting, she exchanged a knowing smile with the other woman.

Indio said, "Okay, Skylar. Would you like the job?"

"Uh, that's it? I love your kitchen?"

Claire chuckled. "Indio, she might want to know what exactly is involved, or at least what she'll be paid."

The old woman waved her left hand. "We'll make it up as we go along. The woman who worked here for years moved away last month. We need a cook."

Skylar said, "Don't you want information about me?"

Indio shook her head vigorously. "Nope. Got all I need."

Claire burst into laughter. Indio guffawed with her. The joyful noise grew louder, until Skylar saw tears stream down their cheeks.

At last Indio dabbed her face with a handkerchief. "Excuse us. We get a little loony when things like this happen. You see, we know exactly why you came in person and why you came today."

An intense desire crashed through Skylar to grab her backpack and make tracks out the door. At some wordless level she understood life was spinning out of her control. She felt as if she were being nudged onto a path she hadn't chosen, a path like the Yellow Brick Road.

Great. Just great. All she wanted was food and shelter, not another flaming journey to the Land of Oz!

She'd leaned forward, ready to snatch up the pack, a "no thanks" forming on her tongue, when Indio fixed those twinkly black eyes on her. Skylar's muscles flapped like wet noodles.

"Skylar, here's what's happening. I can't prepare a cup of tea without help these days." She lifted her braced arm and dropped it back onto her lap. "The Hacienda Hideaway reopens tomorrow with twelve guests, here for dinner, staying through breakfast on Sunday. This is Claire's first experience with a retreat group. She has help with the cleaning, but I promised her that I would cover the kitchen." She paused. "I've been praying for a week for a cook to be here by today." The grin nearly scrunched her eyes shut. "I don't need to know a thing except that our God answers prayer."

Skylar blinked a few times. "Trip out. That's heavy stuff."

"It is. Now, dear, what do you think? Would you like the job? Could you start today?" Indio pressed her lips together and waited, still as a statue.

Forget the gentle nudge. With the likes of the elderly sage staring at her, things had escalated into a definite shove onto that Yellow Brick Road.

Skylar's stomach growled. The cinnamon scent had blossomed into a baking cake. Her legs and shoulders ached.

She liked these women. The positive vibes coming from them could not be denied. Why not give them a weekend? What could one weekend hurt?

"Sure. Why not?" The words skipped off her tongue as merrily as Dorothy and her friends flittering on down the road to Oz.

Three

While her mother-in-law laughed and squeezed Skylar Pierson's hand, Claire studied the stranger who had just agreed to be their cook.

The girl was confident to the point of brashness. Her long, deep-brown hair screamed "dye job." The mama's heart in Claire noted the auburn roots, sprinkle of freckles, and clear green eyes and believed their hint that someone less churlish lived inside her.

But which one was going to show up in Claire's kitchen?

The wife's heart in her predicted Max would go through the roof. Her husband would insist the girl visit his old staffing firm, fill out an app, interview with a professional. For crying out loud, she should be vetted. *"We can't run a business based on my mother's whims!"*

His mother turned to her now. "This job comes with room and board, right?"

Claire stifled a sigh. Working up close and personal with Indio Beaumont was like riding the back of a tandem bicycle. On the front seat a blind speed demon pedaled with all her might, hitting every pothole along the way.

"Right." Claire quickly reviewed the guest rooms. Nothing was available for the next four nights.

Indio said, "The 'oh, by the way' room."

The woman read her mind.

"But it needs—"

"Next week." She smiled at Skylar. "We call it 'oh, by the way' because it's off by itself and small. We usually forget it exists. I do hope you can live here. Serving breakfast to guests requires such an early morning."

"Uh, yeah. Sure. That'd be great."

"Wonderful. Get your backpack and I'll show you your new home. Then we'll eat lunch and start work."

Claire remained on her stool and watched them walk outside into the courtyard. She whispered to herself, "Oh, Lord, what was that all about?"

Indio, like Claire, had intuited that Skylar was hungry and homeless. They'd heard no car. She carried her belongings on her back. Her face was flushed from the August heat. She must have hitched a ride, been dropped off on the highway, and walked up the long drive.

It was bizarre that she had found her way to them.

No. Not so bizarre. Indio had been praying. Of course the girl found her way.

The week before, when Indio injured her wrist, Claire had teetered between panic and exhilaration. The maniac steering the tandem now had only one good arm. Her reply as usual, though, was an energized "God is good. There is a reason for this. Let's see what He's got in store for us."

The woman's faith never ceased to amaze, but Claire's practical side immediately kicked into high gear. She asked her daughters, niece, friends, and part-time housekeeper for weekend help in the kitchen. To a one, they balked. She cajoled, whined, and threatened to no avail. Max offered to cook on his grill everything from eggs to zucchini.

What on earth had ever possessed the two of them to take over the Hacienda Hideaway? Who in their right mind would sign up to expend all their time, energy, and money on a place for strangers to invade? Messy strangers who would, most likely, gripe about grilled eggs?

Claire smiled. Good grief! The answers were so easy. After thirty-some years of growing apart, she and Max had wanted a life together. They wanted to create a safe harbor for themselves, for the family, and for whomever God brought to their door.

Evidently that included people who did not make reservations and pay deposits. That moment at the door when Skylar had said the ad was for a cook, goose bumps prickled all over Claire. She knew then and there that Indio's prayer had been answered.

Indio's prayer: an expression of her faith that God would supply the specific need she requested.

A fleeting sense of remorse went through Claire. She had not prayed for a cook. Her petition had been more of a yelp for help.

"All right, Lord, I get it. This retreat center stuff is off the wall and it's nowhere near simple, but I get it. Thank You." She sighed loudly. "But maybe now we could please have just few days of biking *around* the potholes?"

Four

Sitting on the edge of the single bed, Skylar caught sight of a veggie garden through the open door and an eastern view of rocky hills through the window.

Insane.

Indio said, "It's a good view."

"Yeah," she whispered, feeling like she'd entered Brigadoon.

The house was a humongous U-shaped thing, totally transplanted from a movie set. She and Indio had strolled through a courtyard. The rooms they passed opened directly inside the U onto a wraparound veranda. At the far end they followed a flagstone path, turned a corner, and voilà, there it was: a forest-green door. They walked through it into the "oh, by the way" room, a room that offered the most perfect view she had ever imagined.

It was incomprehensible that she'd just been invited to live there.

Skylar wondered when the bomb would explode. Maybe Indio and Claire were wacko and got their kicks from luring people into their home just to cut them up into little—

"My friends made that quilt for me after the fire."

Skylar noted the blanket draped over the foot of the white wrought-iron bed. "The fire?"

"Oh, I forgot. You said you don't live in San Diego. The fire came through here nearly a year ago now. We lost most of our things." Indio sighed. "We lost everything but the walls and roof."

That explained the new furnishings and the young scrub vegetation. "I'm sorry. That must have been so awful."

"It was beyond imagination awful. But it facilitated a number of blessings. The whole place got refurbished. Claire and Max moved up here from the city to run things. Ben and I don't have to be in charge anymore. I placed that ad two years ago because I knew I wouldn't be able to keep up much longer even then. And now here you are, just in time for us to reopen."

Totally insane. "So, uh, where's your room?"

"We live down the road a piece, in a little house Max built for us. Two of my granddaughters live in an RV on the land." She smiled. "I'm sorry this room is such a mess. We'll get some rugs next week. And a chair and curtains. I am sorry there is no closet either. It's such a tiny space. Hopefully the armoire will be sufficient."

She'd already apologized for the tools piled in a corner, the shower not working, and the dust. "No problemo. I mean there's a bed, a private bathroom, a shower room around the corner, and a phenomenal kitchen I get to play in. What else—" She cleared an annoying catch from her throat. "What else could I want? It's great."

"Okay, then. I'll let you get settled. Lunch is ready, so come as soon as you want. The circus should start about three o'clock, and you won't want to miss that." An impish chuckle burst from her.

Uh-oh. Here it came. The weird thing that would shoo her through the exit door. "Circus?"

Indio smiled. "My grandchildren and their friends are coming for dinner. Counting you, there will be thirteen of us. Claire and Max are going to practice their hosting skills. They're such newbies. Between you and me, they haven't the foggiest notion what they're up against by reopening this place."

"Oh."

"It should be fun. You'll definitely earn whatever it is we're paying you." Two spry steps put her at the door. "See you in a few."

"Indio."

She turned.

"This quilt. It's too special to leave in here with me."

Those ancient eyes stared at her for a long moment. "It belongs in here, Skylar, with you." She turned and hurried away.

"Trippy." Flinging her arms wide, Skylar fell back against a pile of pillows. "Major trippy."

She replayed the so-called interview. It was downright weird. A two-year-old ad still in effect? Women who laughed like banshees? Room and board plopped into her lap, effective immediately?

She'd spent such a long time following one Yellow Brick Road after another, never quite reaching Oz, the kingdom where all the answers would be found.

Skylar grew still, startled by a new thought. There was really only one question she'd wanted answered: how could she find her way home? Somehow between ringing the doorbell and touching a handmade quilt, she had found the way.

Yes, she knew beyond a shadow of a doubt that she was already safely back home in Kansas.

Skylar stood at the island in the center of the kitchen, at the sink. Lasagna noodles drained in a colander. Through the rising steam she watched a dozen different emotions play across Max Beaumont's face, from huffy to friendly, confused to resolute.

Claire had just introduced her to him. After his initial polite hello, she wondered which sentiment he would express first.

The kitchen wall clock struck three in robust Westminster chimes. Indio, that tiny smile coming and going, pretended to nap in her rocker.

Max spun on his heel, hands on his hips, and faced Indio. Macho Man had won out. "Mom, you placed an ad two years ago?"

Eyes still shut, Indio said, "Yes."

"Just like that. Without consulting me? I own a staffing business!" He twisted his head, as if to work out a crick. "Owned."

"Your people wouldn't know the first thing about finding a cook willing to live in the middle of nowhere and invest her life in a center for people seeking deep rest for their souls." She peered at him through one eye. "That's why they publish those caretaker newsletters, for odd-balls like us."

He turned to Skylar again. "That's what you want to do? Cook and live in the middle of nowhere and invest your life here?"

The description sounded like nirvana to her. But how could she explain that to an uptight businessman? He was good-looking in an old-guy, Mel Gibson sort of way. He had his mother's eyes, though, black and piercing.

"Mr. Beaumont, there's nothing I'd like better."

"Why?"

She raised her shoulders. "I love to cook. I love living close to nature and meeting new people." She finished off the shrug. "If I can mix all that in with a job, then yeah, I'll invest my life here. For now."

He scrutinized her. She knew what he saw in her dyed hair, dark clothes, and two hoops in each earlobe with holes for more: alternative and unstable. At least she had cleaned up, put on a skirt and fresh T-shirt, and twisted her hair into a bun.

At last he spoke. "What about your family, friends, home?"

"Dead, scattered, and back in Ohio a long time ago." She almost said back in Kansas, but her ID said Ohio and he would ask for that.

"Do you have an ID?"

"Driver's license, in my room."

"Max!" Claire banged a spoon against a pot on the stove. "Enough with the third degree." She laid down the spoon and turned, glasses askew, hair falling from a clip, her apron tomato streaked. "We needed a cook. Your mom asked for one. Skylar showed up. She's already put together a beautiful salad and fine-tuned this sauce to the point that you'll think you're in Rome. Just get onboard, okay?"

He tried to remain angry, tried to hold on to his twitches and huffs. But after a moment of staring at his wife, Skylar watched the emotions trickle right out of him like water. In an instant his eyes crinkled and a slow grin folded his cheeks. "Okay." He laughed. All traces of Macho Man vanished. "Okay. Welcome, Skylar. And call me Max."

These people were crazy.

"All right. Thank you."

He went to Claire and put his arms around her. "You're looking a little frazzled, sweetheart. What can I do?"

"Hugging is good."

Never mind Diane Keaton and Mel Gibson. June and Ward Cleaver were alive and well and living at the Hacienda Hideaway. Skylar imagined the TV couple from the old sitcom *Leave It to Beaver*. Slip pearls round Claire's neck and twist a tie at Max's, and the resemblance would startle even the most diehard oldies viewer.

Indio caught Skylar's eye and winked.

Claire straightened and sighed. "The first 'guests' will be here in half an hour. Maybe we shouldn't eat dinner with them after all. On the one hand, we want to experience dinner as a guest. On the other, we won't do that with real guests. And what do we do when they arrive? Go to the parking lot? Wait out front? Let them wander into the courtyard?"

Max shrugged. "What's the difference? We say hi. We eat dinner with them tonight because they're our kids."

He might be onboard, but he was still a guy, clueless in the nuances of hospitality. And Claire had been unraveling since lunchtime.

Skylar cleared her throat. "Do you mind if I make a suggestion?"

They looked at her. Claire said, "Please do."

"You hired me to take care of the kitchen, right? So let me do it. Claire, you go get unfrazzled. And Max, really. I mean, a polo shirt and dress slacks at a wilderness retreat?"

Max's brows shot up, his chin tucked inward, his eyelids batting a few times.

Skylar held her breath. Had she already stepped over the line? If so, they might as well call it quits right now. Being mouthy was second nature to her.

Claire smiled and Max chuckled.

Skylar breathed. Home free.

Home? Who was she kidding? The situation was a few nights' stay at best. Once the Cleavers really got to know her, they would easily, without hesitation, make do without a cook.

Five

Jenna squeezed her hands into fists, pressed them against her thighs, and glared at the computer screen.

More precisely, she glared at the icon of her cyberspace mailbox.

It was empty.

Still.

After four days.

Empty.

Four. Days.

"I can't do this." She hissed the words through gritted teeth. "I cannot do this."

"Yo!"

She jumped at the sound and jerked around to face the open classroom door. "Ohmygosh!"

Cade made a wry face and strode to her desk. "Oops. Sorry. Figured you heard me. I was whistling and talking out in the hall. You okay?"

"Sure." Her heart hammered the breath right out of her lungs. "No. Yeah. I am. I'm fine."

"Jenna." Loosening his tie, he squatted coach-style next to her chair and looked up at her. "I think this is exactly what we talked about a couple days ago. It's okay to be not okay. It's even expected."

Her chest felt like the host to a kickboxing match. She nodded.

He smiled, and his brows went up.

Oh, no. If Mr. Ice Guy went soft on her, there was no way the sob could stay inside of her. This was absolutely not what she needed.

"Tell me, Mrs. Mason, what can I do for you?" His voice dropped a notch. "Right now, this very minute, what can I do to help?"

She glanced at the computer screen and felt again the stab of anger. "Tell him to send an e-mail."

He didn't answer for a moment. Then, "When did you last hear from him?"

"Monday."

"You know he can't—"

"Yes! I know! I know he can't write or call every day! And I know there are legitimate reasons why he can't write every day." She bit on her lower lip before she spewed out exactly what she thought of the USMC and of Kevin reenlisting.

"And those legitimate reasons . . ." Cade's voice hushed. "They probably scare the living daylights out of you."

The anger drained as if a plug had been yanked out. It happened like that. A giant rushing gurgle and *pfft*. It was all gone, leaving her limp and unable to fight the fear left in its wake.

She closed her eyes.

"Jenna, they would tell you if Kevin was injured."

"Or killed." She looked at him. "Or missing in action."

His steady gray eyes held hers. "He's on some assignment, out of the office, so to speak. He'll be back before you know it."

A silent moment passed between them.

Cade whispered, "I'm sorry I can't call him up and ream him out. I'm sorry I can't say, 'Hey, bud, your wife needs an e-mail from you *right now.*'"

Something shifted inside of her, as if one of those big chunks of fear had been moved.

As if Cade Edmunds had angled his shoulder under it, sharing its weight, bearing as much as she allowed.

Jenna was suddenly struck with the maleness of this man and realized how much she missed that element in her life. Kevin would have knelt before her in the same way, his face likewise a mixture of compassion and a determination to slay dragons for her. She would get lost within the confines of his arms. The world would be right again.

Cade rose to his feet, and the spell was broken. "There's a group of us going to dinner. Why don't you join us?"

She cleared her throat. "Uh, thanks, but I've got plans. A family thing."

"Maybe another time."

"Maybe." She cocked her head. "What do you mean you can't call him? You are so not a help, Edmunds."

"Yeah, yeah." He put his hands on his hips. "I want you to carefully consider taking tomorrow off."

"I'm fine."

"I'm serious."

"I know you are."

"I don't want to find you in here again cursing at your computer."

"I wasn't cursing—" She saw the glint in his eyes and relaxed. "I'm serious too. This helped. I mean, us talking. So thank you."

A rare grin lit up Mr. Ice Guy's face. "You're welcome."

The late afternoon sun still felt warm on Jenna's face as she stood outside her apartment building. She waited for her brother and his girlfriend to pick her up.

The family thing she'd mentioned to Cade was dinner at the Hacienda Hideaway, the retreat center her parents and grandparents were reopening. It was located up in the hills at least—depending on traffic—a fifty-minute drive from her place. She'd welcomed the ride offer.

A black SUV pulled into the parking lot. Jenna steeled herself. Family gatherings so magnified Kevin's absence.

But then, what didn't? A yawning void filled the apartment, the car, the school, the empty e-mail box. An evening out with coworkers or other friends they shared in common would not exactly be a respite. Anger would bubble and then, like what happened earlier with Cade, fear would take over.

The car braked near her, and the passenger door opened. Her older brother, Erik, slid out. "What's wrong?"

"Besides my entire life?" She returned his brief hug.

"Yeah, besides that." He looked down at her, his poker face a sure sign he was in playful mode. "I mean, you're standing outside your apartment building. I don't have to call you to say we're downstairs." He held up a hand. "Okay, just give me a moment here. This is quite difficult to fathom. The princess is actually waiting for us, actually ready to go?"

"Shut up." Jenna turned to Erik's girlfriend, who moved in for a hug.

Rosie said, "Don't mind him. The prince is feeling a little feisty. He actually worked today."

"He worked? Really?"

Erik said, "Ha, ha."

Rosie smiled at him. His own grin lit up his face, a sight that reminded Jenna of him as a kid.

Erik Beaumont and Rosa Delgado were such an unlikely couple. Her brother, a former TV newscaster, would never have dated the Latina policewoman if he hadn't checked into rehab and gotten over himself. Rosie never would have dated the snob—her own word—if she hadn't nearly killed him.

"Jenna," Rosie said. In spite of her pretty summer dress and her loose, wavy hair, she resembled a cop. It came across in her major-gym-time body and those sunglasses. "Seriously, how are things this week?"

When they first met, Jenna hadn't cared much for Rosie. Why any woman wanted to do a man's job was incomprehensible. She was pushy, intimidating, and outspoken. She honestly did believe the Beaumont siblings were royalty, in the negative sense of being spoiled. Not to mention the fact that she *shot* Erik.

But over the months, Jenna grew to trust and admire Rosie. No question about it, the woman loved Erik. Without her influence on him, Jenna's older brother could easily have become by now a hopeless drunk lying somewhere in a gutter. Yes, Jenna could talk honestly with Rosie.

Jenna exhaled loudly. "The first couple days of school are always nerve-racking. Edmunds stuck me with this totally off-the-wall group for sixth-hour lit. I swear every last one of them will be suspended by next Friday. Which, come to think of it, will give me an extra prep period. Hmm. Maybe I won't complain."

Rosie took off her sunglasses, revealing a deadly combination of terrorist-level interrogation glare and grandma-level tenderness. "When did you last hear from him?"

Jenna twisted the strap of her shoulder bag and tried to smile. "You know, you'd make a great cop."

Rosie touched Jenna's arm. "I'll pray."

That was the other thing that used to bug her about Rosie—how she wore her faith like a scarlet *C* on her chest. *"Everyone take notice. I am a Christian."*

But that was before Kevin's absence had hollowed out Jenna's insides. It was before the void had begun to haunt.

She put her hand on Rosie's and squeezed. "I could use that. Thanks."

Six

"You don't look like an ax murderer."

Skylar ignored the voice behind her. She was busy studying two pans of baking lasagna at the open door of one of the magnificent Decor wall ovens. Claire had declared the kitchen the family's private residence and off-limits to guests, even for tonight's make-believe guests. Whoever was clearing his throat could wait.

Making a mental note of twenty minutes, she slid the oven rack back into place, shut its door, and turned.

A curly-haired guy approached, his hands shoved into the back pockets of his jeans. A pinched expression on his narrow face defeated the easygoing posture.

"Well," Skylar said, "you don't look like an ax murderer either."

The flit of a smile might have been a figment of her imagination.

He put out his hand. "Danny Beaumont."

Not bothering to remove her oven mitt, she shook it. "Skylar Pierson."

"Skylar with an *a*." His hand slid into the pocket again. "I heard. What about Pierson? With an *e*, *a*, and *o*?"

"*I*, *e*, *o*."

He blinked.

Skylar sighed to herself. The guy had to be Max's son. It was clear from his dark eyes to his slender build to his uptight manner.

She said, "P-I-E-R-S-O-N."

"I got it. I just don't get why you're here."

"Um." She shrugged and rolled out her lower lip. "Ad, cook, right place at the right time, kismet, God. Your grandma prayed."

"I don't doubt Nana's prayers. But you have to admit it's all pretty bizarre."

"Yeah." She glanced behind her shoulder, looked at him again, and lowered her voice. "I'm not supposed to reveal this, but I'm really an angel from God, sent to cook lasagna."

"I see. Where did you last work?"

"A coffee shop in Seattle. I'll get references."

His forehead imitated an accordion. He rocked on his heels. Although he must be at least her age, his boyish face resembled one of those cutesy nice guys from an old TV show. Somebody like Wally Cleaver, Beaver's brother. Any mother worth her weight in apple pie would easily approve of him.

He said, "It just seems prudent, for everyone's sake, that we take the traditional route. Application, reference check, so on and so forth."

"You mean drug test."

He moved his head in an odd turtle fashion, in and out. "That's not unreasonable these days. On the flipside, you'll want to know about us, too, I imagine."

"Oh, definitely." She took off the oven mitts and tossed them onto the nearest counter. "First order of business is to give your grandma a drug test."

The nonsmile darted across his mouth again. "I should have prefaced all this by saying my parents and grandparents have been through a lot this past year. They've peaked on the stress charts. I'm just trying to help them cover all the bases. They—"

"Yo!" The shout came from a tall guy in the doorway. "Wow!" Chewing in an exaggerated way, he flung his arms upward, touchdown style, and shut his eyes. "This dip! Spinach, artichokes, garlic, cream cheese. *Magnifico!*"

Skylar smiled, relieved at the interruption and pleased at the reaction to her hors d'oeuvres.

The guy swallowed and opened his eyes. "I repeat: mm-mm. That was beyond incredible. Absolutely exquisite. Are you Skylar?" He strode to her, his hand extended.

"Yeah. I'm glad you liked it."

Instead of shaking her hand, he lowered his head and kissed it. "Promise me you will never leave this place unless it's to marry me and cook in my kitchen," he implored, locking eyes with her.

She laughed. "Who are you?"

"Erik, eldest of the offspring. I work with a production company that makes documentaries." He straightened and let go of her hand.

"How many are there of you, anyway?" Skylar asked.

"Of siblings?" Erik paused. "Four. Myself, Danny here, Lexi his twin, and Jenna. Jen is the one with dark hair like mine and a snobbish look, which is really just a cover-up for being at her wit's end because her husband is a Marine serving overseas. Lexi is the fragile-looking one making eyes at Nathan. Then there's Tuyen, our orphaned cousin whose mother was Vietnamese and her father was killed in Vietnam. Her English is, uh, shall we say, improving."

Skyler hoped she could keep them all straight. Four kids and an orphaned cousin. Parents who could pass for June and Ward Cleaver. And a grandmother who was some kind of Native American squaw with a direct line to God.

Erik said, "I'm so happy to meet you. I'm so happy you're here. By any chance, is there more spinach-artichoke dip?"

"I'm sorry, no."

He exhaled, clearly disappointed. Taller than both Danny and Max, he had startling good looks. Pierce Brosnan came to mind, aka a young James Bond.

"Dan," Erik said, "did you taste it? The spinach-artichoke dip?"

"Not yet."

"Well, you missed out. It's gone now. I guess?" He turned a hopeful expression toward her.

She nodded. "But dinner is almost ready."

"Are you allowed to divulge the menu?"

"Caesar salad—"

"With anchovies?"

She hesitated. Claire had not ordered anchovies because so few liked them, she said. But the delivery man from the market had a jar in his truck and Skylar trusted the subtle tweak their flavor would add.

Erik tilted his head. "Really?" He must have read something on her face. "You added anchovies?"

"Um, yeah, really."

"Bless you, dear! What else can we expect?"

"Garlic bread and lasagnas."

"Lasagnas? Plural?"

"One with sausage, the other with veggies."

The brothers said in unison, "*Veggie* lasagna?"

"Yeah. Tofu and soy cheese. The thing is, there were these extra noodles and I thought, hmm, maybe we should practice for vegetarian guests."

Danny said, "Does Mom know?"

"No." Skylar dug in her self-defensive heels. "She's been busy elsewhere."

"Mom's all for experimenting with gourmet, but she agreed with Nana about vegetarian. They wouldn't bother unless specifically asked to do so."

"Well, I figured the kitchen is my domain tonight. And since I have to pass inspection, I thought I better strut my best stuff."

Erik grinned. "Don't tell our grandfather what he's eating and you'll pass with flying colors."

"But the kitchen is Nana's domain." Danny protested. "She has experience and definite ideas about what to serve."

"Daniel." Erik's voice lowered. "Give the Boy Scout routine a rest. Life is not all black and white. Nana can't do this, and Mom was counting on her."

By now, both of them had their arms crossed, jaws set, eyebrows bunched.

Danny said, "You weren't here the other night. It was the worst yet. Mom and Dad came unglued, over-the-top."

"And they will again before one of two things happens: either they get a handle on running a center or they give it up. Nana agreed to help but she's close to eighty years old, and she always had help. Papa totally quit being involved months ago. Which leaves Mom and Dad. This is a nutso project they've taken on, but it's their nutso project, not ours."

Skylar did not want to hear about family issues. "Hey, guys. Excuse me."

They looked at her.

"As far as I know, I still have this job, which I need to get back to right now." She made a scooping motion. "Shoo."

Erik turned to Danny. "She's kicking us out. Which, technically speaking, is within the boundaries of her domain. We 'guests' were told not to come in here tonight."

The younger brother twisted his lips. He clearly wasn't buying it.

And Skylar clearly wanted to stomp on his foot. Until he had walked into the room, she had a good gig going. She liked Max and Claire. And there was something special—serene, even—about Indio. The older brother seemed like a good guy too. But this hotshot Danny, he was really getting on her nerves. If he spouted off one more disapproving comment, she'd blow it by telling him exactly what she thought of his bullheaded attitude.

But she didn't want to blow it. She didn't want to leave this new-found oasis. Not already. She reminded herself of something she'd read in a magazine back when she thought such boy-girl advice made a difference. Because of her interest in cooking, this tidbit had stuck with her: "Stop swinging the red cape. Just feed the bull and he'll calm down."

She stepped up close to the younger brother, her face within inches of his, and let the red cape of her attitude flutter to the floor. "Your mother gave me permission to create a feast." She spoke softly. "Trust the feast, Danny. Just trust the feast."

He did not back away or break eye contact. There were fine lines at the corners of his eyes, pronounced by a California tan that suggested he spent a lot of time outdoors.

At last he said, "The proof is in the pudding?"

"Exactly." She smiled.

He gave a half nod and walked away.

Erik followed, giving Skylar a thumbs-up on his way out the door.

Seven

Claire removed the fork from her mouth. Her taste buds went on full alert.

Portabellas. Yellow peppers. Oregano, basil, thyme. Tofu.

Vegetable lasagna?

"Oh, my." She sighed the words to herself.

Across the table, in the midst of several simultaneous conversations among family members, her son Erik caught her eye. He smiled and winked.

She raised her brows, took another bite, and wondered how much they could afford to pay Skylar.

With each passing hour, Claire's appreciation for the young woman expanded. God hadn't answered Indio's prayer by sending a proficient cook. Instead, He sent a self-assured, accomplished chef.

Claire smiled. Of course He did.

For the first time in a long while, hope soared. Her and Max's crazy dream just might work. If *real* guests—people she didn't know—responded even to a small degree as her family did tonight, they were in good shape. The Hacienda Hideaway was in the business of providing a safe harbor—and great food.

Kevin's absence left a large hole at the table. Still, it was so good to have her four kids together. They'd grown closer since the fire. At the moment Jenna, Danny, and Lexi were teasing Erik, giving him grief about his video camera on the floor beside him. In recent days it was always within arm's reach. He refused to disclose what he was really doing. He'd say, "It's a doc, you know."

A documentary of family members eating dinner or walking outdoors? Who knew? At least he seemed to be enjoying his work.

Max leaned sideways, his arm against Claire's, his lips at her ear. "This one." He touched his fork to his plate, on a piece of lasagna. The vegetable version. "It tastes a little off."

Her smile fell. Her stomach twisted. Heat crept up her neck. The large table and rustic dining room went out of focus. The chatty voices of ten other people around the table muted.

"Claire." Max hunched forward now, making eye contact. "What did you hear me say?"

She saw the velvety black eyes, the ones that had resembled lava rock for most of their thirty-plus years of married life.

Just over a year ago she had left him.

Just nine months ago she'd struggled to trust him again.

Just two months ago he'd slipped into old work habits, helping his former partner through a rough time, taking a 24-7 stint at the office for six weeks, closing himself off from her. It was temporary and not quite like in their past, but still . . .

Just that morning she had prayed that in the chaos of opening the Hacienda Hideaway, she would not again lose her voice.

Max put his arm across the back of her chair and gently touched the nape of her neck.

Okay. He was with her. She took a deep breath and let it out. Not wanting to draw the others' attention, she whispered. "I heard you say that you don't want to do this."

He tilted his head. "Huh?"

"'This.' As in run the retreat center. You don't like the lasagna, ergo you want to fire Skylar, ergo we can't possibly function this weekend, ergo it'll be a major flop, ergo we'll close up shop by Monday."

"That's a lot of 'ergos.'"

"It is."

"You a little skittish about this venture?"

"Yes, but I don't want to quit."

He smiled. "I didn't imply any of those things."

"I know." She grinned. "What you said simply implied that you wouldn't know good vegetarian if a dump truck backed up and unloaded a ton of it on your head."

He laughed.

She kissed the corner of his mouth. He really did have an awfully nice mouth.

"Eww!" The cry came from across the table, from Lexi, their youngest and Danny's twin. "PDA!"

Erik half rose, whipping his camera to eye level, and pointed like a game show host to his cousin. Half Vietnamese, she was his uncle's daughter who had showed up out of the blue only months before. "Tuyen, you're on! PDA. Definition!"

The young woman, their orphaned niece whose mother had been Vietnamese, smiled. Erik had been her obvious favorite Beaumont since her arrival the previous spring.

"PDA. It mean—" She rolled her blue eyes, very Jenna-like. "It *means*—"

"It means," Erik fairly shouted, "hallelujah, your English is improving every day!"

"No. It means—"

"I'd swear you're from California."

"Erik!" Tuyen gave him a stern look. "Sit down. You tease too much. No. PDA means 'public demonstration of affection.'" She looked at Claire and Max. "And you not want—you do not want to PDA in front of guests. It is in bad taste."

Laughter erupted around the table. The hint of joy impacted everyone. It erased the pain from Jenna's face. It lightened Danny, who'd been in a funk all evening. Lexi did a little bit of her own PDA as she giggled into the shoulder of Nathan, the sweet reporter she'd been dating. Rosie, Erik's policewoman girlfriend, lost her usual reserve in a loud belly laugh. Indio chuckled so hard tears ran down her cheeks.

Even Max's father smiled. He couldn't quite bring himself to fully welcome Tuyen—the illegitimate daughter of his older son BJ—into the family, but at least he wasn't rude to her anymore. His blue eyes twinkling now in her direction gave hope of a softening attitude.

Claire breathed a prayer of thanks. It might work. It just might all work.

Eight

Jenna slipped away from the after-dinner chaos. Enjoyable as the evening was with her family, the walls had closed in on her.

Outdoors, the wraparound porch offered solitude. Soft lights bathed the old wooden planks that had somehow survived the fire. The thunk of her footsteps resounded across the courtyard.

And reminded her of Kevin.

But then, everything reminded her of Kevin.

He liked to wear his cowboy boots at the hacienda. He liked to thump around the veranda and slap against the stone pathways and kick up the dust at the barn. He loved the Hideaway. He loved family meals in the *sala*.

He would love Tuyen and Rosie and Nathan. And Skylar now. He would like her too. He would love her raspberry crisp.

It hurt that he hadn't even met any of them. They'd all arrived after he deployed. When he left, the reconstruction from the fire wasn't near finished. There had been no farewell dinner for him in the sala. Their whole world had changed since he left.

"Jenna!"

At her father's shout, she turned.

"Jen!" He stood in the sala doorway, waving his telephone. "It's Kevin!"

Kevin!

She flew back down the porch, her heart racing. Her husband was calling from the other side of the world where it was already tomorrow!

Her dad met her halfway and handed her the cordless, smiling. He went back indoors as she sank onto a nearby bench.

"Kevin!"

"Hi, pretty lady."

"Oh." Tears welled and her throat constricted. She whispered, "Hi."

"Hi." There was a grin in his voice. "How was the big dinner?"

"You remembered."

"Are you kidding? This is a major event in the Beaumont family."

That was Kevin. Too much Beaumont togetherness provoked him at times. Not having grown up in a close-knit family, though, he appreciated being a member of hers.

She smiled. "Ready to change your name yet?"

His low rumble of a laugh tickled her. "Can I say hi to everyone when we're done?"

"I'm sure that's why you called here instead of home."

"Could be."

"I love you, Kevin."

"I love you, Jenna. And I miss you more than I can say."

A long silent moment passed. Precious time was lost, but it was unavoidable. It happened whenever they spoke. As if on cue, they hit a wordless space, its pain too deep for expression.

"Okay," Kevin said. "Tell me all about tonight."

And she did.

Later that evening, still aglow in the sweetness of hearing Kevin's voice, Jenna rode with Danny in his pickup truck. As they traveled away from the house lights, an impenetrable blackness engulfed them.

She said, "Even Kevin's phone call can't take away the willies this road gives me at night."

"I know what you mean." Her younger brother drove confidently down the long, winding, private dirt-and-gravel road. It led from the recently blacktopped parking lot to the highway, a familiar route on which they'd both learned to drive. "You'd think it'd be in the daytime, when you can see the charred trees, but it's the darkness that does it."

"I can't help but think about what they went through that night." She felt a chill, as she always did, imagining her mother, sister, and grandparents trying to escape a wildfire in the middle of the night. They didn't make it out, not until the next morning.

She said, "I don't know how they can live out here."

"It's only by God's healing grace."

Jenna didn't reply. She adored her brother. He was fun, intelligent, hardworking, and endearingly Tigger-like in his enthusiasm. But sometimes his pat answers drove her up the wall. He resembled Rosie, but his scarlet letter was less a *C* for Christian than a *G* for Got It All Figured Out.

They reached the highway. At last the headlamp beams picked up some tall leafy trees, evidence of the fire's hopscotch pattern.

"Thanks for the ride," she said. "I didn't want to wait for Erik and Rosie. They were so wound up, they could be there half the night. Isn't it great to see him sober?"

He grinned. "Yeah. He actually seems to enjoy hanging out with the fam now too."

"Speaking of the fam, did you hear Skylar refer to us Beaumonts as the Cleavers from *Leave It to Beaver*?" Jenna had insisted Skylar join them for dessert. Her mom's no-kitchen rule wasn't going to fly. Guests would want to meet the chef.

She said, "The perfect TV family. Isn't that wild? Just wait until she gets to know us."

"It seems like we should get to know her first." Disapproval laced Danny's tone.

In the glow from the dashboard, Jenna saw his frown. She recalled his standoffish demeanor as they all ate Skylar's luscious raspberry crisp. "You have a problem with her."

He shrugged. "The circumstances are just too plain weird. There's just something about her . . . It doesn't quite add up."

"Danny, that's not like you. You're the one with a faith as big as Nana's, which to most people sounds just too plain weird. Honestly, when we were little kids, I knew this. I'd even ask you to pray for me before recitals. Remember? You'd grab my hand and start right in. 'O Lord! Have mercy on my big sister. She didn't practice her piano enough!'" She chuckled. "You were so cute, but I never dared tell my friends what you did."

"I still pray for you. And Kevin."

"I know. Thanks." She didn't want to go down that road. "About Skylar. She reminds me of kids who stay out on the fringe of things. They sort of sit back and observe, not sure how to fit in."

"As Erik and Kevin would say, you are a princess. You're beautiful, smart and always wear the right clothes. Those kids on the fringe don't *want* to fit in. For whatever reason, they're anti-everything. Skylar was mocking us, Jen. The Cleavers were hopelessly unreal, television fluff."

"I don't agree. She told me she doesn't have a family. She never knew her dad. Her mom OD'd on prescription drugs and died when Skylar was eighteen. She couldn't afford college. I think Skylar knows we're not perfect, but we have each other, just like the Cleavers."

"Princess."

"Boy Scout."

They rode in silence for a while. The city lay below them now, a vast sea of sparkles. Beyond them, blackness swallowed the ocean.

Danny lived near the ocean and surfed daily, whatever the season. Despite his scarlet *G*, he got along with everyone there from beach bum to tourists who paid for surfing lessons through the shop he owned with his roommate. His main business was software design, which meant he got along with straitlaced business-type clients too.

"Danny, I don't get you sometimes. You were the first one to accept Tuyen and her crazy story about Uncle BJ living in Vietnam for years after being declared MIA. I still catch myself holding back with her."

"Only because you're afraid that Keven might repeat our uncle's history—go overseas to fight a war and be declared MIA, only to discover years later that he fell in love with someone else over there and had a child with her."

Jenna flipped her hand, dismissing his ridiculous opinion. "Whatever. And speaking of Kevin, you welcomed him from the start too. He was basically without a family since they all lived so far away in Indiana."

"Kevin, for some inexplicable reason, adored you. We had to welcome him into the family. You were such a pain as an unmarried princess."

"Ha-ha. What's with the Skylar problem? She and Tuyen are both orphans, in need of a home, which in a sense is exactly what Mom and Dad say they want to provide."

"Tuyen's country disowned her, and she's a Beaumont. We really don't know Skylar's background. She waltzes in with her long hair and sixteen holes pierced in each ear and hippie clothes—"

"Ohmygosh! You just described your old friends, Faith Simmons and Gunther Walker, from college."

"Yeah, yeah."

"Yeah, yeah, *yeah*. You think Skylar is just like them."

"I don't think so. I know she is."

"She told you she's an anti-everything weirdo?"

"She doesn't have to. Her attitude screams it loud and clear."

"And you think *I'm* judgmental, you snob. Whatever happened to Faith and Gunther?"

"No clue."

"You three were best friends from, like, kindergarten until college, right? I always imagined you and Faith would end up together. Didn't she change her name? What was it? Something cheery."

"Farah Sunshine."

"Yes. Well, anyway, Mom and Nana think Skylar is wonderful, so maybe you want to stop comparing her to Farah Sunshine and give her a break."

He didn't reply for a long moment. "Maybe you can walk from here."

Jenna looked at him. "And maybe Boy Scouts sometimes make mistakes."

"Nah. Princesses do, but not Boy Scouts."

"Oh, stuff it."

Honestly! He truly drove her up the wall.

She settled back in the seat, crushed by an onslaught of loneliness. It snuffed out her earlier glow. The frustration she felt with Danny was a joy compared to going home to an empty apartment.

Nine

Skylar expected Max would deliver part two of his third degree. She had only hoped he'd at least wait until after her first cup of coffee. But he didn't. Midmorning the day after the big hoo-ha dinner, he launched into it.

"Skylar," he said, "we need to talk about your salary and job description. Do you have time now?"

She waited a beat, her eyes on the gurgling coffeemaker. She felt like a carafe full of hot emotions. Max had just added more water inside of her and turned up the heat. Things were starting to spit and hiss.

Pulling herself together, she turned to Claire, who sat working at the kitchen's built-in desk. "Do you need me?"

"Not for a while." She flashed her movie-star smile. "Coffee's done."

Skylar poured herself a mug, thinking how she, too, might be done.

She followed Max outside into the sunny courtyard. Still foggy from a dead sleep on clean sheets and under a roof, she savored whiffs of caffeine and wondered what to do. Maybe her best defense was a gracious offense.

"Max, my room is too comfortable. I better get an alarm clock for tomorrow morning or the guests will be fixing their own breakfast."

"There's no clock in there?"

"Not that I can find."

They followed a stone path around flower beds overrun with rosemary and other herbs she planned to use. At the sunlit center of the courtyard they sat in Adirondack chairs. Like the pinewood benches on the porch, the seats were simply constructed, their natural color unstained

Skyla nearly inhaled her first taste of coffee and closed her eyes. The Beaumonts understood the essence of coffee. Fresh espresso beans, grinder, and top-of-the-line maker settled the issue of finding a truly good cup there in the backwoods.

She looked at her interrogator. His brows went up and down. His mouth twisted side to side. He cricked his neck.

He reminded her of the Wizard of Oz yanking his curtain shut, trying to hide his true self. Well, she had seen behind the curtain: Max Beaumont's fierce business persona was all for show.

He shook his head and the phony uptight guy fled the scene. "Details! We don't have enough clocks. We don't have enough hand towels. We don't have enough couches. Good grief. That's the kind of trivial bunk that makes me want to hightail it to my former office." He gestured toward an empty space in front of their chairs. "We don't have a fountain. We won't have a fountain in time for today's guests or even next month's guests because every fountain we choose is either discontinued or on back order. And we don't have flowers. Lexi has worked marvels on the landscape, but this area is far from what the brochure promises."

"It sounds as if you've all worked marvels. Indio told me a little bit about last year's fire and your renovations. It doesn't matter that *Better Homes and Gardens* wouldn't photograph the place, but so what? They're not the ones coming. It's beautiful here and the guests are going to love it as is. They won't miss flowers or a fountain they've never seen. They'll make do without an extra hand towel."

He gave her a quick smile. "I appreciate your encouragement."

"In a way I'm like your first guest." She smiled. "And the pile of tools in my room didn't disturb my sleep in the least."

He smacked his forehead and groaned. "The tools! I apologize. I will take care of them today."

"Hey, no problem. I'm not complaining in the least."

"Skylar." His tone quieted and his brow furrowed. Crossing his legs, he leaned back in the chair, his hands on the armrests, and scrutinized her with marble-hard eyes.

Uh-oh. The businessman was back in the saddle.

She broke out in a cold sweat. Here it came, the third degree. No Claire or Indio in sight to run interference for her. The next few minutes would decide whether or not she got to spend another night in that comfy "oh, by the way" room and work in that kitchen of all kitchens.

Max said, "Where are you from?"

"Ohio?" She wanted to kick herself for the questioning lilt.

"I mean besides that."

"Oh. Um. Here and there." She bought time with a shrug and reviewed the history she'd constructed for just such a moment. Enough truth fused to it so that the gaps were covered.

"Here and there?" He prompted.

She sipped more coffee to unglue her suddenly sticky vocal chords. "Yeah. I like to travel. I'm single. I have no responsibilities beyond myself. So I've worked my way across much of the West. I lived in Seattle for a while. That's where I read your mother's ad in an old copy of the *West Coast Retreat Gazette* and thought, *Hey, why not? I could live in San Diego for a while.*"

"Did you stop between Seattle and here?"

"Not in any one place for long." *Stick close to the facts.* "I'd saved up enough money to travel for a while. I'm not exactly high maintenance."

"Most people your age don't use alarm clocks. They have a cell phone with an alarm-clock tool."

"Now, that's high maintenance." She grinned. Perspiration trickled down her sides, under her shirt. "I bet you've noticed I'm not like most people my age. I don't have a phone, a car, a permanent home, or a five-year plan."

"Did you ever find work through a temp agency?"

She wrinkled her nose and then remembered temporary staffing was his specialty. "Oops."

"It's okay. Many people don't understand my business. But we get a lot of applicants down on their luck."

"I don't think of myself as down on my luck. I get by fine. I cook and wait tables at funky coffee shops. My bosses aren't the type to call Kelly Girl. It may surprise you, but in some circles I'm not considered all that strange."

He chuckled. "It may surprise you that I'm not considered all that strange in some circles either."

Skylar smiled, stretching tense muscles that ached to form words she could not speak. *You're like every other middle-aged hypocrite, acting like you know my world, pretending like you don't think I'm a communicable disease that should be eradicated.*

Max said, "We're not running a funky coffee shop here."

"I don't know." She held up her mug. "The coffee would pass muster."

"My mother's technique. It's been around forever." He uncrossed his legs, leaned forward, forearms on his knees. "Danny thinks we should go through a formal process, the whole shebang. Application, references, medical history, drug tests, fingerprints."

Vertigo crashed over her. Fingerprints?

It's okay. It's okay. It's okay. No prints were on file.

Her stomach squeezed itself into a tight knot. Coffee threatened to work its way back up.

"But." Max's eyes came into focus. They'd lost the hard look. "My son tends to be overly pragmatic." He shrugged. "I don't know where he gets that."

The guy was teasing? He was teasing. Skylar managed to take a deep, slow breath and let it out.

"Anyway," he went on, "I've been around people a lot longer than Danny has. I've been burned, sure, but usually I read character fairly accurately. In my opinion, I can hire you on that alone. Then there's my mother."

Skylar waited, expectant at the mention of Indio. Her heartbeat slowed. Her stomach relaxed. The courtyard stopped swimming before her eyes.

He said, "I don't have her depth of faith. I do have faith, however, in her ability to hear God. She knows when she knows. And she knows you are a direct answer to prayer. So Claire and I want to offer you room and board and a salary." He named a generous amount. "She's working on a job description. Once you see that, you can let us know what you decide. Does that sound fair?"

Skylar sensed the burner under her emotional carafe flip to the Off position. The hot mix would not bubble over. For now she was free to stay at the Hacienda Hideaway.

She nodded. "It sounds totally fair. Thank you."

"You're welcome." He stood and smiled. "For the record, cellular service up here is iffy at best. You're going to need an alarm clock. I'll get one for you right after I get rid of that pile of tools."

She promised herself not to go to seed on the thought that maybe, just maybe, Max Beaumont didn't think she was a communicable disease.

Wouldn't that be something?

Ten

The evening after the family dinner at the hacienda, as the shadows lengthened and the air cooled, Jenna sat at the high school football game on a top bleacher. Several rows separated her from other spectators. Her choice.

It was going to be a long night. According to the scoreboard, there were twelve minutes and twenty seconds left in the game. The *junior* varsity game. The event *before* varsity warm-ups, pep stuff, band stuff, intros, varsity game, halftime, more varsity game, so on and so forth, *ad nauseam*.

The game clock stopped. Twelve minutes and fifteen seconds.

"Hey, Mrs. Mason!" The shout came from below.

Jenna scanned the crowd. People moved about every which way through the stands. As someone sat down, Amber Ames appeared, waving like a lost person at an overhead helicopter. She made a bee-line up to Jenna's row.

Yessiree. It was going to be a really, really long game.

"Hi." Amber smiled and plopped down beside her.

"Hi."

"Guess what I learned third hour? Our husbands are seven thousand, seven hundred thirty-one miles from San Diego. Isn't that the most depressing thing you've heard today?"

"It is. Thanks for sharing it."

"I'm a firm believer that misery loves company. Lucky you." She bumped her arm against Jenna's. "Go ahead, tell me the most depressing thing you heard today."

She didn't have to think long. "Kevin called last night."

"Oh, that's wonderful!"

"It was." Past tense. The glow was long gone. "He said he figured tonight was the first game and he sure hoped I would go to it, sort of as his proxy to encourage the guys he coached last year."

Amber's face was expectant.

"That's it," Jenna said.

"I take it you don't like football."

Jenna sighed. "Watching any sport is like watching mold grow, but . . ." She shrugged.

"I know. It's not depressing that you're bored. It's depressing that a football game makes you just absolutely wallow in his not being where he used to be."

Jenna blinked, surprised at her insight. "Exactly. Not to mention I can also now wallow in the fact that Kevin is seven thousand, seven hundred thirty-one miles from where he used to be."

Amber gave her a sad smile. "See? Now, didn't that feel good? To vent all that negative energy with someone who's just as miserable as you are?"

Jenna looked at the blonde with appreciation. Amber might exhibit a featherbrained persona, but Jenna was beginning to realize Amber was nothing like that. Not only did she teach *chemistry*, she had plucked Jenna's heartstrings with the finesse of a master violinist. Twice.

Jenna said, "Thanks. It did feel good. I have friends. You'll notice, however, that not a one is here tonight holding my hand. My very best friend, Steph, probably would have come but she moved to Dallas last month. Even she, though, can't quite—well, none of them quite get it, do they?"

"They can't. Not unless they can say, 'Been there, done that.'"

"I find myself saying dumb things to defend myself, things like 'Just walk a mile in my moccasins and then you won't think I'm such a shrew.'"

"I keep asking for cheese to go with my whine."

Jenna smiled.

"We could team teach a unit on clichés." Amber chuckled. "So tell me about this mold growth—I mean this game."

"I don't know anything about it. Don't you?"

"Nope, I just came because it was something to do on a Friday night. And since your Kevin coached last year, I thought you might be here. Given we share the same size in moccasins, I figured hanging out with you might give me a respite."

Like a cloud moving in front of the sun, Jenna saw a somberness creep over Amber's face and obliterate its sparkle. The dimples disappeared.

Odd how another's pain took the edge off her own.

"Thank you, Amber."

"Thank you."

"Earlier, when I said that about my friends not being here to hold my hand, I didn't mean it literally."

Amber stared at her for a moment, her face going deadpan. "I'm really glad you said that. I was a little concerned about holding your hand."

"Just so we understand each other."

"Got it." Amber burst into laughter.

And Jenna joined in.

No way!" Amber stretched her mouth into an elongated oval. "You weren't a cheerleader?"

Jenna smiled at her reaction. Amber's exuberance had halved the time it took mold to grow on the football field. Darkness had fallen already and—if she understood the scoreboard—it was almost time for intermission of the varsity game. Intermission? Make that *halftime*. Talk about featherbrained.

"Honestly, Jenna, I took you for Miss Popular when you were in high school. Homecoming queen and all."

"Nope. I played violin and piano. Orchestra, private lessons, and all that. My older brother was homecoming king a couple years ahead of me. He says I was always too bossy to be popular. I think I still am. The guys here adore Kevin. The girls are friendly to me because it puts them one step closer to the hottest coach they've ever seen. For me, they have a nickname." She waited to see if Amber knew it.

"Bullhead Mason."

"Yeah. There might be others."

"I don't know of any, but I have heard my best students talk about how hard you push them. They see that as a good thing. There's respect in their voices."

Jenna shrugged. "You obviously have a good rapport with the kids." Students kept calling out to Mrs. Ames and climbing up the bleachers to greet her. Some acknowledged Jenna as well, more as a polite afterthought, though.

Now Amber shrugged. "You and I have different personalities. I grew up an Army brat, all over the world. I learned early to roll with the punches. My four older brothers made sure of that. I wasn't allowed to whine, cry, be shy, or act bossy. Dating was a nightmare. Joey practically had to win a fistfight with each one of my brothers before we got engaged. Heads up!" She blew out a breath. "Two o'clock."

"What?" Jenna followed Amber's gaze to their right. Cade Edmunds was climbing the bleachers in their direction.

"Speaking of holding hands . . ." Amber leaned toward her and murmured. "He can hold mine anytime."

Jenna studied her face, looking for clues. "Are you serious?"

Amber laughed. "Partly. I mean, I wouldn't *really* hold hands with him, but he is magnetic and inviting in that way. Joey says if I like the bald look, he'll shave his head."

"You told Joey your boss is magnetic and inviting?"

"Sure. It keeps my guy on his toes. Makes him want to come home in one piece to win the magnetic contest. Hey, Mr. Edmunds!" she called out.

"Hey, ladies." He sat down on Jenna's other side and quickly averted his gaze to the field below. "Great game, huh?"

She exchanged a look with Amber and they snickered.

Jenna said, "If you want an enlightened view on that subject, you've come to the wrong bleacher."

"You two don't have a clue." He half stood, punched the air, and shouted a cheer along with everyone else on the bleachers. "Yes! Way to go, guys!"

Jenna smiled at Amber's exaggerated yawn.

Still applauding, Cade sat back down. "You gotta tell Kevin about this. His guys are out there doing what he tried to get them to do all last year. It has come together."

"I don't know what that means."

He shook his head as if he couldn't believe her. "Tell him the offensive line really jelled."

"Huh?"

Eyes still on the game, Cade said, "The offensive line jelled. Think of it as the most exquisite dénouement in some Shakespeare play. That's what you're seeing down there, all the pieces coming together to execute a work of art." He threw a brief smile her way. "Maybe when it's over, you can remember who wins and tell him that too."

She cocked an eyebrow. "I might even manage to memorize the score."

He chuckled. Bracing one foot on the empty bleacher below them, he shoved his hands into the pockets of his lightweight jacket. An elbow touched her arm. "I hear they're doing military salutes

everywhere these days. At concerts, Padres games, the zoo, Sea World."
He paused. "Sundance High football game."

Jenna tensed.

"It was the team's idea. We've got three players with brothers overseas, plus a few dozen other students with some relative in uniform.
Then there's the faculty."

Amber sighed. "Are these boys sweet or what?"

Jenna slid to the edge of the bleacher, put her weight on her feet,
ready to flee. "When?"

"Right about . . ." Cade looked at the scoreboard and counted
down the seconds. "Three, two, one. Now." The horn blared. "Before
the team heads off the field."

The announcer's voice boomed through the loudspeaker, asking
people to remain in their seats for a moment. As he explained what
was going on, Jenna met Cade's stare.

"Jenna, they're his guys. They need to do this." He shifted. His
shoulder pressed gently against hers.

On her other side, Amber hooked an arm through Jenna's, not
saying a word.

Jenna turned to her. The dim light caught the glisten of a teardrop
on Amber's eyelashes.

If not for being tightly hemmed in by Amber and Cade, Jenna
would have bolted down the bleachers and gotten lost in the crowd
rather than hear it again. Like at the faculty meeting, names of military personnel were read along with their family members, first students, then faculty. Amber stood. Just as it seemed they might have
forgotten Kevin Mason, the announcer began to talk about him.

About his accomplishments at the high school the previous year.

About his impact on the boys whose older brothers had gone
overseas.

About his prior service in the Marines.

About his wife.

At last his name was pronounced.

Then Jenna's.

As one, the football team looked up at her and cheered. Spectators joined in and began to stand until it all became an earsplitting ovation.

Amber motioned for her to stand.

She couldn't. She didn't deserve recognition just because she was married to Kevin. All she did was cry, curse the USMC, complain about his absence, and count the days until he would come home. Last fall, when he reenlisted, she had even separated from him for a while and could not imagine how she'd ever remain married to such a man. He looked heroic to some. To her, though, his actions felt like abandonment.

Cade still sat beside her. He slanted toward her. "You can do this."

His face blurred before her. She shook her head.

"The kids need you to." In the shadows he took her hand and helped her to her feet.

The crowd went wild. Jenna bawled.

And Cade Edmunds squeezed her hand.

Eleven

Daniel Beaumont, what is wrong with you?" Claire practically hissed in frustration at her son.

She was keeping her voice lower than low because—as she was quickly learning—guests at the hacienda meant absolutely no privacy for the hosts. None. Not one square inch of it in over three hundred acres.

One woman had chatted with Skylar the whole time the girl baked cookies for tonight's bedtime snack. One couple followed Lexi around as she watered new plants, advising her on the best way to care for the landscape. Another woman had even wandered into Claire and Max's bedroom and caught Max mid-shirt change.

And the weekend was only six hours old!

Claire vowed to order several Employees Only signs. The ones she had vowed not to order. The ones she had vowed not to post would be going up ASAP.

"Mom, I'll carry that." Danny took the empty lasagna pan from her.

They were in the sala, at the buffet near the dining table, cleaning up after dinner. For the moment, no guest was in sight.

She put a hand on his arm. "Don't change the subject."

"Nothing's wrong with—"

"You're bugging Skylar and you're bugging me. Why are you here tonight anyway?"

"I told you," he whispered back, his brows nearly touching above his nose.

That was true. His roommate Hawk had driven up to see Tuyen. It had become evident the two were enamored with each other. Danny said he simply thought he'd tag along and help out.

Claire said, "I'm not buying it. You came to meddle."

"And how exactly do you figure that?"

She pressed her lips together and willed herself to slow down. Danny had challenged her since day one, yelling at the top of his newborn lungs, demanding attention a full five minutes before any of them realized his twin sister waited in the wings.

Unlike with her other three children, solid parent-child lines of demarcation did not exist with Danny. Through the years their relationship had often resembled either argumentative siblings or one of total role reversal. Even as a teenager Danny could play the wise father and chasten Claire. Despite his sometimes legalistic opinions that had grown more exasperating in recent years, his connection with God began long before she understood for herself what it was to relate to the Lord.

And she thought she was growing into the matriarchal role of the Beaumont family, sliding on into Indio's shoes! Mm-hmm, right. In her dreams.

She fixed a stare on Danny now. He was still a cute kid with curly hair and eyes less the color of Max's and more that of her brother's. Her favorite brother, the one who had moved to Alaska to get his head on straight. That was over thirty years ago. He was still there. Oh, how she prayed Danny wouldn't turn out like her brother.

Danny didn't flinch, but stared right back. "Hmm? How?"

"By quizzing my cook. She is part of this household, and you dogging her all evening while she's trying to work is not acceptable. If and when she's ready, she can tell us all about her life, but not this weekend and not to you between courses. Got that?"

He relaxed his hunched shoulders, and his eyebrows separated. "Remember Gunther and Faith?"

"Of course I do." Claire leaned sideways against the buffet. Danny's childhood friends, their families, and the Beaumonts often got together for holidays and birthdays. "I remember it was almost spooky how they changed so drastically. Their whole personalities transformed practically overnight."

"Mm-hmm. Skylar's spooky, too, Mom."

"Skylar?"

"She dresses and acts like them. Behind that whole New Age, bohemian, save-the-whales persona lies a blatant disdain for all things establishment. My old friends wouldn't be caught dead working here with four traditional types and their likeminded guests. Why would Skylar?"

Claire burst into laughter. "You think we're establishment? Good grief!" Her voice lost its whispery level. "Your father sold his life's work and I dropped thirty years' worth of social and volunteer commitments overnight. We moved to the sticks to chase a crazy pipe dream! It is so crazy I may start smoking your grandpa's pipe, even before this first weekend is over!"

"Trust me, your new cook knows where to buy the opium to put in it."

"Danny, that's nonsense. This is all about you. I know you stopped hanging out with Faith and Gunther because they got in too deep, but I also suspect they left you in the dust and didn't bother to look back."

He shook his head vehemently. "It was my decision."

"Oh, honey, they betrayed you simply by embracing things you wouldn't buy into. You can't deny that didn't hurt."

"Okay, okay. So they hurt my feelings. That was eons ago. I'm over it, but I know better now. Their type can't be trusted, and Skylar Pierson could easily pass for their clone."

Claire saw the chink in his armor—a gaping, unhealed wound

she couldn't fix or even address yet. "Methinks thou doth protest too much."

"Mom."

In his resistant tone, she heard immaturity and thought again of her brother. Despite his spiritual maturity, Danny had a ways to go yet to find his true self.

Smiling softly, she patted his cheek. "Whatever. Just please don't move to Alaska."

Twelve

Skylar set a cup of chamomile tea on the island counter and decided against telling Claire she looked like a zombie. "Sit and sip."

"I should—"

"Nope. It's break time. No 'shoulds' for the next ten minutes. Everything is under control. Dishwashers are running. Guests are doing their own thing. Tomorrow's breakfast is all prepped. I will put milk, tea, and cookies on the buffet at nine."

Claire sighed, slid onto a stool, and wrapped her hands around the cup. "Okay. Thank you."

"Sure." Skylar wiped a dish towel across the countertop. "So Danny says you want to take up pipe smoking."

Claire groaned.

Skylar chuckled. When Danny told her that, his mood had actually been mellow. So mellow, in fact, she thanked him for his help with bringing dirty dishes in from the sala. His mouth twitch had escalated to smile status. Briefly, but for real.

She folded up the towel and looked at a decidedly non–movie star version of Claire Beaumont. "Claire," she said, "are you having a good time yet?"

"A good time?" Claire squinted in thought. "Well, honestly, I . . . No, I don't think so."

"It's only your first night."

"Yeah." There was not a hopeful note in her mumble.

"If you don't mind my asking, why did you and Max start this business?"

Claire sighed. "In a nutshell, we desperately needed a new life. After thirty-some years of growing apart, we were either going to divorce or grow back together."

"That's heavy. No middle ground to shoot for?"

She shook her head. "Middle ground was a dead end. Ages ago, when we fell in love, we imagined a shared life of helping others by helping them find work. That turned into his one-man show while my show became kids and the home."

"It's a common scenario."

"Unfortunately, you're right. Anyway, Ben and Indio created the Hacienda Hideaway when she retired from nursing. It was low-key. Advertising was word-of-mouth and local. After the fire came through here, they didn't want to start all over. Max and I saw it as a perfect opportunity for us to start over in all ways."

A faraway expression came over Claire's face. She stopped talking for a long moment.

"The thing is, what Max and I learned during our rough time was that we didn't offer each other an emotionally safe harbor. We should have been a place of retreat for each other, a relationship that offered peace and restoration." Her eyes focused back on Skylar. "That's why we started this. We wanted to create a safe respite where people could retreat from whatever and be healed. Or at least strengthened and encouraged."

A tight feeling crept from Skylar's chest into her throat. Startled at a rare desire to cry, she ground her teeth together and willed it away.

Claire said, "Does any of that make sense?"

Skylar nodded and swallowed with way too much difficulty. "Yeah." She took a deep breath. "The thing is, well, it's not the wallpaper that makes a safe harbor." Again she had to set her jaw and tamp down the buildup of tears.

"What do you mean?"

"In the twenty-four hours I've been here, I've watched you fluff pillows, line dresser drawers with scented paper, color coordinate towels and sheets, replan meals, and arrange flowers. You've created an unbelievably comfortable, homey ambience."

"Thanks." Claire tilted her head. "There's a 'but' in your voice."

"But all that is not the safe harbor." Skylar leaned forward, her forearms on the countertop, her tone urgent. "Earlier I saw you with the cleaning women and the construction guys. You treated them like they were family. Then tonight with the guests you went all stiff, like you've blended in with the wallpaper, like you're just part of the décor."

"I want them to feel like this is home for them for the next couple days."

"Claire, there is no home without personality. You're the personality. You're the safe harbor."

Surprise registered on the woman's face. "Really?"

Skylar nodded.

Claire grabbed a napkin from a nearby holder and held it to her eyes. Skylar gazed around the room, biting her tongue.

At last Claire looked at her with red eyes. "Hon, I'm quite sure we're not paying you what you're worth."

The term of endearment struck Skylar like a blow to the solar plexus. Or maybe Claire Beaumont's very own, thousand-watt grin was to blame.

Either way, life at the hacienda had just gotten way too complicated.

Thirteen

Eight and a half long days after talking with Kevin, Jenna sat on the low seawall—face toward the ocean, sandaled feet dangling above the sand, Cade Edmunds beside her—and she counted the fibs.

Fib number one: she had come to the beach that Saturday because she was shopping in the neighborhood.

Fib number two: knowing Cade would be at the beach had no impact whatsoever on her decision to brave the late summer hordes and sweltering heat or wear her electric blue print sundress that showed a little more of her long legs than her typical school attire.

Fib number three: she wanted to thank Danny in person for taking the time to teach surfing to Cade's special group of juvenile delinquents

Were three fibs enough to send her to hell? Danny would have the answer. Not that she was about to ask him. She needed the lies. Without them she'd be forced to give up the reprieve Cade Edmunds offered, a time-out from a loneliness that had grown unbearable.

"Ha!" Cade chuckled. "Those waves ought to take my obnoxious whippersnappers down a notch or two." He was talking about the four boys he'd brought to the ocean. They were heading out into the water now, surfboards in tow, huge waves in the distance.

Jenna turned to Cade and instantly regretted coming. He was too attractive in his flip-flops, shorts, T-shirt, and sunglasses, his face glistening with sweat. Mr. Ice Guy's rare expression of enjoyment was downright provocative.

Watching the ocean, he said, "Your brother and his friend are something else. Did you know they won't let me pay a dime for the lessons or the boards?"

"That's Danny and Hawk. They both have hearts of gold. When Hawk was a teenager, he was just like these guys."

"A wannabe gang member, huh? I sensed that about him. He had an instant rapport with the kids. Danny's good with them, too, but I bet he's always been a straight arrow."

"Annoyingly squeaky-clean. If he wasn't doing homework, he was surfing."

He smiled, his face toward the newbie surfers.

Jenna watched them as they paddled out into the surf. Danny and Hawk waded alongside them, guiding the boards. The experience should be a treat for the guys, all from broken and poverty-stricken families. They lived a mere twenty minutes from the coast but rarely got the chance to visit it, let alone learn how to surf from a pro.

She said, "I still can't believe you pulled this off."

Cade shrugged. "No big deal. When I mentioned I wanted to give nonfootball players an outlet and you said your brother never did team sports, he just surfed, a light went on. I don't know why I didn't think of it sooner. One phone call to my friend in Sacramento and my four chief boneheads are having a healthy time of their lives." He referenced a statewide program for disadvantaged students. It included a local supervisor who was coming later.

She grinned. "You did emphasize to these guys that Danny's my brother, right? That their sixth-hour English teacher is partly responsible for this great day they're having?"

"You sound desperate to make points with these guys." He took a swig from his water bottle and grinned back at her.

"You think it's funny, sticking me with all four in one class."

"Not funny." He looked at her. "You needed a challenge. You've been skating for six years with the 'Yes, ma'am, whatever you say, ma'am' kids."

She stuck out her tongue at him.

"Trust me, Jen, by the end of this school year you'll have them eating out of your hand."

She held back a smart retort because—fib number whatever—she was not, absolutely not, flirting.

Turning again toward the water, Cade likewise fell silent.

Fib: it was not a comfortable silence between them.

Fib: she would go home soon.

If Kevin were there at home, she would go. If he were calling today, she would go. If she knew there was mail from him, electronic or snail, she would go. If the apartment did not resound with ear-splitting echoes of his absence, she would go. She would.

And that was the truth.

Jenna lingered at the beach.

She and Cade moved to the water's edge. At his insistence, she sat in his low-set beach chair. He plopped down in the sand beside her.

They laughed as again and again the boys tumbled off the surfboards, skinny legs and arms flailing. When one finally managed to stay upright for a few seconds, Cade whistled and cheered.

Jenna said, "You really are great with them."

"Thanks. They remind me of myself at that age. What I want to do is fill in the gaps for them. Be the dad they don't have." It was the closest he ever came to revealing personal background.

Everyone knew he had grown up in a tough Los Angeles area, supposedly fatherless, and carved a way out. His unorthodox approach to the role of principal often took people aback. He got results, though, and the superintendent and board members cut him a lot of slack. He was single but would sometimes bring a date—never the same one—to faculty social events. The man remained for the most part an unknown.

She said, "Who filled in gaps for you?"

He waited a beat, his mouth a straight line. "A teacher here, a coach there, a dean."

Abruptly he stood and stepped ankle deep into the water. Waving his arms, he let out another fingerless, piercing whistle and shouted, "Nelson! Way to go!"

Kevin was like Cade, wanting to save every kid who crossed his path. When he saw boys from his classes and teams graduate and enlist, he felt compelled to go with them. It was why he reenlisted with the Marines. His students would be graduating and enlisting. To continue playing football while they and other young guys went off to war became unthinkable for Kevin.

Men.

Jenna's only goal was to get her students to write a complete sentence and read a poem before the year was over.

Faint music reached her ears above the noise of the surf. It was the theme from the old television show *Bonanza*. Her grandparents were calling?

She pulled the cell phone from her bag, guessing her phone-challenged grandfather was not on the other end. "Nana?"

"Jenna, dear, where are you?"

"At Danny's beach. He's surfing with some kids from my school."

"You're not alone, then?"

"Hardly. It's packed. Nana, you sound odd. What's wrong?"

"Nothing is wrong. Maybe the word is—" Her voice broke. "Emotional?"

"What happened?"

Her grandmother sniffed and took a noisy deep breath. "Beth Russell called."

Jenna felt herself go still inside. She did not know Beth Russell.

She only knew that the woman had been engaged to Uncle BJ. She'd been deeply in love with him. And then he joined the Navy, went to Vietnam, and disappeared. Assuming BJ was dead, Beth married someone else and got on with her life. End of the Uncle BJ–Beth Russell story. Not much to it.

Or too much to it?

"Jenna, she's coming to visit next week. She wants to meet Tuyen."

And this has what *to do with me?* Jenna held back the caustic retort. Her cousin, Tuyen, had turned up out of the blue, news to all of them. Uncle BJ, who'd been MIA for thirty-five years and believed dead, was her father.

"Beth is . . ." Again her grandmother's voice filled with tears. A long moment passed as she regained composure. "Beth is a beautiful woman. It's being impressed upon me that you are supposed to meet her."

Jenna's heart pounded in her ears. The sun's blanket of intense heat enveloped her. The visor pinched her forehead, and the swimsuit cover-up felt unbearably heavy. Her sunglasses cut into the bridge of her nose.

Indio Beaumont's *being impressed upon* did that to people.

Jenna said, "Why?"

"I have no clue, dear. I just hope you will consider it. Next Sunday."

Jenna's throat closed up. She could only whimper, "Mm-hmm."

"Tell Danny, too, all right? He'll want to come."

"Mm-hmm."

"Jenna, I know this is so very hard for you. You're thinking about Kevin and horrible things that could happen. Like getting injured and lost and, oh my, falling in love." She echoed what Danny had said last week.

"How did—" It was Jenna's turn to fight back tears. "How did—" She gave up.

"How did your Papa and I get through it? God. God carried us through BJ's war. He carried us through the news of him being lost. Through thirty-four years of not knowing what happened to him. And through meeting the daughter we didn't know he had in Vietnam. God will carry you, Jenna. I promise you, He will carry you. Just hold on to Him with all your might."

While her grandmother's conversation slid into a prayer, Jenna cried openly. There was no way—no way in the world—she was going to be able to hold on.

And that was the absolute truth.

Fourteen

His feet planted in the sandy ocean floor, a gentle swell breaking over his shoulders, Danny watched his sister fall apart.

It was typical drama-queen behavior. Jenna tore off her sun visor and sunglasses. They fell beside the chair onto the sand. She jammed her elbows against her thighs and buried her face in her hands. Her cell phone protruded from between fingers. Even from this distance he could tell she was crying hard.

Typical and yet . . . Jenna must have just received a phone call. And Kevin was halfway around the world where people blew up other people on a regular basis.

"Dear God."

A humongous wave crashed over his head. Its force rolled him like tumbleweed underwater. Righting himself, he wiped stinging salt water from his eyes and nose and turned. The boys on the surfboards were behind him. They'd managed to dive through the wave. His friend Hawk was treading water between them. Grins and riotous howls and thumbs-up came at him from all five. They were learning quickly and having a blast.

Danny looked again at Jenna. Cade Edmunds was kneeling in front of her. He put his arms around her. Her face went against his shoulder.

Danny swam toward shore. In the shallows he tripped, caught himself, and lunged to where Jenna sat. Prayers and obscenities yammered in his head. How was it he could simultaneously pray for Kevin's safety and curse the United States government up one side and down the other?

He knelt next to Cade. A corner of his mind registered that his married sister snuggled in the arms of her boss was not a good thing.

"Jen? What happened?"

She raised a tear-streaked face and blubbered. "Nana called. Beth Russell is coming!"

Catching his breath, Danny stared at her, dumbstruck. "Huh?"

Jenna nodded.

He groaned, sat down on the sand, and rolled onto his back. His heart bucked like a bronco as he gulped for air. Uncle BJ's girlfriend from *years* before he and Jenna had been *born* was coming? Big deal.

"Danny!"

He tilted his head to look at her. Between gasps he said, "I repeat, huh?"

"Nana says I should meet her!"

"Yeah. So? We knew she might come. I want to meet her. Why wouldn't we?"

"Oh!" She cried in frustration.

Cade still had one arm around Jenna. The dude was beginning to irritate Danny.

Jenna wiped a beach towel over her face. She accepted a water bottle from Cade and took a few sips.

"Jen," Danny said, "it's what I said the other night, isn't it? Your imagination is in overdrive." He sat up. "Kevin is not Uncle BJ. He is not in Vietnam. You are not Beth Russell. He is not going to run off on you and create another life with someone else."

"It's more than that. It's Nana and her—" She pressed her lips together, a combination of pout and wail suppressor.

If the stranger hadn't been sitting right there, Danny would have talked about their grandmother, about how strong she was, about how she'd received Tuyen with open arms because Nana trusted God knew what He was doing. What was a reunion for Nana with her old friend Beth? It'd be a party by comparison.

Cade said, "What about Nana?"

Jenna burst into fresh tears and jumped to her feet. "I'm sorry! I just can't handle this anymore!" She grabbed her bag and hurried away toward the boardwalk.

Danny stood.

Cade rose beside him. "I'll go after her."

"No." He took a moment to look directly at the sunglasses that hid the man's eyes. "It's a brother's job." He waggled a thumb over his shoulder. "The guys are doing great, but you better stay with them."

"Yeah." Cade's jaw worked. "Right."

Without another word, Danny went after Jenna.

Fifteen

On her third Sunday at the Hideaway, Skylar declined Claire's third invitation to attend church with the family. She went for a hike.

It was early September. The never-ending Southern California sun refused to take a break. It heated up the pleasantly cool morning in record time. Sweating, she climbed a winding, rocky path through live oaks and pines, some in full growth, some bare and blackened.

The Beaumonts' church must be a humdinger. Even with guests at the hacienda, they managed to slip away for the service. Even with the imminent arrival of the much-talked-about Beth Russell, they went. Apparently they didn't let anything interfere with what Indio called their corporate worship time.

Skylar rounded a bend and came into a clearing. Max's father, Ben, stood a dozen feet from her, in the center of it, hands on his hips.

He looked her way and raised a hand in greeting. As usual, he wore denim overalls and a plaid shirt with rolled-up sleeves. His shock of white hair was uncombed, his weathered face haggard.

She waved back and walked up to him. "Morning, Mr. B. You're missing church."

"So are you, young lady." His blue eyes reflected the sunlight, and she caught sight of his rare sparkle.

"Are we in trouble?"

"Only with Indio. The good Lord can handle our need to be

elsewhere besides a pew this morning. Have you been to this spot yet?"

She shook her head and studied the wall of gargantuan boulders before them. Down low, a jagged cross had been dug out of the stone. Alongside that, evenly carved letters spelled, "Benjamin Charles Beaumont Jr. – September 9, 1950." Some sort of smudge marred the "eau" of "Beaumont."

Skylar said, "Claire told me about it. It's a memorial to your son."

"Yes," Ben said. "We never knew the date of death." He sighed, a sound so deep it could have been dredged up from the bottom of his soul. "We still don't. They didn't mark the grave in Vietnam. Tuyen says 1982. If her story is to be believed."

"You're not sure?" Claire had told her about that as well. Tuyen, an Amerasian and a complete unknown to them before last spring, arrived with a wild story about BJ being her father. He'd been a Navy pilot, shot down, MIA, alive for years but unable to escape. When Tuyen was little, he and her mother had been killed by Communists.

"Well, I'll tell you what I think, Skylar." Ben looked at her, his twinkle snuffed out by a dark gaze. "I can't believe my son survived for years in that country and had a child out of wedlock. I can't believe it because of one reason. And she's coming here today."

Obviously he referred to Beth Russell. She, too, must be a humdinger to still have the old man's devotion after so many years.

In a way, Skylar was glad that, like the odd mar across the stone's carved letters, the Beaumonts had a few smudges in their history. Such imperfections could mean a longer stay for her own scruffy self.

Sixteen

Claire stood near the parking lot, on the railroad-tie steps. Heated by the afternoon sun, they gave off the tarry scent of creosote. Its pungency played tag with the softer odors of sage and cedar mulch.

A car approached, dust swirls trailing it. Aside from the pavement in front of the house, the lot was still mostly dirt and gravel, as was the incline leading up to the yard, bordered by more ties. Asphalt and bedding plants would come, in time.

Max stood a step below Claire, and Tuyen one above. Indio and Ben were in the parking area. Claire felt part of an odd receiving line. They all waited to greet Beth Russell.

The car stopped now, and the long-ago fiancée of Max's brother emerged. Claire had met her on a few occasions, years before. She remembered a petite honey-blonde, down-to-earth, a quick smile, a little-girl voice. That described the woman in blue jeans and over-sized white shirt whose ponytail swayed as she cried, "Indio! Ben!" and embraced each one tightly, for long moments.

They hadn't seen each other in at least twenty years. Tears flowed freely from all three. Claire looked away.

She heard Tuyen's sharp intake of breath.

Claire turned and smiled up at her. "It's okay."

Her blue eyes—so incongruous in the tall girl with her Asian features—were wide. "It okay? Me here?" Her accent had thickened steadily throughout the week, her words often indecipherable. She dreaded meeting her father's former fiancée—the woman her dad had betrayed by staying in Vietnam with her mom. Surely the woman would hate her, she'd said.

Claire took Tuyen's hand. The young woman wore her sun-yellow *ao dai*, traditional Vietnamese slacks and long, embroidered, slit tunic. She'd had her dark hair cut recently. It flowed in its elegant chin-length style.

Claire squeezed her hand. "It is very good that you are here." She looked again toward the others.

Max stepped forward. "Beth. Hello." He hugged her, his older brother's best friend, the one who had been like a sister to him during his teen years while she was dating BJ.

"And Claire." Beth smiled and moved to greet her.

"Welcome." Mutual emotions held them in a long hug. There was so much to say, but that was for later.

Beth let go of Claire, a gentle smile on her lips and in her glistening eyes. Holding out her arms, she spoke in a foreign language, an Asian ring to it. Claire heard her say, "Tuyen Beaumont."

The frightened woman moved stiffly down the steps and into Beth's embrace.

Claire crossed her arms and cried almost as hard as she did the day Tuyen arrived. She felt Max's hand caress her back, heard his own snuffles.

Beth cupped Tuyen's face in her hands. She said more in the foreign tongue. Tuyen murmured replies. The worry seams across her forehead quickly smoothed out.

Claire recalled that BJ and Beth had studied Spanish in college; they'd planned to live as missionaries in South America. He would fly planes, she would teach. Then Vietnam erupted, and he enlisted. Like Kevin, he could not stand by and watch others go. Since BJ's disappearance, Beth had gone back to school, studied other languages, and become a linguistics professor, wife, and mother.

Beth slid an arm through Tuyen's, holding the taller woman close,

as if she did not want to let her go. "That's all I know how to say in
Vietnamese."

Tuyen giggled in her shy way.

Beth looked straight at Ben. "This is BJ's daughter, Ben."

He moved his head, a subtle shake of disagreement.

"Ben, listen to me." Beth's tone grew urgent, but her voice
remained soft and high-pitched. "I have a wonderful, godly husband.
I have three beautiful children, all in college. And still sometimes I feel
guilty for abandoning my fiancé declared missing in action thirty-five
years ago. For letting him go. For moving on with my life."

Ben bristled, shifting his weight from one foot to the other.
"You were so young. We never thought you shouldn't marry someone else."

"I know, and I always appreciated your support. But the guilt is
there nonetheless. My children's hearts soaked it up. They carry
around my brokenness. They sometimes can't receive God's blessings.
I recognize it now. I've asked their forgiveness. God is healing. I'm
sorry. I didn't mean to preach at you."

Ben lowered his head. Indio smiled.

Claire thought how her in-laws knew firsthand about asking
a son for forgiveness. They were no stranger to brokenness and
healing.

Their sons were opposites. BJ was the ideal kid; Max was the
rebel. Years later, Ben and Indio realized how they'd hurt Max by
comparing him to BJ. Beth squeezed Tuyen's arm. "BJ would have
been happy for me. And I am so happy to know that he was loved
and that he knew the joy of fatherhood. I only wish he could have
seen Tuyen grow up." She looked at the young woman. "Do you
understand any of this?" She added a phrase in Vietnamese.

Tuyen touched her own chest and nodded.

A sob burst from Ben. He stumbled to the edge of the lot and sank
onto a bordering railroad tie. He buried his face in his hands and cried
so very hard.

Indio raised her hands for a split second, her typical quick gesture of thanksgiving, and went to him.

Claire sidled up against Max. Tears seeped from his eyes, but he smiled. Like her, he knew Beth's words had given Ben permission to finally surrender . . . his crazy grip on BJ's moral innocence, his anger at a world that conspired against his son, his hostility toward Tuyen.

Claire thought she heard music, like a distant choir singing.

Maybe it was just her imagination.

Or maybe not.

Seventeen

At the far end of the great room, near the dining table, Skylar silently observed the Beaumonts. The entire clan was there, including even the golden retriever, Samson, and the yellow cat, Willow. Seated in various positions by the stone fireplace, everyone listened with rapt attention to the stranger talk about BJ, the missing one.

Danny broke from the circle and approached Skylar. Uptight as his mannerisms could be, his gait was an effortless glide. His mother said he spent more time on a surfboard than not. Perhaps it came from that.

His mouth split in a bona fide Wally Cleaver grin. "Let me guess," he said in a low voice. "You're a fly on the wall."

Skylar shrugged a shoulder. "Does that bother you?"

"Would it matter if it did?"

"Nope." She refused to explain that his mother had invited her into the room. As a matter of fact, Claire told her the hacienda was her home. She was welcome to enter into family life however she chose.

Skylar would sooner tell Danny to go jump off a cliff.

Evidently unaware of her abusive thoughts, he leaned against the buffet beside her.

The guy annoyed her to no end. He'd been in her kitchen countless times since her first day, probing for information—personal, menu-wise, and everything in between—fidgeting all the while like a hyperactive kid.

At the moment his behavior was atypically calm. He must have skipped his Wheaties that morning.

She turned her attention back to the Beaumont drama unfolding across the room. The presence of Beth Russell might explain Danny's changed demeanor. The whole family seemed a bit subdued.

Beth. The woman was as soft as her name. Skylar deduced that tidbit after exchanging only a few words with her. Although she had to be in her late fifties, she was fresh faced as a little girl, peaches and creamy, cosmetic free. Her eyes were luminescent.

It was something else though, an intangible, that attracted Skylar. With every gesture and spoken word, Beth sent out vibes. It was an aura of—Skylar had no other word for it—*goodness*.

Danny shifted his weight. "For the record, it doesn't bother me that you're here."

She muttered, "Like I care." Thoroughly frustrated with his interruption, she pushed herself away from the buffet. "Excuse me." She walked out the side door and quickly made her way into the courtyard.

So much for learning how the Beaumonts dealt with family smudges. Smudges like a fiancée meeting her dead beau's out-of-wedlock, grown-up daughter no one even knew existed until a few months ago. It would have made a great tabloid headline.

Earlier Skylar had slunk into the sala in time to note Ben's red-rimmed eyes and Jenna's trembling chin. Tuyen sat close to Beth Russell, who often reached over to touch her arm. It was a curious picture.

Whipped right off the page by Danny.

Skylar climbed onto the bottom rail of the fence that enclosed the horse corral. Bending over the top rail, she clicked her tongue. Two palominos stood in languid beauty in shade cast from the barn. They swished their creamy tails and ignored her.

She made another clucking noise. "Hey, Reuben. Moses."

An ear twitched on Reuben's golden head. Moses winked.

"Aw, guys."

It was a hot afternoon. They were avoiding the sun.

As diligently as she avoided the heat of Danny's search beams.

The other week, when Claire went into her "just part of the wall-paper" act with the first guests, Skylar had easily recognized what was going on. It was a trick she herself had mastered in the recent past.

Eighteen months past, to be exact, but who was counting?

Disappear in plain sight and no one cares who you are.

Except nerdy dudes who had no life.

Like the one who most likely belonged to the footsteps now approaching from behind her.

Skylar threw a scowl over her shoulder, but he missed it. A moment later he hoisted himself up beside her.

He remained quiet for all of three seconds. "Do you ride?"

"Do you play 'Twenty Questions' with everyone or is it just me?"

He chuckled. "Mom says I bug you too much."

"Your mother is a wise woman."

"I guess that means you agree. Okay, I admit I probably do bug you and interfere with your work. I apologize."

She squinted at him sideways. "Why?"

"Why apologize?" He shrugged. "Forgiveness is in the air today. I'm hoping to grab some for myself."

"You say it's in the air because of all that going on in the house?"

"Mm-hmm. Do you know the story? About Uncle BJ and Beth? About Tuyen?"

"Yes."

"Sticky wicket, as Erik calls it. My grandfather has not been able to accept that Uncle BJ would do such a thing. Stay in Vietnam and have a child? No way."

"Holy cow! BJ was in a war. How could Ben judge—" Too late she heard the barrage and stopped herself.

"Exactly."

They exchanged a glance.

Of connection?

He said, "And now, lo and behold, Beth believes BJ probably did exactly that. She totally accepts Tuyen. Totally forgives BJ."

"Forgives BJ? How can it be his fault? I mean the guy didn't try to get shot down and survive in some foreign jungle he couldn't possibly escape without being killed or captured."

"I totally agree. But people were hurt. Call it forgiving him or the Viet Cong or our government. Whoever or whatever. The choice to forgive simply releases a stranglehold on someone's heart. My grandfather's, in this case."

Oh, man. "I suppose you're one of those, you know, *vocal* Christians."

He laughed. "I suppose I'm still bugging you."

"You suppose correctly."

"So do you."

"Easy call. It was either that type of Christian or you're part bulldog, and since you don't walk on four legs . . ."

"I've been tagged worse names."

She gave him a mean smirk. "You have no idea how much I hold back."

"I might." He looked at the horses. "So do you ride?"

Skylar felt like she'd been thrown off a horse and had the wind knocked from her. His swing of mood and topic was going to give her whiplash.

She blurted, "Yeah. I love riding."

Uh-oh.

She'd already decided fatherless kids from Ohio with drug-addicted moms did not ride horses. It was a rich person's hobby, not even a remote possibility under the scenario she'd presented.

"I mean," she said, "I got to go. A few times. As a kid. Big-sister program or something." *Shut up, Skylar. Shut up.* "Your grandfather said he'd take me sometime."

"Or I will. Moses and Reuben here are the best choice. The others are unpredictable. I think they're still spooked from the fire."

A wave of homesickness nearly bowled her off the fence.

It wasn't an ache for *home*. It was an ache for moments, for the freedom of those moments.

She did ride. She loved to ride. She loved the wind in her hair. The keen sense that the powerful animal could whisk her to the ends of the earth at her command.

Skylar stepped down from the fence. "I have work to do."

Without a backward glance, she hurried away.

Danny Beaumont was not a nuisance. He was a danger, the hound that would sniff and sniff until he caught scent of her true identity. He would make it impossible for her to remain in the Kansas, the home she'd just found.

Locating a pay phone was a major hassle. Skylar spent most of the drive down from the hacienda cursing cellular technology. It pigeon-holed Americans, forcing them to carry phones on their hips, thereby eliminating convenient public phones for all those people who could not afford or simply did not want to carry phones on their hips.

She stood now at a pay phone in a bus station and placed a collect call. As she listened to the ring on the other end, relief at actually finding the phone got lost in a press of other emotions.

There was the strain of fabricating a grocery need in order to borrow a car for a quick run to town. Claire always graciously offered hers, but driving the sleek foreign model with its fancy gadgets on the curvy hills did a number on Skylar. GPS doohickey aside, navigating around an unfamiliar area was a pain. And there was still that lingering homesick ache she'd felt while watching the horses.

Which explained why she stood there staring at dirty cracked linoleum, battling a nervous breakdown.

The ringing stopped. "Rockwell residence."

Skylar shut her eyes. "Mom. Hi. It's me."

"Laurie!" The low-pitched voice conveyed surprise layered heavily with wariness. "Are you all right?"

"Yeah. I'm good. I have a job, as a cook. And I met Wally Cleaver."

"Who?"

"From TV. Not really. He just reminds me of—how are you?"

"Fine."

"How's Dad?"

"Just fine too. He's at the hardware store."

"Any news?"

A slight hesitation. "No."

"Okay. Well, I just wanted to check in."

"Okay, thank you."

"Sure."

"Take care."

"You too. Bye."

"Bye."

Skylar hung up the phone, shuffled to a nearby bench, and sank onto it.

Replaying that voice, she heard the usual relief in the "Take care." If she listened hard, really hard, she could almost make out regret in the "Bye." Almost.

Most likely, though, it was simply her imagination filling in gaps with what she'd never, ever in her life heard in that voice.

Eighteen

"How did you do it?" Jenna gazed at Beth Russell. She'd been watching her all afternoon. She could not look away from such an enigma.

They sat alone outdoors, in wicker chairs tucked between a low boulder and a young sycamore tree at one end of the courtyard. A black streak marred half the trunk from the ground up, but wide leaves rustled and their odd scent wafted in the afternoon breeze.

"How did I do it?" Beth's smile eclipsed the fact that they had met only a few hours ago. The heart connection between the two women was ages old. "You mean, how did I get out of bed every day while the love of my life lived in a war zone the other side of the world?"

"And not lose your mind?"

Beth reached over and placed a hand on her arm. "Oh, dear heart."

On any other day, Jenna would not be conversing with the likes of a woman who said "dear heart" and reeked of such utter compassion—most especially one her grandmother practically demanded she meet because of one of her visceral conclusions.

But today was not any other day. Today was the day she'd awoken from a vivid, explicit dream of lovemaking with Cade Edmunds.

Jenna said, "I've heard the pat spiritual answers."

"Indio."

"Yes. They don't seem . . . available to me."

"Your grandmother lives in the mystery." Again the gentle smile, the eyes so sparkly they were of no particular color. "God is real, Jenna. He is our only hope for sanity."

"But how?"

"Talk to Him. I talked to Him nonstop after BJ left. I determined to expect Him to show up in the everyday."

"But what did that look like in the everyday?"

Beth giggled. "You are your father's daughter, and I mean that as a compliment. Max was always pushing for answers. He kept me and BJ on our toes." She paused. "It looked like friends offering to be with me. It looked like opportunities to grow in my studies and work. It looked like camaraderie with other military girlfriends and wives."

Jenna thought of Amber and her invitations to dinner and movies and gatherings with other Pendleton wives. She thought of the list of names tucked in a drawer, names of local women whose husbands were in Kevin's squad.

Beth said, "I remember I stopped watching the news and reading the paper. I still cried at least once a day, but the images of war grew less immediate. I stopped saying 'God, keep him safe' with every other breath. I prayed instead, 'Thank You for being with him.'"

"And when you heard . . . ?" Fear, thick as the grossest of phlegm in her throat, strangled her voice.

"When I heard . . . That's when I entered hell." She squeezed Jenna's arm. "There is no escaping the pain. It becomes the focus of your life the moment he enlists. Right?"

Jenna nodded.

Beth looked at the sycamore near them. Fine lines appeared around her eyes, giving her a look of weariness. "I'm like this tree. My black streak from a long-ago fire is still obvious, but so is new growth." She turned back to Jenna. "You're in the fire now. You can't escape it or make any sense of it whatsoever. It's scorching through you, leaving its mark. The question is, will you let it consume you . . . or will you let God bring about new growth through it?"

Now Jenna tore her gaze away from the woman, unable to view such a raw display of brokenness.

M idweek, early in the morning, Jenna trekked again up into the hills to the Hacienda Hideaway. She would miss half a day of school. Cade hired a sub for her, no questions asked.

She had one giant of a question.

Parking between Danny's truck and Erik's Mustang, she pondered it. Greeting the entire family in the courtyard, she pondered it. Hiking the steep trail behind the barn, she pondered it.

Why in the world had she come?

A subdued bunch trudged along the path with her—her parents and grandparents, Erik, Danny, Lexi, Tuyen, Beth Russell, and Skylar Pierson. The whole gang was there in honor of September 9, Uncle BJ's birthday. They made their way to the wilderness area her grandparents had dedicated to their eldest son.

It was an odd sort of commemoration for him. But then, what exactly was a family to do with a member's birthday when they didn't know if that person was alive or dead? No address for mailing cards and gifts. No grave marker for placing flowers.

What would she do if Kevin didn't come home and yet didn't get killed?

They reached the spot. Scrub vegetation. Dirt. Rocks. A boulder. On its face toward the rising sun was a crude carving of a cross. Beneath it, in neatly grooved letters and numbers, was his name, Benjamin Charles Beaumont Jr., and his birth date.

The ritual began. Papa, almost formal in his collared shirt and bolo tie, laid a small wooden figurine he'd carved on the ground. Nana set down a bunch of sunflowers picked from her garden. Max placed a small stone in a pile. They all sat on blankets in the dried grasses. Claire prompted Nana to tell about the day BJ was born. Nana spoke, her face aglow with sweet memories.

Once more Jenna wondered why she had come. She hadn't been since childhood. Usually only her parents came with Nana and Papa. Why the pull on her heart to come this year?

She looked over at Beth Russell, who sat close to Tuyen, an arm around her fiancée's daughter.

And then she knew the answer.

She had come to see the impossible: proof that God was real in the midst of unspeakable pain.

Hey, Princess!" Beth's youthful voice rang out across the hacienda's front yard. "Wait up!"

Jenna turned, car key in hand, fifth-hour American lit in mind.

Beth reached her, grinning broadly and catching her breath.

Jenna groaned. "'Princess'?"

"Danny referenced you that way. And then the Lord gave me a word for you."

Try as she might, Jenna did not shut her eyelids quick enough to conceal their flutter.

Beth laughed. "I know. I am weirder than your grandma. Hear me out?"

"I need to get to—"

"I know. I'll be brief."

It was impossible to say no to the woman.

Beth wiped a sleeve across her perspiring forehead. "Here goes. They've been calling you 'princess' forever, right?"

"Mm-hmm."

"Nicknames get imprinted in our hearts. We totally buy into them. Deep down, we believe that's who we are."

"I know I'm spoiled, fairly close to rotten." With anyone else, Jenna would not have cringed at the huff in her tone as she did now.

"Exactly. I mean you've been taught the negative side of 'princess' and that's how you see yourself—spoiled rotten, selfish, snooty."

A hot stab of pain shot through her chest.

"Jenna, I want to challenge you. Try this 'princess' on for size: you are royalty. You are the King's daughter. As His child, you are indeed privileged and adored and gifted to serve others. That's what He wants you to grow into. And that, dear heart, is how you do it, how you live through this season." Her eyes shone, two stars unbearably bright. "Okay?"

Even if she could form a coherent thought, she could not have expressed it. All she could do was lean into Beth's embrace and notice in the shimmering distance a row of trees with their charred trunks . . . and branches heavy with green leaves.

Nineteen

Three weeks had passed, weekdays full of learning the ins and outs of running a retreat center, the weekends with the goofiest bunches of high-maintenance guests imaginable. Skylar's first complete day off came none too soon. The emotional garbage heap to process had grown to the size of Kilimanjaro.

She steered Claire's foreign-built dream machine into a downtown parking garage space, cut the engine, and listened to U2 sing about peace on earth. The power clicked off. She sat in the silence, enveloped in a pleasant squishiness of leather and a sweet scent of some high-end department store perfume.

The music was compliments of Erik. He'd delivered a stack of CDs to her one day, thinking she might grow weary of his parents' narrow selection of classical and oldies.

And that was just the tip of the garbage pile.

For her first day off, Claire had given her the car keys along with a credit card, *"For gas or for whatever you need."*

Lexi and Tuyen had her over the previous night for dinner and chick-flick fest.

Indio gave her a one-handed knitting lesson and two hours' worth of Kumeyaay folklore.

Ben took her horseback riding.

Max not only removed the tools from her room and fixed the shower; he delivered a clock radio and comfy armchair.

Jenna smiled at her and told Danny to lighten up. Coming from the wife of a guy on the front lines, the gestures meant a lot.

Danny lightened up to a small degree.

Hideaway guests went out of their way to praise her cooking and baking.

All that didn't even begin to address her freedom to roam three hundred acres and work in the vegetable garden and play in that kitchen of all kitchens.

Not to mention Beth Russell who—if Skylar bought into childhood Sunday school stories—could be a stand-in for the Virgin Mary.

Skylar could find no emotional space to store all that was coming at her with gale-wind force. She thought she'd answered an ad for a cook. What she got was a family. And it felt . . .

She didn't know how it felt. She only knew she needed a day off.

Skylar spotted Danny a split second before he spotted her, not enough time to slip away through the crowd.

With a slight lift of his chin he noted her presence, checked both ways for traffic, and made a beeline across the street to her. Like her, he wore sunglasses and a ball cap. Hers was forest green, plain. His was black with deep-blue embroidery of a curling wave around the words "Ro-Bo Shop." His curly hair spiraled out from beneath it.

"Hey, Skylar." He hopped the curb to where she stood.

"Hey, Wally."

He smiled. "Ah, Wally Cleaver. The Beav's brother. The handsome, truly cool one."

She couldn't help but laugh. "Or the goody-goody nerd."

"Now, that sounds like a Lexi description of yours truly."

"You do work with computers, so you have to accept the nerd part. Moving right along . . ." She pointed to his hat. "What's Ro-Bo Shop?"

"I guess Lexi only told you about my conservative three-piece-suit side. You've met Hawk Roman?"

"Yes." Hawk was Danny's roommate, the guy Tuyen could not stopping talking about the previous night. Evidently they were an item.

"We own a surf shop. Ro-Bo, as in Roman and Beaumont."

"What about the computer stuff?"

"Software design. It's how I spend most of my time. Hawk runs the shop. Come on down and we'll give you a board and lessons, on the house."

Again with the family fuzzies. "Thanks."

She glanced around. They stood on a downtown street with at least a couple hundred people lining both sides of a block. The scene would have suggested a parade was on its way . . . if not for the signs some carried.

Bring 'em home now.

Peace.

End the war.

Stop the killing!

Not exactly parade slogans.

She said, "I can't believe you're here."

"The nerd image doesn't fit in, does it?"

"Your brother-in-law is a Marine, fighting overseas."

A muscle twitched in his jaw, and he didn't reply.

Skylar said, "I suppose that could be all the more reason for you to be here at an antiwar march."

The sun glinted off his glasses. Skylar looked away.

The tails on those family fuzzies had fishhooks on them. She felt one now sink in under her skin. The Beaumonts carried a distinctive pain.

Danny said, "Kevin knows I don't agree with the war. He also knows I pray every day for his safety."

"What about Jenna?"

He gave his head a slight shake. "She's totally apolitical. It's too much of a personal thing for her. The rest of the world does not compute with her. She's still stuck on how to forgive him for reenlisting. Kev's a great guy, don't get me wrong, but I'm a little stuck on how my viola-playing sister who scored a 1500 on the SATs and has two master's degrees in lit fell for a dumb jock in uniform."

Danny was such a *guy*. She clucked a noise of disbelief. "There's just no accounting for love, is there?"

Ducking his head, he eyed her over the tops of his sunglasses.

She shrugged. "Been watching chick flicks with Lexi and Tuyen."

"Now, that surprises me. Your being here doesn't, but that does."

"Whatever." Skylar gazed down the street, wondering how to politely disengage from the conversation with her least-favorite Beaumont. Why she even considered propriety when it came to Wally, she had no clue. It probably had something to do with that fishhook.

"Cops are here. And news vans."

She said, "Guess that means it's a gathering of note. Well, it's been fun, but I'm going to—"

"There's Rosie." Danny waved an arm.

Skylar peered between shoulders and saw a policewoman head their way. She never would have recognized the woman she'd met at the hacienda in the reflective sunglasses and navy-blue uniform, hair pulled severely back in a bun. Suddenly Erik's girlfriend was an honest-to-goodness *cop*.

Skylar's jaw went rigid. She rubbed it, searching behind her own dark lenses for an exit route through the crowds.

Rosie reached them. "Hey, Danny. Skylar. I half expected to see you two here."

Danny turned to Skylar. "Officer Delgado should make detective any day now."

Rosie laughed. "Danny, you've shared your opinions often enough. And Skylar, take no offense at my profiling here, but you've got 'peacenik' written all over you." She quickly sobered. "Do you guys know what's going on here?"

He held up two fingers in a peace sign. "We do this at passing cars. It's a regularly scheduled program."

"Not this time. The demonstration organizers got a permit to march." She pointed over Danny's shoulder. "Down there, to a church."

"That's different."

"We thought so." She paused. "There's a funeral scheduled to start soon inside that church. For a Marine. Not to be overly dramatic, Danny, but put Kevin in the coffin. Put Jenna and your family on the sidewalk, going inside to pay last respects. Would you want to read these signs and listen to the shouting?"

"I . . ." Danny chewed his bottom lip. "That's . . ."

Skylar felt sick to her stomach. "That's really ugly."

"Mm-hmm." Rosie scanned the crowd, her face in profile. "It could get uglier. Somebody's got an agenda. Somebody wants to agitate things. Did you notice the television crews? They got wind of something?"

Danny said, "They're not usually here. Nor the police in full force."

She nodded. "Listen. I totally respect your right to disagree with the government's foreign policy, but do you really want to be a part of this?"

Skylar cleared her throat. "You got me with the coffin visual. I'm out of here."

"Yeah." Danny shrugged. "Me too."

"Thanks for the heads-up, Rosie."

"No problem, Skylar. You owe me some spinach-artichoke dip."

"Anytime."

With half nods and waves, the three of them parted in different directions.

She heard Danny call out, "Skylar?"

Pausing, she looked back. He made a tipping motion at his mouth, as if inviting her for a drink, and mouthed the word "coffee."

With a brief shake of her head, she scurried the opposite way. She'd spent enough time with Danny for one day . . . or month.

The entire city lay before her, ready to be explored via a fancy car. She'd packed books, swimsuit, and blanket. Reading at the beach sounded great. Not Danny's beach, though. Where exactly was it Lexi said he lived? Just her luck, she'd plop down in the sand right outside his door.

Actually, he wasn't that bad of a guy, not nearly as deplorable as she'd first thought. As a protestor, he couldn't be too saintly.

As she wove her way between people, her mind registered a familiar movement . . . a lanky arm bent in a gesture of urgency.

She stopped dead in her tracks.

Not ten feet away stood a guy. He was in profile, but there was no mistaking his identity. Finley Harrod. A fictitious name, of course. He'd told her it meant "blond-haired soldier and conqueror." Ironic how the violent nature of that name found its way to this demonstration, this sublime whimper for peace.

The sight of Fin chilled her to the bone. Heartbeat hammering in her throat, she struggled frantically for a coherent thought.

Her sudden halt on the sidewalk was a stupid, *stupid* move.

Okay. Okay. Think, Skylar, think.

The ability to disappear in plain sight was ingrained in her. Like an adoring puppy she had learned the tactics from this master. Time and again since leaving him, she had used them. She knew how. She *knew.*

If only she could breathe.

If only she had not begun to let go of the past, to let down her guard, to believe she'd arrived at last in Kansas.

Slowly, so as not to draw attention to herself, she hunched her shoulders and moved sideways, melding into a nearby group, angling herself behind a cardboard sign. *Peace now!* Shortening her typically long strides, she made her way back around to where she'd talked with Danny. Resisting the urge to peek over her shoulder, she doddered along, staying close to people.

Advantages raced through her mind. Eighteen months was a long time. She looked different. Although her last dye job was several months old, the telltale auburn roots in her hair were covered by the ball cap. A trendy So-Cal ponytail bounced through the cap's opening. She wore—thanks to Lexi—blue jeans that did not bag and a nondescript light-brown shirt that did not scream "flower child."

And, if she could catch up to him, her new best friend Wally Cleaver just might buy her a cup of coffee. Even the most annoying Beaumont seemed to know how to offer a safe harbor.

Twenty

I have to say, Wally—I mean *Daniel*." Skylar smiled. "That is one major scowl you've got going there."

Danny relaxed facial muscles that had instantly contorted at the sound of her annoying nickname. Whatever had possessed him to invite her to have coffee? Every time the woman spoke he felt like hives erupted all over his body.

She said, "You don't like the moniker?"

"It's probably more the tone than the name."

"You're kidding. This is my teasing tone."

"Hmm. What does your derogatory tone sound like?"

"Like this." She slouched, sneered, and exhaled huffily. "Wally sodding Cleaver." Straightening, she smiled again. "Hear the difference?"

He raised his hands in surrender. "Got it."

She laughed and eyes the color of sunlight through a Perrier bottle twinkled. The splash of freckles across her nose danced.

He steeled himself against another stab of attraction. Green eyes, intriguing face, and common pro-peace grounds were not why he'd invited her. No way. It was solely because he did not trust her. Better to know an enemy than not.

But her looks were appealing.

She made him laugh.

And . . . okay . . . hives aside, her personality was growing on him. Why wouldn't he want to tango with her over a cup of coffee and explore the recesses of her wacky mind?

He said, "You started to say something?"

"Yes. I was saying that I have to say, you surprise me to no end." She held up her mug in salute. "Funky nonchain coffee shop. Antiwar demo. Total acceptance of your uncle's illegitimate Vietnamese daughter. Not in the office on a Friday."

"My apartment is my office. I'll be working tonight. Probably tomorrow too."

"You get my drift."

"Not exactly."

"The bona fide nerd who is also an in-your-face Jesus freak doesn't do funky. He doesn't do anti. He doesn't do out-of-wedlock."

"For all your freethinking, Skylar, that really is a narrow-minded attitude."

She pulled off the billed cap, ruffled her hair, undid her long ponytail, reassembled it, and slid the hat back into place. Her eyes reflected its green. "Yeah, I agree. It is shockingly intolerant."

"Hey, you're supposed to argue with me."

She flashed the grin again, the one that crinkled her nose and set the freckles in motion.

He said, "What makes you think I'm an in-your-face Jesus freak anyway?"

Skylar opened her mouth as if to reply, then closed it.

Danny took a wild guess. "My twin didn't used to talk so much."

"Lexi didn't use those exact words. She just confirmed what I already assumed. I mean, you haven't hit me up with the plan of salvation—yet—but you did give me a spiel on forgiveness the other day."

Danny leaned back in the overstuffed chair and crossed his legs, ankle to knee. "I don't understand the world's problem with forgiveness. There's such a commonsense side to it. I mean, if everyone extended and received forgiveness, wouldn't that lead to world peace?"

"Maybe, if we didn't have to include Jesus. He's the divisive factor."

He wasn't going there with her. "Did you grow up going to Sunday school?"

"Hasn't every American over a certain age?"

"Then what?"

She frowned. "Then what, what?"

"Then you stopped going to Sunday school, to church. You stopped wanting to hear about Jesus."

"Why would I want to hear?"

"Because He was real to you or real to someone close to you."

She shook her head.

"You want to see my surf shop?"

"See your—Danny, you just jumped in one breath from world peace to Sunday school to your business. I'm getting whiplash here flipping over the segue gaps."

He grinned. "I promise not to hit you up with the plan of salvation. Unless you want me to."

"Uh, no thanks."

"No thanks to the speech?"

She nodded. "Heard it once or twice."

"How about the shop tour?"

"We just got our coffee."

"In to-go mugs."

"I'm trying to imagine you sitting still at a computer."

"Baffles the mind, doesn't it?" He wondered at her hesitation. She didn't seem the type to weigh a lot of consequences in her decision-making process.

The resemblance between Skylar and his old friend Faith kept knocking him off balance. It went way beneath a similarity in outward appearance. It went to the core.

And he knew Faith's core. She'd rejected everything he believed in, everything she had said she believed in the first twenty-one years of her life. Despite the day's momentary connection with Skylar, he suspected she, too, at her core, rejected not only God but all that was good and hopeful in the world. If so, there was no reason she would choose to work at the Hacienda Hideaway.

His grandmother would say Skylar behaved as she did because of wounds, hurts that God wanted to heal, pain through which He would call out the true Skylar Pierson. The thing Nana didn't get was that Faith Simmons refused to receive from God. There was no reason to believe Skylar would not do likewise.

"Danny."

He blinked and saw that Skylar was standing, mug and sunglasses in hand.

"Let's go see your Ro-Bo Shop."

He uncrossed his legs and slowly got to his feet, surprised she would accept his invitation. "You don't have anything better to do than hang with Wally Cleaver?"

"Of course I do." She shrugged. "But making points with the bosses' son is a priority."

There was more truth than joke in her remark. He really did not trust her. She was all about herself.

Meeting her eyes, he forced a smile. After all, it was the honey that attracted the bear. "I didn't drive here. You don't mind a bus ride, do you?"

"No."

"I'll drive you back later to the garage where you parked Mom's car. After what Rosie told us, I'd rather avoid the protest area and that church."

"Yeah, me too." The typically confident voice warbled. Skylar spun abruptly on her heel and headed toward the door.

Danny followed, reminded that despite their current teasing rapport, despite her good work at the Hideaway, Skylar Pierson was an unknown.

As they walked along the sidewalk, he glanced at his watch. "It's one-thirty-six. The bus should be—"

A rumbling noise cut off his speech. It was distant, but he

immediately comprehended that it did not belong. In the vicinity of airstrips for F/A18 Hornets and commercial airliners, it did not belong. Near rails for the Amtrak, it did not belong. In an area familiar with earthquakes, it did not belong.

Something was terribly awry.

Twenty-one

There was no warning, just an abrupt, thunderous boom that shook every inch of the old church.

Before Jenna's eardrums registered the explosion, a glass sliver pierced through the sleeves of her polyester black suit jacket and white silk blouse and embedded itself into her left forearm. The splinter came from the huge stained-glass window at the end of the pew, a colorful depiction of a dove, a rainbow, and the ark.

Before her mind registered the injury, the world slid into a state of suspension. Her thoughts wandered backward, over the events that led to her being in that particular place at that particular moment . . . on a Friday afternoon with hundreds of mourners and a flag-draped coffin flanked by Marines in dress blues and gloves so white they almost glowed in stark contrast to the surrounding dark-stained woods of paneling, altar, rail, and pulpit . . .

Amber had been at her all week to attend the funeral. Not a lunch, prep period, or hall sighting went by without an Amber exhortation

"Come on, Jenna," she had said. "Keep me company, please, please. It's not like I know the widow either. Except we did attend that book club last month and shared similar views about *Empire Falls*. By the way, did I mention how much you with your literary background would add to the group? I hope you can make it next time. This woman is a sweetheart. Not that it matters if she's sweet. She lost her husband. I'd go anyway, as a show of support. We're all in this together, you know? All us military families."

Jenna might have withstood Amber's onslaught if not for other forces at work.

Cade was one of those forces. On Wednesday he'd asked her to step into his office. "Jenna, Friday afternoon is a professional half day." That meant no classes, just faculty business. "If you need to do this thing with Amber, don't worry about missing a department meeting." His eyes did their ice melt.

Via e-mail, she poured the dilemma out to Kevin and, on Thursday, he replied.

> Jen, I can't put into words what it would mean to me if you went. I know all this military stuff is still new for you and it's so hard for you to make sense of it. I wish I could call you, cuz this will probably come out wrong and I can't fix it online. But here goes. If you attend a fallen comrade's funeral, it'd be like you've really come on board. You know? You are my Pretty Lady and I love you. Kev.

Seven thousand, seven hundred thirty-one miles away, the guy turned her to mush. Still, a corner of her heart resisted that "really" coming on board business. Images of doing everything alone and talking to him only long distance haunted her. That's what coming on board meant.

Like pretending those things didn't describe her life right now could make it all go away? Who was she fooling?

The final push came indirectly from Beth Russell. *"God is in the gatherings with other wives . . . He wants you to step into your 'princess' role, to give to others . . . He will take care of you."*

Friday morning she had not yet decided, but she put on her black suit, white silk blouse, and pearls and went to school.

And then the bell rang. First hour began. Her thoughts already on John Donne, she went to shut her classroom door. A straggler shuffled down the hall, his back to her. She recognized him. Last year she had attended his brother's funeral. Not long after that, Kevin reenlisted.

How the boy must ache, unspeakably ache.

Maybe Donne had it right. Maybe no man was an island.

Maybe she ought to find a bridge and take a hike across it.

She would go to the funeral . . .

The world spun again, slamming Jenna into a state of nauseating vertigo.

"Oh God! Oh God!"

Was that her scream?

Amber came into focus, her face a hairsbreadth from Jenna's, her voice nearly lost in the din of a thunderous echo.

Jenna gasped for air. "Huh?"

"I said hang in there! We're okay. We're fine—no, lie still. Lie still. There's glass everywhere."

Amber's hair glittered, sparkly stained-glass beads dotted its curls. She was kneeling beside Jenna, looking downward, smoothing Jenna's collar, the jacket, her skirt. "There's a cut on your arm, hon. Otherwise"—she flashed her signature smile—"you're good to go. We better wait for medics, though. I hear sirens."

Sirens. And screams. Shouts. Cries. Moans.

"It shouldn't be long, hon." Amber's calm voice silenced the chaos for Jenna. "Help is on the way."

"What . . . what . . . ?"

"Two simple bombs. Just large enough to pop out a couple windows." Again the quick smile. "Walls are still standing. Homemade, my guess. Type my chem whizzes could make, no sweat. Planted outside this window and that one up a few rows." She indicated the direction, tilting her head. On her neck a trickle of blood appeared, ominous in its sudden, steady seeping. "I really don't think it's a major terrorist attack—"

"Amber! You're bleeding." Jenna pressed an elbow against the floor. "Help me sit up."

"You shouldn't move." But Amber supported her to a sitting position. "I tumbled us both to the floor. Comes from four brothers whose favorite game was always 'duck and cover.' Jen, keep your jacket on."

"Your neck." Jenna struggled out of her sleeves. The left one caught on something and a sharp pain shot through her body. "Ah!" Tears sprang to her eyes as she worked her arm out. Now her blood-soaked blouse sleeve came into view. Her stomach lurched.

"Sit still. You're hurt. Wrap the coat around your arm."

Instead she wrapped the coat around Amber's shoulders. Her friend, dressed in skirt and short-sleeved jacket, was shaking uncontrollably. Jenna leaned back against the pew and pulled Amber into her arms.

"Lord, have mercy," Amber whispered. She slumped then, dead weight against Jenna's chest.

"Christ, have mercy." Jenna Beaumont Mason burst into tears.

Twenty-two

Hands on her hips, squinting against the afternoon sun, Claire gazed up at the fountain in the center of her courtyard. Above the sound of rushing water she called loudly to Max standing beside her, "If you hurry, you might be able catch the delivery guys before they reach the highway."

He chuckled. "Trevi Fountain comes to mind."

"The one in Rome? Nah. Ours isn't that, uh, big."

"Or gaudy. There are no mythological gods."

"Still."

"Exactly." He shrugged. "But let's look on the bright side. It's not cracked and it's not on back order."

"I just didn't have giant flying sea bass in mind, spurting forth rivers. Just a pleasant, hushed, ambient gurgle."

"I think they're Chinook salmon."

She sighed loudly.

"I'm sorry, sweetheart."

"I know. It's not your fault."

"I'll play with the water pressure." He bent and flipped a switch on the fountain's side. Sudden silence engulfed the courtyard.

Claire eyed him as he straightened. Mr. Handyman he wasn't. He'd proven that time and again since they'd started the remodeling project. "Your dad can help, right?"

"Before or after I break something?" Max smiled. "I'll see if he and Tuyen can lend a hand."

Claire slipped her arms around his waist and leaned against him. The blossoming relationship between Ben and Tuyen was a beautiful sight. They'd become inseparable that week, since Beth Russell's visit. Every inch of the Hideaway's three hundred acres held a memory of BJ that Ben couldn't wait to tell and Tuyen couldn't wait to hear. Time and again Claire had come upon them inside the house or courtyard, at the barn or heading out on the horses. Ben would be saying, "I remember when your dad . . ."

"Phone." Max kissed the top of her head and strode over to the porch where she'd left the cordless. "Nobody would call on a Friday afternoon to plan a Saturday getaway, would they?"

Smiling, she shrugged. As fun and rewarding as their first weeks of company had been, she and Max were anticipating a weekend of empty guest rooms. As a couple, they were overdue for some alone time.

Word was spreading quickly in local circles that the Hacienda Hideaway was open for business. Still winging it policy-wise, they hadn't yet decided how much lead time they needed for a reservation. Literally speaking, the place was ready. Fresh linens were in place. The freezers were stocked with some of Skylar's goodies.

Max picked up the phone, checking the ID display. "It's Erik." He answered it. "Hey . . . What . . . No . . . Yeah . . . Hold on. Claire, do you know what Danny was doing today?"

She heard the hesitation in his voice and walked over to him, shaking her head.

Max said, "There's an antiwar demonstration."

Claire tried not to read panic in his widened eyes. He knew as well as she did that Danny attended those things when he had the time. Growing up with an MIA uncle, their son adopted at a young age a deep compassion for soldiers and a deep distrust of reasons for war.

Max said, "Erik, we don't know . . . Okay, yeah. Thanks, son." He clicked off the phone, his face creased into a tight frown. "We need to turn on the news. There was an explosion just moments ago."

"Oh, Max!"

"It appears it happened outside a church. The TV crews were already there for the demonstration. And Rosie's there."

"He talked to her?"

"No. She's not answering her cell and neither is Danny. She told Erik last night about her assignment. She said they were expecting some problems."

"Is anyone hurt?"

"Some people inside the church. Apparently the demonstrators weren't at that spot right then."

"So Danny would be okay?" She was clutching his hands.

"It sounds—"

"But Rosie—"

"Is trained for this sort of thing. Let's go inside and turn on the TV. The news is covering—"

Claire cried out. Her breath felt ripped from her chest. In the recesses of her imagination she heard the echo of a wind.

"Sweetheart, God is with them. They are in His hands."

"Oh, Max!" Sudden tears streamed down her face.

He wrapped her in his arms and held her tightly. "It's okay. It's okay."

She could not have spoken if she had to, but Max knew what was going on inside her. In a few days, they would mark the first anniversary of the devastating fire that tore through the estate and emotionally scarred them all horribly. With the approaching date, she had been on edge, grateful for so many positive outcomes but reliving fear-filled moments.

She and Max had talked again of his experience, how he survived that long night not knowing if his family was alive or dead.

Like . . . Ben and Indio with BJ. One long night that lasted thirty-four years.

Oh, God! There's too much pain. Just too much. How are we supposed to do this? Live in this world of hurt?

Max's voice reached her, calm, soft, steady. He was praying.

After a bit, her tears slowed, her lungs filled with oxygen, her faith in Someone else's control put down a new root.

Claire, we know where everyone else is." Max pulled a polo shirt over his head. Behind him a commentator on the television described a scene full of emergency vehicles.

"I just need to hear their voices." She looped a belt around her tunic top while sliding her feet into sandals. Her jeans and boots lay in a heap. "Right now."

"Before we leave? Not from the cell phone when we get down the hill?"

Yes, right now! Again and again she tried poking the belt prong into a hole. It kept missing. *Lord, don't let him quit on me. Please don't let him quit on me.*

Max gently pushed her hands from the belt and buckled it for her. "I'll dial the numbers for you."

She gave him a small smile. "I don't think we can reach Skylar."

"Skylar's on your list too?"

"Why wouldn't she be?"

He kissed her cheek. "We can't get Dad and Tuyen, either, you know. They're out on the horses. Mom first?"

She nodded and they sat on the couch.

They talked briefly with Indio, who was in her house down the road. Her prayers, of course, were set in motion.

Lexi was at the office of the landscape firm where she worked part-time now that they needed her help on the hacienda grounds. Claire let Max break the news to Lexi and then she spoke with her.

"Hon—"

"Mom! Danny's there! He told me he was going." More resolution than panic filled her voice. "But don't worry. He's all right. I know it."

"The twin thing?"

"Yeah. With some faith thrown in too. I'm leaving right now. I'll catch up with you down there."

Max called Jenna's high school and was put on hold. He clasped Claire's hand. When a male voice came on, she could hear most of what he was saying.

"Mr. Beaumont, Cade Edmunds here. We just heard the news. Um, Jenna, um . . ."

Claire had met Cade Edmunds a few times. The man did not say "um." Her stomach twisted.

"Uh, um, there was a funeral at that church."

They knew that. They'd heard that on the news. A Marine . . . A *Marine.*

No.

"Jenna and another teacher went . . . went to the funeral. I've been calling . . ."

Claire was out the door before Max hung up the phone.

Twenty-three

Breathless, Skylar ran alongside Danny, anxious to know what had happened, equally anxious not to know.

They couldn't pinpoint the direction from which the noise had come, but—like others racing ahead of them—deduced that the rally site must somehow be involved.

What insanity possessed them all to run toward the sounds of chaos rather than away? She thought of videos of tumbling skyscrapers, still frightfully vivid after so many years.

They couldn't see anything yet except for stopped traffic and racing fire trucks and police cars. The coffee shop was at least ten blocks from the demonstrators. Skylar slowed to a jog. Surfer Dude might be able to run the whole way, but she couldn't.

"Danny, what are we doing?"

He matched his pace with hers, his breath nowhere near as ragged as hers. "Rosie's there. Other people I know."

"Rosie will know what to do. You told me you warned your friends about what she said even before I caught up with you."

"That doesn't mean they left like we did. I have to make sure they're okay. I have to make sure Rosie's okay. I should call Erik—no, not yet. You don't have to come."

No, she didn't. But at the same time, yes, she did. She knew people there too. At least one, anyway. If God wanted to wreak a righteous vengeance, that one should be lying on a stretcher. She

should have said something. She should have said something! Deep
down she'd understood he was not there just to carry a sign.

They reached a corner. A few blocks ahead, every kind of
emergency vehicle clogged the street. Their lights flashed, the sirens
winding down. Firefighters and people in military uniforms looked
like fish swimming upstream against a tide of people exiting a
church.

A church. The one Rosie mentioned? The one holding a *funeral*?

Skylar saw a curl of smoke and followed it downward to a side
wall of the big old, gray stone building. Where stained-glass windows
should have been there were, instead, two gaping holes, giant eyeballs
staring blankly.

Insane.

There were no visible flames. Skylar surmised that an explosive
device had blown out the windows. Or blown them in. To prove a
point?

Or to maim and kill?

"Skylar." Danny grasped her arm and they stopped. "You look
ready to barf. I said you don't have to come. I'll show you how to loop
around this block and get to the parking garage."

She shook her head vehemently. "I have to come."

Beneath the sunglasses, his mouth twisted in a quizzical expression. "Suit yourself." He let go of her arm and they resumed their hurried pace.

She'd heard the anger in his voice, felt it in his fingers digging
into her arm. It matched her own.

This should not have happened.

Skylar and Danny reached the edge of the chaos. Someone jostled
her and she fell against him. Police were cordoning off paths, allowing people exiting the church down ramps and steps one way,

emergency workers up another ramp. Looky-Lous like themselves were being turned aside.

They stepped off the curb and found an empty spot to stand, in between two parked cars. Their owners wouldn't be driving off anytime soon.

"I don't see Rosie." He pulled off his sunglasses and continued scanning the hordes.

Skylar's throat ached at the sight of mourners stumbling along the sidewalk, some so close she could have reached out and touched them. They were all dressed in black, a new horror etched on their faces that had nothing to do with burying a loved one.

She whispered, "It's not right." *He goes too far. How did I ever . . .*

"I want to punch somebody," Danny muttered. "I want to tear somebody's head off."

"No, you don't."

He turned to her.

"You don't, Danny. Don't say that. Don't say that kind of stuff."

He looked away.

A medic backed out of the church's double center door. He guided a wheeled stretcher over the threshold. A fireman came into view, holding aloft tubes and an IV bag. Another medic followed at the other end of the stretcher. They moved toward a handicap ramp down one side of the steps.

At least a face was visible on the stretcher. It wasn't covered with a sheet. It wasn't in a body bag.

Skylar heard faint music. "Your phone's ringing."

"Huh?"

"Your phone."

Danny dug into his back jeans pocket, pulled out his cell, and flipped it open. "Erik . . . Yeah. Mm-hmm . . . I talked to her earlier. It's a mess now. I don't see her, but she's fine. The damage seems to be inside the church. She wouldn't have been in there . . . *What*?!"

At his shout, Skylar looked at him. The tanned cheeks had drained of all color. "What is it?" she asked.

He ignored her, listening intently for long moments. "I'll find her." He snapped the phone shut.

"Danny?"

"Jenna's inside the church."

Skylar's knees buckled. She sank onto the bumper of one of the cars, watching him stride up the curb and roughly elbow his way between people, powerless to go after him. Acid burned its way up from her stomach into her throat.

Images battered about in her mind, snapshots of herself. Lonely, toddling behind her older sister and brother, never catching up. Confused at her parents' disinterest in her. So sad in that redwood forest, heartbroken years before she was old enough to understand man's destructive ways. Angry with the unfairness she met at every turn, at the crimes committed against people and nature. Growing quiet and secretive and fearful. So naive even when she was old enough to understand. Running. Running.

Explosion after explosion echoing in her head.

Skylar jerked upward, quickly scanning every direction, assuring herself that the noise had been in her imagination. Disorder filled the area. Those clad in black still inched their way past her. People crushed against each other, shouting. Sirens screamed.

The blasts were all imagined . . . except for that one, the one that swirled Kansas, the Land of Oz, and the yellow-brick road all together and right on out into oblivion.

She faced a choice: stick with the Beaumonts or hightail it out of San Diego. Claire would forgive her for using the credit card to buy just one tank of gas, wouldn't she? When that ran out, Skylar would stick the card in the glove box and abandon the car. The police would eventually find it. Max would retrieve it. By then Skylar would be long gone. The family would think it all rather curious and simply get on with their lives.

Oh! She nearly shouted a curse. She did not want to leave! The Hacienda Hideaway was not a movie set. The Beaumonts were not a sitcom family. They were a safe harbor, *her* safe harbor, unlike any she'd ever had in her life. The least she could do was jump into the fracas with Danny and help him find his sister.

And what of Fin Harrod, the ghost from her past? The one who could very well be—most likely was—at least partially responsible for the mess before her? For any harm that had come to Jenna?

Skylar hesitated.

What would Indio do? What would Claire do?

Those two women who welcomed her as a family member would not back down. They epitomized feminine courage.

More than anything else, Skylar wanted to be like them.

She sprang up the curb and pressed herself into the crowd. "Excuse me. I have family inside the church. Excuse me."

Skylar found Danny behind a parked ambulance, its rear doors open.

"Hey," she said.

He whirled around and tossed her a passing glance as he hurried by. She kept pace with him.

"She's not here. She's not there." He waved his arm in the direction of other ambulances. "I don't see her on the street. She's got to be inside."

Or on her way to the hospital. Skylar didn't want to say that aloud. "Who would be with her?"

"No clue. Jenna doesn't hang out with military people. She hasn't even admitted that she is one." His face was crimson. The anger almost masked the fear so obvious in his eyes that darted every which way. "I can't imagine what she's doing here, how she got here."

"Who said she was here?"

"Her principal."

So Jenna had left school to attend a military funeral. Maybe the family was somehow related to the faculty or a student? But wouldn't she have said something to her own family if the school were affected like that?

In the confusion she and Danny easily bypassed police and firefighters still trying to cordon off the sidewalk. On the church steps, Skylar climbed slowly behind Danny, squished against a railing by people descending them. They made it to the main double doors.

A helmeted fireman blocked their path. "You need to turn around, please. Only emergency personnel allowed inside."

"My sister—"

"Sorry, bud. Everyone needs to clear out. We don't know the extent of the damage. It's not safe in there—"

Danny was on his toes, jabbing the air with his finger. "Are there people in there?" He was just shy of going ballistic.

"Medics are bringing out the injured as quickly as possible. Please, sir, move away."

"I'm not going—"

"Danny!" Skylar grasped his elbow and pulled as hard as she could. Getting close to his ear, she whispered, "Come on. Maybe there's a back way in."

Avoiding the side with the blown-out windows, they went the other way and passed one door with a cop helping people exit it. They rounded the back corner. Ahead, nearly hidden in an alcove behind wide-leafed tropical plants, a door opened. Clergymen emerged, followed by a woman, two little kids, and an elderly couple. They were all clothed in black, all with blank expressions that seemed to say the moment was totally beyond comprehension.

Danny hurried across the narrow stone path, moving quickly to the door that kept automatically closing on people. He took hold of the handle. "I'm so sorry for your loss."

Waiting off to the side in the grass, Skylar stared at him. Was he for real? In the midst of his own anxiety, gracious words fell from his lips in heartfelt tones.

Marines backed out through the door now.

They carried a casket.

God, if You're for real, would You just wipe everyone responsible for this right off the face of the earth?

Twenty-four

Jenna gripped the medic's gloved hand and pulled it from her wrist. "I'm fine!"

"Ma'am, please sit still—"

"Take care of her! Take care of Amber!"

The man beside her on the pew got into her face, blocking the view of her friend on a stretcher in the aisle. His haircut resembled Kevin's quarter-inch buzz. Kevin's post-enlisted haircut. Had this guy joined up too? Where was Kevin? She should tell him she was all right. He would worry. He was like that.

"Jenna, stay with me here."

She blinked a few times. The room still spun faster than her eyes could follow. Her ears still rang.

"Amber is being taken care of." The medic's head came into focus. He was bent over her arm, holding her wrist again. "Okay? There's plenty of help around. We need to take care of you too."

"But she's hurt!"

"And this"—he gently lifted her blouse sleeve—"is a figment of my imagination. Mm-hmm, right. What do you do for a living, Jenna?"

She leaned sideways. Amber looked dead. Pale. Motionless. An oxygen mask covered most of her face. A dressing covered that spot on her neck, the spot where blood had trickled. Two medics still worked on her, conversing with each other, talking at her. She didn't answer. She looked dead.

"Johnson!" A voice barked.

Jenna nearly jumped off the seat. A burly policeman moved along the row ahead, directing his attention to the guy next to her.

"We gotta move out right now. They're not so sure about that wall."

A rustling noise came from the stretcher. Amber was talking, her voice muffled, and she tried to push aside the mask.

One of the medics lifted it. "What?"

"Solid masonry." She rasped. Her eyelids fluttered, but didn't completely open. "No problem. Bombs went *pop, pop*. Do about as much damage as a skeeter on an elephant's behind." Instantly Amber returned to her deadlike state.

The medics chuckled, put the mask back in place.

Then the policeman was slapping his palms against the pew's back, gripping its edge, and leaning over it toward Jenna. "What does she know about the bombs?"

Jenna heard the voice and saw the big man's square jaw, his scrunched lips, but nothing registered. There was too much else going on in her mind. The spinning. The noise.

"What do *you* know about the—hey!" The cop shouted again, this time to Amber's group. "I need her ID."

Someone called out the name of a hospital.

Johnson, the medic with Jenna, still held her injured arm. He'd put something around it. "That one is Amber Ames. This is Jenna Mason, on her way to the same place. They'll be there awhile." He moved closer again, his eyes commanding hers to focus on him. "Let's try to walk, okay? We'll catch the next stretcher that comes by."

"Can't we wait here?" Her legs felt like overcooked noodles. "Amber said the walls are solid. She's really a smart woman. Knows all about explosives."

"Yes, but—"

"Jen!" A familiar voice shouted. "Jenna!"

She looked up to see Danny. From the front of the church, he was climbing over pews, making his clumsy way to the middle where she sat. Relief flooded through her. Danny would know what to do.

"Who is this?" The cop wouldn't let up. He spun around, flung out an arm, and stopped Danny in midstride over the final pew. "Who are you?"

"What? That's my sister."

"Who are *you?*"

"Daniel Beaumont."

"Were you in here for the funeral?"

Jenna rolled her eyes. Like somebody would wear ratty blue jeans, T-shirt, and Ro-Bo Shop cap for a funeral.

"No," Danny said. "Excuse me, Officer."

"How'd you get inside?" A notebook was in his hand now, and he was writing.

"Walked through a door." Danny sprang over the back of the pew and reached her. "Jen, you okay?" He looked beyond her shoulder. "Is she okay?"

"She'll be fine," the medic replied. "She's fading in and out a little. Has a bump on her head. There's a sliver of glass in her arm. Doc will have it out, no sweat. Jenna, let's take that walk."

They helped her to her feet. Whatever her last meal had been rumbled in her stomach.

The cop growled something about not letting them out of his sight.

"Danny." She tried to bring him into focus. "Call Kevin. Tell him I'm all right, but I have to go see Amber at the hospital. Tell him to meet me there, okay? This nice guy here knows where."

"No worries."

She began to sink back down.

Danny scooped her in his arms. "Mmph. You gaining weight?"

Probably. Since Kevin had left, meals were not exactly balanced or timely. Since Kevin . . . left. Shipped out . . . Deployed . . .

She rested her head on Danny's shoulder. "Kevin can't come, can he?"

"'Fraid not today, sis."

Jenna closed her eyes.

Twenty-five

From behind an ornately carved altar, between two huge, still-standing brass candlesticks atop it, Skylar watched Danny hurdle the pews. The bulldog was back.

She had stopped trying to keep up with him moments before. It was the startling sight of a cop shouting at Jenna that froze her in her tracks.

Did Jenna know something? Did the police know something? Did they know Fin Harrod was there? Did they know that Skylar knew the bomber—

No! That was crazy. Nobody knew anything, including herself.

She held on to the table, wrinkling its linen cloth between her fingers. She inhaled deeply, fighting down a wave of panic.

The scene before her added up to nothing except that all of them were in the wrong place at the wrong time. Happenstance, that was the word. Pure happenstance.

Now the cop was screaming at Danny. What was going on?

Skylar focused on Jenna. She was speaking and moving, but her forearm was swaddled in some gauzy stuff. A paramedic was holding her good wrist.

Skylar felt ill again, nearly sick to her stomach. What was a Beaumont doing at that place, at that time? *God, that's not fair. That is so not fair!*

Her mind in overdrive registered somewhere the odd fact that she was in church, talking to God.

And wanting to throw up.

The church was nearly empty. Some people were still in the same area where Jenna was, where the most damage had occurred. It was an enormous, old-fashioned church. The gaping holes where windows had been were larger than average.

Most of the people appeared in shock. Many had white bandages stuck to some body part. Medics and firefighters were gathered around them.

Was it a good sign that Jenna had been relegated to the end of the line? Did that mean her injuries were the least in terms of needing urgent attention?

The medic and Danny helped Jenna to her feet. She slid right back down.

Why didn't they get a stretcher for her?

Danny whisked his sister up in his arms and followed the medic down the aisle, the cop dogging his heels.

Sirens wailed anew. Skylar hadn't realized the relative quiet until now. Ambulances would be transporting the injured. A good sign. The dead didn't need sirens, right?

Would one wait for Jenna? Danny didn't have a car there. Skylar had Claire's car. Should she go get it?

Skylar sank to her knees. Too many questions swirled in her head, making it too heavy to hold upright. She rested her forehead against the back side of the altar.

"Oh, God. Take care of her. Take care of them all."

Now she was talking out loud to Him?

Tears seeped from the corners of her eyes.

She was in a sacred space. At least that was what the Sunday school teachers had told her long ago. The bema was for holy things, they said, for the bread and wine and water. It was for those who taught from the Word. It was where Christ lingered, where His broken body lay and His blood poured out. An atonement . . .

Was it true? Could it be true? How could it be true? She was looking at polished wood and red carpet placed by human hands at one end of a room in a building.

Exhaustion coursed through her. She was so tired of fighting, so tired of the struggle. But if she let go, if she put down her guard . . . then what?

Lost in her thoughts, she felt a prickly sensation on the back of her neck. It grew stronger, increasing to a gentle but urgent pressure, nudging her downward.

Unable to resist, Skylar moved with it, folding, collapsing, bowing low, and still lower, until her face lay against the carpet.

And she wept.

Eventually Skylar's tears stopped. She rose unsteadily to her feet behind the altar and stretched the cramps from her legs. Wiping her sleeve across her eyes, she glanced across the church. A few people still straggled at the main entrance. Police and firefighters inspected the holes in the wall.

She slipped quietly through a side door and down a hall that led to the exterior door she and Danny had used.

Outside she walked around the church. Order appeared to have been restored. Police guarded the front entrance. Firefighters were climbing into trucks. She wished she could find Rosie. She even almost wished she had a cell phone.

There was no question in her mind but that the thing to do was to find Jenna and be with the Beaumonts.

Skylar went to the nearest emergency person, a female cop, and asked her where the injured had been taken. The woman told her the name of a hospital and patiently gave her directions on how to get there as well as to the parking garage.

Huddles of people grouped here and there along the blocks she walked. There was the eerie feel of disaster all over the place, that weird sense of camaraderie that enveloped strangers after a tragedy struck.

Skylar hurried past them. Whatever had happened behind the altar was weird enough for her to handle. She wasn't up for listening to wild rumors that must be flying between those hanging around.

"Hey, Annie Wells!"

She slowed and turned toward the voice.

Why did she slow? Why did she turn?

It was him. Fin Harrod. Six feet between them.

She felt her eyes bulge, her lips part, her throat close up, her heart boom. At least her sunglasses hid the most obvious reaction.

She turned back around and picked up her pace, like someone who'd figured out the "hey" wasn't intended for her.

"It's you, isn't it?" he said.

She looked over her shoulder and shook her head. "Sorry," she said, lilting a British twist to the word.

He laughed.

He knew.

And he knew that she knew he knew.

Keeping up the charade, she continued down the sidewalk, dipping slightly to add a swing to her stride. Before she reached the corner, she checked both ways for traffic. The light was against her, but the street was clear. She went straight across it, not turning where the policewoman said she should.

Resisting the urge to see if he followed, she walked another block, grateful for more clumps of people to wind through. At the next corner she turned right. There was a chain coffee store ahead. Centered between office buildings, it was the only place she might conceivably enter.

She'd be stuck.

She continued, almost jogging now. Holding firmly to the mental map she'd drawn of how to find the garage that held Claire's car, she began a circuitous route. She went forwards, sideways, and back again. After a time she started checking over her shoulder every so often. No one followed.

Skylar ran and ran and ran.

Twenty-six

The ER doctor said she had a slight concussion.

Jenna huffed in his face leaning over her. If that meant she couldn't stay with Amber, she was not buying into it.

Her mom squeezed her arm. Claire hadn't let go of it through the entire ordeal. Nor had her dad let go of her hand. They were on her right side. The left side she did not even want to think about.

Claire said, "Honey, you'll come home with us, at least for one night."

"I need to be with Amber, Mom. She doesn't have anybody here." Jenna's entire body felt numb, but she shivered uncontrollably beneath a thin blanket.

The fifty-something, gray-haired doctor handed a clipboard to the nurse beside him. He did not follow her from the room, but slid off his reading glasses and pinched the bridge of his nose.

"Jenna," he said, "there's a bruise on the back of your head the size of Iowa. You've just had fifteen stitches sewn into your arm. Not to mention the trauma you experienced while sitting twenty yards from an exploding bomb. What you need is some very serious rest, young lady."

"Later. Her husband is overseas somewhere. Mine's in Iraq." She had already told him that, but it suddenly seemed important to repeat those facts. "We have to stick together."

As he slipped his glasses into a breast pocket, his entire demeanor changed. Rigidity left his face and shoulders. His eyes shimmered. It was as if a mask peeled away the doctor and exposed raw compassion. "Thank you for your service."

Jenna stopped the habitual *tsk* already forming on her tongue. Her typical whine—*It's not me! I have nothing to do with his madness!*—died in her throat. "You're welcome."

He gave his head a slight nod and told them all good-bye.

Jenna looked at Danny standing in a corner, his arms crossed. He'd been her rock, taking care of details that registered themselves like vague threads from a dream. She remembered he put her on a stretcher and rode beside her in the ambulance. He called their parents. At the ER he intercepted a clerk and dug in Jenna's purse for an insurance card.

It wasn't until after they arrived at the ER that he fell apart. She had watched him lean back against the wall and slide down it until he sat on the floor, curled like a ball, face buried in his hands. Everything grew fuzzy after that, her mind wandering off into some misty place.

Now Danny eyed her, a curious expression on his face.

Jenna shrugged.

He said, "It's okay. It's where you should be."

"I don't want to be."

"I understand."

Their dad cleared his throat. "Anything we need to know?"

Danny chuckled. "Nah."

Jenna had no words. What could she say? Something had shifted inside of her. Maybe it was fact finally ruling out the dominance of emotion. She hated that Kevin was a Marine. She hated with a passion that they were separated because he was in the military. Therefore she did not *want* to be associated with the military. But she was. Danny understood that.

He walked to the bedside. "I'm sorry you've got a brother who participates in antiwar protests. I'm sorry you got hurt at one of those protests."

"It wasn't your fault. You're not an extremist. You're not responsible for their actions."

He touched her cheek. "Want me to find her?"

"Thanks." She smiled. "Amber Ames. Mrs. Joseph Ames."

Jenna's dad helped her sit up on the hard table, unbelievably referred to as a bed. Its paper covers twisted noisily beneath her. The room started a slow spin.

"Honey," her mom said, "you don't have to move yet."

She must look as green as she felt. The numbness lessened. Her teeth began chattering.

"The doctor said to lie still until the nurse checks us out."

"I'll be okay." Still shivering, she leaned heavily against her dad as he half carried her to a chair. She sat and rested her head against its back. "Rosie's okay, right? That's what Danny said?"

"Yes, honey." Claire rolled a stool over to the chair. "He talked with Erik. Everyone is fine." She resumed alternately patting and massaging Jenna's right arm.

"Mom, I'm really here."

Claire kissed her hand. "Max, hand us that blanket."

Chuckling, he picked it up and draped it over Jenna. "She's going to chase us out if we don't stop hovering."

Jenna smiled. They'd hovered through x-rays, injections, an extraction of stained glass, and stitches. All that was left to hover about was clothing and a wheelchair ride to Amber's room.

"I need a top." She wore the hospital's blue print cotton shirt, its back open, and her black skirt. Her stockings had not survived, but her shoes were on the floor. The blouse was long gone, minus the left sleeve the medic had cut away while it was still on her. "You haven't seen my jacket?"

"No. They'll have a spare T-shirt for you. Jen, seriously, we can find out about Amber, but then we need to go straight home. I'll bring you back tomorrow."

Jenna admired her mom. They were friends in the way that a mother and daughter could be, open and direct with each other.

Real. Things like hovering and whining did not upset their rapport.

But Jenna felt a new determination crackle through her, almost a physical straightening of her spine. Her husband was overseas. Why did she keep repeating that? She was the wife of a Marine. Certain things, certain obligations, were expected of her.

"Mom." Jenna shivered, chilled as if she'd been dunked in a tubful of ice. Her head throbbed. Her left forearm felt like a hot knife sank into it. "I am staying with Amber."

Claire stared at her for a long moment. "Okay. Then I'll stay with you."

Jenna smiled. "Dad, when did that guy say Kevin would get your message?"

"He couldn't say for sure." Max's brow creased. He never could hide his worry very well.

"Bet you already told me that too." She had lost track of several conversations.

"This is why—"

"I'm better now. I'm here. I'm really in the moment."

"Yeah, well if you don't stay put longer than three minutes this time, you're going home."

In unison, Claire and Jenna broke into song, an old family joke the women employed when the guys acted overly tough. "Macho, macho man."

Her dad shook his head.

The door opened, and Danny entered with Skylar, both of them grinning crazily. "Hey," he said. "Look what the cat dragged in."

Skylar reached over and tugged the brim of his cap until it covered his face.

"Ouch!" He chuckled.

Jenna exchanged a glance of surprise with her mom. Had they just witnessed friendly banter between the two people who had yet to share a smile? Danny must be feeling the rush of relief if he was able to act natural with Skylar.

Skylar gave Danny's hat a final tug and stepped over to Jenna's side. Concern quickly replaced the grin as she knelt next to the chair. "Jenna, I am so sorry."

"Thanks."

Max said, "How did you find out?"

Skylar cringed. "I-I was there. With Danny."

Well, wasn't that tidbit interesting? And Danny hadn't breathed a word to them about it.

Claire groaned in an exaggerated way. "You were both at the protest. I guess that means we have *two* of you pacifists in the family."

Skylar inhaled sharply, loud enough for Jenna to hear. She looked at her closely. There was something different about her. The sixties throwback look was gone. Her jeans and shirt weren't her usual baggy style. Her hair was caught up in a ponytail, not twisted into a makeshift knot. Only one hoop hung from each earlobe.

But it was more than that, something behind the physical image. Jenna couldn't pinpoint exactly what it was. She sensed, though, that the distance Skylar always kept between herself and the family was somehow lessened.

"Claire." Skylar's eyes were wide, her lower lip quivered. "I'm not family."

"Why, of course you are, honey."

Skylar started crying softly.

In one fluid motion, Claire moved from the stool to the floor and pulled Skylar to herself in a hug. "Oh, Skylar. Of course you're family."

Twenty-seven

Of course she was family?

As she sat on the hospital floor, Skylar hiccupped little sobs into Claire's shoulder. The woman's words echoed in her mind. They reverberated in her heart. The sentiment, however, could not find a place to take root. There was no fertile ground inside of her, only what felt like huge slabs of concrete.

Danny's voice came from behind. "We'll make you an honorary Cleaver. We've already added a few extra members to the family. What's one more?"

Jenna laughed weakly.

Skylar raised her head from Claire's embrace and wiped a sleeve over her face. The whole thing was totally insane. She could be a Cleaver. It didn't matter. Pierson wasn't her real last name. She might as well add another to the list.

If they only knew who she was, what she was. What she had done.

"What?" Danny teased. "No retort?"

Claire stood. "Hush. Leave her alone."

"Aw, Mom. You always did like her best."

Skylar couldn't join in their laughter. It was too much an inside joke, a family thing. And no matter what they said, she wasn't one of them.

She stood and gently touched Jenna's wrist. Above it the skin was discolored and swollen. A gazillion stitches followed a long, crooked line. "Does it hurt?"

"I can't feel a thing." Jenna's eyes fluttered at half-mast, the lids and under-eye areas nearly as brown-black as the irises. Her hair was matted and disheveled. She was the type of female who looked sophisticated in whatever she wore—except, apparently, for a hospital gown over a skirt.

Skylar felt like crying again. "I'm sorry."

"I look awful, don't I?"

"Yeah."

Jenna gave her a loopy smile. "It's not your fault."

But it was. In a roundabout way it was. If Skylar had found Rosie at the rally after she first spotted Fin and said to her, "Hey, there's this guy here who spells trouble. He likes to blow things up . . ."

Right. Then Rosie would have asked how Skylar happened to know him.

Maybe Fin wasn't responsible.

There was a sharp rap on the door and it opened. A cop stood there. His shoulders all but grazed the door frame. He entered and the tiny room shrank to breathing space only.

"Excuse me." The foghorn voice sucked up most of the air.

Like a tiny slug poked by a finger, Skylar curled into herself, sinking back down to the floor and folding up against Jenna's chair.

Max said, "Can I help you, Officer?"

"Nope." He nodded toward Jenna. "Mrs. Mason, I need to ask you a few questions."

Max moved next to Claire, forming a mom-and-pop brigade in front of Jenna. "I assume you're the officer who talked to my daughter at the church?"

Skylar recognized that the cop's size and gray hair matched those of the one she had seen follow Danny and Jenna. Evidently they'd told their parents about him.

The man gave a slight nod. "I'm Officer Brayson. What's your name?"

"Max Beaumont." Max cleared his throat, a noise akin to a lion's menacing rumble.

Over the past few weeks, Skylar had witnessed Max in a variety of roles, from gracious host to total left-brained manager, from laughing gardener to grousing horse stall cleaner. Some new energy vibrated from him now, though, some undefined edginess.

He said, "You asked my daughter questions while she sat there bleeding, a glass shard stuck in her arm, ears ringing from a bomb blast. You are not going to bother her now."

"That's my call, sir. This is a police matter and time is of the essence. She has information about the bombing." He looked at Danny. "And I need to know exactly how and when you got inside the church."

Max crossed his arms. "I don't think so." His low voice sounded almost primal in its intensity.

A long silent moment passed, the glares proverbial dart throwers.

Officer Brayson blinked first. He glanced over at Jenna and then met Max's gaze. "I'll wait until your daughter is up to talking."

"She's a high school English teacher. Her husband is a Marine. She went to a military funeral with another teacher, a Navy SEAL's wife. You can't possibly think these women had any prior knowledge of the bombing."

"Like I said, I'll wait." He closed up his notebook, slid it into his breast pocket, and leaned sideways against the wall.

Max took two strides and was in the man's face. "All due respect, Officer, you can wait elsewhere. This room is for family only."

Brayson waited a beat, his eyes almost shut. "Sure. No problem, sir. I'll be in the hall." He turned and walked out.

Max shut the door behind him.

This room is for family only.

The room in which Skylar sat.

Twenty-eight

As the door shut behind Officer Brayson, Danny wondered if he needed a lawyer. Had he broken a law by circumventing a police cordon? Poor Jenna. All she did was go to a funeral and get hurt.

His mother blew out a loud breath. "Max Beaumont! You can't talk to a policeman like that!"

He grinned at her. "'Course you can. He was bothering my kids for no good reason."

Danny said, "Dad, there is a good reason."

"Well, it can wait. It's not like you guys know anything that will speed along the investigation. You walk in through an unguarded door to help your sister. Jenna's friend teaches chemistry and knows a thing or two about explosives. So what? There are plenty other witnesses not in the hospital who heard and saw the same things. Anybody want some dinner?"

The door opened again. A nurse's face appeared. "Jenna Mason, you are good to go. We need the room ASAP."

"Thanks!" Max called out as the door shut.

Jenna flung aside the blanket. "Let's go to Amber's room."

From the looks of her fluttering eyelids, Danny figured she was sailing away again. She should sail on all the way to the hacienda for the night and forget Amber. The cop's interrogation had upset her. Or maybe it was their dad. He'd clearly won the most points for belligerence in that round.

Danny tuned them out as his parents and sister made plans to head upstairs. He wasn't hanging around any longer.

Skylar rose from the floor, sort of crawling backwards up the wall. Her eyes, still red from the earlier crying jag, were wide as full moons.

She saw him watching her.

Danny winked. "Wasn't that fun?"

"Tons."

"What do you think? Shall we go talk to Brayson, get this over with?"

"What do you mean 'we'? You have a mouse in your pocket?"

"Actually, I was wondering if I should have a lawyer in it."

"You didn't do anything."

"Which I need to tell the police."

"Suit yourself." Her breathing sounded like gulps from a person too long under water.

"I said 'we' because it will come out that I didn't enter the church alone."

The freckles on her nose stood out, the skin beneath them paling. "Whatever."

His dad turned around from Jenna. "Hey, I don't want either one of you talking to anybody tonight. We'll sort it all out tomorrow. Got that?"

Danny held up a hand. "Give me a minute here, Dad. I just have to get over this feeling that I'm six years old."

Max twisted his head, a quick jerk to the side. "Sorry. But we're family. We need to support each other. That includes you, Skylar."

"Thanks." The soft, reverential tone didn't sound like any other that had come out of her.

Danny said, "Dad, if you don't need me here, I'm heading home."

"Go ahead. You, too, Skylar. Thanks for your concern."

Danny and Skylar said their good-byes and left the room together. "I just realized I don't have any wheels. I came in the ambulance. Would you mind swinging by my place?"

She shook her head.

"Well, it's not exactly a swing by. It's out of the way. I'll buy you dinner." *Huh?* Where had that come from? "On the other hand, I can take a cab—"

"You don't have to bribe—" Skylar halted abruptly, looking down the wide corridor. "There's Rosie."

He followed her line of sight. The ER was a busy area, but he easily spotted Rosie in uniform, talking with Brayson.

He said, "Jiggers, it's the cops! And they're blocking our escape route!"

"Your dad said not to talk to *anyone*." She spoke quietly, haltingly, not joining in his banter.

Where had the smart-mouthed, flippant chef disappeared to? Apparently Skylar was more disturbed than he thought.

"Yeah well, Rosie's not *anyone*. She's like you—Family. Capital *F*. Let's go."

She winced and then quickly frowned as if trying to hide the look of hurt.

"What?" he asked.

She shook her head and strode forward. He hurried to catch up.

Rosie saw them as they neared. "My favorite peaceniks."

"My favorite hard-nosed cop." He threw Brayson a glare. The returned glare made him swallow the teasing remarks about Rosie being tougher than the big guy.

Danny whispered to Skylar, "If I have to, I'll sic Dad on him again."

They reached them and stopped.

Rosie said, "Is Jenna all right?"

He nodded. "Some stitches, and she's a little loopy. But that could be the pain medication, or the concussion, or just plain old Jenna."

"I'll go see her. It could have been so much worse. There were only cuts and bruises. Her friend is the only one in serious condition. How about you two? Are you okay?"

"Fine," they said in unison. He added, "Bye."

Brayson said, "Hey! Three questions."

Rosie rolled her eyes. "Allen, I told you it's my boyfriend's family, they're good guys. Dan Beaumont, Erik's brother. Skylar Pierson, their employee at the retreat center."

"How'd you get inside the church, Beaumont?"

He looked at Rosie. "Do I need a lawyer?"

She raised an eyebrow. "Do you?"

Danny tingled with exasperation. He snarled a reply. "I was at a coffee shop a mile away when I heard a big boom. I went toward the noise, saw the holes in the church wall. Erik called my cell phone right then and told me Jenna was inside. I walked around the church, saw an open door, and went through it because my sister was inside a building that had just been bombed!"

Rosie touched his arm. "It's okay. Calm down."

He took a deep breath. "I came in behind the altar and saw Jenna in a pew. End of story."

Rosie looked up at the other cop. "End of story."

He ignored her. "Did you see anyone? Did you see anything suspicious?"

Rosie's help aside, Danny figured the sooner he answered, the sooner they'd get out of there. "I saw people leaving out the back door: the priests, the family, the coffin, the pallbearers. That's it. Nothing weird if you don't count the whole freaking scene."

"Were you alone?"

"That's four questions."

Rosie's glower at him matched Brayson's.

Danny relented. "Skylar was with me, from coffee shop to altar. And now we are leaving."

Rosie grabbed him in a hug. "Thanks." She gave Skylar a quick hug too. "Take care."

They hurried off, weaving a path around clumps of people in the hallway, people in the waiting room, people coming in and going out the ER doors. Even the stinking sidewalk had people on it.

He'd been weaving his way around hordes of people all day long. He wanted to be home. No, he wanted to be in the water, just him and his board, the sky and the swells.

But he wasn't there. He wasn't even close to home. First came a forty-minute drive with an odd woman he'd met only weeks ago who seemed as upset as he was.

He tamped down his emotions and aimed for a neutral tone. "That went pretty well, don't you think?" He missed the mark, heard the defiance, pressed on anyway. "At least they didn't arrest me."

Wordlessly, Skylar slipped her arm through his and steered him into a parking garage.

In that moment when he ached so badly to wrap himself in solitude, the warmth of her touch felt right.

Incredibly right.

Twenty-nine

From her seat in the wheelchair, Jenna lifted a defiant jaw and reminded herself she could do cool, calm, and collected. Even with the Iowa-sized knot on her head, ugly raw stitches holding her torn flesh together, and pain meds roiling in her stomach and fogging her brain, she could do serene.

"I'm going in there."

Standing on either side of the chair, her parents hummed "honey" and coughed their embarrassment. Claire and Max had witnessed her "attitude" since she was a child—in private, though, not in public, not toward a person in charge.

That person was a middle-aged nurse in a white top and slacks that swished with every gesture. She blocked the entrance to the ICU. "I'm sorry. As I said, only family is allowed."

Obviously Jenna's teacher persona was not going to get the job done. She pushed aside the thought of Amber lying beyond those doors, all alone, unconscious. Lingering there would only make her bawl.

Better to take a lesson from Kevin and douse her thoughts with testosterone. Act like a tough roller. Act like a coach. Act like a Marine. Act like—

Or just *be*. Be that military wife whose duty it was to take charge of things while the guys were gone.

Jenna pushed herself out of the wheelchair. Her dad's hand grasped her elbow, which prevented her from plopping right back down.

"Nurse." She peered at the woman's name tag. The letters blurred. "Um."

"Cathy."

Jenna met her gaze. The woman knew the whole story. She knew that the hospital had called Amber's emergency contact number, that it was the Navy, that her husband was incommunicado, that they were doing what they could to locate him. She also knew that Jenna had talked with their principal and that Cade was still trying to connect with Amber's parents in England.

"Nurse Cathy," she said. "My husband and Amber's husband are in the military. They're both overseas. They don't know each other but we know each other. That makes us *family*. I will see her now. I will tell her she is not alone."

The nurse's eyes filled.

Oh, don't do that. Don't do that. Jenna's legs wobbled along with the surge of adrenaline.

Cathy's nose twitched and her eyes cleared. "Can you walk unassisted?"

"Yes."

"Come with me." She looked at Claire and Max. "Family only, you understand."

Max let go of Jenna's arm. "Of course."

Her mom patted her shoulder. "We'll be here, honey."

Jenna followed Cathy through a large set of doors and down a hall. She missed Amber, missed her perkiness, her bubbly chatter, her smile. What if she died? Was it Jenna's responsibility to tell her husband and parents? The military knew how to do those things. They had special people who knocked on the door. They read from a script. Like a spouse didn't know what they were going to say. *He's dead. She's dead.* What else was there to add?

This was all backward, the spouse safe at home getting hit by debris from a bomb. It wasn't supposed to happen this way.

Of course Amber had other friends. She was the sort of person who never met a stranger. She seemed close to a biology teacher, a history teacher, neighbors in her apartment building. She had friends in a Camp Pendleton wives' book club. Two of them had been sitting on the other end of the pew.

Were they all right? Would her other friends know yet what had happened to Amber? Except for the teachers, they were all nameless to Jenna. Should she call someone?

The sense of hospital overwhelmed Jenna. Antiseptic odors. Soft beeps and hisses. The squish of rubber soles against linoleum. Harsh lights. Muted voices.

The nurse stopped in front of an open doorway. "Five minutes, Mrs. Mason."

"What . . .why . . ."

"They didn't tell you?"

Jenna shook her head.

"The doctor removed a teensy piece of glass that entered through her neck. It made its way up into her head and interfered with the blood flow. There is some swelling of the brain. She's in a medically induced coma. Now we wait. And believe in miracles. Five minutes, okay?"

"Okay."

"Prepare yourself. Her appearance may upset you."

Jenna nodded.

"Please talk to her. I'm convinced my patients can hear."

"Thank you."

Just inside the door, Jenna halted. She clenched her teeth and fought down the impulse to dart right back out.

Amber was nearly hidden beneath tubes, wires, machines, and bedding. Thick, white dressing swathed her head.

"Oh! Your beautiful blonde curls!" Jenna slapped a hand to her mouth. Had they shaved her head? Probably.

I'm convinced my patients can hear.

She should be upbeat.

Jenna moved to the bedside and found a place to lay her hand on Amber's shoulder. She took a deep breath. "But hey, it's only hair, right? I've heard you say that. It grows back in no time, you say. And just think, for a while you and Joey can have matching 'dos."

Oh, dear God. Dear God. I don't know what to say, how to pray. Please tell my Nana to pray. Let her know.

Then she remembered that her mom had called her grandmother. Yes. They had talked. Nana knew. Nana was praying. Nana was carrying them.

Jenna forced her voice into a lilt. "The nurse said your parents are coming as soon as they can get here from England. Of course Joey will come too." She didn't mention that he had not yet been contacted. "Those military bigwigs are going to be really ticked at you. What a way to get your guy back home, huh? Brilliant on your part, my dear."

She talked on, filling the precious five minutes with upbeat words, hoping with all her might that Amber could hear them and take comfort in knowing she was not alone.

Thirty

Outside the hospital, Skylar kept her arm linked with Danny's. Apparently Wally Cleaver had gone AWOL. She figured he could use some literal support.

They stepped from evening's dusk into the hospital's brightly lit parking garage. She blinked a few times, but it still looked like a maze of metal.

She halted. "I don't have clue one where I parked your mother's car."

"That would make two of us. Got the key?"

She pulled it out of her jeans pocket and handed it to him.

His smile was a jagged slash across his narrow face. "We'll hit the panic button. That's appropriate, don't you think?"

They continued up the ramp. Danny held the key aloft, pressing the tabs, and singing to an old childhood tune, "Oh, where, oh, where has my Volvo gone? With its hood so sleek and its trunk so square . . ."

Definitely AWOL.

As they rounded the corner, a car halfway up the next ramp burst into action. The horn honked, all the lights flashed, an alarm sounded, the trunk popped open.

"Found it." Danny pressed the buttons some more until at last the car went quiet. "Expresses a mood of panic rather succinctly."

"Are you okay?"

"Never been better."

At the car, he held the key out to her. "You should go home. Dump me off at the cabs by the front door."

Skylar shook her head a little too vigorously. Okay, so she maybe had gone AWOL too. She slid her arm from his. "I don't want to drive anywhere just yet. I'll take you home first."

"If I drive?"

"Right. Then later I can get myself home." *Home. Oh, God!* The cry of lament, so foreign sounding, swirled and swirled in her mind.

"I'm really not okay either," he said.

"I know. You're royally ticked off and upset about Jenna. But it's your mom's car."

A corner of his mouth lifted. "Besides that, I'm the better driver. The guy always is."

"Not necessarily, but that stupid remark proves you're calming down."

A full-on smile appeared. He strode to the passenger door and opened it with a flourish. "Mademoiselle."

A sense of relief washed through her. At long last the insane day was over. She'd bumped into her past and one burly cop who, if given half a chance, would have peeled back the layers of that past.

And she'd survived. To top it off, she'd been referred to—by Claire and Max—as *family*. Maybe Kansas was for real.

Before getting into the car, she paused in front of Danny. His demeanor with her had undergone a major flip-flop, as had hers toward him. Naturally the terrifying experience linked them together now. It'd probably fade away in no time but for now, past and future did not enter into the picture. In all honesty, she just did not want to be alone in her rattled state.

She said, "Can we get a pizza?"

His brows rose in surprise. "You eat pizza?"

"With Canadian bacon."

"No way."

"Yes, as in pork. But don't you dare talk about Wilbur."

Their eyes locked. Skylar saw understanding dawn in his.

He *tsk*ed. "Charlotte would be sorely disappointed in you."

"She can take a number." Skylar got into the car.

Danny, you surprise me." Skylar wiped her hands on a napkin.

"Let me guess. Because my place is clean?"

"No." She leaned forward and snagged another piece of pizza. The carton sat on a coffee table between his seat on the recliner and hers on the couch. "I didn't figure you for a peacenik, but neatnik? For sure."

"Yeah, it is obvious. I've asked others to pray for me."

"Seriously? About being overly tidy?"

"The key word is 'overly.' Jesus was zealous about cleaning His Father's house, but I don't think it was because of dust." He crossed his leg, ankle to knee, and balanced his empty plate on his shin. "Sorry. Don't mean to preach. What surprises you about me, then?"

Skylar fingered the slice of pizza on her plate, taking a moment to gather thoughts scattered at his abrupt reference to Jesus. Of course, that was part of the surprise, part of his bouncy nature that pinged from hissing at a cop to referencing Jesus and God like he would any other dude and his dad.

She looked around the room. Danny lived with his business partner, Hawk, in a small cottage a block up from the beach, two blocks from their surf shop. She'd heard the story from Lexi, how Danny the computer whiz kid had earned enough money by the time he was twenty to buy what had been a dump. By twenty-five he'd upgraded the place and invested in the shop with Hawk.

The house sat between an alley and a gardenlike walkway between two rows of similar bungalows packed closely together. One tiny parking space was allotted to each, necessitating their leaving Claire's car blocks away. No matter the smallness, Danny owned a prime piece of real estate that someone would pay several times over what he had—to tear it down and build new.

He was a little Max in the making . . . but he went to antiwar rallies?

He said, "You don't have to explain yourself."

"I'm trying to put it into words. I mean, you're this successful business guy, devoted to family, dead-set against hiring me without going through proper channels, noisy about your faith—"

"Vocal." He winked.

"Okay, vocal. And . . . and . . ." Her mind hit an air pocket. It wasn't the first time that evening.

She shut her eyes. It had nothing, absolutely nothing to do with the black lashes sweeping over brown velvet that shone with ethereal light.

"You were describing a traditional boor," Danny prompted.

She looked at him. "In a sense."

"Ah, don't hold back, Sky. I'm counting on your unequivocal candor."

Sky? With an effort, she swallowed a few "uhs." "Yes, you exhibit gung-ho apple pie-slash-mom-slash-flag traits. But then, whammo. Wally Cleaver morphs into the Fonz. You're a dyed-in-the-wool radical."

"The protest?"

"And going toe-to-toe with a cop. Your hair is more long than short. You wear T-shirts, jeans, and flip-flops. You don't work when you don't want to. You play this . . ." She waved a hand toward a speaker in the corner and listened for a moment to the music that had been playing softly. "Leonard Cohen?"

Danny's smile, the genuine one, spread from one ear to the other. "You know his work?"

She ignored the question. "And earlier was Marley and Tom Waits. I just . . . just . . ." *Just sound like an idiot.* She slowed her speech. "I just find you're full of surprises, that's all."

He shrugged.

She shrugged and changed the subject. "I wonder if Jenna talked with her husband yet. I don't know how she keeps on, with him over there."

"Me neither." He stood. "I'll call her."

"Find out about her friend too." She had heard about the other teacher from him, how Jenna insisted on finding her in the hospital. How she was more hurt than Jenna.

While he talked on his phone, he walked around the house. The guy never sat still for long.

Skylar cleaned up, crossing paths now and then with him as she moved between the kitchen and living room areas, which were in one open space. She eavesdropped and rinsed their plates.

He set the phone on the counter.

"She didn't talk with him?"

Danny's shoulders heaved. He blew out a breath. "Not yet. Not to wish her a worse injury, but maybe a broken arm would bring him home."

"How's her friend?"

"Amber had surgery. So far, so . . . so nothing. They don't know. She's in ICU."

"Maybe her husband can come home?"

Danny gazed at her. "They don't know where he is. He does special ops. He goes under the radar for days at a time."

Tears stung Skylar's eyes. She quickly turned and rinsed the plates again. Jenna was hurt but okay. Everyone else was okay. Except the friend. Amber was an unknown.

What of the emotional side? Posttraumatic stress would impact every single person who was inside that church.

And Skylar could have prevented it.

Maybe.

She couldn't go down that road. She wouldn't. *Please, please let them all be okay.*

Now she was praying?

"Skylar, the plates are clean enough."

"Okay." She turned off the water and picked up a towel. "I better go before I fall asleep on my feet." *Or plain fall apart.*

"I'll walk you to the car."

Outdoors, they passed open-air restaurants full of people loudly enjoying a Friday summer night. Danny gave her directions to the freeway as he took them through a labyrinth of streets. He chatted on, pointing out landmarks of shops and bars. Claustrophobia set in, tightening her chest. She longed for the wide-open spaces of the Hideaway.

"Oh, man," he muttered. "I hope we can find the car."

She tried to smile but it wouldn't stick. Out of the corner of her eye she saw that he was watching her.

He said, "Call me when you get home."

"You're joking."

"No. It was a rough day, and you've got a long drive ahead of you. I want to know when you get there."

"That's ridiculous."

"Pretend like you're my sister and I'm your fusspot brother."

She scoffed. "We are not related, and I can take care of myself."

"You don't have to."

"Yes, I do."

By now they stood beside the car, on a side street, in shadows. His voice had risen; hers surpassed his.

It was like they were dancing. It was what they'd been doing since the moment they met . . . dancing around each other, moving in close, swinging back away, never quite touching.

"No," he announced with finality. "You don't have to."

"Bug off!"

In one flawless move, Danny enveloped her. He held her tightly, close to himself.

The only sounds were those of whispering ocean waves and her muted sobs against his neck.

Thirty-one

Kevin's voice was faint and even indistinct at times. There was interference in the line. Jenna didn't know if her dad's cell phone was to blame or if the problem was on Kevin's end, wherever that was, whatever his equipment was. Maybe it was her blubbering that stopped up her ears.

She thought she heard him say "pretty lady." She thought she heard him curse at the so-and-sos responsible. She thought he said he had been briefed on the situation.

Briefed? Like she'd participated in some covert operation?

Jenna sat in her dad's car, parked curbside at the hospital. Her parents waited inside the lobby, giving her privacy. Night had fallen. Tears of frustration soaked her face.

"Jen." The line suddenly cleared. "I can get leave. Come home for a while."

"Home! You can come home?"

"For a while."

"Meaning you'd have to go back?"

"Yeah."

She kneaded her forehead. How long was a while? They'd have to go through the good-byes again. Would the agony be worth a week together? A month? Six months? No matter. Every single day would be a day of sheer anticipation of his leaving.

"Jen, do you want me to do that?"

"No. Yes, but no. Does that make sense?"

He sighed. "It does."

"I have to let you go, Kev, like I think you've let me go. I don't mean in a permanent way. Just in a way that admits and accepts that this is our life for now. We'll get through it."

He whistled a note of appreciation. "Who are you and what have you done with my wife?"

"Blew her up with a bomb."

The line went so quiet she thought the connection was lost. Then she heard him crying, taking big, man gulps for air.

She curled up and lay sideways on the front seat, her head on the console, the phone pinching her ear. She tilted the mouthpiece so he would not hear her. The cries felt wrenched from her, as if a hand reached down and pulled them from deep inside her stomach.

Come home, Kevin! Come home. Come home. Come home.

Minutes passed.

"Kev."

He sniffed. "Yeah?"

"You asked me if you should come home. You *asked.* You actually brought it up for discussion."

He chuckled softly. "I guess I did. Maybe I've learned a thing or two about being a husband. Hey, while we're at it, I got another question. I was thinking about getting another tattoo."

"In your dreams, bud."

"Aw, you didn't give me a chance to ask."

"It would be such a waste of breath."

"I love you, Jenna. I love you so much. I am so sorry I'm not there."

"Kevin Mason, that will not change my mind about tattoos."

The sound of his laughter echoed long after they said their good-byes. It comforted, hurt, and submerged her under an ocean of fear all at the same time. It solidified the reality of what she'd done.

She'd told her husband not to come home.

Jenna."

The voice came to Jenna in a dream. It was Kevin's, steady and assured. Wave after wave of warmth rippled through her, flooding her with a sweet sensation of deep contentment, flowing even into the corners grown cold.

"Jenna."

Consciousness crept in, pushing aside the fog of sleep. She hated waking up from such dreams, of leaving that safe cocoon where she felt wrapped in Kevin's presence.

"Jenna."

A touch on her shoulder startled her. She jerked and opened her eyes to a dim light. Where was she? Her cheek pressed against hard padding. She lay on her side. More hard padding supported her back. It was a couch. She was on a couch.

In the hospital.

"Sorry." Cade Edmunds came into view. "I would have let you sleep but—"

"Amber!" Jenna struggled to sit up. She was tangled in a rough blanket. "Amber."

"No change. She's the same." He sat beside her and tried to help her straighten the cover. "You always wake up like a bear?"

"Oh!" Frustrated, she shoved the blanket aside and rubbed her face, brushing hair out of her eyes. Her heart was about ready to burst from her chest. And what was she wearing? An oversized T-shirt and skirt. "What are you doing here anyway?"

"Couldn't sleep until I'd seen you and Amber with my own eyes. Not that they let me see her. Unlike others, I wasn't deemed 'family.'" He paused. "Joey Ames is on the phone."

Jenna emitted a low moan.

"Will you talk to him?"

"I can't," she whispered, gesturing to ward off his request. "No. No. I can't."

"Shh." Cade grasped her flailing hand and squeezed it gently. "He's talked with the doctor. He's heard all the medical info, but he needs a firsthand account. Joey Ames deserves a firsthand account. You were there."

Jenna wanted to kick and scream like an out-of-control toddler in a candy aisle.

Cade said, "If it were you lying in the ICU and Kevin were on the phone, he would want to talk to Amber. Right? You would want him to hear Amber's voice because it was the closest to your own."

She gasped to catch her breath.

"Jenna, you can do it."

The shaking had started again. She gritted her teeth together to keep them from chattering. What had happened to her earlier resolve? All that gung-ho military wife bunk she'd spouted to her parents so forcefully that even her mother left?

Cade reached around her and picked up the blanket. He folded it and draped it around her shoulders. "Come on." He helped her to her feet. "I'll stay with you. We'll do it together."

She leaned into his sideways embrace and let him lead her across the waiting room.

Let wave after wave of warmth ripple through her . . .

Jenna sat with Cade in a small room. The door was shut. The walls were covered in blue floral-print wallpaper. A single piece of artwork hung. Her sister, Lexi, would be appalled at the paint-by-number depiction of sailboats on a glassy turquoise sea under an azure sky.

On the end table were a low-wattage lamp, a box of tissues, and a telephone base. Five padded armchairs were shoved together into a tight square.

Jenna wondered if doctors delivered horrific news to only four people at a time. If he stood while he did it, though, he could talk to five people. Were such things limited like that?

Between random thoughts about the furnishings, she prayed what her grandmother called "pings": *God, help Joey. God, help me. God, wake Amber up.*

She held Cade's hand, or rather clung to it as if it were a lifesaver, the thing that kept her from going under.

She held the phone to her ear.

And she listened to Joey Ames cry.

Cade gently pressed a tissue to first one of her cheeks, then the other.

Jenna froze. Cade did likewise, his hand midair, centimeters from her face. He knew as she did that an unspoken boundary had just been crossed.

But it was a moment for the unusual.

She flicked her eyes toward him, sending the message, she hoped, that she would not hold it against him.

Through the phone line, Jenna heard Joey clear his throat. "I'm on my way."

They had already talked about what happened. He kept addressing her as "ma'am" and "Mrs. Mason" until finally she snapped, "Stop it!"

He'd known who she was, of course. Amber had told him all about her, probably like she'd told Kevin all about Amber. Maybe not quite the same. While Jenna said, *"She's such a flake, Kev,"* Amber probably said, *"She's absolutely clueless when it comes to the military, Joey."* Then she would add, in her inimitable half-full style, something kind and positive.

Unlike Jenna.

How had the two of them ever sidled into a friendship?

Because Amber was Amber.

Now she said to Joey, "When will you get here?"

"I don't have the schedule yet. I'll let you know. Can I have your number?"

She gave it to him. "When she wakes up, you know she'll chew you out for coming."

The sound from halfway around the world was part chuckle, part sob. "Yes. But she'll just have to deal with it because *I am coming.*"

Jenna heard the steel in his voice. The guy would have to be made of reinforced armor to match Amber's personality.

"Thank you, ma'am—Jenna. Thank you."

She nodded.

"Okay," he said. "Good-bye."

"Bye," she whispered.

Cade took the phone from her.

Steel. Why was it that Kevin's steel led him to enlist, to go away, to leave her and be a hero to others?

Why was it that her steel led her to say, "Don't come home"?

She curled into herself, legs folded on the seat, blanket wrapped around her. Cade's chair was tight against hers, his shoulder right where she needed it. She leaned across the chair's arm and nestled into him. He enclosed her in his arms, resting his chin atop her head.

In the midst of her worst imaginable nightmare, the comfort from such an unexpected source warmed her once more.

Thirty-two

Claire heard voices out in the courtyard and looked down at the bowl on the island countertop. Eight unbeaten eggs would not be enough. She pulled another egg from the carton and once again thanked God that they'd had the foresight to black out the weekend for guests.

Next week marked the first anniversary of the wildfire that had torn through the area. Even before Jenna's tragic incident, Claire's emotions had gone haywire, inexplicably and uncontrollably at times. Seeing to guest needs might have put her over the edge. Right now, just figuring out how many eggs to cook felt like an insurmountable task.

Max entered through the open kitchen doorway.

She sighed. Having him nearby was making all the difference. "Are Lexi and Tuyen here?"

"Dad too." He arched his eyebrows. "Checking on the mums. Ready for breakfast. If there is any."

"Got it covered, so wipe the angst off your face."

Walking toward the island, he glanced toward the other end of the large kitchen. Skylar was stretched out on the couch facing the fireplace, her head on Indio's lap. His mother, eyes shut, stroked the girl's hair with her good hand and hummed softly.

Max laid some rosemary cuttings on the counter. "This was supposed to be a quiet weekend." He spoke in an undertone. "You and me."

Claire cracked two eggs, one in each hand, against the mixing bowl. "Ta-da! Look at that. Am I getting more efficient or what?"

Max breathed heavily at her shoulder.

"I learned this trick from your mom. I also learned"—she eyed him over the rim of her glasses—"that we go with the flow or forget about trying to run a retreat center."

"No whining?"

"None."

"That was Danny on the phone." Max had just been talking on the cordless outside. "He already picked Jenna up from the hospital."

"Really? Hallelujah! I still can't believe she spent the night in a waiting room. How is she? How is Amber?"

"No change in Amber. Jenna, he said, is wiped out." Max kissed her cheek. "They'll be here in twenty minutes."

Claire laughed. "Then we'll make French toast, too, her favorite. After breakfast, we'll tuck her into bed and hide all the car keys. She needs to stay put for the weekend."

"I suppose God had a hand in this."

"You think?" she teased.

"Yeah. We tell guests not to come. We tell our kids not to come and look what happens." He sighed dramatically.

"They didn't make it happen."

"Doesn't matter. They're boomerangs. Won't they ever move away and stay there?"

"Oh, I hope not."

He chuckled with her. Their remarks echoed recent conversations they'd had about surrendering outdated parental roles. What did it look like to let their adult children go and yet . . . *not let go of them?* Where was the balance?

He said, "'Tis a quandary for the ages."

Claire smiled and pulled two more eggs from the carton. A vague feeling of happiness tugged at her again. She'd been trying to tamp it down since the hospital visit last night because it seemed sort of demented. The truth was she was overly happy that Jenna needed them. But her poor baby needed them because she'd gotten hurt. *Huh?*

She beat the eggs and sent Max to search the freezer for French bread.

The vague happy feeling snowballed into an onslaught of pure delight. She giggled and sighed.

Maybe she was just tickled because Jenna was joining them for breakfast. And Danny. And Lexi. Tuyen as well. Skylar too, even. What was Erik doing that morning? A truly grand time would be if he came and brought Rosie with him. And Nathan, Lexi's friend, who already seemed part of the family, might get a ride with them . . .

Claire smiled. When she told Max she hoped the "boomerangs" would never leave for good, she only half teased. Yes, the kids needed to spread their wings and fly, but the thing was, her mama's heart sang whenever one of them paid a visit to the nest. Arias resounded if they stayed overnight. Entire operas poured forth if all of them were there together at the same time.

An opera couldn't be bad thing, could it?

They sat around the kitchen table on chairs and the L-shaped bench seat. Jenna snuggled against Claire, Skylar against Indio. Max refilled coffee cups. Danny appeared tired. Ben was gregarious, Tuyen quiet but not withdrawn. No one moved yet to clear the breakfast clutter.

Lexi was talking about Nathan. "Remember that follow-up article he wrote about the fire victims?"

Max said, "When you two started dating?"

"Yeah." She smiled in a dreamy way.

Claire smiled too. Little Alexis had blossomed into a lovely young woman, counting more battle wins than losses against an eating disorder, falling crazy in love with a wonderful young man, and thanking God for it all.

"Well," Lexi went on, "he's doing another article about where we all are now, a year later. He's coming up today so he can file it before the actual anniversary date next week. The article is basically done, but I'm taking him along the escape route, sort of for ambience. Not that it'll be the same with the sun shining." She wrinkled her nose, her only negative expression about that awful night of the fire. "Mom, you don't have to come along, but you're welcome to. Same for you, Nana. Papa."

Claire froze. Images of thick smoke filled her imagination. She could smell it. She could hear the roar of wind, the crackling rush of fire. Her heart pounded.

Ben startled her with a chuckle. "Thanks but no thanks, Lexi. Being able to hike up that path a year ago was a miracle, thanks be to God. I see no reason to ask Him to perform it again."

Indio smiled. "Amen. That trek was indeed a supernatural event. The good Lord will have to do a powerful lot of talking to my heart to get these old bones moving like that again."

Max said, "Physical abilities aside, I don't know that you'd all care to relive that night in other ways. Lexi, are you sure you want to?"

"I do." She nodded. "I've thought a lot about it. I am totally ready now."

"Must have something to do with *The Guy* tagging along?"

"Dad." Lexi blushed whenever her dad teased about Nathan.

While everyone else laughed, Max locked his eyes with Claire's.

Her heart's mad thump slowed. Hearing her family's reaction to the thought of retracing that night's steps calmed her. Hearing Lexi proclaim that she was ready to face that demon encouraged her tremendously.

Claire had faced it some time ago, taking Max with her along the escape route. They'd driven through a large portion of the estate's rough terrain, parked, and then hiked up what she would have deemed impassable rocky hills. She'd even crawled into the hole when she didn't have to . . .

Yes, she'd relived it with her guy beside her. She understood now that the Lord had been there, too, singing songs of deliverance over her the entire way. It was finished.

Claire turned to Lexi. "I don't think so, hon."

"Been there, done that?"

"Yeah."

Lexi smiled. She knew her mom's story.

"I'm glad you're ready."

"Me too, Mom."

Danny announced he wanted to go along. He invited Skylar, who perked up at his request. Tuyen wasn't interested, but suggested they call Erik. Jenna, her eyes nearly shut, asked which room she could sleep in. Max declared he was back to Plan A, which included no hikes, no guests, no family. Claire hushed him with a fierce glare.

Ben cleared his throat loudly. "While we're announcing plans to revisit the past, I have one to add."

All eyes turned to him. Voices quieted. Ever since Beth Russell's visit, Ben's old compassionate, confident self had reemerged, a change welcomed by all.

Ben sat up straight in his chair. "Tuyen and I are going to Vietnam."

Claire felt her eyes go wide.

He said, "She'll show me BJ's grave. Where he lived. Where he died. We want to go as soon as possible." He snapped his jaw shut.

He had no more words, nor did anyone. Long, silent moments passed.

Then Indio sighed, a sound of release.

Everyone began to speak at once. Finally Max's voice rose above the others.

"Dad, you won't hike your own back forty but you'll fly halfway 'round the world and somehow get to some obscure village up in the mountains during monsoon season?"

Ben stuck out his lower lip and nodded.

"Then I'm going too."

Claire exclaimed. "What?"

"Yep." Max nodded, still looking at his dad. "We'll go. We'll take care of it once and for all."

Ben gave another nod, quick and final.

Claire met Indio's gaze. The black eyes were inscrutable.

Her mother-in-law sighed again. "It's a good plan. Necessary, like Lexi's walk. If we don't revisit the past that haunts us and banish it, its control over us will never end."

Claire shut her eyes and thought of that tandem bike ride with her wild mother-in-law. Indio wasn't steering this situation, but she might as well have been. Her respected opinion powered up the pedaling and jerked the handlebar. Claire felt as if they'd just rounded a curve and hit a pothole at full speed. The impact threw her equilibrium completely out of whack. The wind whistled in her ears.

She knew what Indio meant. Claire had revisited her own haunting memories, from the night of the fire to childhood traumas to emotional affairs with other men. She'd received forgiveness and healing through Christ.

Now, if she understood Indio's wink, Ben and Max were headed down that rewarding but most difficult of paths: surrendering. They had to let BJ go once and for all.

Claire looked around the table. Her eyesight felt different. She saw all of them letting go . . . Jenna of the life she had wanted with Kevin. Skylar of whatever it was that kept her from settling down. Danny of his prejudices. And Lexi now, in trekking up to the gold mine, would let go of the terror from that night of the fire.

Perhaps even she herself would do some surrendering. The thought of Max being gone triggered old resentments from his many absences through the years. Why not let them go?

"Claire." Indio smiled at her. "We just pray, dear."

Okay. The matriarch prayed. She would. Just at soon as she let go of her fear that Indio was passing the tandem's handlebars to her.

Thirty-three

After the family breakfast, Jenna wanted to join Lexi's hike with the others. She wanted to be excited for Papa's travel plans. But wanting did not supply the necessary energy. She went to one of the Hideaway's guest bedrooms and crawled between cool, crisp sheets.

They were blue floral.

They reminded her of the small room at the hospital.

She kneaded the pillow beneath her head and looked up at oak beams across the ultrawhite plaster.

They reminded her of Amber looking up at ugly, gray ceiling tiles. Not that she could see them. As of a few hours ago, her friend still lay in a coma at the hospital.

Jenna rolled onto her side. Outdoors the sun shone, making for a miserably hot September day. The old hacienda room was comfortable, though. Its thick adobe walls and shuttered windows locked in the previous night's cool. Mingled scents of wood furniture and lavender sachets added another layer of serenity.

Nothing like the antiseptic odors at the hospital.

The guest room was at the farthest end of the courtyard, away from the family commotion taking place in the kitchen. She would sleep.

Just as soon as she forgot about the hospital with its gruesome odors and the blue floral print wallpaper . . .

Had she really kissed him?

Jenna shut her eyes, but the mental video recorded last night rolled on . . .

After talking with Joey in the middle of the night, Jenna laid her head on Cade's shoulder. She did not cry more. Her tears had been all used up, shed while on the phone first with Kevin, then with Joey. Nor did she sleep. Her earlier nap on the couch in the waiting room had taken the edge off her exhaustion.

What she did was move into a new space. All defenses and pretenses fell away, leaving her more *real* than she'd ever been in her life. As she had told Kevin, it was time to admit and to accept their current situation.

Like writing a grocery list, she listed the elements with a cold practicality.

One, Kevin was overseas, fighting in a war.

Two, she was on her own, teaching, and befriending Amber. At long last she was embracing her role as a Marine's wife, which meant, basically, that she lived day in and day out inside an emotional combat zone.

Three, people offered their appreciation, privately and publicly, for her and Kevin's sacrifice. They honored them.

And they exploded bombs near them. Both of them. At home and over there.

Four, damage was done. Physical, mental, emotional. Untold. Irreparable. Collateral.

Five, steps were taken to ease the pain. Stitches were made, comas induced, phone calls exchanged, rules broken, prayers offered, courage summoned, comfort sought.

The list was finished, its elements admitted and accepted. She understood that she was a casualty of the emotional combat zone in which she lived.

Coherent thought fled, taking with it the ability to step back and coldly assess the damage. Pain crashed through her, physical, mental, emotional.

She could take meds for her arm and for her head. For that deeper, unfathomable hurt she could only turn intuitively to the comfort close at hand.

She tilted her face up toward Cade, her mouth centimeters from his.

"Jenna." The dim lamplight cast shadows over his eyes, but his tone was clear. It cautioned.

But she didn't move.

He waited.

She waited.

He lowered his face. His lips grazed hers.

Her hurt began to ebb away.

And then she kissed him back . . .

The mental video ended.

In the safe harbor of her parents' home, Jenna rolled to her other side, angling her left arm so that it would not be squished underneath her.

Yes, Cade had kissed her and she had kissed him back. For long, sweet moments, the intimate contact eased her deep ache.

Now, in the light of day, she saw it as the result of a glitch in the system. When a happily married couple was torn apart and thrown into the chaos of war, one or both could quite easily turn for desperately needed comfort to another.

Like Uncle BJ did in Vietnam. Away from his beloved Beth Russell, he turned to a woman who comforted him, the one who would in time give birth to Tuyen.

Jenna thought her heart stopped right then and there.

That which she so feared had become her reality.

Of course Kevin could—if put into Uncle BJ's position—respond the same way. Of course he could. Danny kept saying it would never happen. But it could.

And of course she herself, surviving a bombing and watching over a comatose friend, could respond in the same way. *Had* responded in the same way.

Similar way, she corrected herself. Similar. Not the same. A few kisses of comfort from Cade Edmunds did not signify a thing. The physicality was morally wrong, yes, but also the result of a glitch in an unfair system.

It was, even, part of the whole abominable scene. She shuddered at the memory of the funeral, the explosion, Amber falling against her, both of them bleeding, the ambulance ride. The needles, the pills. Amber's head swathed in white. Listening to men cry on the phone. Cade being there at that precise moment.

Yes, Cade's comfort was for the time of utmost anguish, a time that was past. She'd reached the other side of the glitch.

Jenna succumbed at last to sleep.

Thirty-four

The pickup truck hit a rut at what would be considered full speed on a country highway.

"Ouch!" Skylar clutched the side of the truck bed and bounced. Even with a thick layer of blankets beneath her, she felt every bone jarred loose.

Danny's arm rammed against hers. "Lexi always did have a lead foot. The story goes she almost outdrove the fire that night." He half turned and banged on the back window. "Lex!" he shouted. "Slow down!"

His sister and her friend Nathan rode inside the cab, Lexi at the wheel. They both looked over their shoulders at Danny and Skylar, cupping a hand at their ears as if they couldn't hear.

Danny turned back. "Two pods in a pea."

She raised her brows in question.

"Lexi used to call us twins 'two pods in a pea.' I think the phrase applies to them now."

"You mean those moony, gooey-eyed lovey-doveys?"

He grinned.

Skylar couldn't help but smile in return.

Dog tired, guilt ridden, and spooked at the thought of her old acquaintance Fin being in the same city, she *smiled*. What was it about these crazy Beaumonts that got to her?

Indio loved on her like she'd been hurt as badly as Jenna. Claire fed her and reiterated that she was not to cook or clean for others, no matter how many people showed up that weekend. Everyone accepted her at the breakfast table as if she were *family*. They talked freely in front of her about deep hurts and tragic events and their plans to address those things.

Last night—

No. Smiling had nothing to do with last night and Danny's holding her while she bawled. It had nothing to do with his concerned voice on the phone later when she had called him as promised after getting home. It had nothing to do with his invitation that she join them on this hike that began with a bumpy truck ride.

For certain it had nothing to do with his dark eyes peering at her now from under the brim of his ball cap. Or the way his curls stuck out every which way. Or the mouth that really did have Wally Cleaver's smile down to a *T*.

He broke eye contact and looked toward the end of the truck bed. "We'll be parking soon. The trail gets too steep and rocky for driving."

Skylar studied the rough terrain. Every shade of green vied with blacks and grays. New life was forging its way through death and destruction. But there was evidence of old-growth chaparral killed. Manzanita that looked from their breadth to be maybe a hundred years old lay broken. Thinking about the loss of vegetation and wildlife added weight to her heart already heavy with grief.

"How did the fire start?" she asked.

"Wind blew down a power line in an uninhabited area. Conditions were just right for one spark to take off before anyone spotted it. Actually it started several miles from here, going a different direction. Then the wind shifted."

"And Lexi, your mom, and grandparents were trapped?"

"Yeah. Along with three firemen." He looked at her again. "Let's jump to the happy ending. They all got out safely."

"Where were you?

"In some sort of limbo hell. There was no communication with them. Dad, Jenna, Kevin, Erik, and I got up as far as that lookout turnout along the highway. We could see entire mountains on fire."

"How awful! And they were out here, in the middle of the night, fire all around them, trying to escape?"

"Yeah."

She shuddered involuntarily. "Why couldn't they get out?"

"There's just the one road in and out, the driveway. The fire had circled around and felled trees across it. Hindsight says they should have left sooner, even though there was no direct threat."

"It could happen again."

"Sure. It's happened often. The fires just never hit the house or barn. Papa grew up here, you know. He's evacuated plenty of times. Nana, Dad, and Uncle BJ too. Based on past experience, Papa thought they were okay. I remember evacuating once when I was a kid staying up here for a couple weeks. We could hardly see the smoke, but Papa said he knew best." Danny smiled wryly. "It's one of the perks of living surrounded by all this peace and beauty."

She bit a fingernail, seeing that night in all its vivid horror. It did not take much effort to imagine. She knew firsthand the roar of fire . . .

"Skylar, what's wrong?"

"N-nothing."

"You look scared."

"I'm fine."

"The night did have a happy ending."

"So you said."

"And this year we've had above-average rainfall. Conditions are nowhere near what they were. Papa and the neighbor are working on a path between the properties. It really is safe to live here, I promise. Safer than going to a protest. You won't leave, will you?"

"What?"

"You won't leave the Hideaway? Mom says she'd have to close up shop if you left."

Skylar's throat tightened. She was on overload and dangerously close to spilling again.

"You are upset."

"Stop telling me how I feel—"

"Did you sleep last night?"

"That's none of your business."

"You could have stayed home. It's obvious you're worn out."

"Danny, don't you ever shut up?"

"Not much." He went quiet.

In the silence between them she heard something. Like birdsong that was there all along but undetected until a noisy lawn mower was turned off, she heard it.

It was the sound of Danny's unspoken thoughts.

The guy liked her.

Skylar scrunched herself as far into her corner of the truck bed as possible. Next time she'd let him yap as long as he wanted.

Five minutes into their hike in some far-flung corner of the estate's three hundred acres set in the middle of nowhere, Skylar accepted the fact that avoiding Danny was not a possibility. She didn't exactly have anyplace else to go for the time being.

Like a tour guide, Lexi led the way up unmarked rock-strewn, almost-vertical paths and described—not without a few tears—what had happened the night of the fire. Nathan stayed close beside her. They all carried water bottles; the guys carried lanterns as well.

Skylar liked the lovey-doveys. Lexi was quiet; when she spoke she had something to say. Nathan was, in Lexi's words, the boy next door—simply an all-around nice, solid guy.

The strenuous climb tired Skylar. The emotional story pouring from Lexi zapped every last ounce of her energy. She should have skipped the whole thing.

But sitting back at the hacienda would have meant wallowing in regrets and fears about Jenna and Amber. Which she was not doing now. *God, please.*

God?

Oh, man. She was losing it.

Danny appeared at her side. "Don't bite my head off."

"Don't have the breath for it." She opened her water bottle and took a swig.

"I'm not saying you look ready to keel over, but tell me if you need to sit for a while."

"Sure." She watched in her peripheral vision. He took off his cap, wiped sweat from his brow, replaced the hat. The gesture had a hint of anxiety in it. "You haven't come up here before?"

"Not since the fire. Lexi and I used to play up here as kids. I came partway once, got as far as the back there." He referred to his grand-father's other truck, the one driven the night of the fire. It was a burned-out shell. Because of its remote location, they'd put it last on the postfire cleanup list.

She said, "No further?"

"It seemed like, I don't know, a sacred ground or something. A place closed off until Lexi was ready to take me to it."

"You two are really close."

"Most of the time." He smiled softly at his twin's back a short dis-tance ahead of them. "Excuse me." With the grace of a deer, he bounded up to Lexi and Nathan.

They were too far ahead for Skylar to overhear what he said to her. She saw Lexi smile and slip an arm across Danny's back.

Danny had a bit of all-around nice, solid character himself.

Sometime later they reached their destination at the top of a steep incline. Danny and Nathan knelt on the ground before a pile of rocks against the hillside and began pulling them away.

Lexi and Skylar sat down nearby and drank water.

Skylar said, "This is it?"

"Yes. Behind those rocks is the mine. Do you want to come inside?"

She shook her head. The sight of Lexi's tear-streaked face affirmed her decision not to follow that far. Lexi's revisit to that spot should be a private scene between her, Danny, and Nathan.

Lexi nodded.

"You'll be okay."

She nodded again and wiped the corner of her eye. "Happy tears. I'm so grateful that God kept us safe that night. I'm so grateful for the whole awful thing, even."

"Why?"

"It forced me to face some hard truths about myself and learn how to trust in God. I am in such a better space than I was a year ago. And, in a roundabout way, it brought Nathan into my life."

Skylar smiled.

"There it is." Lexi nodded toward the hillside. A hole no larger than a crawl space had been opened.

"It doesn't look like a gold mine entrance."

"It was a back way in, probably a hundred years ago. The tunnel ends at a cave-in where our great-great-something grandfather was killed. Danny and I discovered the place when we were kids. If Papa had known what we were up to, he never would have allowed us beyond the barnyard. He almost caught us once when we didn't put his flashlights back." She chuckled. "We had so much fun playing 'gold miners' inside here."

"Just the two of you?"

"Yes. Erik preferred hanging out with the horses. Jenna was always sitting in the sala with a stack of books."

"You and Danny sound like the holy terrors of the family."

"In my defense, I have to say he was. I just tagged along." Lexi stood, resolve written evident in her stance. "And I'm really glad I did. Otherwise we probably wouldn't be here today."

Skylar watched her step over to the entrance, pick up a lantern, and then drop to her knees. Lexi crawled into the opening and disappeared from sight. Nathan followed with the other lantern.

Danny looked back at her. "You're sure?"

She nodded. "I'll wait here."

"Okay." A moment later he was gone.

Skylar was left alone in the hush of high desert broken by dissonant echoes of sorrow. How could she ache so strongly for something she'd never had?

Maybe it was because now she understood that growing up within the safety net of a loving family would have made all the difference. All the difference in the world.

Thirty-five

"Ma'am, as I've already said, I am not allowed to give out patient information. That means none at all."

Jenna squeezed her eyes shut. Her fingers ached from their grip on the telephone.

The person on the other end of the line was a nurse at the hospital and she absolutely refused to say if Amber was dead or alive or even still in the ICU.

Jenna's voice warbled like a sick seagull, but she pressed on. "When will Nurse Cathy be in?" Maybe the woman who had let her see Amber the previous night would answer her questions.

"Ma'am, all I can tell you—again—is that she's not on duty at this time. Now, if you'll excuse me—"

Jenna hung up on the loathsome voice, struck with her own rudeness. Compared to life's tragedies, though, being rude to a faceless stranger did not matter.

She balled her hands into fists and stared at a small section of tiled wall, the backdrop to the kitchen's built-in desk. "I will not cry." She shoved her palms against her eyes and wondered if she'd ever get hold of her emotions again.

A short while ago, she'd stumbled out of the guest room, still groggy with sleep. It was late afternoon. The hacienda was quiet, the courtyard and kitchen alike vacant. She had no idea where anyone was, nor did it matter. Her only thought had been to find out about Amber.

But she couldn't.

Did Cade know anything?

At the hospital earlier, after what happened between them—that moment, that *glitch*—they had left the small room with its telephone, its chairs shoved close together, and its blue floral-print wallpaper. They sat in the cafeteria, across a table from one another, and sipped tea, talking of everything but what happened between them in the small room. Then Cade had walked her to the parking lot where Danny waited in his truck and promised to check in on Amber later.

At the hacienda, after breakfast with the family, Jenna had fallen asleep to her own promise not to mix it up with Cade again.

But she needed to know how Amber was!

Oh, Lord, please don't let her die. Please don't let her die.

Nearly ill from exhaustion and worry, Jenna admitted it would be idiotic to drive herself down to the city. Her dad had already declared at breakfast that he would not take her anywhere until Monday, no matter how much she whined. Her mother agreed.

Jenna had no choice but to phone Cade.

Her cell didn't work at the hacienda, but she used it to find his number and then called it with the house phone.

He answered on the first ring. "Edmunds."

"Cade, it's me. Jen—"

"Jenna, are you all right?"

The overt concern in his voice was too loud. It tore through her, shoving roughly at her fragile sense of equilibrium.

"Jenna?"

"How is Amber? The hospital won't tell me anything."

"I talked with her parents a couple of hours ago. They said there's been no change, which is good news for now."

"Are they coming?"

"They'll be here tomorrow night."

"Joey?"

"They talked with him. He should make it here by late Monday."

"Will they call you if . . ."

"Yes. Or they'll call you. I gave them your number too—cell, home, and your parents' house."

"Okay." *Okay, okay.* Everything was under control. For now.

"Please tell me how you are."

"I'm . . ." She took a deep breath. "Fine."

"You slept?"

"Yeah. Is there more on Amber?"

"Only what the nurse told you before. They'll keep her in the coma until the brain swelling goes down."

"And when will that be?" Jenna wiped at her damp cheeks. "Huh? When?"

"They can't say."

"Oh, Cade! How did this happen? Why did this happen?"

"It just happened, Jenna. It just happened. It is what it is."

Suddenly she knew that he was no longer talking about Amber. He said, "It can't be undone." There was a hint of defeat in his voice.

"I-I know."

"We move on."

"I agree. Like two ships passing in the night."

After a silent moment, he said, "My favorite English teacher is speaking in cliché?"

Jenna closed her eyes. "Your favorite English teacher is a total basket case."

"That's obvious. Go back to sleep. I'll call if there's any change with Amber."

"Promise me, Cade?"

"I promise. By the way, don't you dare think about coming in next week. Your favorite sub is counting on five days in your classroom. Understood?"

She heard the subtle change in his voice. Mr. Ice Guy was back.

Before replying, she waited for a twinge of disappointment to work its way out. She cleared her throat, humming around for the perfectly impassive tone. At last she said, "Understood."

And she did understand what he said: as far as he was concerned, life was back to the way it had been before the night in the small room with the blue floral-print wallpaper.

Thirty-Six

*Y*our favorite English teacher is a total basket case.*

Jenna's words stopped Danny cold in his tracks in the doorway. His sister spoke toward the wall, her back to him, her teacher voice carrying easily backwards across the kitchen.

"Promise me, Cade?"

Cade. The name rooted Danny to the floor.

Jenna's voice hushed, her good-bye lost to his hearing. He watched her hang up the phone and cross her arms on top of her head as if in exasperation.

He cleared his throat so as not to surprise her. "Jen."

She turned. "You're still here?"

"Seemed the thing to do with everyone being a little on edge."

"Take me to the hospital?"

"No."

"Didn't think so." She lowered her arms to the back of the chair and laid her chin on them.

He walked to the island and leaned against it. Jenna appeared even more vulnerable, in her crumpled sweats and disheveled hair, than she had in the bombed-out church. "How are you feeling?"

"So-so. I called the hospital but they wouldn't tell me about Amber. I called Cade; he'd talked to her parents."

She called the hospital first? That order of events helped, but not much. "And her parents said what?"

"No change. They say that's good." She sighed. "How was the hike to the gold mine?"

At her question, he felt it all again, all the discomfort he'd felt earlier on the dusty trail and inside the damp tunnel. It was an empathetic fear for his mom, Lexi, Nana, and Papa. "I don't know how they did it the night of the fire."

"Oh, Danny, there's just too much going on. I feel like the world is crumbling all around us."

"Where does Cade fit in?"

She jerked upright. "What do you mean by that?"

"Come on, Jenna. You hang out with him at the beach. He spends the night with you at the hospital. First thing you wake up, you call him."

Her face reddened. "I've worked with him for years. He's our friend. Mine, Amber's, and Kevin's. He's concerned about all of us."

"'Your favorite English teacher'?" He heard the harshness in his mocking tone but couldn't let it go.

"It's a joke."

"The flirting kind."

Jenna stood abruptly and walked by him. "I expected more from you, not this stupid judgmental attitude insinuating that somehow I'm disloyal to Kevin. You're the only one who hates this war as much as I do. You should understand."

He followed her with his eyes to the doorway.

She stopped and turned. "I'm getting one of those bumper stickers that says 'Marine Wife' and I'm going to proudly display it on my car. If you make one snide remark, I swear I'll stop talking to you."

"Hey, if 'Marine Wife' means 'Hands off this chick,' go for it. Make sure what's-his-face sees it."

She puffed a noise of disgust.

They were badgering each other now exactly as they'd done all through childhood and adolescence. But Danny felt obligated to speak his mind. Who else would tell Jenna she was headed for major trouble? Her overly defensive tone confirmed his suspicions. Cade was clearly much more than friend and boss to her.

"'Marine Wife' means," she said, tossing her hair like a prancing mare, "all that *semper fi* stuff. Fortitude. It means that my husband and I are in this together. That he has my full support. That I can take care of myself while he's gone."

"In other words, 'Hands off.' That's good, Jen."

"You are so full of yourself, Daniel." She spun on her heel and walked out the door.

Jenna was a snot, so full of her—

His anger drained away. Jenna was so full of fear.

Why hadn't he figured that out yet? He'd been preoccupied with praying for his brother-in-law's safety, not grasping the fact that Jenna lived in a war zone too. Although different in nature, it was every bit as dangerous to her well-being as Kevin's situation was to him.

Lord, I'm sorry. Forgive me for not listening to Jenna's heart. Please keep Kevin and her safe. Draw her to Yourself. Help her to look to You for her peace and comfort. You alone and not what's-his-face.

He should go after her. Apologize and tell her he understood.

Then again, maybe not.

On a good day Jenna was not very accepting of his faith and his attempts to incorporate it into everyday life. As a young girl she would ask him to pray about her piano recitals, but the request was similar to rubbing a rabbit's foot for good luck.

That wasn't his take on Christ. Yeah, He was there to help, but He also taught about turning from sin. Jenna never wanted to hear about that.

And, too, there was the real possibility that if he heard Jenna defend Cade Edmunds again, he would blow his cool to such a degree he'd push her over the edge. Asking her the tough questions was one thing, but losing rapport with her was not what he wanted.

Just like he didn't want to lose the fragile rapport he had going with Skylar. He knew without a doubt that she'd run as fast as she could if he openly declared his thoughts. True, she reminded him less and less of his old friend Faith, and yet he couldn't completely trust her—no matter how right that hug had felt last night.

Lord, I need some direction here. He'd prayed for Skylar as he did for Jenna, that God would give her faith to see Himself. *It's backfiring. The more I pray for her, the more she's on my mind. And that's a bit too much even for me to see You do.*

He should go home, surf, clear his mind.

But the thought of being near Skylar was doing a number on him. Could be there weren't enough waves to clear his mind of her—or to get a handle on his feelings.

Thirty-seven

The courtyard was midnight quiet. Low-to-the-ground solar lamps lit stone pathways and threw the fountain into a tall shadow. When guests slept at the hacienda, the gentle flow trickled throughout the night. Not this night, though. This night was for family and for remembering. For remembering and letting go of the old.

Skylar sat in a wicker chair near the fountain, wrapped in Indio's quilt. She hugged herself, rocking back and forth without benefit of rockers. She twisted a long strand of hair around and around, aware that she was neither guest nor family.

Kansas was growing complicated.

"Skylar." Danny's voice startled her. He came into view, moving up one of the side paths to her. "Sorry."

"I thought you left."

He sat in another chair and propped his feet on the fountain's edge. "Jenna might wake up and think she can head to the hospital to see Amber. I don't want her driving in the middle of the night. I don't want her—" He abruptly stopped talking.

"Don't want her what?"

Leaning back, he tilted his chin toward the starlit sky. "Nothing." He paused. "There was a guy with her at the hospital this morning. I don't want her depending on him for help."

She set her bare feet on the chair and hugged her knees. "You are quite the brother."

"Granted, I'm a brother. What does 'quite' mean?"

"Cleaver-like." She laid her forehead against her knees, blocking the view of his shadowy face, too spent to keep up her facade.

Not a good situation.

"Skylar, when you refer to us as the Cleavers, I wonder if you're poking fun. Those sitcoms were about clueless dorks."

"True, but the great thing was they all hung together through thick and thin."

"So you think we're jerks who have loyalty down pat."

She turned her head sideways and gazed at his profile. "No. I think you're the most amazing family on the face of the earth. 'Quite the brother' means you watch over your Lexi and Jenna like a guardian angel. You probably do Erik too. I wish I had been born a Beaumont."

The starlight caught a flash of white. He was smiling. "Thank goodness you weren't. I couldn't have handled another sister."

Skylar buried her face again.

Jenna might very well sleep through the rest of the night until noon tomorrow. Her body was in dire need of restoration. And yet there Danny sat, available. Like he'd been for Lexi earlier that afternoon on the hike. She and Nathan had emerged from the mine, laughing and talking nonstop. Danny had appeared several moments later, uncharacteristically subdued. Skylar understood that he had entered Lexi's nightmare and taken it on as his own. He would always be there for her.

The guy had guardian angel written all over him.

He said, "Why are you still awake?"

She sighed to herself and looked again at his profile. "Let me put it this way. If I drank, smoked, or did drugs, I'd be asleep."

He swung around to face her.

As she knew he would. "Gotcha. You figured I did drugs, didn't you? Because of the unconventional way I dress and talk. Because of my gypsy roaming."

"Guilty, I confess."

"You really should do something about those preconceptions of yours, you know? The world is not a black-and-white place."

"Has my mom been talking to you?"

"She doesn't have to point out the obvious. I mean, you protest the war. Lexi is all about protecting wildlife and the environment. Which puts the three of us in agreement on several points. But there's a huge difference. You two happen to look like a goody-goody TV family while I resemble a 1960s Haight-Ashbury leftover."

"I apologize, Skylar. It's been my experience—oh, never mind. It doesn't matter."

"Yes, it does."

"Okay, okay. I had a couple of really close friends. When we went off to college, they totally embraced the anti-everything lifestyle, complete with drugs and the hippie look. The point is, I thought I'd met your type before, because of the resemblance. In all honesty, though, I've never met anyone like you. I'm sorry for prejudging."

"Apology accepted."

"So I guess we're both awake. Anything in particular you want to talk about?"

Pick a topic.

She probably knew the identity of the bomber.

She'd packed her bag.

She could never go home.

She could not stop thinking about Danny holding her.

Which was the only thing that kept her from bolting.

Not exactly subjects to discuss with him.

It was time to calm down and slip on the facade again. Her foray into being real hadn't chased him off, but if she kept going down that road, decisions would be made for her. Decisions she didn't want to face in the middle of the night with Danny Beaumont, who had just said in a tone of *admiration* that he'd never met anyone like her.

Now, *there* was topic for discussion, but she said, "No. Anything you want to talk about?"

"Nah. We could just sit here, watch the stars, and not talk."

"Did you actually say you'd sit still and shut up?"

He laughed softly.

Silence settled between them. Comfort as deep and warm as the quilt enveloped her heart and, for the moment, pushed aside all the complications Kansas could serve up.

Bells and smells." Danny nodded sagely at his mother. "Skylar is going to be impressed."

"Oh, hush." Claire frowned. "Why are you still here anyway? It's Sunday morning."

"People keep asking me that." He shrugged. "I have no idea."

Skylar sipped luscious coffee and watched the two of them fuss back and forth. It was interesting how Danny unraveled Claire unlike her other children could.

His mom, at the kitchen island, shook a finger very near his chin. "Let's get one thing straight. Just because you're here does not give you permission to pester Skylar."

Skylar snickered.

Claire turned toward her, eyebrows raised.

Skylar said, "It's okay, Claire. He's not pestering."

"See, Mom?" His eyes danced. "Sky and I got it all worked out last night. She basically told me I'm judgmental, and I apologized. Profusely."

Skylar said, "Huh-uh. Not profusely, but enough to remove the pester moniker."

He smiled.

Claire swiveled her gaze between them.

Skylar grinned. "He does get to you, Claire."

She sighed. "As I was saying, our church is liturgical, but not overly formal. You don't have to feel that you must go through all the motions. Danny doesn't. Everyone is friendly but they're focused on God. They don't care who's kneeling or not."

"It sounds similar enough to the church I went to as a kid. I'll be fine. No worries."

Claire nodded. "I have to check on Jenna before we go." With that she left the kitchen.

Danny said, "If you're not fine during the service, we can leave."

"Why wouldn't I be fine?"

"Well, why is it you decided to go today? Mom said you didn't seem interested in going before now."

She hid her face, taking another drink of coffee, and thought of her packed bag inside her room. She was so torn.

Inadvertently she'd inflicted damage on the Beaumonts. She had brought evil into Kansas. It was time to go. But then they all showered her with unconditional love. And last night Danny had accepted her. When they parted ways at 2 a.m. he whispered, "I hope you don't leave." As if he knew . . .

He knew somehow, more than he had words for, but he knew. He saw beneath the surface of things. His ability frightened and comforted her at the same time.

Danny took a step nearer her, but stopped an arm's length away. "Can I take a guess why you want to go to church today?"

She lowered the cup. His dark eyes no longer danced. They'd softened to a velvety concern. She shrugged.

"You want to go for the same reason most of us do: because none of us are fine. We hope to get fine by being part of this age-old tradition of corporate worship where we're reminded that God dispenses forgiveness."

Lowering her chin, she gave him a sarcastic look. "It's that simple?"

"It's that simple."

Danny thought getting fine at church was simple. Twenty minutes into the service Skylar wondered if losing the ability to breathe was part of the guy's "simple" process.

The old church was straight out of some Zorro-era movie with all the wood, stained glass, candles, and crosses. She sat in a pew, Danny on one side of her, Claire the other. Max, Indio, Ben, Lexi, and Tuyen filled in the remainder of the row.

The Beaumont row. Nice and cozy. Homey.

She couldn't breathe. It wasn't so much the nearness of half this clan that claimed her as family. Nor was it candles or perfumes that robbed her lungs of needed oxygen. The windows were open. It wasn't even her inexplicable warming toward Danny.

No, the problem was the air itself.

The air was alive, a living, breathing entity that she could not escape. It felt thick, layers and layers thick. It felt as if it propped her up, keeping her body rigid. It pressed against her, scrabbling for a way inside.

Danny turned and waggled his brows, asking in that gesture if she was okay.

She whispered, "I can't breathe."

He leaned in, his ear close to her lips as if he hadn't heard.

"I can't breathe." Her voice came like spurts from a tire pump. "The air is too thick."

He angled his head and made eye contact with her. A smile started at one corner of his mouth and spread slowly until the lines at his eyes crinkled. Then he put his lips to her ear. "It's not thick. It's thin. You're in a thin space, Sky."

A thin space? Not air so thick it enveloped her like a suit of armor? *Thin?*

Danny put his hand over the one she had splayed on the wooden seat between them. His touch sparked a shock wave, a current racing up her arm and throughout her body. In a flash she understood.

What felt like air thick enough to touch her was exactly that: a touch . . . an embrace from the unseen . . . able to reach her because in that space of corporate worship, the separation between the visible and the invisible had thinned to *nothing*.

If not for the belief that if she stood she would fall, Skylar would have torn down the aisle and never looked back.

Thirty-eight

"Danny." Claire grabbed her son's arm. "Let her go."

They stood in the hacienda's courtyard, watching Skylar scurry off like a deer at the first bang of a shotgun.

Claire felt Danny's resistant strain against her hold, but he didn't break away. "She'll work it out, hon."

Skylar reached the far end and turned the corner toward her room.

At last Danny relaxed. "I thought we were making progress." Frustration laced his tone.

Claire let go of his arm. "We can't push these things. It was clear that church moved her in some way. But that's between her and God. She doesn't need lunch with us to help Him." A memory flashed and she chuckled. "I can't tell you how I used to loathe coming here for lunch after church with Nana and Papa. I carried around so much guilt and hurt that their talk about what went on in the service only made it worse, no matter how good their intentions."

"I never knew that."

"It was before you were born. Later I got fairly adept at faking it." She smiled. "You probably can't relate. You were born with Tigger's bounce and St. Paul's faith. Why would anyone not accept what Jesus taught? Why wouldn't they want to hang out with the likes of you and Nana and wax eloquent about His life-changing truths?"

"Well." He shrugged. "Why not?"

"Because she's not ready just like I wasn't ready. The Spirit has to work in her. I suspect that like with me, there's a lot of heavy baggage in there that's been piling up."

"I could at least take lunch to her."

"Danny, are you not listening? Give her a break."

"But—"

"No buts. Besides, Jenna's ready to leave. I'll pack you a lunch and you can take her home. Then maybe you could take yourself home."

"Mom." He protested, a pinched expression on his face.

She felt a Danny collision in the making. What was going on with him? In the faith department he'd been light-years ahead of her his entire life. He knew more Scripture than she would ever even have time to read. As a toddler he'd pray about everything—Lexi's lost paintbrush, rain, a parking spot for his mom, limping seagulls. Why would he lose sight over an obviously hurting young woman?

Unless . . .

Claire studied his profile. He gazed toward where Skylar had been, his eyes half-shut. A jaw muscle twitched. His hands on his hips expressed a sense of determination, as if he'd hound her until she was his.

Danny was falling in love with Skylar?

Okay. That would take some adjustment on her part.

Danny was her traditional, most-like-Max child. He focused on his two businesses and spent downtime with friends from his church. His church—where all the young women were traditional, focused on their careers, and spent their downtime with friends from church. Couples kept forming within that circle of friends. Danny seemed destined to hook up with one of them sooner or later, whenever he got around to realizing that sharing life with a special woman beat rooming with Hawk.

Or was that a mother thinking with her heart?

Skylar was a free spirit who did not have an interest in career. She resembled Danny's dearest childhood friend after she had abandoned the traditional route and broke his heart.

Skylar carried a whole lot of baggage. Absent parents. Poverty. Much like Claire had herself when she had met Max.

Oh, my.

Her most-like-Max child.

Ohhhhh.

"What did you say?" Danny was looking at her.

"Nothing." She kissed his cheek. "Let her be for now." Turning, she walked toward the kitchen and breathed a soft prayer. "Lord, have mercy."

Max grinned across the kitchen table. "In love with Skylar?"

"I really think so," Claire said.

"That's, well, that's . . ."

"Exactly."

He took a bite out of his tuna sandwich.

They ate in silence for a few minutes. Danny and Jenna had left; Skylar had not reappeared after they got home from church; Indio and Ben, Lexi, and Tuyen had gone to their respective homes on the property.

Max said, "We let it go."

"I like her a lot. I would hate to try to run this place without her. She's giving, loving, quirky, but—"

"Sweetheart." He touched her hand. "We let it go. Do you know how often you tell me that? It's all about surrendering, you say. Give up the past; it's over. Give up the future; it may never come. Live in the moment."

"But—" The whine grated on her nerves. She lowered her voice. "She has baggage."

Max laughed. "I can't believe you said that."

"Well."

"Like none of us have baggage?"

"That's not the point. What if Danny's coming at this relationship, consciously or not, with the attitude that he's going to rescue her? He couldn't rescue Faith, but now he can make right that failure. He'll just hurt her and himself in the process. They're too different on every level to become one."

Max squeezed her hand. "Listen to yourself, Claire. What do you hear?"

"A concerned mother who just wants the best for her son."

He shook his head. "It's fear."

Her stomach twisted and she heard the truth in his statement.

"This is why we reserved the weekend for us, right?"

She nodded. "We thought the memory of the fire might do a number on us. What do you think?"

He smiled gently. "What do you think?"

She closed her eyes. Things crept in now and then and undermined her peace. A sense of unreasonable fear. A sense of not being able to cope with the everyday. A sense of reluctance not to do something innocuous. Flashbacks of dark and smoke that triggered a rush of panic.

Max knew of such episodes. Often he was the one who pointed them out to her, much as he'd done just now about her overreaction to Danny and Skylar.

She looked at him. "Why isn't it finished yet? God has brought me so far, but . . . it has been worse these past couple weeks."

"It's the same time of year. The earth is at its hottest and driest. Nothing like last year's condition with the rain we've had, but similar enough for your unconscious to react to."

She sighed. "I just accept and give myself a break."

"Yep. Still."

"Where are you?" Although Max's experience with the fire was not hers, that night had been his worst. He'd had to process emotions as well.

"Ever since I told Dad yesterday that I'd go to Vietnam with him, I've regretted it. It seems the right thing to do for him and for myself, so why the worry? It finally came to me in church. It's all about fear too. I'm afraid of being away from you. I'm afraid you'll need me and I won't be able to get to you."

"Like that night. I've had similar thoughts."

"I'm sure." He leaned across the table, his eyes locked on hers. "I do believe it's the right thing. I need to deal with this bag of trash— say good-bye to BJ and let go of my anger toward the government and the Vietcong."

She winced. "I agree. I don't like it, but I think I'm supposed to push through this one. Your absence doesn't mean abandonment to me like it used to."

"You're not just being stoic?"

"No." She smiled. "I don't do that anymore."

"Okay." He straightened. "Did you and Mom decide if you want to formally mark the passing of this year?"

She'd been avoiding the subject like she'd been avoiding mention of his spur-of-the-moment trip idea. She sighed. Enough with the ostrich mime routine.

"Yes. We want to make a memorial, kind of like BJ's, leave some mementos. Your mom has a stone angel. I have a wrought-iron garden cross. The gold mine seems the most appropriate place, but it really is too difficult for your folks to get there. We decided—" Her throat closed up.

"Aw, sweetheart." Max moved to her side of the table and knelt beside her. "You decided what?"

That night rushed at her. Ben kept driving the Jeep up to a high point. From there he could see the fires in the far distant mountains. Although he knew what shifting winds could do, he initially believed the fires would not reach them.

She had ridden with him one time to view the scene. And that was where it all started, the gnawing deep inside of her that the world was being flung out of control.

"Claire?"

"Your mom and I decided to go up to that spot where your dad watched."

Max nodded. He knew the story and the place. "I've got something to add. Wait here."

He went through the side door, into the laundry and mud room. A moment later he reappeared, a twist of blackened metal in his hand. He walked over to her.

"It's a cross," he said. "Not very pretty but I made it from—" Now his voice cracked. "From your car."

Her car. They'd had to leave it in the parking lot when they evacuated. It burned, its trunk and backseat loaded with Indio's special things.

"Oh, Max!"

"I remember that morning, when we drove up behind the ambulance. The first thing I spotted was your car. It was just a black shell. All I could think about was if you'd died." He laid his gift on the floor and pulled her into his arms.

And then they both cried.

Thirty-nine

They were beyond Estudillo Corners in Danny's truck and on the downhill stretch into San Diego before either of them spoke. Not that Jenna was going to breathe a word unless her brother did first.

"I'm sorry," he said.

Jenna stared at him.

"I forget how awful this is for you, having Kevin fighting in that . . . that far-off war."

She heard the unspoken expletive in his stutter. Despite his love for Kevin, his anger at the situation was always there just beneath the surface.

Danny reached over and touched her injured arm. "And now this. Truce?"

She was too tired to argue with him anymore. "Sure. Okay."

He flicked on the turn signal. "Mind if we turn off for a few minutes?"

Every nerve in her body screamed in protest. "Yes, I mind! What are you doing?"

The truck slowed. "I need just a minute here." He turned left onto a side road.

Jenna recognized where he was taking them, and her anxiety jumped another notch. "The lookout? Now?"

"You do know what the date is, right?" He glanced at her. "Or maybe not, considering."

The date? All she could think of was Amber lying in the hospital. Or the morgue. Or wherever it was they took—

"The fire, Jen. It happened a year ago this week. I have to, I don't know, have a moment of silence or something."

Exasperated, she tilted her head back with a thump against the headrest.

"It's good to remember," he said.

"It's one of the worst memories I have. Why would I want to remember?"

"To mark its passing. To thank God for keeping us all safe through it."

"Oh, Danny! Can't you do it some other time? I am so worried about Amber."

He pulled into a parking lot along the side of the road and braked. "I want to do this with you. Dad says he's coming later. Erik's bringing Rosie up tonight."

Jenna looked through the windshield. A panorama of mountains stretched forever toward the east. It was an incredibly gorgeous sight—one she had avoided for an entire year.

The afternoon sun threw the most distant ones into a purple haze; the nearer ones glowed in Technicolor: vegetation greens, blue-grays of rock . . . and black scars beneath it all.

"Oh, Danny," she said again.

"Come on." He got out of the truck.

She joined him at the edge of the lookout, at the low stonewall where one year they'd had a family photo taken for Christmas cards. It was a favorite spot of their mother's.

Jenna linked her good arm with Danny's and leaned her head against his shoulder. "Mom loved this spot."

"I think she still does. It was bizarrely appropriate that we gathered here that night."

She shuddered. The memory sprung upon her, fresher than the one of her mom bringing coffee to her that morning.

That night of the fire, the road up to the hacienda had been blocked off just beyond the lookout. No one had been allowed up to Santa Reina or even Estudillo Corners, the turn for the hacienda. Emergency workers and vehicles had filled the place where they now stood.

Jenna and Kevin had joined Danny, Erik, and their dad. The five of them waited through the cold night, huddled together, inhaling thick smoke, ash collecting in their hair. They flailed about in a no-man's-space, having not one clue whether their mom, Lexi, Nana, or Papa were dead or alive. A firefighter pretended to update them; in truth he only repeated again and again, "No news. We can't get in."

It was such an unbelievable nightmare.

Danny unlaced his arm from hers, draped it around her shoulders, and hugged her tightly.

As he had done that night.

"Thank You, Lord," he prayed, "for keeping them safe."

As he had done that night.

She looked at him. "Danny, you prayed those words before we got to them. Before we even knew."

He nodded.

"It was more than your twin mojo, right?" Through the years he and Lexi had often felt things about each other from a distance. That night he'd sensed that if Lexi were not safe, he would somehow know it.

"Yes." He smiled. "More than the mojo. It was faith." She saw a shimmer in his dark eyes.

"How do I get it?"

"You have it, Jen. You know God's real. You recognize Him in this vista before us. In Nana's love and wisdom. In your music and literature. The thing that takes practice is recognizing when He speaks to you."

She didn't bother to ask how and leaned her head against his shoulder. Danny was a mystery to her, which probably explained why he made her nuts at times.

After a moment he said, "Just now you *knew* my prayer that night came from something besides my connection with Lexi. That's how faith is. When you *know* something in that intangible way, trust it. Go with it. Be open, and God will reveal Himself."

She closed her eyes and tried to conjure up a knowing, an intuitive sense of something being true.

Her arm hurt. Bottom line, it hurt because the world was messy and unfair. Her heart ached. Same reason. Her husband was too far away. Same reason. She was afraid for Amber. Same reason.

Everything had a reason. She knew nothing by faith.

She felt the soft cotton of Danny's T-shirt against her cheek and viewed the mountains from an angle. For the moment she was at peace, content to be still in the presence of her goofy brother who for once was still himself.

The two of them at that awful place of remembrance and yet at peace? She couldn't explain that one away. Did that make it faith?

She highly doubted that conclusion.

Danny braked near the hospital's front entrance. "You should go home."

She gathered her bag of clothes and opened the truck door. "Your reluctance is duly noted."

"I can wait."

She sighed. They'd already been through the argument of whether he would take her to her car or to the hospital. She would pop, she'd told him, if she didn't see Amber as soon as possible. Given the fact that her car was still parked by the church, which was way beyond the hospital, he'd finally agreed.

"Danny, don't wait. I'm sure others will be here by now. She has so many military wives for friends. I'll get a ride to my car." She smiled.

"That's what we Marine wives do, you know. We help each other out. We stick together. We semper fi."

He chuckled. "But have you met any?"

She scrunched her nose at him. "Not yet."

"I'll wait."

"Danny! Go home." She slid from the car.

"If you need to, take a cab home and I'll get you to your car later."

"Good-bye."

"You don't look yourself."

"Do I care?"

"Usually."

Jenna imagined what he saw. She'd done her best. Thanks to Lexi and Tuyen, she wore a knit black skirt, a long-sleeved sea green top, sandals, and makeup. She really didn't care. She had work to do. The love of her life was seven thousand, seven hundred, and thirty-one miles away.

"I showered," she said.

He pointed to his eyes. "You need to recuperate."

"Go home, *Mom*." Jenna slammed the door and walked off, never glancing back.

She entered the hospital. Finding her way to the ICU floor required almost too much effort. The building was a maze. Every staff member she begged directions from asked if she were family because if she weren't, she may as well forget about going there.

At last she recognized a hall and began eyeing nurses in hopes that Cathy—the helpful one who'd allowed her into Amber's room— would be on duty again,.

"Jenna."

At the sound of Cade's voice, she turned. He approached.

And then, like a sudden clang of cymbals in a symphony, she heard what Danny was saying in all his words about not going to the hospital. He figured there was a chance Cade would be there again.

She had figured the same thing.

Danny was concerned about their connection.

So was she. Now that she saw him.

He smiled easily and stopped before her. "Amber's the same. Don't look so frightened. They keep saying 'same' is best for now."

Jenna nodded, her throat too tight for vocalizing.

Not that she really had anything to say.

Mr. Ice Guy was in place. The smile belonged to him, the steady gray eyes. The proper space between them was his doing.

But it didn't matter. She'd gotten more than a glimpse behind that cold persona. The lips she now watched moving in speech had kissed her.

"It'll get easier," he said.

She jumped. "What?"

"Us. It'll get easier." He spoke in a low voice. No one else was near them in the hall.

"Huh?"

"Neither one of us wants to go down that road." He cocked his head.

She nodded, then shook her head. Yes, she agreed. No, neither wanted to go there.

"I came here for two reasons: to check on Amber since they won't tell you a thing on the phone, and to see you. I didn't want this to happen at school. There's nothing between us, all right?"

"Mm-hmm. No." She looked down at her feet. She needed a pedicure. Those heels she'd worn the other day mussed the polish.

Cade cleared his throat. "Your nurse friend is here."

Jenna raised her chin and focused beyond his shoulder. "Cathy."

"Yes. She informed me that you're family, but I'm not."

"Is anyone else here?"

"No real family yet. There were some friends, but they've gone. You might get in to see her if you want."

Jenna nodded and moved.

Cade grasped her elbow. "The other way."

His touch burned her skin. A heat wave engulfed her.

She wanted to fall into his strong arms. She wanted to depend on him. He would take care of everything. Amber's situation. The hospital staff. Jenna's classes. A ride to her car or straight home. The loneliness . . .

She knew all those things, *knew* Cade Edmunds could fill every empty space, calm every anxiety.

Was that faith?

Probably not.

God, help.

Jenna said to him, "Thanks." She moved away. His hand slipped from her arm. She walked. And kept on walking.

She walked toward the nurses' station. She would find Cathy. She would sit with Amber and talk to her. She would take a cab to her car and drive herself home. She would fix herself dinner. She would make new friends who were in the same swamped military boat as she. She would wait for Kevin to come home.

All of that she *knew* was impossible.

Which could mean, perhaps, if Danny was right, that she had just recognized God speaking to her.

Forty

"Dear." Indio beamed at Skylar across the tiny table.

Skylar couldn't help but return the smile. Indio's endearments always ignited a warmth within her. It didn't matter that they sat in a fast-food chain restaurant eating a questionable taco. Its fried breaded fish was of undetermined variety, its overly white cabbage of the mechanically shredded sort, done nowhere near the premises nor within the past week.

"Look at this." Indio held her taco up in both hands, obviously happy to have her cast off.

Skylar had driven her to the doctor's office. They'd stopped for lunch at this horrid place because Indio declared she hadn't had good junk food in ages. It was Monday, the day after Sunday, the day after church. A part of Skylar lingered in the twilight zone, unsure what was real and what wasn't. She probably would have said yes to a request from Indio to fly to the moon.

Indio said, "God is so good. Maybe I broke my wrist just so you and I could meet."

"How do you do that, Indio? Add an optimistic sidebar to everything?"

"Might as well as not." She shrugged a shoulder and munched on her taco.

She was a curious sight in her "going to town" outfit of suede-fringed skirt and vest. Her hair in two long, thick braids accented her pudgy face. Skylar had noticed passersby either stared rudely or smiled in delight at her. The latter, she figured, related because they had their own senile weirdo hanging from the family tree.

A quirky appearance meant nothing. Indio was the farthest thing from senile or frail or wacko that Skylar could imagine.

"Anyway," Indio said, "I was afraid that once my wrist healed, you might think we wouldn't need you any longer at the hacienda."

Skylar saw the gleam in those bottomless pools. As she so often did, Indio was talking about more than the obvious, drawing upon a knowledge she gained by who knew what. It was like she had an osmotic relationship with some unseen entity.

Entity? She might as well admit it: Indio was all about God.

A chill went through Skylar. She thought of her knapsack, still packed, still shoved under the bed. Somehow, Indio *knew*. Like Danny. Uncanny the resemblance between grandmother and grandson.

"Skylar, I must confess, I don't have the energy or interest in doing what I promised Claire I would do to help run the center. I've spent most of my life in that kitchen. It's where I first met my mother-in-law, Lord rest her fractious soul. She reluctantly passed her home on to me. Then I raised my boys there. Then Ben and I turned it into our retreat." She sighed. "Now I believe that season is over."

"I can't promise—"

"Oh, dear heart, I don't want you to! And I am not laying a responsibility on you. Claire will understand. And as my son says, he knows the staffing business. He can staff the Hideaway kitchen like that." She snapped her fingers. "No, I just want to say that you have been a godsend in countless ways."

A too-large bite of tortilla worked its way down Skylar's throat. "Thank you."

"Thank *you*." Indio tilted her head. "Do you mind if I talk straight?"

Skylar stirred a plastic fork through the glob of lardy refried beans on her plate, waiting for her heartbeat to slow. She looked at Indio. "Do you ever not talk straight?"

"You have no idea how much I hold inside."

Skylar burst into laughter. The woman won. The woman would win every time Skylar dared try matching wits with her. "You play with a stacked hand, Indio."

Her smile was nothing less than enigmatic. She understood what Skylar meant although Skylar herself did not. At work was that unseen entity for which there were no words.

Indio said, "Yes, indeed I do."

Skylar knew it was pointless to hope for a sudden drenching of senility to hit Indio and make her forget what she'd been saying. She didn't bother trying to change the subject.

"As I was saying, Sky—Danny calls you that, doesn't he? 'Sky.' It's nice. It makes me think of endlessness and timelessness, kind of like God." She smiled. "But I won't steal Danny's nickname. Anyway, you've been a breath of fresh air to him and to all of us. We adore you. We hope you'll stay just because you're you, not because you're the best thing that's ever happened to that kitchen."

"I'll-I'll think about it?" Her voice went up. What was with the wavering? She couldn't stay. She simply could not stay. "M-my schedule isn't quite set yet. I'll, um, I'll let you know?"

"That's all I can ask. I just wanted you to know what we were all thinking." She winked. "I took a poll. Even Nathan and Rosie agreed."

"How come?" *Uh-oh.* Skylar was falling where she didn't want to go. "I mean, why would they all—I am not a good person, Indio! You must know that."

Indio reached across the table and patted her hand. "Jesus wiped your slate clean, Skylar, like He did all of ours. You must know that. Now." She smiled. "Let's have some of that fried ice cream."

Skylar pressed her lips together and blinked, gazing about the dining area. At last the garish colors and faux Mexican décor came back into view. Indio had put her through a wringer once again and now it was time for dessert.

"Fried ice cream." Skylar nodded. "Sure."

Whatever. Maybe she could remain at the hacienda a few more days.

Skylar neither unpacked her bag nor put back in the clothes she removed from it to wear day by day. She felt like she had one ruby-red-slippered foot in Kansas and the other on the Yellow Brick Road leading out of town.

Was Fin searching for her? How could he ever track her down? More to the reality of his ability, how long before he tracked her down?

Maybe, though, maybe, maybe, *maybe* he doubted the person he'd seen was, after all, her. There was that chance.

By Thursday evening her equilibrium was, in a word, *off*.

As she poured red cake batter into the last of three round pans, Danny entered the kitchen from the courtyard door.

A reddish puddle formed on the countertop and she cursed softly.

"Oops." He strode over and slid a finger through the spilled batter she clumsily spooned into the pan. He licked his finger. "Yes. Nana's recipe, right?"

She didn't bother to reply. Yes, it was Nana's recipe. With both hands free, Indio had been spending more time cooking at the hacienda. She was a phenomenal hybrid of Rachael Ray, Paula Deen, Julia Child, and some unknown wise herbalist.

"Sorry, Sky." He crossed his arms on the counter and leaned on it. "I'm here to help, not to pester."

"Really? Then you might want to take a hike."

"Your enthusiasm astounds me."

She carried one of the cake pans to the wall oven, opened the door, and slid it inside.

"Right behind you."

She sighed and gave Danny space to put in the other two pans.

"Thanks." She shut the door and set the timer. "I'm sure that's all the help I need."

"You haven't left us."

Brushing past him, she returned to the counter, picked up the dishcloth, and began cleaning the mess. Maybe if she ignored him, he would get lost.

Obviously she hadn't left them. Too much unfinished business interfered with her plans, adding too much confusion.

There was no change in Jenna's friend, Amber.

Claire expected her largest group of guests tomorrow. Even with Indio's added help, they were scrambling.

Max, Ben, and Tuyen were preoccupied with their upcoming trip.

Lexi wasn't around much either. After the hike with Nathan last week, she had spent most of her free time with him in the city. Since first meeting the two, Skylar had seen hints of forward strides in their romance.

Erik was just downright fun. But busy. His activity seemed to revolve around filming a documentary. Although no one knew what it was about, he made everyone swear not to mention it to Rosie.

And so Skylar needed to stay. For now. To see what happened with the Beaumonts. To dwell in that space where the echo of Indio's welcome enveloped her like a fleece blanket.

She lived deeply in each moment, acutely aware of every sight, sound, smell, and texture. Her bedroom felt like a queen's palace with luxurious towels and sheets and quilt, a full view of her kingdom right outside the door. Every time she entered the kitchen, she thought she must have said, "Open sesame" to have such a treasure at her disposal.

She tucked the moments away for future comfort. The weight they added to the constant expectancy that she was leaving nearly broke her.

"Skylar."

She jumped at Danny's voice. He was at her shoulder, taking the dishcloth from her. She realized she was standing completely still, unaware of his presence or the mess on the counter.

He rinsed the cloth in the sink and then wiped the countertop. "Nana thought you might leave after she got her cast off."

"She told me."

"Evidently she doesn't want her kitchen back." He dried his hands on a towel, inspecting his work. In profile his lashes were long. They curled upward.

She didn't remember noticing them before.

He turned. Standing very close, he seemed taller than she'd imagined him.

"It's after ten o'clock, Danny. Why are you here?"

"I know you like the kitchen to yourself late like this, after my folks are usually done for the night."

She should walk away right now. Go to her room and not come out until the cake was done. He would most likely be gone by then.

But she didn't want to walk away. Danny brought with him a peace that she realized had been missing all week.

He said, "I wanted to say some things in private." He stood still, not saying anything.

In the silence and motionlessness, Skylar sensed words and movement. Something was happening, something intangible.

When at last he moved, she was ready to receive the soft kiss he gave her.

"Mm." He straightened, a tiny smile on his face, and whispered, "That was why I drove forty-five minutes up here tonight."

Smart retorts about if it was worth the gas money fizzled long before they reached her vocal cords. A smile kept slipping out of place.

Danny pointed a thumb over his shoulder. "I guess I'll go take a hike now."

She nodded.

He nodded and backed away. "Uh, take care."

Again she nodded.

He turned and walked out the door.

Several deep breaths later she heaved an enormous sigh.

That, *that*, was why she hadn't yet left the Hacienda Hideaway.

Forty-one

Jenna gazed out the window of the fifties-themed diner and saw, not twenty feet away, a man standing at the very end of the Oceanside pier. A fishing pole was propped against the rail beside him. He resembled a dried fig wearing a ball cap. One gnarled hand curled around a knife, the other around a hunk of fleshy bait. As she watched, he skewered a piece of it onto the pole's hook.

Jenna looked down at her shrimp salad and her stomach turned.

A cute young woman seated across the table clanked her spoon against a water glass. "I'd like to make a toast." She held up the glass and smiled. "To Jenna."

As Jenna watched, the seven other cute young women at the rectangular table raised their glasses. "To Jenna!"

"I didn't do anything," she protested.

Beside her Miranda smiled. She had sun-kissed light-brown hair and dimples that showed whether she smiled or not. "But you will do something, right? You promised to buy us all lunch."

Jenna laughed with them. True, lunch was on her.

She wished she could do so much more. Buy them groceries. Take them shopping. Send them to a resort, day care included. Her new sense of semper fi had unleashed a host of maternal emotions toward the younger wives.

The women knew each other. Most of them lived on the base at Camp Pendleton. Miranda at twenty-five was the oldest, but she, too, like the others, looked to be eighteen. Their little kids—a whole slew between them under the age of three—played together.

Their husbands were deployed with Kevin, all members of his squad. As their sergeant, he was their leader. Which meant he was concerned about their wives. Which meant he figured his wife should hang out with them and be an influence on the younger women.

In his dreams.

Jenna had met them before the guys left. She had names and phone numbers. She had even spoken on occasion with Miranda or one of the others, most often to turn down an invitation to a potluck. No, Jenna did not have the slightest interest in spending time with Marine wives.

Until now.

Jenna's cell phone rang. She pulled it from her bag and checked the ID. Amber's husband's name and number showed. She had programmed it in days before.

"It's Joey," she announced.

A silent glance went around the group, then a shared nod in her direction. She had told them all about the bombing and about a Navy SEAL whose wife lay in the hospital. It didn't matter that they'd never met or even heard of Joey and Amber Ames. They connected the instant they learned the story. Looking at their faces now was like looking at one big heart that beat visibly with compassion.

Jenna left the table, answering the phone as she strode to the exit. Although they were all eager to hear news about Amber, she wanted to receive it in private.

Not counting the dried fig of a fisherman.

She went outside, moving toward the rail, not far from him. "Joey?"

"She's awake."

Jenna yelped. "And?"

"And she's fine. She's fine. Just fine."

Jenna heard the tears in Joey's voice and imagined the guy she had met at the hospital. It took some effort to match this soft side to his bricklike, compact build. He reminded her of the hero action figures her brothers played with as kids, complete with colorless slits for eyes. If Amber didn't adore her husband, Jenna could have easily avoided him.

But he cried. The ocean blurred before her now. She looked down at the wooden rail, gave up finding a spot clear of bird and fish droppings, and put her elbows on it. "Oh." The word came out as one long sigh.

Joey chuckled. "Yeah. There's not much else to say."

"My grandmother would say, 'God is good.'"

"I think Amber would too."

"She hasn't yet?"

"I guess she has, in her own way."

"When can I see her?"

"She's pretty weak, but you know her. She'll be bouncing around in no time. The doctor wants to keep her here a couple more days anyway, with only me and her parents allowed to visit, but you can come tomorrow afternoon. That one nurse and Amber think you're family."

"I talked to my mom about you two staying up at the Hideaway. There's a room for you anytime during the weekdays."

It had been Jenna's idea that Amber and Joey spend a few days up in the hills, pampered by her mom and grandmother, feasting on Skylar's cooking. Her mom loved the plan.

He said, "My in-laws will stay until the end of next week. Maybe the week after?"

"Whatever works. How long . . ." Her voice trailed off. She didn't want to know the answer yet.

Joey supplied it anyway. "A month. Now that she's awake, they'll give me a month here."

A month. What she wouldn't do to have Kevin beside her for a month! A week, even. The good-bye agony would be worth it.

Joey said, "I need to ask a favor. Would you mind letting your principal know what's going on?"

Call Cade? "Of course I wouldn't mind. Let me take care of school-related issues for you. She'll want to know who her sub is."

"Thanks, Jenna. Amber always says you're the greatest."

She looked down at her forearm suspended fifty feet above the ocean. Her sleeve inched up, revealing some of the stitches. They would come out next week, but the mark would still be visible.

She thought about the night at the hospital.

You're the greatest.

Yeah, right. Amber might think Cade was hot, but she sure wouldn't be happy about her friend turning the fantasy into real life.

After talking with Joey, Jenna debated whether to share his good news first with the women inside the diner or Cade.

That decision took about ten seconds.

As she hit the speed dial number for the high school, the old fisherman moved closer, smiling and nodding. Startled, she canceled the call.

The man smoothed a towel across the top of the rail, pointed first at his elbows and then at the cloth.

She returned his smile. The towel appeared as grimy as the rail, but at least it would prevent snagging her blouse. She stepped over and rested her elbows on it. "Thank you."

His kindness touched her. The kindness of her new acquaintances—Amber, Joey, Beth Russell, the women inside—touched her. It was Beth's words about camaraderie with other wives and Amber's belief about just doing what was expected as a military wife that kept Jenna going. Those things would keep her treading water. No matter how fast her feet spun, though, her head would not remain above water except for the kindness that Cade offered. It gave hope like a gulp of air to a drowning person.

She needed them all. Was that God at work? Providing others to ease her journey? The stranger on the pier, Amber and Joey, the women who shared her same day-to-day fears, and Cade who centered her. Each and every one a gift.

It was Friday, a school day. Cade was busy, most likely not even in his office. She should leave a message with his secretary.

She glanced at her arm again.

And then she dialed his cell phone number from memory.

He answered immediately. "Jenna."

At the sound of his calm voice, she closed her eyes. "Hey. Guess what. Joey Ames just called. Amber woke up and she's fine!"

He laughed. "That's great news."

They chatted. She told him everything Joey had told her.

She told him where she was, what she was doing.

Then she told him about her favorite Italian restaurant where she planned to eat dinner that evening by herself at seven o'clock in celebration of Amber's recovery.

And then she told him good-bye.

Jenna smiled at Cade, wondering if it was the candlelight or pasta carbs that had softened the ice in his eyes.

"I'm ready to come back on Monday," she said.

"Don't hesitate to change your mind. Sarah's on standby."

"Okay, but I'm fine."

He gave her a concerned look.

"I am! Now that Amber's okay, I'm okay."

"Besides that, you're a control freak when it comes to lit lessons."

She laughed.

He grinned.

It was easy to laugh with him, to let go. She was so glad he had shown up at the restaurant.

He had come in after she was seated, Mr. Ice Man's persona evident on his face and in the set of his shoulders. It took awhile for him to relax. No matter. She basked in the reality of him, his masculinity, his kindness in giving her his free time, his concern about her well-being in the classroom.

"Jenna, I need to say something."

"The answer is no. This chocolate gelato is all mine. You could have ordered your own." She put a spoonful in her mouth.

He shook his head, his expression an unfamiliar one. It seemed almost vulnerable. "Seriously. It's why I came tonight."

"Okay."

"Do you know how enchanting you are?"

She set down her spoon.

"I consider myself a fairly well-disciplined guy. The other night, emotions dismantled that belief. However, I know that under normal circumstances when two of my best teachers aren't hurt in a domestic terrorist attack, I'm still a well-disciplined guy. But I have to admit, I am fast approaching a line here." He leaned forward. "What exactly do you want from me?"

Jenna swallowed with difficulty. The taste of chocolate was thick on her tongue, the ice cream cold in her throat.

She wanted Cade Edmunds to take Kevin's place, pure and simple. That was ridiculous, but that was exactly what she—total princess that she was—wanted. Simply put, life was easier when Kevin was around.

She masked her response by taking a stab at one of the many rumors surrounding the mysterious Cade Edmunds. "Maybe you could tell me about your girlfriend."

Cade's jaw muscles worked as if he held in a reply.

She realized he would never say it until she spoke to his question. "After lunch today, I walked home with Miranda—the one I told you about."

He gave a slight nod.

"She lives in town, not far from the pier. Two doors from her house she spotted a black car parked at the curb. It practically screamed 'military.' She sat down, right then and there, on the sidewalk. She could hardly breathe." Jenna's voice caught at the memory.

"Miranda thought they'd come to tell her that her husband had been killed."

Jenna nodded. "I sat down with her, on the concrete. We both cried and cried, even though we could see the car was empty and we knew that they certainly wouldn't be waiting inside with her babysitter and kids."

"I'm sorry."

"I just . . . I just . . ." She wiped beneath her eyes. "Things don't hurt so much when I'm with you. Life isn't scary. I'm sorry. Today I couldn't get a handle on it. Amber's development is so good but so draining. I'm sorry. That's just the way it is. Just the way I am."

Cade reached across the table and took hold of her hand. "I can't take his place."

"I know," she whispered and looked down. He rubbed his thumb gently across the back of her hand. She focused on it until, after a time the sharp edges of fear and pain dulled.

Cade muttered something, his words indecipherable.

She looked up at him, questioning.

He shook his head. He was not going to repeat it.

Jenna thought she heard, *I do not understand how he left you.*

Maybe she heard wrong.

Forty-two

Five weeks passed after the anniversary of the fire. Through September and into late October, Claire felt life settle into a new routine, a pleasant one full of running a retreat center. Guests multiplied, eager to enjoy the prerainy season. Skylar grew more and more indispensable. Danny's visits increased, but his bugging of Skylar lessened.

The only abnormal activity revolved around helping Max pack for a trip to Vietnam. Now the day of departure had arrived.

Claire melted into Max's embrace. His chest muffled her voice. "I'm trying not to have second thoughts."

He chuckled. "Yeah, me too."

"It's already tomorrow in Vietnam. I can't fathom that you'll be in another day . . ." She stopped speaking the lines they'd already said over and over too many times. Still though, the anxious thoughts circled in her mind.

How could she handle a separation of this magnitude? Since before Thanksgiving almost a year ago they hadn't spent a night apart. In the past, Max had traveled fairly often on business but never overseas. But it wasn't only the physical aspect that disturbed her. Just the simple anticipation of his absence triggered old resentments of how often he was gone, if only at the office.

She groaned. Already the battle had frazzled her nerves.

They stood in silence for a long moment, locked in each other's arms, blotting out the surrounding hubbub.

Most of the family had gathered in the parking area to send off the travelers. Erik and Rosie wore chauffeur hats, white shirts, black ties, and slacks. They'd borrowed a friend's limo and were driving Ben, Tuyen, and Max to the airport in style. Lexi and Skylar had baked cookies and created elaborate snacks that they now tucked into the carry-on bags.

Not everyone was there. Danny hadn't driven up for the send-off but planned to see them at the airport. Jenna didn't want to miss any more school activities and had said her good-byes the previous evening.

"Ma'am." Erik rumbled loudly at Claire's ear. "Sir. We simply must get this show on the road. Hugging time officially ended five minutes ago. Buck up now. All is well that ends well."

Max released her and grinned. "And this is all about ending well. Right, sweetheart?"

His face blurred. Yes, it was all about that. *Say good-bye to BJ. Comfort your father. Love on your brother's child.*

And come home soon.

Claire snapped shut the violin case and glanced at her watch for the umpteenth time that night. Or morning now, technically speaking. One-thirty Tuesday morning. Max, Ben, and Tuyen were somewhere over the Pacific Ocean.

Yawning, she combed her fingers through her hair, tired but nowhere near ready for bed.

Max had called from Los Angeles. He would not call again until they reached Hong Kong, the last stop before Ho Chi Minh City. That would not happen until after lunchtime. Why was she still awake, as if waiting for something to happen?

Easy: anxiety about their trip. A stomach bloated due to her ingestion of half a bag of tortilla chips, half a carton of salsa, and a few cookies. Okay, six cookies. Loneliness because Indio, Lexi, and Skylar had better things to do than sit with her. Fear at the thought that the four of them, although within close proximity of each other, were divided by pitch blackness and howling coyotes. And last but not least, a throat raw from a crying jag over Max's absence.

She sat down in the kitchen's rocking chair beside Indio's wall of crosses. Strands of a Bach piece still hummed in her mind. When was the last time she had played to her heart's content as she had tonight?

Another easy one: when she and Max had been separated last year, on the verge of divorce, she had played often and to her heart's content.

"Ouch."

She set the rocking chair in motion.

"Why is that, Lord? He likes to hear me play."

I still hold back.

"Nah."

Yeah.

Tears burned again. "I have to sleep. I have a full week getting ready for guests. I don't want to think about this."

The thing was, she missed Max so much already. They had so much time to make up, time lost because they had traveled different paths for a long time. "Lord, we're just getting together. Getting it together. Why this major thing for him right now at this time? Why did he have to go away, and so far?"

I know the plans that I have for you. It was her voice still, but she recognized it was not a thought of her own making.

God knew what He was doing. God knew everything that concerned her.

She dabbed at her eyes with a sweatshirt sleeve. "I'm listening."

She did hold back with Max, but only because she wanted a balance they hadn't enjoyed most of their married life. Was that being clingy? Was that stifling the newfound freedom between them, freedom to be real with each other?

"The thing is, Lord, I don't want to be okay without him." She paused. "Good grief. That sounds absolutely absurd. It is perfectly all right to be all right without him. It is all right to miss him but it's also all right to stay up all night, eat junk food, make music, be fearful and lonely."

She rocked for a few moments, listening to the night sounds of house and nature and anxious heartbeat.

"But I will be fine, right, Lord? I will be fine because You are here and You are with Max, Ben, and Tuyen. I will get through this a better person for the struggle. We will all benefit from the stretching time." She sighed. "I just don't understand why You have to make this life a nonstop journey the whole entire way."

A couple days after the send-off, after Max's upbeat phone call from Vietnam—friendly, helpful people, beautiful scenery, great weather, on schedule—Claire drove her car along the highway, heading home after shopping in the city.

With a start she realized something was missing. What had she forgotten? Her mind raced through the list of supplies she'd purchased for the guests coming that weekend. She'd had inklings of feeling proficient in her role as manager of the Hideaway. Indio and practice were perfect teachers. What could it—

"Oh, good grief."

She hadn't forgotten a thing. The missing something was simply a feeling: the awful dread that Max was not at home.

The first thirty years of married life had felt like one long day that Max lived at the office, consumed with his business, away from her. It had been a wedge between them, one they'd been chipping at for almost a year. And now . . . well . . .

She smiled. "Thanks be to God. This is indeed progress."

Okay. There it was. Further proof that she could weather Max's absence.

With a laugh, she lowered the windows and turned off the radio.

The wind blew her hair back. She imagined riding that tandem with Indio, watching her every move, mimicking, letting go of her own handlebars.

She drove Max's car. Skylar had gone to town as well to help with errands. Claire smiled. The woman seemed to have settled down a bit after last week's turmoil. She insisted on using Claire's car, saying she dared not sit in Max's "baby," the old black Mercedes he pampered, let alone drive it.

As usual, there was no other traffic on the highway. The two-lane meandered east through rugged terrain and past a few scattered ranches. It wound its way up into a mountain pass and then straightened out on the desert floor beyond. Eventually it intersected with a major thoroughfare.

An odd sight came into view. Not too far in the distance, where the hacienda's gravel drive met the highway, stood a man beside a parked car.

Claire slowed and double-checked the door locks.

She sighed. Fear had not been totally eradicated from her. The fire experience had created it. Now it was like leftovers in a container shoved to the back of the fridge, forgotten until some innocuous event knocked off its lid. Then the stench spewed forth.

Of course, having Rosie the policewoman around didn't help matters. Despite the young woman's faith, she saw far too much ugliness to be casual about certain situations. One of which was meeting a strange guy in a lonely place. And so Claire heard Rosie's voice in her head, listing the precautions to take, the details to take note of.

She zipped the windows back shut but rejected the idea of driving past the man. He was near her home which was, after all, a retreat center, a place where strangers gathered.

As she made the left-hand turn onto the gravel drive, she braked with her left foot, keeping her right foot on the gas pedal, keeping the gear in drive. The unfamiliar car was white, small, nondescript like a rental. The man was thirtyish, lanky, tall, dressed in blue jeans and a plain black T-shirt. Medium brown hair, medium length. Dark glasses. A ready smile.

She lowered her window just enough to be able to talk through. "Hi. Do you need some help?"

"Hi. Thanks for stopping." He did not approach her car. His voice carried a trace of an accent. "I'm looking for an address." He rattled off the Hacienda Hideaway's number.

Claire's stomach muscles clenched. No one used the address. They had a Santa Reina post office box for mail. Directions to the place went by landmarks and mileage.

There was no mailbox or sign to indicate the retreat center or the house's number. There was no welcome sign to the retreat center. Because they didn't want looky-lous wandering up the drive, they'd placed it in the parking area, out of sight from this point on the main road.

Guests were scheduled to arrive tomorrow.

They were all women.

Claire said, "This is that address."

"Oh. This road here?"

"Yes."

"I'm looking for someone, an old friend. Annie Wells. Last I heard from her, she said she'd recently gotten a job here. Said it was a wonderful place." He shrugged a shoulder. "I'm down from Seattle. Thought I'd look her up while I was in the area."

Everything but the name described Skylar Pierson. Was he talking about her?

It didn't matter if he was or not. Claire did not like this guy.

Rosie said sometimes it was best to trust the sixth sense that communicated the abstract.

Claire said. "A job?"

"Yes. She's a great cook."

"That's curious. This is our family home. Grandma and I cook."

"You never hire outsiders for anything?"

"A professional cleaning service now and then." She rolled her eyes, a gesture lost on him since she wore sunglasses, but it felt right as she improvised. "I haven't been able to find just the right one yet. Perhaps your friend came with one of them and sort of embellished her story."

"Perhaps. Which services have you used most recently?"

None of your business, she thought, but wanting to play out the helpful role, she offered a half-truth. "Nina's and the Housekeeping Experts." She had tried both of them several months before she'd found another that fit her needs best. She shook her head. "It seems a lost cause."

"Undocumented foreigners probably work best for you."

She couldn't help but smile at the innuendo she often heard. "I'm not touching that with a ten-foot pole. Are you with the INS?"

He grinned. "No."

"Well, good luck. Sorry I couldn't be of more help."

"Thanks anyway." He gave a little wave.

Claire drove off.

About ten feet later, the shaking started.

With all the restraint she could muster, Claire resisted the urge to cannonball up the winding gravel road.

The guy at the bottom of the hill spooked her.

Reminding herself how Max drove his car, she slowed sensibly at curves. At an agonizing snail's pace she drove past the charred tree stumps and new growth browning in the late summer heat, past the bend in the road where Indio, Ben, Lexi, and Tuyen's homes were located. At long last she reached the parking area and stopped beside their discreet sign—Hacienda Hideaway ~ A Place of Retreat—and looked over her shoulder.

He had not followed.

Claire drove slowly to the other end of the blacktopped lot and followed the narrow gravel driveway to the back door. She parked, grabbed her purse and the nearest shopping bags, hurried inside the kitchen, and locked the door.

Skylar, also gone for the day, had helped her lock everything before they both left that morning. Although the construction people still worked some days, today wasn't one of them, so she and Skylar had closed up more tightly than usual.

The hacienda was a conglomerate of doors. The kitchen, sala, and each bedroom had their own exterior doors that opened onto the U-shaped wraparound porch. All those had been locked as well as the huge front doors that closed off the entryway that was open ended to the courtyard.

At the back and sides of the yard there had been a perimeter wall, but it had been destroyed by the fire. Repairing it was at the bottom of a still-too-long list of projects.

The whole place suddenly felt too open for comfort.

Claire sank onto the rocker next to Indio's wall of crosses, looked through the tall windows toward the parking lot, and struggled to catch her breath.

Max and Ben were half a world away.

Tuyen was with them, of course. Lexi and Indio were gone for the day at a garden show. Skylar was running some errands with her and then meeting Danny.

Claire picked up the phone from the lamp table and called Danny. "Mom?"

Thank goodness he answered. "Hi, Danny." Her voice warbled.

"What's wrong?"

He shouldn't have been her first choice. Erik would have steered the conversation until she regained control.

"Mom!"

"Yeah. Um, something odd just happened." She told him about the incident with the stranger.

"Skylar."

"I think so. He didn't say 'She's the cook at the Hacienda

Hideaway.' He said she's a 'great cook.' I got the idea that she didn't actually talk to him."

"I agree. If she wanted to see an old friend, she would have made arrangements to meet in town. She would have told you if he was coming to the house."

"But then how did he find her?"

"I don't know." He was silent for a moment. "We shouldn't tell her. Not yet."

"Why not?"

"She'll freak out. She'll . . . leave."

Claire heard his undertone. "Danny, don't go Messiah on us. You can't save her. If she needs to leave, we can't stop her."

"But we can protect her. For now. You and Dad always talk about the Hideaway being a safe harbor. Isn't this what a safe harbor is all about?"

Oh Lord, this child is trying. "That's an emotional thing, Danny! Not this—this unknown threat."

"Of course you're feeling physically vulnerable. Just call the sheriff, Mom. Ask him to patrol the area. I'll call Rosie. Erik and I will spend the night up there. Maybe Rosie can too."

"How do we explain that to Skylar?"

"You're lonesome and I'm—" He paused. "I'm crazy about her."

"You are, aren't you?"

His silence was all the reply she needed.

Claire closed her eyes, overcome with a stab of a mother's anxiety. The thought of Danny losing his head and heart over a troubled soul was worse than knowing there was a weirdo at the bottom of her hill.

Forty-three

Skylar studied Danny's back from a distance.

What, what, *what* was she doing?

If he turns around, I'll stay.

"That's totally juvenile."

But . . . she waited there on the boardwalk, probably fifty yards from where he sat on the seawall facing the ocean. It was a crowded place, people walking and jogging and biking between them.

"It's also totally asinine," she murmured.

Behind her was the parking lot. They'd agreed to meet there because she could not remember how to find his place. He said it was complicated. The area was a maze of beach houses, condos, apartment buildings, shops, bars.

Danny wore a cap, white T-shirt, dark green cargo-type shorts. His physique did not personify "hunk." No, it was more "Southern California—So-Cal—surfer dude." Comfortable in his skin. Confidence born from riding the curl of a wave.

And he was just cute. Okay, *adorable*. If she had a mother who baked apple pie and grasped the significance of a flesh-and-blood Wally Cleaver, this guy would be at the top of her short list for son-in-law.

"Sky."

What was she doing? Did she—

"Sky." Danny appeared, stepping around from behind her, grinning. "Hey."

She glanced back and forth between him and the figure on the wall. Yep, the real Danny was standing in front of her. No cap. Blue jeans, not shorts. T-shirt was the same. "Where did you come from?"

"Other side of the parking lot. What's wrong?"

"Nothing."

The subtle lift of his brows unnerved her.

"I thought that was you over there." She pointed.

He looked. "Hmm. Close resemblance. Bunch of clones at this beach. I don't know how they all got my genetic info." The brows drew together. "Why didn't you go over to him?"

"I was on my way."

"You've been standing here a good five minutes."

"And how do you know that?"

The forehead smoothed, the mouth corners indented, the eyes crinkled. "Been standing back there for five minutes watching you."

Unnerved could not begin to describe the state she leapt into now.

He said, "And I was thinking really idiotic, moony things like 'If she likes me, she'll sense I'm here and turn around.'"

"You are such a Wally." Her heart was not in the quip. *Too far gone,* she thought. She was just too far gone. Not good. Not good. "I didn't turn around."

"But you wanted to." Danny extended his arm, palm up. "Are we to the hand-holding stage yet?"

Until that moment, Skylar had no idea sweetness thick as honey could fill the empty corners of a heart.

She put her hand in his, went up on tiptoe, and kissed his cheek.

He squeezed her hand. "Hello-kiss stage too?"

She nodded.

"I'll buy that." He smiled. "Want to walk?"

Again she nodded.

There really were no words to say.

Skylar found plenty of words to say as she and Danny walked barefoot at the ocean's edge. That honey-thick sweetness she'd felt earlier seemed now to coat them, glazing her spoken thoughts with a depth and truth long missing from her conversations.

Truth as in the big picture. Neither she nor Danny mentioned their life's laundry lists. Topics like names, dates, and places were not exactly ignored. Instead the focus of their dialogue transcended the particulars of parents, siblings, schools, jobs, travels, and friends. They talked about the war, music, God, what lay on the other side of the waves that lapped at their feet.

Skylar kept Scarlett O'Hara firmly in the driver's seat. Tomorrow she would think about all the junk, all those particulars, that if spoken aloud would send Danny hightailing it on down the beach. He'd hide himself quicker than the little sand crabs burrowing themselves lickety-split into the sand before them.

Danny said, "Can we talk about us?"

"There's an 'us' to talk about?"

"Exactly."

"Let's sit."

They moved up onto the dry sand and sat. The sun was in its late-afternoon slot above the horizon. More surfers were entering the water.

"Danny, I think—"

"Hey." He bumped his shoulder against hers. "I brought it up first. I get to go first."

"Okay, okay."

"We haven't seen each other for a week."

"Five and a half days."

"But who's counting?"

She smiled.

"Anyway," he went on, "I needed space after the kitchen kiss. That's why I hadn't called or come up again. You've thrown a major monkey wrench into my life itinerary."

"You don't have a life itinerary."

"I do. An itinerary and a strong belief that the color gray does not exist."

"That's pathetic."

"Yes, it is."

"Seriously."

He met her gaze. "Seriously. I'm going to make X amount of dollars before I'm thirty-five. If a woman looks like a Haight-Ashbury, hippie leftover, she must be a drug addict. You get the picture."

"Yeah."

"You've shaken things up already. Which means, in my mind, that 'us' is a good thing."

Skylar bit her lip. The words were gone again.

He said, "Good for me, anyway. Maybe not so much for you."

She opened her mouth, closed it, and waited. The thoughts were there, but not the right words. *I think you're the cat's meow. You're the Tracy to my Hepburn. I'd follow you to Timbuktu.*

How lame was that?

"Sky?"

And his nickname! A name based on a name that wasn't even her real name!

"Danny, there's so much you don't know."

"We're just at the beginning. We're friends."

"I can't be more than that." *Ever. Not ever.*

"You have an itinerary, too, you know." His gentle voice soothed. He touched the corner of her eye, his little finger diverting the tear from her cheek. "Wally Cleaver is outside your relational experience. You must be absolutely dumbfounded trying to figure out why you're sitting on the beach with him."

Her laugh sounded like a choke. "Yeah, okay, I admit it. You've thrown your own monkey wrench."

"Good. I prefer to be on equal footing with you."

His grin nearly blinded her.

have to go," Skylar said as they retraced their steps along the beach.

"We reenter practical life." Danny blew out a loud sigh. "Which reminds me, I told Mom I'd come up to the house tonight."

"Really?" She winced at the excited schoolgirl voice.

"I think between the anniversary of the fire and Dad being gone, she's feeling afraid to be alone."

"I'm there. She seemed fine the last few nights."

"It's the trauma thing. Comes and goes. And besides, you're not exactly a macho presence."

She groaned. "Here it comes: the macho card."

He bent his elbow and flexed his biceps. "Yes. I do have one of those in my back pocket."

Skylar's giggle started from deep inside her, in a place that had been locked up for a very long time. It bubbled up, frothed, spilled over. It grew to a full-on laugh. It sang out into a sidesplitting belly laugh.

Danny paused in his silly display, his face a question mark. Slowly its furrows evened out. His dark eyes shown in a way eyes had never shone in Skylar's direction.

If it hadn't been for the honey-thick sweetness holding her heart together, it just might have burst apart from this infusion of pure joy.

Forty-four

Jenna smiled at Amber. The two of them sat in Jenna's classroom long after the students had gone home on Thursday. "You look as perky as a freshman."

"Except for the hair."

"Well, yes, except for the hair."

Amber cocked her head at a jaunty angle and touched the fashionable straw hat she wore over a scarf. "Joey and I are having a date-to-die-for tonight." She pursed her lips, allowing for a pregnant pause. "Wig shopping and sushi."

Jenna chuckled.

"If it doesn't work out, can you take me on Saturday?"

"Sure. If you promise to go with blonde and curly."

"You sound just like Joey. I'm thinking Angelina Jolie in her early days. Long, straight, dark, and full."

Jenna groaned. "I want my Amber back."

"Talk to God about that."

They both grew somber. Amber had told her about the nightmares, the headaches, the dread already of telling Joey good-bye, the fear even of returning to her classroom. She had stopped by to check on things in her classroom long after the students and sub had left.

Jenna said, "I am talking to God about it. So is my mom and gram."

"Danny too?"

She rolled her eyes. Amber knew all about her brother's propensity to pray. "Danny too."

Amber stood. "We'll be all right then."

"We will."

They hugged each other tightly for a long moment. Their goodbye was wordless and almost tear free.

After she left, Jenna sat back at her desk. Three weeks back in the saddle and she still had too much work to catch up on. It helped, though, being in the routine.

Being near Cade.

Not that she saw more of him than any faculty member did on a given school day. But knowing he was in the same building kept emotional extremes at bay.

Tomorrow, Friday, she would go up to the Hideaway. Nana would give her some ancient herbal remedy for the scar on her arm. She'd sleep in Tuyen's room as Lexi had suggested. She'd help her mom with the guests. Throughout the fall they'd been coming most weekends. It was probably time Jenna stopped distancing herself from her parents' new lifestyle, uncomfortable as it was to see strangers in their home.

On Sunday she would swing back up to Oceanside and eat dinner with Miranda and a couple of the other wives. She would fill the hours between Kevin's sporadic e-mails and phone calls.

She would be all right.

Jenna's cell phone rang as she walked into her apartment building. As usual, hypervigilant to calls just in case it was Kevin, she had her phone handy in a front pocket of her handbag.

It was Miranda.

She answered. "Hi—"

"Jenna." Miranda sobbed.

Halfway up the exterior staircase within a courtyard, Jenna sank onto a step, hugging her book bag. *Dear God, no. No.*

At last Miranda found her voice again. "It's Evie."

Evie. Flaxen hair, spiked in every direction. Turned-up nose. Big blue eyes that sparkled whenever she mentioned her twin boy and girl, two years old, or their daddy, Nick. Everyone said he was a sweetheart.

Fear clutched at Jenna's throat. She scanned what she could see of the parking lot, glanced up at her door. No somber military guys lay in wait for her. *Thank You, God.*

"What's wrong?" she asked.

"I don't know exactly. She's sort of gone off the deep end. I've never seen her so distraught. She can't seem to handle not hearing from Nick for days at a time. It's like she's just given up."

And what am I supposed to do about that? Jenna wanted to scream.

Miranda went on. "We're all in the same boat, you know? But she's hit a wall or something. Some of us are helping her with the kids. Her parents are on their way from Idaho. They're driving, though, so it'll take a couple days. I . . ." Her voice choked up again. "I just wanted you to know, Jenna."

She masked the curse on the tip of her tongue with a loud moan. "It is so awful, this whole lousy scene we're living in." She exhaled loudly. "What can I do? I'll come up. Should I come?"

"Oh." The word was a long sigh. "Would you? It would mean so much to Evie."

"Okay." She thought about the freeway, about traveling north at four thirty alongside half a million other people averaging thirteen miles per hour. "I'll be there as soon as I can."

After tearful good-byes, Jenna scrambled up the steps. She fumbled with the front-door key and burst into her apartment, eyes going straight to the answering machine on the kitchen counter. It wasn't blinking.

No message on the machine.

No voice mail on the cell phone.

No e-mail.

Again, too much time had passed between the last communication and this moment.

Exactly how long did those faceless people in charge expect them all to go on like that?

Exactly how long did *Kevin* expect her to go on like that?

Jenna was totally "there" with Evie. The line between nightmare and reality grew dimmer by the day.

She grabbed the cordless phone, dialed her mom's number, sat on the floor, and burst into tears.

Far too many hours passed from the time Jenna heard about Evie's emotional collapse until she heard her own husband's voice.

She spent the time at Miranda's house with four other wives. Instead of lifting each other up, they wallowed in self-pity. The hours were not filled with shared encouragement. Tears and angry outbursts flowed freely as if anguish were a contagious virus.

Now she walked in tight circles around Miranda's front yard, cell phone at her ear. The damp night air soaked her shoes. A street lamp cast eerie shadows.

"Jen." Static accompanied Kevin's voice as it traveled seven thousand, seven hundred, thirty-one miles to Jenna's ear. "Calm down. I said I'm okay. I'm fine."

"Oh, Kevin."

The repetitive conversation did little to compose her shredded nerves.

He sighed heavily, wearily. "Are you okay?"

"I'm at Miranda Bell's house, crying with four other wives. Evie's asleep, heavily sedated. Her parents are driving all the way from Idaho."

"Are you okay?"

"Of course I'm not okay!" she snapped. Her voice rose to a screech. "How did this happen?"

"Calm down, Jen."

"Stop saying that. It doesn't help one iota!"

"I don't know what else to say. This is just the way life is for now. It's beyond incredibly difficult. Some days I think it's easier to be in the battle over here than in the one you ladies are fighting back home."

She rubbed at her eyebrow where a headache had begun to pound. Despite the words, his tone made her feel like a kid on the football field during a losing game.

Whenever Kevin had gone off to do his macho stuff—coach 24-7 during the fall, play some sort of ball himself every season of the year, *reenlist* in the Marines, even—he kept her separate from that side of life. Even so, he made her feel a part of him in other ways. In the way he looked at her, the way her spoke to her, he communicated that they were one entity.

Until now. Now the war slithered up between them, a palpable energy that breathed destruction.

"Jenna, we guys are doing our best to stay in contact. It's impossible to describe the schedule. We're don't go off to work from eight to five with phones at our elbow and computers at our desk. We don't go home and flip on the computer while dinner cooks. It's just not like that."

"I know, I know, I know!"

Silence filled the line for a moment.

He said, "I'm not sure how to say this. I don't have words for it yet. At the risk of sounding just like your grandma, here goes." He paused.

"What?"

"God is real, Jen. He truly is real. I tell Him all about you, and I ask Him to take care of you. Then this sense of peace sort of wells up inside of me, like He's hugging me and telling me He's with you." He chuckled softly. "I'm Nana in desert cammies."

Jenna kneaded her brow. The hammering had spread. Kevin's

version of Nana's faith was too much to swallow. Like her, he'd always acknowledged God's existence. They trusted that He loved them, that He even answered prayers, albeit in His own way and time. But up close and personal like Nana and Danny espoused? Not exactly.

She had only one word. "Huh?"

"Yeah, blows your mind, doesn't it? What I want to say is just try to rest in Him, okay? He's involved in our lives, Jen. I think He wants us to act like it. Hey, it's late and you're way up in Oceanside. Go home, please. You need to take care of yourself."

"No way, José. This is your semper fi in action, wife-style. I have to be here. We're helping each other through this even if it looks ridiculous to you nonemoting types."

He sighed loudly. "All right. Do what you have to do to get through this. I gotta get off—"

"Wait! Wait a sec! I have to tell you! Amber woke up and she's fine."

"Really? That's great news. See, God is at work. My time's up."

"I love you!"

"Love you, too, babe. Bye."

Click.

Babe?

Babe!

What happened to *pretty lady*? She hated *babe*. He never called her—

"Do what you have to do to get through this." What did that mean? Don't bug him with details about how she coped? How she got through the hours of every day? Just talk to God about it like apparently he was doing all of a sudden?

She felt it again, the war sliding in between them, taking up permanent residence in their relationship.

A glitch in the system? That explanation did not begin to account for the darkness just unleashed.

Forty-five

Claire debated with herself about Danny's idea that they keep Skylar in the dark about the stranger on the highway. Somehow the guy had connected the hacienda's street address with Skylar. Who knew? Maybe he was an old friend and Skylar would like to see him. Worst-case scenario, he was not a friend and Skylar needed to be warned.

"Claire." Rosie waved a hand in front of her face. "Are you on the bus?"

"What? What bus?"

A chuckle went around the sala. Erik, Rosie, Danny, and Skylar sat with her at the fireplace end of the room. A fire blazed in it, warding off the night chill and Claire's shivers that had little to do with the temperature.

She frowned. "You know, you guys really make me feel old with those inside jokes of yours. Why would I be on a bus?"

They howled with laughter, a welcome sound, even if it did mean she now understood why Indio got lost in a conversation with Claire and Max, the "young" ones, and had no desire to learn how to work a DVR.

Rosie said, "Sorry, Claire. It's just a silly way to ask if you're mentally present here with the rest of us. You're obviously preoccupied with what Jenna told you about her friend."

Claire felt a heaviness in her chest. Jenna had sobbed hard on the phone, but she wouldn't come up to the house. Claire worried about all the men's wives in Kevin's unit. And the husbands. How did they cope? The emotional strain on everyone had to be stretched to the limit.

She had been continuously praying for all of them. Fortunately or unfortunately, the added stress gave more credence to her emotional state in front of Skylar. If the girl thought about it much, she would not have believed Claire was undone solely by Max's absence and the anniversary of the fire.

Rosie said, "We don't have to talk about this."

Erik scowled in his dramatic way. "Should you be talking about this anyway?"

"I can share what we've already told the reporters."

"Officer Delgado." His deep newscaster's voice resounded. "I do so love it when you talk cop-speak in that tone of authority."

Rosie turned deep red but tried to look nonchalant with an eye roll.

Erik grinned at Claire. "Isn't she adorable?"

Claire laughed with the others. Even Rosie smiled. The obvious deepening relationship between her son and this woman was a definite bright spot in the evening.

On the other hand, the obvious deepening relationship between son number two and the mystery woman cast a shadow.

Danny said, "So what do the reporters know?"

"That the bomb was a small, simple one. Any kid halfway familiar with combinations of accessible chemicals could put it together. Pack it all up in cardboard and voilá. The good news is it wasn't made into a pipe bomb, which would have resulted in much more damage."

Claire winced.

"Sorry, Claire. I get carried away imagining how a criminal's mind works. Like, why didn't he make it bigger? I guess his motive was to disrupt the funeral, to make a sick protest against the war without taking out a city block and killing—sorry. Again. Anyway, they figure the bomb was hidden sometime before the demonstration began. The grounds are fairly private along that side of the church, with a lot of vegetation."

Danny said, "How was it detonated?"

"A fuse."

"So someone had to light it during the funeral?"

"Right. Again, with the secluded area we're talking about, it was easy for him—or her—to do that unseen."

Danny cocked his head. "This is helpful information?"

Rosie grinned. "Yeah, it is."

"It sounds like a beginner's crossword puzzle, the kind anybody can solve."

"But there's always a tricky clue that makes or breaks a successful completion. Not just anybody will be able to do it, or at least not easily."

"You're saying there are things about this situation that reveal not every kid in Chem 101 could pull it off?"

"Maybe."

Erik said, "Ah, we stray into restricted territory."

Rosie winked at him.

Claire tried to smile at them, but all she could think about was Jenna needing more stitches.

"Mom." In that one word Danny communicated that he picked up on her distress. "You don't have to keep us company. Go to bed."

Skylar cleared her throat a few times, as if she had trouble finding her voice. "The kitchen looks disorganized, Claire, but there is a method to my madness. If you touch anything, the lunch for tomorrow's guests won't happen until dinnertime."

Claire wondered how these two bossy, control-freak natures had been able to mesh. "Mind if I get a glass of water?"

"Not at all."

Claire smiled, bid everyone good night, and left the room quickly, shutting the door with the hope that her stress stayed put on the other side.

Rosie caught up with Claire in the courtyard. "I needed some fresh air."

"Rosie, I'm really okay now that all of you are here."

"You're not morphing into Cleopatra, are you?"

She'd heard that one before. "Queen of Denial? All right, honestly I'm not exactly okay, but I am less upset than I was, now that you're all here. Do you have your gun?"

"In my purse, behind the couch."

"That's handy."

"I know where Erik gets his smart mouth."

"That's my nerves talking."

"I understand." She paused. "My vanity is talking for me. The reason my gun is not tucked into my waistband under a big shirt is because I'm trying my best to resemble a svelte model."

Claire laughed. "Rosie, he's nuts about you. His svelte model days are so over."

"You're sweet to say that."

"It's true." She gave the young woman a one-armed hug as they walked. "The gun is on my mind because Indio and Lexi have Ben's shotgun loaded. Lexi planned to sleep with it on the hide-a-bed in Nana's front room."

Rosie groaned.

"Ben taught both of them how to use it years ago."

"And I'm sure they practice diligently." She shook her head. "I'll check on them later. Claire, I know we talked already, but I need to go over a few things. Did the guy threaten you in any way?"

"No. He was friendly." She rehearsed the encounter yet again in her mind. "But afterward, when I was driving away, I felt like I do after I've spotted a rattlesnake and made it to safe ground."

"By then your body was on adrenaline overload. You did an amazing job talking to him."

"I kept hearing your advice."

"Good."

They stopped on the wraparound porch outside the master-suite door. The fountain was not running, but every solar light along the paths and wall lamps by guest room doors were turned on, providing soft glows. The corner spotlights bathed most of the courtyard in a bright light.

"Claire, will you describe him for me again?"

"Tall and—"

"Erik tall?"

"No. He was rangy. I think that made him seem taller than he really was. Does that make sense?"

"Absolutely."

"Somewhere between Erik and Danny. Otherwise he was just medium. Medium-brown hair—"

"Medium Danny's hair?"

"No. Darker than Danny's. Shorter than Danny's and straight. Narrow face. Pointy chin. Blue jeans, black T-shirt. He seemed at least thirty."

"You said he wore sunglasses so you didn't see his eyes. Tell me about his accent again."

"It was very slight. It made me think Canadian. You know how some of them do that thing with their vowels, sort of round them off?"

Rosie chuckled. "I know what you mean. Anything else?"

She shut her eyes and pictured him again. What was it? When he turned briefly and nodded up the road. "A mole." She opened her eyes. "Below, almost behind, his right ear."

"Okay. Thanks."

"Do you think it's right not to tell Skylar?"

Rosie did not reply, but Claire had been around her enough to recognize when she was measuring her words before speaking.

At last she said, "This is the restricted territory, but I consider you as in the need-to-know column. The physical description you just gave me matches one we got from a witness who saw a guy emerging from the side of the church shortly before the bomb exploded." She paused. "Enough time to light a long fuse and get out of the way. So, yes, it's right not to tell Skylar."

Claire leaned against the door. "Oh, no."

"Try not to worry, Claire. From Danny's report, I really don't think she could have been part of this. I suspect that her path crossed with this guy's at some point in the past. 'Annie Wells' and 'Skylar Pierson' are most likely pseudonyms. Nothing shows up under either."

"Can't you just ask her about it all?"

"Not yet."

"I should have listened to Danny. He didn't trust her from the start. We should have gone the traditional route. Application, background check, so on and so forth."

"Well, I like Danny but I trust your mother-in-law more. I trust Indio's insight, her intuition. I think you do too."

"Yes."

"Skylar was a direct answer to prayer. And I trust what you see. You've seen Skylar's heart."

Claire gazed at the young woman, awed as she had been before at Rosie's own insight. "You have too."

"Yep. Now get some rest."

Claire almost laughed in her face.

Indio." Claire whispered into the phone as she snuggled under the covers on her bed. "What do we do?"

"Pray, of course," her mother-in-law whispered back.

Claire had her own need-to-know column, and Indio was most definitely in it. She had told her everything she'd learned from Rosie without the policewoman's permission.

"Dear," Indio said, "you knew that, didn't you?"

"This one is a stretch for me. I mean this is all about domestic terrorism, Indio. The police are involved. Jenna was hurt, her friend hurt worse, half a dozen others injured, part of a church demolished. And I talked face-to-face with the guy who was probably responsible!"

"You feel afraid."

"Yeah!"

Indio began to pray softly. She thanked God for His goodness. She asked Him to camp angels around the property. She prayed for the healing of Skylar's soul. She prayed that the creepy guy would come to accept the Lord's love for him. She asked for God's peace to rest on them all.

"Amen." Claire breathed out the anxiety. Hearing the breadth of Indio's faith in her prayers always produced a calm. Would she ever get to that point of complete expectation that God would respond?

Claire said, "Should we tell Danny?"

"Rosie didn't?"

"Not that I know of."

"Technically it's her place."

"I think he's in love with Skylar."

"Yes, he most certainly is."

"Certainly is? Indio, how do you know that?"

She chuckled in her enigmatic way. "Just let it go, Claire. Let it all go and get some rest."

Maybe she could now.

As long as she didn't ponder the question of how she would ever make it through life's journey without holding Indio's hand.

Forty-six

The kitchen clock chimed eleven. Skylar let it resonate through her, hoping to find solace in the somber repetitive tone.

It didn't happen.

She poured chocolate batter into a baking pan. The brownies weren't needed until noon the next day, but if she stopped working she would go insane.

Rosie's report had burst over her like fireworks. Mesmerized, Skylar sat rooted to the chair, watching each flare light up and illuminate her guilt, shame, and fear. As the flames died out, hot ash rained down on her. It singed every exposed emotion, cauterizing them until she felt nothing. She spoke and moved by rote, eventually leaving Danny and the others in the sala.

Now, alone in the kitchen, she felt a burning sensation. Frantic for a salve to ease the pain of her wounds, she scurried about doing unnecessary chores. There was absolutely no way she could hoof it to civilization this time of night. Not because of mountain lions, snakes, and coyotes but because, at the moment, she really wasn't sure she could find her way out of a paper bag. The thought of maneuvering the Hideaway's three hundred acres with its neighboring ranches of thousand-plus acres and the dark highway void of traffic made her want to puke.

Danny would say pray. Indio would say God was good. Claire would beam and say God was listening to the prayers of her heart.

What did they know? God might answer *their* prayers but they were all *good* people. They didn't know what she knew.

She knew what Rosie had explained. She knew way more than what Rosie had explained.

Fin Harrod made the bomb. He knew the chemicals, how to combine them, how to pack them. He'd chosen a cardboard tube this time, deciding by some sick logic that he'd forgo the pipe bomb. Major destruction was not his purpose.

He hid the bomb in such a way as to protect it from the elements. He may have dismantled the church's sprinkler system. The bomb's fuse was long enough so that after lighting it, he had time to walk— not run—away.

Skylar picked up the baking pan and headed across the kitchen toward the wall oven.

That tricky clue Rosie had mentioned?

Wishful thinking on the cops' part. Fin didn't leave a signature or a calling card. He was one of the truly evil ones. He did not want to get caught. He bragged to no one but his closest friend, Duke, who would have been, without a doubt, in the crowd at the protest.

Duke, who could tail an FBI agent and not get caught.

Duke, who could have easily tailed Skylar to the parking garage and Claire's car, noted the license plate, traced the number—

"Skylar."

She nearly jumped out of her skin. The pan slid from her hands and crashed onto the floor. Batter flew everywhere. "Danny!"

"Sorry. We should get a bell on that door."

"You could just knock!" She knelt and turned over the pan. What chocolate hadn't splattered across the floor and cabinets lay in a puddle beneath it. "Look at this mess."

"At least it wasn't a glass pan." He hunched down beside her, a dishcloth in his hands.

"Would you just get out of my kitchen?"

"Why don't you get out of it?" He sopped up a glob of batter. "You don't need these brownies tonight."

"Thanks for the news flash."

"I thought you were coming back in the sala to play cards with us."

Play games? Yeah, right. She ignored his comment. "Bring over the paper towels. The whole roll. And the mop."

They worked side by side on the floor, wiping it and the cabinets, not speaking.

At last he said, "I am sorry, Skylar. I'll finish. I'll even whip up another batch of brownies and bake them. I'm not totally lame in following a recipe off a box mix."

The sound of his too-familiar voice talking about inane subjects began to soothe her nerves. Wally Cleaver was just such a *nice* guy. Had they really held hands and talked like friends that afternoon? It seemed like a lifetime ago. Somebody else's life.

"It's not from a box," she muttered.

"Hmm. That's explains the nuts and chocolate chips and melted caramel." He sniffed a paper towel. "And German chocolate cake? Just leave the recipe out."

"It's out and you're hovering."

"Yeah, but you love it now that we're, well, you know."

Three hours ago she would have given him a flirty glance and offered a smart remark. Not now. Probably not ever.

Just when they were getting started.

He bumped his shoulder against hers. "Seriously, get out of here. I promise I won't eat more than one brownie when they're done. And I won't let Erik have more than three."

"I can't—"

"Give it up, Sky." He dried his hands with a paper towel. "Come on. I'll walk you home."

The waterfall sound of his tone had become the salve she longed for. It covered her wounds, diminishing the pain so that now she was able to feel the exhaustion and to hear the voice of reason. Did it really matter that she alone took care of the kitchen? Did it even matter that the brownies burned or were underbaked or if he and Erik ate the whole pan?

Did it matter that she knew the bomber?

Danny pulled her to her feet and steered her out the door. She didn't resist.

They walked through the courtyard in a comfortable silence, passed the last guest room, and rounded the corner. She remembered the first time Indio had walked this route with her.

And she wanted to cry.

At her door, Danny gestured with a flourish. "Ta-da. The 'oh, by the way' room, m'lady." He leaned over and planted a sweet kiss on her cheek as if it were the most natural thing in the world between them. "Sleep well."

"'Night." She turned the knob and pushed the door open.

"You lock your door, right?"

"No."

"Will you tonight?" He stood only inches from her, but his face was hidden in shadow.

"Why?"

"I forget," he murmured.

She sensed the shift in the tenor of his voice. "Danny, you really don't know the first thing about me."

"You keep saying that like I give a rip. We are the sum of our past, mistakes and all. The sum that I've experienced in you is one that I care for deeply."

"I don't want to hurt you."

"I don't want to hurt you either, but I will. It's part of life, but you know what they say. It sure beats the alternative."

In the darkness she felt more than saw his gaze on her. She knew she should step away from him.

But his words offered her such hope, his presence such security, his low rumble of a voice the promise of a physical expression of it all and more.

He touched her cheek gently, cupped her face in his hands, and then he kissed her. He kissed her again. And again.

That solace she craved was freely poured into her. She swam in it, soon lost to all pain and fear.

When at last they parted, she thought she must be dreaming. She'd never felt so incredibly cherished.

He laughed softly. "Whew." And then he walked away.

Skylar carried the gift he'd given her through the door and into her little 'oh, by the way' room.

How was she ever going to leave?

Forty-seven

"Ms. Mason."

Jenna looked up, surprised to see two students standing at her desk. Aliah and Kaiya, best friends who cruised through English, totally complacent with pulling down average grades, yet capable of reaching the stars.

Jenna twiddled a pen in her hand. After the previous night's crash course on group grieving, she had made it through her first Friday class drained of patience and energy. Hitting a neutral tone was out of the question.

She said sternly, "I thought the bell rang and my prep period started."

The girls exchanged an uh-oh glance. Their flat-ironed hair resembled stiff brooms, one magenta, one peacock blue. That was this week's color.

Kaiya, of the blue shade, turned a determined expression to her. "We wanted to try out a couple of metaphors."

"Or similes," Aliah added. "We get them confused."

"'Kay," Jenna replied. That idiom was foreign to her, but it was how Amber talked. Modeling her friend's lingo and attitude seemed the easiest way to make herself more approachable to the kids. "Bullhead Mason" ranked right up there with "Princess" as the identity she most wanted to lose.

She smiled at the girls. The fact that they actually stayed after class to talk with her proved that change was in the air. "Go ahead."

243

Aliah cleared her throat. "You look like something the cat swat-ted, mauled, and dragged in. Is that metaphor or simile?"

"Uh." She blinked. "What do you think?"

"Simile because of the word *like*."

Jenna nodded. "Good."

Kaiya said, "How about this one: if you were a towel, it'd be past time to put you in the rag drawer. Metaphor?"

"I think you know. What's going on, ladies?"

Again the exchanged glance. The eyes they turned back to her, though, glistened.

Kaiya said, "You don't look like yourself. Is your husband okay?"

Jenna bit her lip. She'd gotten to bed about two that morning after returning home from Miranda's. The short hours between two and six hadn't exactly been a beauty rest. She'd thrown on slacks and cotton shirt, no jewelry except for a pair of earrings, her hair in a need-a-shampoo-yesterday ponytail.

The girls were right. Their worry touched her. That made three of them on the verge of bawling.

She chose the teasing route. "He's fine, but I'm miffed now. You're really more concerned about him than me, aren't you? Probably because he's cuter than I am."

They giggled. Aliah said, "Mrs. Mason, he is sooo hot."

Kaiya sighed dramatically. "What's it like being married to him?"

"Honestly, right now our marriage is a royal pain in the neck." *Whoa. That might have been too much information.*

"Cliché, right?" Aliah grinned.

Jenna rolled her eyes.

Kaiya's smile changed quickly to a grimace. "We are really sorry that he's overseas."

Not sure what might come out of her mouth next, Jenna stuck to nodding.

Aliah said, "And class was a major bore today. You might as well go home and let the sub take over again."

Kaiya gasped and pulled on her friend's arm. "I can't believe you said that. Gee whiz. Mrs. M, can we have a late pass? Please?"

Mrs. M. Jenna liked that. She would have given the girls passes to a rock concert.

After they left, she remained at her desk, too exhausted for physical exertion. The girls were right about the way she looked and the boring class. What counted at the moment, though, was that Jenna was there, plugging forward, not giving in.

Two things had haunted her through the night: the image of a hopeless Evie and the unsettling phone conversation with Kevin. They still shadowed her when she finally got up after the sleepless hours.

As she had stood unseeing in front of her closet, she recalled a conversation with Rosie. Jenna had asked the policewoman about the horrible time the previous spring when she had shot Erik. Although Rosie acted in self-defense and Erik survived, the mere thought of the incident still sent shivers through Jenna. She could not understand how afterwards Rosie was able to go back to the streets, back to her regular job.

Rosie replied that long before it happened, she had learned to compartmentalize thoughts and feelings. She would simply lock the intrusive ones inside a mental closet, freeing her mind to focus in the here and now.

The trick was working fairly well. One class down, four to go, the boring aspect didn't count. What was it Kevin used to say to get himself pumped? *Ooh-rah.* That was it. Well, ooh-rah for Jenna.

At the sound of a rap on her open door, she looked up to see Cade.

"Hey." He strode across the room. "Got a minute?"

"Sure."

He pulled a student chair to her desk and straddled it backwards. "I'm tracking down rumors. Quote, 'Mrs. Mason is boring today and she doesn't look right,' unquote."

"Yeah, that's all true. So what?"

"Jenna, this is when you go home."

"Huh-uh. I am not giving in. This idiotic war will not get the bet-ter of me. I have a job to do here." *Ooh-rah.*

Cade gave her two thumbs-up. "Way to hang in there." He crossed his arms on the back of the chair. "Still. It's only second hour."

She nodded slowly. After the hearty outburst, her sails were flagging.

"What happened?" he asked.

The protest didn't make it to her vocal cords. He knew. Some-how he knew.

She said, "One of the wives had a major meltdown last night. Evie. Sweet. A mom. Twenty years old. I was up in Oceanside with her and some others until almost two this morning." Jenna shook her head. "Her eyes were—the light was out. Nobody was at home."

Cade shut his eyes. A long moment passed before he looked at her with gray eyes turned dark. "I'm sorry."

"It's like a torture. This not knowing day in and day out if he's dead or alive." Her voice was tight. She heard fear and anger in it. The mental closet had been shoved wide open. What would Rosie do with that?

He stood abruptly, reached over her desk, and pulled the stack of papers from under her arm. "Get your stuff. You're out of here. If the sub can't make it by the start of next hour, I'll cover for you. Where's your lesson plan?"

"I am not leaving!"

"I'm not asking if you are. I'm telling you that you are." The steel in his voice nearly scared her.

She gathered the papers from him, straightened a few things on the desktop, got her bag from a drawer. Her hands were shaking.

"Lesson plan?" he said.

It took her a moment to uncover it. "Here."

"Can you drive home?"

"Yes." She stood and rummaged in the bag for her car key.

"Jenna."

She looked at him.

"You're still recovering. Go home and stay there. The world will go on without you for a few days."

The sensibleness of his words struck her. She was thinking of what she needed to do if she wasn't staying at school: go to the doctor, go to Evie's, call the sub herself, go help her mom, call Amber, grade papers, stop at the dry cleaners, check e-mail again for a note from Kevin. A wave of relief loosened all that anxiety.

She said, "I'll go home."

"You can bet your next paycheck you'll go home."

One anxiety remained, though, a yearning so strong it physically hurt.

She wanted Cade to hold her.

The fact that such a possibility was totally out of the question only amplified the feelings.

They walked across her classroom, not even their arms close to touching.

He said, "I'd escort you to your car, but I have a sub to call ASAP."

"I don't need to be escorted."

At the door he stopped. "It's more about what I need." There was a fleeting hint of a smile on his lips, a softening in his icy gaze. "I'll check in on you later."

She savored his words and the expression on his face. It was the closest thing to a hug he could give. It would have to do.

For now.

Forty-eight

Ah, normalcy returns." Claire sipped her first cup of coffee, seated at the island counter.

Skylar eyed her over her own mug. The movie-star image had returned, smile and sparkly eyes intact, outfit unwrinkled. She said, "Normalcy, except that Danny's still here and Max and Ben aren't and we don't have enough brownies for lunch."

"True. But you look better today, honey."

She waited a beat for the yank on her heart to subside. "Thanks. So do you."

"It's been difficult with Max and Ben gone this week. Not even talking to him since they got there has been harder than I imagined. And you and I did a lot of extra work. You're even helping Lexi with the horses."

"No problem."

"I talked to Jenna. I don't think she's going to make it up this weekend. She wants to spend time with that group of Marine wives in hopes of moving beyond the 'misery loves company' phase."

"I can bake cookies," Skylar said.

"No. Danny ate the brownies, Danny can run into Santa Reina and buy all those special ingredients, and Danny can mix them up."

"Then he can get out of our way and I will bake them."

Claire smiled.

Skylar felt like crawling under the table. "Claire, I'm sorry." The words tumbled from her without thought. "For not being up front with you." She caught herself in time before saying enough to get her booted down the road.

Booted down the road?

More like locked in a room until the sheriff got there.

"Skylar." Claire's face softened to an expression of pure compassion. "Indio and I both realized that you were in trouble the moment you showed up. Generally speaking, people do not appear on our doorstep in the middle of the boondocks without a car, no cell phone in their pocket, carrying all their earthly goods on their back. Yes, we believe that God brought you to us, but not just because we were desperate for a cook."

"Why . . . why else?"

"Because you needed us, too, for food and shelter, for a safe harbor."

"I don't deserve it."

"None of us deserves such good things. We totally ignore our Creator. That's why He sent Jesus, to be our intermediary. The more we accept how we are continually being reconciled to God—in our past, in our everyday ways of ignoring Him—the more real His love and acceptance becomes. And the more we live in the reality of being His precious child."

Precious child? Precious? Child? The words spun in Skylar's head, sounds from some dead language she'd never learned.

Claire got off her stool and stepped over to Skylar. She wrapped her in a big hug. "It can be a difficult concept to grasp. Just know that Indio and I love you. We love you unconditionally, as if you were our own precious child."

Skylar's defenses all but vanished. Danny's expression of care, Claire and Indio's tenderness, the security of the Hideaway, the beauty of the land, the comfort of her own room . . .

The threat that emanated from Rosie's report dissipated, a river of doubt and fear spreading across a floodplain.

Forty-nine

Danny folded his arms across his chest. "This is a bad idea."

Jenna stomped her foot. She was in definite princess mode. "Come on, Danny. All I want is a guy's take on how the toilets flush and the garage door swings."

He shook his head in disbelief.

They stood on the front walk of a vacant house for rent. It was only minutes from his place, a plus for him since he seemed to be her go-to guy in recent months. The house's upscale Southwestern style, lush vegetation, and quiet neighborhood suited his sister, but it wasn't right.

"It's just not right," he said, "You can't move while Kevin's overseas."

"Why not? He and I have talked about it since we got married and crammed all his stuff into my dinky apartment. It's not like I'm buying a place. It's a one-year lease."

"You can afford this?"

"Yes, now we can."

Danny felt himself recoil at her words. Kevin was getting paid extra for combat duty. Combined with Jenna's salary, they were doing all right.

"So why not?" she said.

"Because Kevin needs to be able to imagine where you're living. He'll need familiarity when he comes home. It'd be like you shaving your head, piercing body parts, and gaining a hundred pounds. 'Hey, welcome home to your wife, big guy.'"

"Or like getting tattooed without telling him?" Her eyes narrowed. "Or quitting my job and joining the Marines without telling him?"

Whoops. Wrong tactic. From her point of view, she was not doing anything Kevin hadn't already done without consulting her.

She said, "That is not going to fly with me, Daniel. I'm feeling like a cooped-up hen in that apartment. Not to mention every inch of it reminds me of him. And no, I do not want to be reminded of him because that only makes me think all the more about how he's not there!"

He patted the air and whispered, "Bring it down, Jen. The neighbors will be signing a petition against you moving in here."

She clamped her mouth shut.

"You have the key?"

She turned on her heel and walked up toward the door.

Danny followed, vowing to limit his comments to toilets and garages. Jenna needed him more or less to okay what she'd already decided. An agent had shown it to her earlier. She had called Danny soon after. It was perfect, she said, and it was going to go fast. She couldn't wait for their dad to get back from his trip to help her, and Erik was all thumbs when it came to the practical side of life.

Women.

Like Skylar. What was he going to do about her?

Since last Thursday when their mom had been so upset about the strange guy, Danny and Erik had tag teamed spending weeknights up there. Their mom grew less anxious. Skylar grew more subdued.

As his attraction deepened toward her, he feared she would wig out on him. Like Faith Simmons had years ago. Was that why he was moving so quickly?

Jenna held her arms wide. "Perfect, huh?"

He looked around. The layout was bright and airy, combining

kitchen, living, and family rooms. A hallway presumably led to bedrooms. French doors led out to a back patio and fenced yard.

An impression flashed through him, flooding him with a knowledge. He knew what he wanted to do about Skylar: he wanted to
bring her home.

He blinked. He had no clue what that meant.

"Danny, can I get some response? Anything?"

"It's great."

"You really think so?"

"You really think I'd pretend?"

She grinned.

"Jen, you were right about Faith Simmons."

"How'd we get from a great house to Faith Simmons?"

"Pretending." He might as well admit the Faith connection. "I
did pretend about her. I never had the hutzpah to admit I loved her,
either to myself or her. She became Farah Sunshine and was gone."

"Oh, no kidding."

"No kidding." He would not pretend with Skylar. He would have
to find out more about her with or without her help, just to prove to
her that no matter what, he cared—no. He loved her.

Danny swung his laptop around so that Rosie could see the photo
on its monitor. "Meet Fin Harrod."

Her face registered surprise, but she quickly hid it behind her professional mask. "What are you doing?"

"Have a seat." He pointed to a chair beside his in front of his
desk. They were in the spare room he used as an office.

Rosie sat.

It was Sunday evening. She was off duty and had come at his
request. Erik was busy with Nathan working on a documentary, the
topic of which they kept to themselves.

He said, "Skylar's name is Skylar."

Rosie blinked, a slow movement that left no doubt who was in charge.

He couldn't help but smile at the attractive Latina. "You totally level Erik with that look, don't you?"

She laughed, but didn't say anything.

"You are so perfect for him."

"Thank you. Now, you were saying?"

He expelled a breath. "I-I'm in love with Skylar."

"I noticed."

"No way."

Her brows went up.

"Anyway, she keeps saying I don't know her. That if I did, I'd hightail it the other direction. I think she cares for me too."

Rosie's brows rose further.

"Okay. So you noticed that too. The thing is, she won't open up with me, but I've been taking notes." He tapped his head. "She's basically been on edge since we saw Jenna in the hospital after the bombing. I don't think that's because she's all that close to my sister."

"Which leaves?"

"Something about the bombing incident itself. A week ago, the night we were all up at the hacienda and you told us about it, she looked like she was going to be sick. Then she disappeared into the kitchen where I found her a total wreck. Back up two and a half months ago to the weird way she first appeared, like a fugitive might. No car, cell phone, address. Her family is all dead. She has no local friends. Convenient, hmm? What is she running from? Simple. Her past."

"Interesting." She pointed at his computer. "Who's this guy?"

"Your bomber. Harrison Feinstein, a.k.a. Fin Harrod. I started cross-referencing the bomb you described with attacks in California, Oregon, and Washington. This guy is a suspect in several unsolved bombings. A few cardboard and two pipe, the latter at logging companies, because he was seen in the areas. Years ago he was an ace chem student at Berkeley, arrested for dealing drugs, served time, dropped out of sight."

She stared at him. "How did you do that?"

He smiled. "The Internet is my life."

"Mm-hmm. Okay, anything else?"

"This is the guy my mom talked to."

She chewed the inside of her cheek.

He said, "Mom's description matches, even if he does have long, blond hair in this picture and you can't see the mole. Which means this guy knows Skylar, and Skylar knows him."

"I talk too much."

"What?"

"I told your mom. I shouldn't have. I'm sorry. Can you just forget—"

"You told my mom what?"

"What you said—she didn't tell you?"

"No."

"She's a good woman." Rosie paused. "Danny, we zeroed in on Fin Harrod. A witness at the church described someone much like him. I had your mom's description. No-brainer."

Danny blew out a breath. "He called her Annie Wells. There's no record of Skylar Pierson or Annie Wells or any combination of those names being born in Ohio about thirty years ago. No record of those names around that age having ever lived in Ohio."

"I know." She smiled. "We cops do have some Internet expertise."

"Sorry. So now what?"

"Now we play around with the names. Like Fin Harrod here, people most often take a part of their real name for a pseudonym. My guess is 'Ann' is Skylar's real middle name. 'Wells' is part of her last name."

"We should just ask her. Warn her about this guy."

"Is the sheriff still keeping a close eye on things?"

"Yeah."

"Is there a chance she could have seen Harrod at the protest?"

They exchanged a stare.

He shrugged.

She said, "That could explain his tracking her down. I don't want to scare her off, Danny. She's obviously on the run from something involving him. These guys always have groupies hanging around. We need more information before we can move in."

Move in? Danny felt his leg muscles turn to gel. This cop needed more information about Skylar. But was he ready for more?

Despite his gallant words to her, vowing that he cared deeply for her no matter her past, he wasn't so sure.

Fifty

The phone rang late Sunday night. Skylar, alone in the kitchen, answered it. "Hacienda Hideaway."

"Hello there, Annie Wells."

In the two seconds it took Fin Harrod to rumble the sentence, Skylar's safe harbor became a thing of the past.

She slid along the pantry door to the tile floor. "Sorry. Nobody here by that name."

"Right." The chuckle embodied the word *malicious.* "I heard the whomp in your chest all the way from Santa Reina to—well, we won't get into where I am at the moment. That witch in the Mercedes didn't know Annie Wells either."

Witch in the Mercedes? Claire had driven Max's car several times since he left, leaving her own car available for Skylar. But when did he—

"The funny thing is," he went on, "license plates don't lie. They're registered to Claire Beaumont with an address. The tricky part was linking the address to the Hacienda Hideaway and tracking down a new phone number. But you know me when it comes to a tricky part. And you do know me, don't you?" Again the chuckle. "You did good, kid. I'm proud of you getting yourself all situated at a retreat center, probably as cook, probably making new *friends.* But I'm sure you know I have a concern."

She had spotted him near a crime scene.

"Well, Annie Wells, it's been nice chatting with you. Take care now."

The line went dead. After a moment, the dial tone returned.

Skylar listened to its droning, the phone pressed to her ear, her forehead pressed to her bent knees. And she listened to his unspoken threat.

He was long gone from San Diego, but he knew where she was and that she had friends. If she went to the police about him, her friends would be endangered.

The sad truth was that he'd already hurt one of those friends.

"Skylar?"

She looked up to see Claire.

"Are you all right?"

"Yeah." She held out the phone. "Somebody wanting a reservation, but we're booked every weekend he asked for. It got me to thinking about this Friday's guests. Mind if I use the car tomorrow? I have some new menu ideas and Costco has the ingredients."

Claire smiled. "Of course I don't mind. I'll take Max's car to the airport." The travelers were returning the next afternoon. "We'll have a houseful for dinner—Rosie, Nathan, and even Hawk."

"Let's serve those chicken casseroles in the freezer."

"Perfect. I don't know if Jenna will feel like coming after that funeral. I really should be with her there."

"Claire, you can't do everything at once."

She sighed. "Thanks for the reminder. My goodness. You take care of reservations, menus, grocery shopping, and my emotional well-being. I don't know how I'd get along without you, honey."

Skylar managed a smile in response. Claire would figure out soon enough how she'd get along without her because Skylar's stint in Kansas was, without a doubt, over.

Skylar packed her bag in the dead of night. Given the fact that she'd not completely unpacked it, the chore did not take long. She carried it by starlight out to Claire's car and stowed it in the trunk.

The shadows spooked her unlike before. Fin Harrod had managed from miles away to suck the safety right out of the estate. Tonight she would have welcomed Danny or Erik's presence in a guest room. After a week of watching over the women, though, neither one was there now. Both had early morning appointments—

Watching over the women?

Because Claire was nervous with Max gone, left alone with the fire memories?

Or because she'd encountered a weirdo asking for Annie Wells?

Would the sheriff make frequent trips up the lane just because Claire was nervous?

And what was that business about Lexi staying with Indio? Even the dog Samson seemed to have relocated down there.

Skylar was losing her touch. How had she missed the clues?

By getting lost in Danny's attention. The evenings he'd spent at the house were the happiest times she'd had since—maybe since ever.

Was he for real?

She'd never know now.

Monday morning Skylar hugged Claire good-bye and ignored the surprise in her friend's eyes at the unusual display of emotion.

And then she cried most of the way to Oceanside.

The city drew her for two reasons: train station and funeral.

The police and military presence around the church was thick. Skylar assumed that although no antiwar protest was involved, the officials were taking extra precautions. She was glad she'd worn a Lexi hand-me-down. The black skirt and loose black sweater over a brown shirt was comfortable without giving her the hippie appearance certain people in uniform might notice.

She entered the church and slipped into a back pew just as things were getting under way. It was a packed house. She craned her neck searching for Jenna. At last she spotted her, near the front.

Skylar released her breath. It made no sense why she was there. Guilt, maybe. Or a need to make some lame attempt at restitution. She only knew that she could not leave town until Jenna had made it safely through a military funeral.

Nor could she make much sense of why Jenna once more attended the funeral of a stranger. She had become downright militant with her newfound semper fi attitude. She had never met the guy in the casket nor his family. She only knew that he had been a Marine and that she was not about to let the previous funeral's experience keep her away from any subsequent ones.

And so Skylar went, too, and sat through music and eulogies that would squeeze tears from a Raggedy Ann doll. She tried not to ponder the fact that the boy was almost ten years younger than herself.

The funeral had not yet ended when Skylar left, but she had a schedule to keep.

She drove to the train station, retrieved her bag, put the key under the driver's-side mat, and locked the doors. At the automated machine she bought a one-way Amtrak ticket to Chicago, dismissed the thought that she could not avoid a possible random ID check, and got on the train.

Fifty-one

Jenna's mind wandered and she let it. She welcomed it. She aided and abetted it. If not for chasing mental rabbit trails, she could not have sat through the funeral.

She thought of Kevin, of course. He had e-mailed that morning, his one and only communication since his phone call the night Evie fell apart. "Indescribable schedule" would be his excuse.

She thought of his e-mail. Short. Terse, even. He wrote that morale lagged, but they were getting through it. Doing better every day. Ooh-rah. So-and-so had pulled a practical joke, too gross to describe in writing, but it had made them laugh. He figured she was handling things in her usual strong way. He signed off with a standard "Miss you, love you." And a new addition: "Remember God is with both of us."

To keep from screaming, she imagined that between the lifeless lines, Kevin was saying things like he was sorry for forgetting to call her "pretty lady" on the phone, that he couldn't wait to come home, that he was proud of her for embracing the role of military wife.

As the pastor spoke from the podium, Amber reached over and took her hand. On Amber's other side Joey was holding hers.

Jenna smiled in appreciation.

Amber leaned close. "You okay?"

"No," she whispered.

"Me neither." She squeezed her hand. "We'll press through, though, huh?"

Jenna nodded. They would press through

It had been Amber's idea to attend another military funeral. Jenna was so tired of resisting in general that she gave in to her friend's convoluted thinking that it would help them work through that other funeral. It didn't matter that neither of them were acquainted with the deceased or his spouse or his parents or even a distant friend. Military was military.

This church was nothing like the other one. This one was Protestant with padded pews. Not much in the way of stained glass, but they sat in the center anyway, far from the few small windows.

She and Amber didn't look like they had when they sat at the other funeral. Jenna wore a gray dress, not a black suit. Amber wore a wig of long, straight, dark hair, nothing like her bouncy blonde curls. Both bore scars.

They weren't the same women they'd been two months ago at the September funeral. Amber had said they were older and wiser. Jenna tweaked her phrasing. "Less gullible and more angst ridden," she'd said. Her friend did not disagree.

They were surrounded by prayers this time too—her mother's and grandmother's. Joey was there with them, GI Joe-slash-Transformer in the flesh. Nothing was going to hurt them this time.

Not even that rotten, pointless, adolescent e-mail from Kevin. The jerk.

Eulogies, prayers, music, Marines in dress blues, flag-draped coffin, a widow in black . . . Jenna only used one hankie and six tissues. Tombstones, flag snapped crisply into folds just so, rifles blasting . . . only eight tissues. Casseroles that swam, children of one absentee parent laughing with innocence, their older relatives drinking too much beer . . . she was in the bathroom going through a roll of toilet paper, congratulating herself for not bothering with mascara that day.

She would press through. She would make it.

Fifty-two

Claire snuggled with Max on the love seat in the master suite. It was their first moment alone in two weeks and she relished in it.

Earlier at the airport, she'd wept at the sight of three glowing faces. Max, Ben, and Tuyen physically displayed the healing that had taken place in each of them while in Vietnam. Max's stories during their few short phone calls had not been able to capture the reality of such peace.

"Jenna won't be here for dinner?" Max asked.

"She's not planning on it after that funeral."

"And Skylar's not cooking?"

She chuckled. "She needed some time off. But no worries. We have plenty of her goodies left over from the weekend meals. Our guests were not big eaters."

"Hmm." His murmur bordered on a snore.

Claire smiled. He was exhausted after the trip and lunch downtown where the three of them had poured out immediate reactions to the whole experience. Indio wept through it all, tears of joy and sadness.

Tuyen sensed a release from her past. With her uncle and grandfather at her sides, she felt like a person for the first time in her homeland. She was an American with a Vietnamese heritage.

While overseas, Max had described to her how BJ would have deeply loved her mother and her. He was that kind of guy. Ben believed that her mother was the kind of woman who loved BJ deeply, as evidenced by how she nursed him back to health and protected him. The tragedy that had been their short life together resulted in the wonder of a life in Tuyen.

According to Max, such words could not have been spoken or received until the three of them stood where BJ had been buried. The reality of his last years spoke to them almost audibly.

Ben had been ready at last to hear such a reality. The beauty of the people and the country touched him. The image of a humble, tiny mountain village broke his heart. He began to grasp the conditions that condemned BJ to a life far from home.

Max found himself admiring his brother to the point of awestruck. He'd spent most of his life knocking BJ off the pedestal his parents placed him on. By the end of the visit, he believed BJ belonged on one.

They had called Beth Russell from the restaurant. Max briefly filled her in on developments. He told her that the remains would be sent for burial in San Diego. She said she would come.

Claire listened now to Max's rhythmic breathing, her ear against his chest. She would stay put while he napped, grateful for how God had brought healing to the wound that had remained open in the Beaumont family for so many years.

Claire clasped Max's hand on top of the dining room table and smiled. "I'm having a hard time letting go."

"Me too." He glanced around the semi-raucous crowd eating dinner. "Is it just me, or is this a cross between a celebration and a wake?"

She surveyed the group.

Ben, surprisingly fresh after the long flight from Ho Chi Minh City, sat with Indio on one side, Tuyen on his other. A new peace had settled about him. Indio appeared tired, but content. She'd made sure to be in on Ben's phone call to Beth Russell, in which he told her all about the trip. Closure was written all over Indio's face.

Tuyen and Hawk had eyes only for each other, but along with Lexi, Nathan, and Erik, they kept the conversation lively.

Danny kept leaving the table and checking the grounds for any sign of Skylar.

Jenna hadn't made it either. Max caught up with her on her cell phone. She was far too upset to visit.

Rosie was missed; she had to work.

Claire said to Max, "Nope, it's not just you. We're all so happy to be together again, but at the same time it's a sad occasion because you've just come from BJ's grave."

He nodded. "Dad's been such an inspiration to me through all this. Watching him let go of the past at his age and grow spiritually by leaps and bounds is not something you see every day. Remind me when I'm eighty that it's not time to sit back and watch the world go by."

She smiled. "I could have married you just for the privilege of having your parents as mentors."

"Thanks." He laughed. "So what should we do, if anything, about Skylar?"

She glanced at her watch. "I don't know. She said she'd be back for dinner, but sometimes she still shies away from special family times."

"The problem, though, is that business with the stranger on the road." Claire had filled him in on the incident. He had been upset that she hadn't told him on the phone when he called from overseas.

Danny leaned across the table, his forehead wrinkled. Evidently he'd had one ear on their exchange. "I agree."

Claire blinked in surprise.

"I know, Mom. I figured it out. That guy knows Skylar. I think something's wrong. I'm calling Rosie."

Even as he pushed back his chair, there was a knock on the sala door and it opened. Rosie walked inside. "Hey, everyone."

Behind her came the sheriff. "Hey."

Neither of them smiled. Both were in uniform.

A third guy entered. He looked out of place and official in a black suit and tie.

Everyone quieted at the table.

Rosie said, "Where's Skylar?"

Danny shook his head. "We don't know."

Erik stood. "Rosie, what's up?"

She sighed. "We have a warrant for her arrest."

The man in the suit was an FBI agent. Even seated by the fireplace, sipping a cup of tea, he looked out of place to Claire.

But then, the whole scene looked out of place.

Rosie sat on the hearth and, after convincing the agent that, yes, all the Beaumonts and company needed to hear some of the story, began to talk.

Claire snuggled against Max on the couch. He held her close. Although Rosie had probed gently about what Claire knew of Skylar's whereabouts, she was shaken.

Danny paced while the others sat in various places. Everyone was subdued, even Erik. While Indio had made tea, Rosie and the other two made phone calls. The entire county was now on alert to the make, color, and license number of Claire's car. They also had a description of Lexi's hand-me-downs that Skylar was wearing.

Rosie said, "Skylar's real name is Laurie Ann Rockwell." She looked at Danny, who stopped and stared back at her.

"Annie Wells," he said.

The name the stranger had used with Claire.

"And Skylar Pierson. Piers is a form of Peter, which means *rock*."

He said, "She was adamant about the spelling of Pierson. How did you find out?"

Rosie shrugged. "I like to play around with names. Baby name books are a great resource. Skylar I don't get, though. It means *sheltering*. I guess by then she just went random."

"Not so much," Danny said. "All she wanted was a shelter."

Claire began to weep softly.

Danny went back to pacing.

Rosie cleared her throat. "She grew up in San Francisco. Her dad is a wealthy owner of a construction company, her mother a socialite type. Both came out of a late-sixties-type hippie lifestyle. Skylar has an older sister and brother. She went to Berkeley for a while, then just seemed to drop out of sight. Her parents don't know where she is. We—"

Indio gasped. "My word! Her parents don't know where she is?"

Rosie read from a notebook, "Quote, 'She calls now and then,' unquote."

"For goodness' sake!" Indio did not conceal her indignation. "That poor baby. Something was not right in her home."

Rosie took a deep breath. "There are a string of coincidences that link her with Fin Harrod. One is that they were at Berkeley at the same time. Eighteen months ago there was a bombing at NorCal Lumber Company, up north. The place was demolished. We believe Harrod was behind it. He's a known ecoterrorist, part of an underground network. We believe he had accomplices. According to our source, a young woman going by the name of Annie Wells used to hang out with him."

Max said, "How can you arrest Skylar with all that hearsay?"

Rosie glanced at the FBI agent. He nodded. She said, "We have one partial fingerprint from—from the incident. It matches one we took from Danny's apartment. I'm sorry." She looked around at everyone. "It's enough to go on."

Max said, "If Harrod's an ecoterrorist, what's he doing blowing up a church that's hosting a military funeral?"

Rosie eyed him like she would a pesky gnat.

He shrugged. "Can you tell us?"

The agent shifted in his chair. So far he had let Rosie do most of the talking. "Harrod no longer fits the typical profile. Ten months ago we connected him to a bombing at an event that had nothing to do with the government, environment, or the military. Since then we suspect he participated in other unrelated explosions. He's not interested in a cause."

Ben said, "Except his own sick cravings."

The agent nodded.

Max said, "Did Skylar have a clue what's been going on here, that you were investigating her?"

Rosie said, "Not that I'm aware of. Neither Danny nor Claire told her about the stranger, who we're convinced was Harrod. There is a chance she saw him at the demonstration."

Claire said, "But that was, like, six weeks ago, and she didn't leave."

Rosie smiled and the professional mask melted away. "Claire, she stayed because you all loved on her like crazy. Of course she stayed as long as could. My guess is it's taken him this long to track her down and that now he's contacted her."

Claire remembered how she found Skylar seated on the floor with the phone in her hand. "I think he called her last night." She related that scenario.

Ben said, "That's it, then. She's done hightailed it out of here." He took hold of Indio's hand. "Love, I hope you weren't planning on sleeping tonight. We have some heavy-duty praying to do."

"Yes, we most certainly do." Indio grinned. "It's what got her here in the first place, you know."

Claire sighed to herself. The tandem ride was in motion, zooming at full speed toward blind curves.

She stole a glance at Danny. His face was scrunched up like it did when he was a tyke, just before he screamed an unholy roar. Without a word, he marched out the door.

She listened, but heard nothing.

Oh, Lord, where do we begin?

Fifty-three

Jenna sat in her car parked outside a condominium complex. As faculty members, she and Kevin had been there a couple of times for cookouts at the principal's home.

The buildings were not new. Views were of freeways and shopping malls. But it was nice, in a central location not far from school. Not far from Jenna's apartment. She remembered his unit's décor as tasteful, no frills. Definite bachelor pad.

Her cell phone rang. She recognized his number and answered. "Hi."

"Do you want to come inside?"

Obviously he had spotted her through a window. She hadn't told him she was coming. She didn't know it herself, not until after she'd negotiated the I-5, thinking she needed to turn on the windshield wipers for her tearful downpour. The sun went down about the time she ran out of tears and tissues.

Not much thought had been put into her destination. She had told her dad she planned to go home, but instead she simply zipped past her exit and took the next one. Nor was much emotion involved. She was drained of emotion except for that insatiable ache to feel safe.

The only place she knew that would be real was in Cade Edmunds's arms.

"Yes, I want to come inside."

The light above his front door lit up. A moment later, she reached it as he opened it. She paused on the threshold, her heart beating too hard, too fast.

He was dressed casually in khakis and knit shirt. He waited, hands in pockets, his expression soft, concerned, patient.

Stupid glitch in the system. Ridiculous e-mail. Senseless twist of events that ripped her husband from her side and filled the space between them with darkness that grew more impenetrable by the day.

"I'm sorry," she whispered, whether to Kevin, Cade, God, or herself she did not know. What she did know was that when Cade held her, the ache would go away.

She stepped inside.

Fifty-four

Rosie had dropped her bombshell on Monday night. Danny lived in a red haze through the following days.

Daylight hours were spent in the water surfing, nighttime ones at the desk researching domestic terrorists. He forgot to eat, forgot to work, forgot to listen for God's voice. His prayers became tirades against loggers and environmentalists alike, warmongers and antiwar demonstrators, the whole entire unfair world at large.

The anger never went away.

Friday morning his roommate, Hawk, got in his face and said Jenna had called him at the store because Danny didn't answer his phone. Hawk said that probably had something to do with Danny's phone being turned off.

Jenna sounded off. She needed to see Danny at the rental house now.

He picked up his cell phone, saw ten missed calls from Lexi and would have headed to the surf if Hawk weren't blocking the door. In their many years as friends, Danny still wasn't sure if the guy was a curse or a blessing.

His twin would have to wait. He only had energy for one sister at a time. He called Jenna back and learned nothing more than what Hawk had told him.

He drove to the rental house, thinking of how Kevin e-mailed less often these days. His references to increased fighting weighed heavily on Danny. Jenna's pleas had broken through the roar in his own head.

Jenna opened the door.

"Why aren't you in school?" he said.

"I got the house." Her face didn't reflect the gladness he figured would accompany that announcement. "I took the day off to get started on the move."

"What's wrong?"

"Nothing."

"You look like you've got prerecital jitters."

She shook her head. "I'm not asking your permission to move in here, but aren't you the least bit happy for me?"

"Did you tell Kevin?"

"Not yet.

"Jen—"

"How am I supposed to tell him if he doesn't call? I'm not doing it in an e-mail, thanks to you. You convinced me he's going to be upset. I need to tell him face-to-face. So to speak."

Danny slowed himself down. Agitated vibes fairly hummed off of Jenna. There was something different about her. Eye contact wasn't happening. She didn't stand still. Her hands flittered in nervous gestures.

"Anyway," she said, "I'm sorry about Skylar. How are you doing?"

"Let's change the subject. Why did you want to see me?" he asked.

"Mom's coming. She hasn't seen the house. She's in the city interviewing a chef at Dad's old office. Do you want a juice or soda? I brought a cooler."

"Sure."

They took cans from a cooler in the kitchen. He noticed boxes on the floor as well, marked in her neat handwriting. A coffeemaker sat on the counter, two mugs next to it.

He followed her through the patio doors. They sat on lawn chairs.

"So Mom's coming," he prompted.

Her eyes darted around the small yard. "I can't handle her by myself. You always know how to handle her. That's why I called you instead of Erik."

He frowned. "What do you mean by 'handle'?"

"Sometimes it's not like she's your mother. She's just another person."

"Why don't you want a mother?"

"Because she makes me feel responsible and accountable." She swiped at her eyes. "Like I should be able to deal with Kevin's absence better."

"Jen, did you forget? Mom left Dad because she didn't want to deal anymore with his absence."

"But then he made this huge sacrifice for her and they've been like honeymooners ever since. She gets this dose of religion and sounds more adamant than you and Nana put together about living by faith and getting through the tough times with flying colors."

Danny sensed that Jenna talked around what was really going on inside of her, but had no clue how to zero in on it. "Do you want me to pray before she comes, like I did before your recitals?"

"No! I just want you to run interference. I mean, life is just really, really hard for me right now. I'm dealing with it the best I can, okay? I don't need anybody's advice."

Even in the midst of his own confusion and hurt, he heard hers. A renewed fear for Kevin emerged, and for their marriage.

He didn't need his sister's permission to pray.

Lord, please take care of Jenna and Kevin. Preserve their marriage.

Unlike Danny, Claire oohed and aahhed in all the right places over Jenna's house find.

He watched the women. Jenna's complexion carried a shade of their dad's Native American heritage, but there was no mistaking a resemblance between mother and daughter. Perhaps it was a touch of the musician's personality, an obvious bent toward detail, toward dotting all the i's and crossing all the t's.

"It's great, Jenna," Claire said as they sat again on the patio. "Are you sure you don't need your dad to help the movers tomorrow?"

"I'm sure, thanks."

Danny listened as they discussed mundane details of moving. Jenna crossed her legs; they bounced with nervous energy. Their mom was obviously worn-out. She had hired two women to help with that weekend's guests, but the loss of Skylar in the kitchen multiplied her distress.

When she had arrived, Claire reported there was no new news. Her car, discovered at a train station Wednesday, was still impounded by the police. They presumed she got on a train. There were a zillion directions she could have taken.

Skylar had not called. *Like that was going to happen,* he scoffed to himself.

"Danny?" His mother eyed him in a distinctly motherly way.

"No, I'm not doing so hot." He answered her unasked question. "I'm like Jenna. Life is just too hard to talk about today."

"Are you both giving yourselves permission to feel that to its fullest extent?"

He and Jenna exchanged a surprised glance.

"I mean," Claire went on, "to let yourselves feel tired, hurt, violated, hopeless, all that junk? To grieve? Fighting it doesn't help. Or pretending that it's not there, eating away at your insides."

He said, "You're supposed to smile and tell us it'll be all better soon and that you're praying. And maybe take two aspirin while we're at it."

"Well, you both know I'm praying. I pray that you'll trust that God is carrying you through. I pray that you'll be able to extend forgiveness to Skylar and Kevin for the choices they made that hurt you. That as you stumble in your pain, you will not be hurled headlong off the path."

"Psalm something or other."

She nodded.

He gave her a sad smile.

Jenna had grown still as a statue. "What's the path exactly?"

Claire tilted her head back and forth. "Of going in the right direction, I suppose." She stood. "I have to go. Jen, I can help you unpack next week."

"Thanks."

"You're taking off all next week?"

"Monday and Tuesday, anyway. Cade said to take more, but I've spent too many days out of the classroom already. It's like you said, Mom. I'm giving myself permission to quit pretending that life is normal."

Danny tuned her out. He'd heard more than he wanted. There was an odd tone, almost a false note, in the way she referenced Cade.

In her pain, had his sister stumbled so badly she'd hurled herself right off the path?

How could she?

And how could Skylar run off without a word? How could she have committed even a fraction of what she was accused of?

An ache pierced him, so sharp it nearly took his breath away. He suddenly saw himself as a legalist consumed with the black and white of rules, with no space in his heart for grays.

Grays? Maybe it was grace.

Fifty-five

After Danny and her mother left, Jenna sat in the dark on a lawn chair in her new dining room, reviewing the days since her self-propelled hurl off the path of going in the right direction.

Her mother's prayer must have been said too late.

Monday night Cade had provided all the comfort and respite Jenna craved.

Tuesday, in the wee hours of the morning, she slipped away while he slept. At home she called in another sick day and spent thirty minutes in the shower attempting to scrub off the shame.

Wednesday she returned to school and successfully avoided him until he called out as she left the building that afternoon.

"Jenna, wait up a sec."

She kept on walking across the parking lot. As she opened her car door, he grasped its frame.

"Talk to me."

She tossed her bag onto the front seat. "I really don't have anything to say."

"Well, I do," he murmured and then barked a laugh, shouting, "Hey, Turner, way to go!"

Jenna glanced across the lot and saw another teacher. The two men bantered in loud voices for a brief moment.

She forced herself to meet Cade's eyes. "I can't do this."

"I know." Mr. Ice Guy was absolutely nowhere to be seen. "But let's put some closure to it. Tonight." He named a casual chain restaurant. "Meet you there at seven." Then he turned on his heel and walked off.

Wednesday at six-thirty she received the call that the rental house was hers. It helped. It offered a glimpse of hope, of a future. It lessened the image of herself in Evie's shoes, living with her parents, resembling a dead person walking.

She met Cade. They ordered dinner at the counter, sat in a back booth, and began to talk.

She said, "I shouldn't have gone to your place Monday night."

"And I shouldn't have opened the door. But you did and I did. It's over. We will not wallow in what might have been."

She shivered at his authoritative tone.

"Jenna, I crossed several lines I always promised myself I'd never even consider approaching. For starters you're married, a faculty member, and in a vulnerable situation. I cruised right on over without a backward glance." He stopped talking.

"Wh-why?"

His chest rose and fell in rhythm with audible breaths. "Because I'm a little bit in love with you."

In love with her? In love? Love had never entered her mind!

"Yeah," he said, "surprised me too. I realize, though, that because of it, I can say, 'Whoa.' This ends now. Having an affair is not what's best for you. Me offering a shoulder for you to cry on isn't either. We have to recapture a professional distance."

She whispered fiercely, "I committed adultery!"

"With me. I'm sorry. I am so sorry, but I can't change that fact."

"I don't know how to live with that fact!"

"It doesn't mean you're a horrible person, Jen."

"Then why do I feel so *filthy?*" Her low voice nearly screeched.

The compassion on his face made her want to cry. "Do you have someone you can talk to? Family member? A pastor?"

She shook her head.

"These things happen, especially when our world is falling apart.

None of us are perfect. We need to forgive ourselves. Sometimes we need help doing that."

He was going spiritual on her too?

"That's why," he said, "there are counselors in the world. The military probably has all kinds on staff. I will help you find one. I will find the best substitute teacher for you so that you can take all the time off that you need. I will do whatever I can, Jenna."

"Except hold me."

He nodded, his lips pressed together.

They eventually ended the conversation, her schedule set to take time off in order to move, his eyes losing the softness to which she had grown accustomed.

Fifty-six

Oh Max! I just want to gather them like a mother hen with her chicks." Claire stretched her legs across the love seat and Max's lap.

He chuckled. "I know you don't mean that."

"I do! I swear I do!"

He kneaded one of her bare feet. "Sorry, sweetheart. We're into 'push them out of the nest' season. Don't worry. They'll get those wings a-flapping before they go splat on the ground."

She glowered. "Ha-ha."

"Seriously, I've been thinking about our safe harbor here. It's not enclosed on all sides. It's a big hug, open for anyone to sail into or out of, a port in a storm."

"That's a better analogy than going splat."

He smiled and massaged her aching feet.

It was late Saturday night. They were huddled in the master suite with a fire in the fireplace and tea. It was their treat to themselves, bidding good night to six guests and a cook who—bless her heart—agreed to stay over until Sunday noon.

The phone rang near Claire's elbow. "Hello. Hacienda Hideaway."

"Claire? It's me."

She bolted upright. "Skylar?"

"Yeah." The voice was small. "Can I come home?"

"Oh, honey." Claire burst into tears. "Of course you can!" Blubbering, she handed the phone to Max.

"Skylar?" he said. "Yes . . . yes . . . all right. Yeah. We'll be there. And Skylar . . . I'm glad you called." He turned off the phone.

Claire blew her nose. "What'd she say?"

"She's at the train station downtown." He paused. "She asked if we'd bring Rosie instead of a stranger." He stood and held out a hand to her. "We better get dressed. One of your chicks needs you ASAP."

Fifty-seven

Skylar found herself in Galesburg, Illinois. Literally she was there on Thursday, but figuratively it was where she realized *who* she was.

It felt like being smacked over the head with a pair of ruby-red slippers.

The train's regularly scheduled stop south of Chicago turned into a six-hour delay due to tornadoes, thunderstorms, and debris blown onto the tracks. She could have hitchhiked to the Windy City by the time the train got going again.

Instead she prayed.

Sitting now in the San Diego train station she smiled to herself. Evidently she'd been majorly bummed to resort to prayer.

She had talked to God like Indio had told her she could, in everyday language, eyes open. She wanted desperately to believe—like Indio said—that He longed for her to talk to Him, that He would laugh out loud with joy when He heard her voice directed to Him.

And so she talked to Him. About all the Beaumonts, plus Kevin, Rosie, Nathan, and Hawk. About the horses, even. About Amber and her husband. She talked most especially about Danny.

Then, after a time, she knew deep in her heart two things, without a clue how she could possibly know them.

She knew God laughed.

And she knew what she had to do.

The first step was to get back to California. The Beaumonts had

paid her well, so money was not the problem, just train schedules. The
return trip took awhile.

The second step was about to present itself right now. Claire,
Max, and Rosie walked through one of the train station's big open
doorways.

Rosie must have been on duty. She was in uniform. Another uniform walked beside her. He fit Rosie's description of her partner, with
a wiry build and an intensely blue glare.

Skylar stepped into Claire's arms spread wide. For one long
moment nothing else mattered.

Max hugged her. "We'll get a lawyer."

"No, I don't need one. I did it."

Rosie said, "Skylar—"

"I did—"

"Hold on. You don't even know what we're arresting you for."

"Of course I do. I did it." She held out her hands, wrists together.
"Let's go. Somebody get my backpack, please?"

Max grabbed one of her hands, Claire the other. He said, "Rosie,
we'll be her handcuffs, okay? She's not a flight risk."

"Sure. Wait, we gotta do the Miranda thing."

The partner rolled his eyes. "Delgado, you're losing it."

Rosie flicked a finger across her damp cheek. "Give me a sec,
Bobby."

Claire sniffed back tears. "Officer Gray, would you mind carrying
Skylar's backpack?"

Eventually they moved to the door, an odd group walking
through the station and onto a broad sidewalk. One cop cried, the
other carried her bag. Max and Claire clung tightly onto each of her
arms, not because she was a flight risk, but because they loved her.

Skylar's courage did not waver through the ride in the back of
the police car, the formal booking, the good-bye to Claire and

Max, the entrance to a cell where a motley group of women hung out.

The hard part, the scary part, was the phone call. That was when her courage wavered.

She knew no lawyer to call; Max promised to take care of that anyway. She needed to hear Indio's wisdom, but Skylar couldn't call the elderly woman in the middle of the night. She thought she should call her parents, but Claire said she would do it the next day, a better time to hear such news.

And so Skylar followed her heart. She called Danny.

"H'lo." He'd been asleep.

"Danny." She bit her lip.

Silence hung between them.

"Is this Annie Wells or Laurie Ann Rockwell?"

She rubbed her forehead. "I'm sorry I lied to you."

No reply.

"I'm at the San Diego police station. I-I turned myself in. Your mom and dad met me at the train station. I just wanted to say I'm sorry."

Another moment of silence passed. He said, "I don't know what to say."

"You don't have to say anything."

"Why did you come back?"

"God told me to." She could hear him breathing and imagined the fire in it. He would have a ton of things to say, but he was suppressing them all.

Totally un-Danny-like.

She rubbed her temple. "I'm sorry."

"Yeah, you said that already."

"Okay. I-I'll let you go. Bye."

"Ciao."

The line clicked.

Her heart clicked and then it clacked. It was the sound she had listened to on the trip halfway across the country, train wheels against rails, over and over. The words she couldn't say out loud to him now had echoed in her head the whole way.

I love you, Danny. I love you, Danny. I love you, Danny.

Fifty-eight

The judge set bail." Jenna ripped a long piece of packing tape from a box. "I still can't believe it."

Seated at the kitchen table, helping Jenna unpack in her new house, Amber said, "I can't wait to meet her."

"We can blame the bump on your head for that bizarre thought. The bump, I might add, that Skylar or whatever her name is helped put there."

"Oh, pshaw."

Jenna frowned at her and pulled a skillet from the box.

Amber sighed. "'Pshaw' was supposed to make you laugh. You're not quite yourself."

"For good reason."

"Yes, but that aside—"

"I'm not like you, Amber. I can't just forge ahead and keep smiling."

"You were, though. You got into ICU and watched over me. You've been caring for Evie and the other wives, offering smiles and tears."

"Ooh-rah. I was faking it."

"No, you weren't."

Jenna didn't reply. If not for Amber's familiar chatty voice, she would have quit listening an hour ago.

"Jen, what can I do for you besides put away dishes?"

"Get a blonde wig instead of that dark one?" Her tone didn't quite ring with the flippancy she'd hoped for. She shouldn't have invited Amber over so soon. She shouldn't have agreed to her mother's crazy plan.

The doorbell rang.

Too late.

A moment later she opened the door. Skylar Pierson stood there, regret in her pained expression obvious.

"Hi, Jenna."

"Hi." She hesitated over the name. "Skylar. Come on in." She scanned the street as Skylar entered. "Where's my mom?"

"Doing some errand down the street."

"That's okay?" Still amazed that the woman was out of jail, Jenna recalled the terms. Her parents had not only posted bond, they took full responsibility for Skylar's not fleeing before her court date.

"Yeah." Skylar closed her eyes for a second. "That's okay. It's allowed. Look, I know this is probably really trippy for you, but I had to apologize in person."

Jenna saw the woman she knew as a friendly, offbeat, topnotch chef. Her hair was less deep brown. Lexi had colored it for her, trying to match the long tresses with the natural auburn roots. Skylar wore only one pair of earrings. Her freckles stood out against abnormally pale skin. Shorter than Jenna, she seemed smaller than before. Vulnerable, even.

This was a bona fide terrorist? "Trippy to the max," Jenna said.

A smile fluttered across her lips. "I'm sorry."

Jenna was sad that her family had been deceived by Skylar, but her heart was too raw to feel malice. She hugged her. "I know you are. Come meet Amber."

They walked into the living room where Amber greeted them. She held out her hand and clasped Skylar's. "I'm Amber Ames."

"I'm sorry." Skylar's voice was low, husky.

"Thank you. Skylar. Is that what we should call you?"

"Please. I-I like it best."

Jenna watched Skylar visibly relax under Amber's gaze. Amber's magic touch struck again.

Skylar said, 'Laurie' makes me feel like an unwanted brat. I dropped it a long time ago and didn't become 'Skylar' until after—oh. I'm not supposed to talk about things like that."

"I just wondered. Let's sit. Can we sit, Jen?"

"Sure." She chose a chair while Amber and Skylar sat on the couch.

Skylar said, "Jenna, is your arm okay?"

She looked at the ugly mark. At least the stitches were out. "It doesn't hurt. The doctor said that most of the scar should eventually go away. The nurse told me to try cocoa butter. You might want to buy stock in it."

Amber smiled. "Kevin will be impressed. It's like a tattoo."

"Not funny." She noted Skylar's questioning glance. "Kevin had one tattoo before we met. *One.* I told him I hate tattoos. He got two more after we got married." That was nothing now, though, compared to his enlisting.

Skylar turned to Amber. "Are you all right?"

"I can't complain. I get my hubby home for a whole month, and I get to wear this Angelina Jolie wig."

Jenna rolled her eyes.

Amber winked at her. "Joey likes it." She turned to Skylar. "Emotionally, it will take some time. But since I woke up, I haven't had any physical problems whatsoever. Not even a slight headache."

"Thank God," Skylar whispered and took a deep breath. "I saw the guy at the protest."

"Hold on. Should you be telling us this?"

"No, but if I don't confess, I-I'll crack up. More than I have already." Tears streamed down her cheeks.

"Hey, I'm cool with being stand-in priest. I won't tell a soul—"

"But you have to tell! If you end up in court, under oath."

"Okay." Amber grasped one of Skylar's hands. "I know you saw him and you think you're responsible for my injury. That's debatable, but God has already forgiven you and so have I."

Skylar wiped her sweater sleeve across her face. "Indio says confession opens the soul up to Christ's healing like nothing else can."

"She would." Amber smiled at Jenna. "I insist on another basking visit with your grandmother. I'll even pay next time."

"Sure." Good grief. Her grandmother, mother, and these two could start their own church. Amber and Joey had spent a couple of days at the retreat center, compliments of the Beaumonts. As expected, Amber, Claire, and Indio connected like constellation stars.

Shaking off her own load of guilt, Jenna said, "Skylar, we really don't blame you. I can't connect the dots between you spotting him and what followed."

"I should have told Rosie when I saw him. I should have grabbed the nearest cop."

Jenna said, "And then what? You know he wasn't working alone. Things were already set in motion. His cohorts could have set it off if he'd been detained."

Skylar nodded sadly. "Maybe. I knew him as an eco-terrorist, not a peacenik. He—we never got involved in this kind of stuff. But I knew he made bombs. I *knew* he was up to no good. If I had listened to that intuition instead of how afraid I was of him, maybe you two and those others wouldn't have been hurt. That poor family could have had a funeral. I am so, so sorry."

Amber scooted closer and wrapped her arms around Skylar. "You are forgiven, hon. God forgives you." She began whispering. It sounded like she was praying.

Jenna wrestled with a sense of being on the outside looking in.

Later that evening, after the others had gone, Danny stopped in to help Jenna move furniture. She liked that he lived so close.

His face red, his brow sweaty, he dropped the mattress into place with a grunt. "I thought your hired movers were supposed to do this."

"They did. I just changed my mind about where I wanted the bed."

"The Princess can be fastidious and finicky."

"What's wrong with that?"

"Nothing that calling your older brother wouldn't fix. Dresser over there?"

"Yes." She watched him push and shove. "Erik wasn't available. He keeps disappearing these days with Nathan. Did they interview you yet for their documentary?"

"Yeah. Still don't have a clue what it's all about."

"They just asked me to describe my first meeting with Rosie."

"Me too. And Lexi. They're tightlipped about it." He repositioned a corner of the dresser. "How's that?"

"Fine."

"Uh-oh. I'd like a 'perfect' if possible."

"It's just fine."

"I don't want to come back tomorrow night. Tell me, what would make it perfect."

"If Kevin were sleeping in it tonight."

"In the dresser?"

"You know what I mean."

Danny slid down along the dresser and sat on the floor. "Give it up, Jen. You're married to a Marine deployed overseas. Period."

"I'm doing the best I can! I've been to two military funerals. I've spent hours on end with a woman who could have been one of my students *yesterday*, watching her lose touch with reality and totally relating to *why* she was. I've given grocery-store gift cards to most of the wives whose husbands are with Kevin because they all have little kids and hardly enough money. I check in with some of them *frequently*! What else is there?"

He clapped.

"You are such a snot."

"I am. I didn't mean to make fun. I really do applaud your efforts, Jen. I couldn't do what you're doing. But you're fueling them on resentment. Is it all aimed at Kevin?"

She sat on the bed. "If Kevin walked through that door right now, I admit we'd have to go see a marriage counselor, but I wouldn't leave him. I'm so afraid he's leaving me, either because the trauma will change him forever or because he's going to get killed."

"That's a lot of fear going on there. True, he's in a combat zone. He's in danger. You can count on the trauma doing a number on him. He will never be the same, not totally."

"Thanks. That helps a lot."

"Let me finish. 'Not the same' has its positive side. Kevin's a strong guy. He'll come through a better person in the long run."

"I'm afraid of the long run too."

"Well, he needs you to hang in there no matter how hard it is. Being afraid or resenting the situation only makes it harder on both of you. It doesn't reinstate you to princess status."

"That's for sure. Which leaves Cinderella, and I'm not so good in that role, taking care of others' messy needs."

"Without complaint." He smiled in a sad way. "You're fine in it, Jen. You've been taking care of kids' literacy needs for years. Totally messy endeavor. Now your sphere has expanded to include a group of hurting wives."

"Beth Russell told me a princess is gifted to serve others." Jenna paused, recalling the conversation. "She said I'd heard the nickname for so long it was imprinted on my heart. I'd come to believe that's who I was, a princess everyone else was supposed to take care of."

"'Your Royal Highness, you are the fairest in the land and always right and deserving of the best'?"

She wrinkled her nose. "Something like that. She encouraged me to record a new message in my heart and tell myself that being a princess means I am in a unique position to help others."

"And not just by cleaning ashes from their fireplaces."

"Yeah. Beth said . . ." Jenna bit her lip. "She said helping others is how I would make it through this season of Kevin's absence."

"There you go. That's what you are doing."

"Sort of." She wondered how that night with Cade fit into anything other than selfish indulgence.

"Jenna, God sees you as that good-hearted princess, not the snooty one. That's His message written on your heart."

"It's in invisible ink. There's a prayer for you: I need that special light that makes the ink show."

"You can pray that."

"Your prayers always work better."

"It just seems like they do." His voice rose a notch. "The only difference is I've practiced more than you have. I don't know what it is you're waiting for."

Taken aback at his agitated tone, she felt a stab of fear. In all her avoidance of God, Danny hung in there, always eager to pray for her. What was wrong?

"Jenna, what are you waiting for? There's no right or wrong way to pray. You've heard Nana say that enough. For crying out loud, just talk to Him."

"I don't know where He is."

He opened his mouth and closed it. They stared at each other in silence.

At last Danny spoke. "Turnabout is fair play. You're in love with a Marine overseas. I'm in love with a felon. Go ahead and say it: tell me to give it up."

"Give it up," she whispered.

He shook his head. "Two plus two doesn't equal four anymore. Black is white, and white is black. I don't know where God is either."

Hearing Danny question his faith sounded like a death knell to Jenna. When all was said and done, his prayers had always been the most real to her. Nana's scared her in how they transcended known entities. Amber and even her mother were too new to Jenna as prayer warriors to make an impact on her.

And her prayers? They were like quicksilver, flowing in unpredictable ways, incapable of reaching the target.

Fifty-nine

In the thirty-some years Claire had known Indio, she had seen her furious on rare occasions. She had never, though, seen her throw something and curse. Until now.

The laundry basket sailed across the kitchen, its contents spilling out onto the floor. The swear word flung behind it sang out loud and clear.

"Indio," she said with some concern as she scooped dirty towels from the floor into the basket.

"Jabberwocky!" Indio resorted to the less profane. She plopped her hands on her hips. "How on earth can a mother not come see her own daughter? I was by no means a perfect mother, but I swear I never, *never* would have ignored my sons if they asked to see me."

"Well." Skylar appeared in the doorway. "That's Marlie Rockwell for you."

Indio flung her arms wide. "Oh, child."

"You can hug me, but you can't blame my dysfunctional family for my stupid choices."

"Wouldn't dream of it." Indio bundled the young woman to herself.

Claire sighed. She had just informed Indio about the third phone conversation she'd had with David and Marlie Rockwell, Skylar's parents. They kept changing their flight. Now they'd changed who was even coming to San Diego to see their daughter in her dreadful hour of need.

The saddest part, which she dared not tell Indio, was their flippancy about the whole matter. *"Laurie's done it again."* Claire knew Laurie-aka-Skylar had never been arrested, so that could not be the 'it' they referred to, but she didn't ask. *"We always expected she'd crash and burn. She was weird as a two-year old."*

Not one word was said about reimbursing her and Max for the bail money or for hiring a lawyer. It didn't matter. They loved the girl.

She shuddered at the things they'd had to consider in recent days. Claire now even knew where the nearest FBI office was. Skylar had spent hours inside it being interviewed yet again by agents.

Skylar straightened from Indio's hug. "We might get lucky and my dad won't show either. Claire, you told him they'll send me up north as soon as they figure things out?"

"Things" referred to facts like Skylar's having nothing to do with the San Diego bombing and that her abandoning Claire's car was not grand theft. The fact that the event that took place eighteen months ago was in the northern part of the state, in a different judicial district.

Claire bent over to retrieve a dishcloth. "I told him."

"And?" Skylar prompted.

She set the laundry basket on the bench near the mudroom door. Then she sat down next to it. "And he backpedaled about coming down here since you'll be up there sooner or later."

Skylar's smile was neither happy nor sad. It signaled acceptance of an unfortunate situation.

"Sit down, honey."

Skylar and Indio sat on stools at the island.

"I realize," Claire said, "that you don't want to blame anyone for your actions, that you want to take full responsibility."

"Yes." She glanced at Indio. "Confess your sins one to another. James, right?"

"James chapter five, verse sixteen. And pray for one another."

They exchanged a knowing smile. Indio had been giving Skylar a crash course in Bible study. She said the girl soaked it up like a dried sponge. No doubt Indio had reiterated her promise to pray.

Claire said, "But you need a lawyer just to guide you through the system."

"Max keeps saying that but all I want to do is go, 'I'm guilty.' I don't want off the hook. I can say that by myself to a judge." Her zeal was a sight to behold, her eyes bright and clear, no longer hiding anything. "Max even said it was answered prayer and not the court-appointed loser lawyer that got the judge to grant bail."

"Yes, but things will get more complicated. One consideration is a plea bargain. They may ask for information in exchange for a reduced sentence."

"I don't want special treatment—"

"Skylar!" Claire was ready to throw the laundry basket herself in frustration. "It's not special. It's part of negotiating and cooperating. The bottom line is you can go to prison all you want, but we prefer it be for less than twenty years!"

"Twenty?" Skylar whispered.

"That's what this lawyer said today. It's a possibility."

Skylar bit her lip.

Against Rosie's recommendations, Skylar had given Claire and Max some of the details of the event in question. Eighteen months ago, Skylar had driven that Fin character to a lumber company office and waited while he planted pipe bombs. She did not fully realize what she was participating in. He said they were simply going to slow down the logging process. She agreed to help, desperate to save her beloved redwoods. And yes, desperate to be noticed by the likes of an antihero.

It was the only time she'd gone on what he and his group called "missions." It was to have been her ticket to be his number one, his "moll."

Until she saw the night lit up with explosives and walls tumble down . . .

Claire said, "Max told this man that you intend to plead guilty. He agreed to take your case."

"Oh, Claire. Max hired him already?"

"Yes."

She pressed her palms against her eyes. "You all do too much for me."

Indio said, "This is what family is supposed to do. Deal with it."

Skylar moved her hands. "Deal with it?"

"You heard me." Indio giggled.

It was a catchy sound. Skylar and Claire joined in, releasing tears of silliness.

Claire waited in the parking lot, holding a shawl tightly about herself. The sun had set. It was Thursday evening, the first week in November. With rainy, cooler weather and Thanksgiving on the horizon, guests' reservations had dwindled to one weekend for the month, a welcome respite considering the present upheaval.

She watched the headlights of Danny's truck approach and prayed for him and Skylar. He planned to talk with Skylar. Claire wished she could be a mouse beneath a chair as they spoke. She prayed for herself too.

She'd feared Danny's increasingly black-and-white attitude toward his faith would lead to his undoing. Either he'd turn into a whole-hearted legalist or experience a major meltdown. She should be happy for the latter. It held promise of a rebuilding.

Danny parked and climbed out. "Mom. You cutting me off at the pass?"

"If that smart tone of yours continues, you can get right back in—" She closed her mouth. He was doing it, goading her, and she was falling for it. "Let me start over. Hi."

"Hi. I'm sorry. I'm on edge."

"We all are." She took a deep breath. "I wanted to talk a minute, before you go in to see Skylar."

"I don't want to hear excuses for her."

"Danny, for goodness' sake! Let me finish one thought, please!"

He folded his arms, leaned back against the truck, and crossed one ankle over the other.

She watched him for a moment to see if he'd stay put. Except for the jiggling of his top foot, he seemed still. "I'm glad you called to say you were coming up. I'm glad you're going to address things with Skylar."

He gave a slight nod.

"But it's none of my business."

His foot stopped moving.

"When your dad and I moved up here, and then Lexi and Tuyen soon followed, I really hoped that somehow you and Jenna and Erik would fit into life here too. He was in rehab; he needed a safe place to start over. Jenna had been so lonely without Kevin. You could do your work from anywhere. We could all live here. Why not? It's a huge place, especially with the new bungalow and the mobile unit. We could make it work."

"The ocean is—"

"Shh." She scowled briefly. "It was my mama's heart yearning to be near my babies. It didn't matter how old you all are or if one of you needs to surf every day. The point is that's how I felt. Irrational? Totally."

She shoved her hands into the pockets of her cardigan and looked around. A few stars twinkled in the darkening sky. The scents of pine and mesquite and cooling earth filled her. Floodlights bathed the sign, Hacienda Hideaway ~ A Place of Retreat.

She fiddled with a key in her pocket. "I heard a sermon. I tried to ignore it, but you know how that goes." She smiled. "The part I didn't want to remember had to do with a mother and a son and a wild man. The wild man is locked up in a cage, the son is intrigued by him, the mother keeps the key to the cage under her pillow. It's time for the boy to go off with the wild man and learn the mysteries of manhood. Will he have to steal the key, or will his mother give it to him?"

Danny gazed at her, his face in shadows. "You haven't held me back."

"I have." Her laugh was uneven. "I just told you I wanted you to live here with us. I've also worried that you would fall in love with Skylar and she would break your heart. So here." She pulled the key from her pocket and placed it in his hand. "I officially give you the key. Unlock the cage and go with the wild man."

He didn't move.

"I said go."

"What's the key really to?"

"I think a padlock on the barn. The fire burned the lock. Papa had an extra key."

He smiled, leaned over, and gave her a hug. "Thanks, Mom."

Lord, I release him. Will You be his wild man?

Sixty

Skylar paced in front of the sala's large stone fireplace. Huge logs burned brightly behind the screen, warming the room.

She paced because Danny was on his way to see her.

How often he had come under the guise of helping around the hacienda. His visits had increased in the three months since she arrived at the hacienda, but he never admitted to coming specifically to see her. She was sort of like the "oh, by the way" room. *Oh, by the way, Skylar's here.* They might as well hike or ride the horses or talk into the wee hours by the fountain or kiss under the stars.

He had held back, always keeping a part of himself closed off.

As he should have. She'd warned him he did not know her. Well, now he did. And now he was coming specifically to see her.

"Lord, have mercy on me a sinner," she murmured the prayer Indio had taught her to say when she had no words of her own. When the fears and doubts overwhelmed, she was to speak simply to God, acknowledging His presence and her need of His mercy.

What else was there?

Skylar shortened the prayer, stringing the words together. "Lordhavemercy."

One of the heavy doors was opening. Skylar stopped midstride. Her heart thumped in her throat. She did not expect a smile or a hug from the guy whose smiles and hugs had become her greatest source of hope.

Indio's voice played in her mind. They had talked about her feelings toward Danny. *"Dear, you know that God is your greatest source of hope, not Danny. My grandson is a hottie and what feels like hope is simply your drooling over him."*

Skylar had nearly rolled on the floor in laughter over that one. Indio was a hoot, even more so since the truth had come out. She and Claire had been, if anything, even freer in expressing their love for Skylar. They held nothing back. They were Christ's hands and speech to her. They were the ones she should look toward, not the grim, uptight Danny walking through the door.

Evidently he'd lost Wally Cleaver somewhere on the trip up.

"Hi," she said, cringing inside at the hesitancy in her voice.

He shut the door and turned back around. "Hi."

"I'm sorry."

He held up a hand. "Let's settle this one point. I heard you the first time on the phone Sunday morning. You don't have to say it again."

Skylar bristled. "I just want that to be the premise of this conversation."

"Duly noted." He walked toward the fireplace, not looking at her.

That confirmed that no hug would accompany the no smile. She strode to the table, poured two mugs of tea from a pot, and carried them to where he sat.

He accepted one from her. "Thanks."

She sat opposite him, in the other wingback chair in front of the fire. "Thanks for coming."

"I figured we—I—uh." He cleared his throat. "Closure was needed."

Her stomach tightened. The finality of the word scared her. "Maybe some venting too."

He thrust out his lower lip and shook his head. "Hawk got that part."

"Lucky Hawk." She paused. "It'd help me if you vented."

"It'd help me if you'd been truthful."

"I told you that you didn't know me and you said you didn't give a rip. What was it? 'We are the sum of our past, mistakes and all. The sum that I've experienced in you is one that I care for deeply.' What was that? Hot air from the heat of a lustful moment?"

"I could not imagine . . ." He ran his hand through his hair. "You're going to *prison*."

"What did you expect, Danny? The usual? Sex, booze, and drugs? Would that have been acceptable to you? Sorry to be such a disappointment." She pressed her lips together, her outburst ricocheting in her chest.

He gazed at the fire, not saying anything.

"What do you need for closure?" she asked.

"Remember I mentioned to you about some old friends who influenced my judgment of you?"

"Yeah."

"There was a little more to it than that." His eyes flicked in her direction. "Faith Simmons and I were close from kindergarten through high school into college. I mean, we were tight, totally connected on everything. We even went to church together and youth Bible studies. I kept thinking it was purely platonic. She dated others. I dated others. I loved her, though, but I couldn't admit that even to myself until a few weeks ago."

"What happened to her?"

"She went flako. We were both just this side of alternative, you know? Music, movies, protests, et cetera, et cetera. Christians, but refused to limit Jesus. We explored His radical side and tried to put that into a contemporary setting." He shrugged. "She dropped out altogether, rejected everything that hinted at God. Dyed her hair, then just shaved it off. Pierced so many body parts she looked like a cheese grater." He paused. "Changed her name."

Skylar didn't know what to say.

"Sometimes I wondered if I was pressing in with you because I never took the chance with her. The resemblance was uncanny. Was I loving you or her? Or do I just have a thing for hurting females who are way out there?"

Now he was doubting that he cared for her at all? *Lordhavemercy.* "Why did she change so drastically?"

"Her father was a tyrant. I suspect more was going on than anyone knew. She had to break away. Why did you break away?"

Her memories were like wisps of smoke from fires she had not fanned in many years. She almost believed her mother was a dead drug addict buried in Ohio and that she did not know who her father was.

"My brother and sister seemed to have turned out fine. They're regular-type citizens." She shrugged. "I was the third, the unwanted runt. Ugly as all get-out. Uncoordinated. Sick all the time. Thumb-sucker and bed wetter until I was seven. We had money. We traveled. One time we were here in San Diego, at the zoo. I was eight. I got lost. They didn't miss me until they were back at the hotel. It was dark by then." She shook her head, shoving similar memories away. "My parents were ex–flower children. They gave up the VW bus but not the pot. They were glad to see me go off to college at eighteen and never come back. I only checked in with them now and then so they didn't report me as missing and sic the cops on me. Waste of a calling card, I'm sure." She wiped roughly at the tears on her face. "Sad enough for you?"

He rubbed his temple. "Yeah. I'm sorry."

"Yeah. No excuse—"

"It is. It is an excuse. Not for your choices, but for having been dealt nothing but junk." He sounded angry. "The cards were stacked against you from the get-go. It wasn't right or natural, Skylar. You can't let your parents off the hook. Don't wallow in the past, but go ahead and blame them for the beatings they inflicted on your psyche."

"Shouldn't I forgive them?"

"Of course. Forgive them and whoever hurt them. Just stop letting the past define you." He exhaled loudly, as if he'd run out of steam.

The moments passed. Danny stood abruptly and threw logs into the fireplace. They thumped loudly, sparks flew. He jammed the poker against the logs. The fire hissed and popped.

Skylar wiped her nose and gulped tea. She hadn't even told Indio or Claire the details she'd just revealed to him. He drew from her deep heart.

"Danny, I started praying in Illinois."

He sat back down, his face red.

"And I know God heard me." She tried to smile. "You'd get religion too if you were in my shoes."

He didn't respond.

"You helped me see myself as someone He could really love. Thank you."

"He loves everyone. I've always believed that."

"And He forgives everyone and asks us to do the same." She leaned forward. "Will you forgive me?"

"I forgive you."

She shut her eyes. *Thank You, God.*

"Those are easy words for me to say. Maybe too easy. Too automatic."

She looked at him. "I'm not asking for anything more. The FBI could show up here at any minute and whisk me off to San Francisco. Then they'll lock me up for a long time. That doesn't leave much space for a relationship."

"Thanks for letting me off the hook." Sarcasm laced his tone. "The truth is we both botched this from the beginning. We both pretended you were someone you weren't. So." He stood. "I plan to split too."

"What?"

"Out of the country. Maybe I'll surf my way around the world. Ireland. Portugal. Australia. I might even stop off in Baghdad and see old Kev."

Skylar couldn't move. He was leaving his family? Work and

friends? Her, for sure. She didn't realize she was clinging to a slender thread of hope until just now. It snapped almost audibly. The falling sensation was so real she clutched the arm of the chair.

He said, "I don't exactly know how to say good-bye."

"Just go." She was about to lose it, but refused to do it in front of him again.

He held out his hand to shake hers.

"I said just go, Danny. Just get out of my sight."

"Yeah." He looked at her for a moment, turned, and left the room.

Skylar's angels found her, a messy heap on the braided rug in front of the hearth.

"Oh, child." Indio patted her back.

Claire helped her stand. "Let's sit on the couch. Nana's knees aren't up for the floor tonight."

She sat squished between them, held upright by their shoulders. She laid her head on Claire's shoulder. Indio held her hand.

"He's so hurt," Skylar sobbed.

Claire dabbed tissues on her face.

"I'm so sorry I hurt your son." She tilted her head to see Indio. "Your grandson."

"Well," Indio said, "it was bound to happen. Better by someone we love than some hussy."

Claire said, "His faith has mirrored Indio's since he was a little kid. But somewhere along the way this dogmatic streak got hold of him. When Max and I had marital struggles, he practically disowned us. 'Under no circumstances do Christians couples separate' was his thinking." Her sigh conveyed sorrow and resolve. "His inability to see grays was bound to undo him, but he has to work it out for himself. He's so much like my brother. He's not going to Alaska, is he?"

Skylar shook her head. "Australia."

"Oh, Lord."

Indio said, "He'll be all right. God's not going to let him out of His sight."

"Can we pray for him?" Through her tears she saw the two staring at her in surprise. "What?"

Indio looked at Claire. "I told you. She's growing by leaps and bounds."

Claire smiled. "And how do we pray for you, honey?"

Skylar hesitated. Danny's admonition had made it clear what she needed, but she didn't want to go there. She really didn't want to go there.

But . . . of course she had to.

"Danny said I need to forgive my parents for how they hurt me."

Indio nodded and stroked her hand. "Danny understands."

Claire hummed softly for a moment. Max had apologized to all four of their adult children for being an absentee father. "Parents can send signals to our hearts that name us in ways God never intended. When we forgive them, our hearts can heal. God can then plant His own signal in us. We can receive our true name from Him."

Did that mean her true name was not 'unwanted runt'? "What's mine?"

"Precious, cherished daughter of the heavenly Father."

Skylar closed her eyes. How she longed to hear those words spoken in her heart!

Claire and Indio prayed—for Danny . . . for her. And she knew they carried her to the throne.

Sixty-one

The computer screen shone brightly in the dark room. It displayed Monday flights to Australia. Under that window were others: client-related files, Ro-Bo Shop spreadsheets, bank accounts, and unfinished e-mails. The clock in the low corner read 2:21.

Danny had always been able to juggle countless thoughts and tasks simultaneously. A spur-of-the-moment checking out of life, however, was proving to be freaking impossible.

It was the emotions. An avalanche of *feeling* buried any clear-cut order.

All he had to do was click the "Buy now" icon, pack a pair of jeans, wetsuit, and board, hand off work details. He had enough money. He had a passport.

Laue, the young guy he mentored, had been chomping at the bit to take on more. He even had a rapport with clients. As far as the shop went, Hawk ran it by himself with a few hired college kids. Tuyen no longer needed his computer lessons; she had a job in Santa Reina.

So why did he hesitate?

He needed to talk to someone.

His roommate, Hawk, would laugh and say, "Welcome to the club, dude." The guy was head-over-heels with Tuyen, a match Danny still couldn't fathom.

Erik? Ditto. There was a sense of permanency about him and Rosie.

His dad? His hero, the guy he wanted to be a clone of? He'd sold his business last year to make hot chocolate with his wife for retreat guests.

His pastor? He'd point him to God.

Danny knew only one person who could hear him, give him new eyes, and make him laugh at himself.

But she was going to prison.

He clicked the icon.

Sixty-two

Speechless, Jenna listened to Danny on the phone. He was leaving the next day for Australia?

"You can't." She walked down the hall, into her bedroom. "You just can't."

"Give me a break, Jen."

"Oh, I don't really mean it. But still." A fresh wave of abandonment washed over her.

"I gotta get my head on straight."

"Good grief, how old are you anyway? You were supposed to do this when you were in high school! Lexi will have a fit."

"She didn't. She has Nathan now. Moving right along, how are you doing?"

She huffed and sat on her bed. "Fine."

He waited.

"Better. I have made conscious efforts to sit still and talk to God. Three times. For about a minute and a half."

He chuckled. "Each?"

"Yes. I think I'm almost to the point of believing He's close enough to listen."

"That's great progress."

"And I'm throwing a barbecue even as we speak. Marine wives and children. Amber's here too. Joey left yesterday, so she's bummed."

"The benevolent princess gathers her kingdom."

"Shut up."

"Bye, sis. I'll be in touch."

A lump filled her throat. She whispered, "Bye."

She turned off the phone. Why did he have to go too? The brother she counted on to pray for her, even when she wasn't interested.

Maybe it was her turn to pray for him.

"God, if You're listening, please screw his head on right and keep him safe."

Jenna, I really think you'd like my church." Amber pushed the automatic ice dispenser button on the refrigerator door. The machine cranked into gear and ice cubes plunked into the bucket she held. "Wow." She raised her voice above the noise. "You sure scored with this fridge, didn't you? Niiiice rental."

Jenna paused in tossing a salad and narrowed her eyes at Amber until the racket stopped. "Which question do you want answered first?"

Amber smiled. "I only asked one. Don't get bent all out of shape. The church comment was a comment."

"You've never made such a comment before."

"Hmm. Must not have been time until now." She set the ice bucket on the countertop. "You have mentioned how your parents' church is too small and traditional and Danny's is too big and odd. Mine might be just right, Goldilocks. But I really am impressed with this fridge."

"I don't know if I'm ready."

"Fair enough. You will—know when you're ready, I mean. You're welcome anytime. I'll take this tray outside."

"Thanks. Be there in a minute."

Everyone was in her backyard. She could hear their laughter. The house was perfect for entertaining with its gas grill, patio table, and a grassy area for a wading pool that Jenna had bought for the kids. Not to mention the automatic ice dispenser.

With Danny she had teased about the one and a half minutes

with God. In truth, she had been sensing something different most of the time since they had talked Wednesday night.

Maybe it had something to do with Kevin's two e-mails since then, his expressions of love.

Maybe it had something to do with caring for others. Preparing for the barbecue with her new friends had energized her. Having them in her home calmed her.

Maybe it had something to do with confessing her adultery to God every single day. She didn't know if it would ever "take," if she would ever be relieved of the shame, but whenever she prayed, there were slivers of light in the darkness. It was enough to keep her functioning one day at a time.

The phone rang. She picked up the cordless and noticed the caller ID. It blurred except for one word: *Govt.*

No, no, no!

"Hello."

"Is this Mrs. Jenna Mason?" It was a female voice. "Wife of Sergeant Kevin D. Mason?"

"Yes." Her voice was barely a whisper.

"I'm sorry, ma'am. Your husband has been injured."

The world careened off its axis.

Jenna moved like an automaton responding to the directions of others. "Drink this. Eat that. Sit down." Their questions, asked in hushed voices, were endless. "Where's his mother's number, honey? What jacket do you want to take? Do you want this handbag or that one? How about a hot bath? A salad?"

Her new little house was wall-to-wall people. Amber, Miranda, and two other wives were still there—friends without children in tow. Jenna's parents, grandparents, Lexi, Erik, Tuyen, Skylar, Danny had all arrived within the hour. Rosie and even Nathan had stopped in at some point.

"It was an IED. Improvised explosive device."

By now Miranda had heard from her husband. He was fine. The others were fine. They'd been on foot patrol, Kevin a few steps ahead of one of them.

A few steps ahead. Which put him in that exact spot at that exact time, ensuring that he took the impact, received the wound.

A chill went through her.

He didn't choose.

He got chosen. Like being given some cosmic assignment, *he got chosen.*

Did they know which part of his body was injured? He had been walking, a guarantee—despite flak jacket and helmet—that it was bad. How bad?

"How bad?" she had asked Miranda.

"He only said it wasn't his head."

She sat on her bed now, clutching a pillow to her stomach, and watched. Lexi pulled clothes from dresser drawers and closet. Her mother folded them and tucked them into a suitcase.

Lexi said, "Jen, where's your passport?"

"I don't know. I don't think it's unpacked yet."

"No, I'm sorry, ma'am, I don't know the extent of his injuries."

Lexi said, "So it's in a box, in the garage. Marked 'desk' or 'personal files'?"

Her sister seemed suddenly older. Her face came into sharp focus. The shy girl disinterested in clothes and makeup was gone. She was succinctly putting together Jenna's travel wardrobe and cosmetics.

"Lex, you feel . . . solid."

Lexi gave her a quizzical look. "Mind if I put Skylar on the passport hunt? She's looking for a job to do and I don't think she needs another ID."

Claire *tsk*ed.

"Just kidding, Mom. She likes it when I do."

Jenna said, "It's in a plastic tub. Files."

"Mrs. Mason, is anyone there with you? Can I call someone for you?"

Amber had been the first to hear her cries from the patio. The others rushed in right behind her and swarmed about her. Jenna didn't have to do a thing but sink to the floor and be hugged. Somebody took the phone from her. Somebody gave her water. Somebody helped her to the couch and wrapped an afghan around her. Somebody turned off the oven. Somebody called her mom.

Very princess-style.

"He's in emergency surgery in Baghdad. Getting the best care in the world. As soon as he's stable, they'll medevac him to Germany. You can meet him there."

Her mom sat down beside her. "Honey, are you sure you don't want Dad to go with you too?"

"I'm sure."

"Danny will take good care of you, I know."

Lexi said, "You should have seen him go at it with Erik's boss that night at the news station." She referred to the time Danny was watching the local news and saw his brother the newscaster, drunk as a skunk on live TV. By the time the program ended, Danny was at the station, chewing out the manager for letting Erik go on-air in such a condition. "Nobody but nobody was going to hurt his big brother. He will definitely take care of you."

"It's impossible to say how long."

Claire pulled Jenna close and leaned back against the headboard.

Jenna shut her eyes. She hadn't cried. No more tears were needed. She had wept incessantly for six months over the possibility of what had just occurred. It was over.

Jenna sat, zombielike, in an armchair. Everyone circled about. Everyone insisted on one thing or another.

Danny declared he was going with her to Germany. He was

packed already and had changed his ticket. There was nothing to discuss. Her mother and grandmother would spend the night. Her dad would drive them to the airport in the morning. Lexi would take care of her mail and yard. Amber would call Cade. Papa advised Jenna to take something to help her sleep.

I can't be knocked out. Her mind screamed. *What if they call? What if they come here, those special Marines in their special car to pay me a special visit?*

It was late. Jenna wanted them all to go home, but her mind would not stop racing long enough to insist upon her own things.

What did she know about IEDs? They blew up. They did indescribable things to people, things that her imagination now displayed in full color.

Miranda, her new friend with the dimples that never went away, crouched down in front of her. "We're going home. Promise to call me if we can do anything."

Jenna nodded.

The dimples deepened. "Ooh-rah, girl."

Two more wives hugged her, one at a time, each whispering, "Ooh-rah."

Ooh-rah. Yes, ooh-rah.

Jenna was the wife of a Marine. There were things she had to finish before she went to be with her husband.

She thanked her family, but sent them all home. It must have been something in her firm tone that silenced any protest. She asked Amber to stay a bit longer.

They sat on the couch. Jenna said, "You called Cade?"

She nodded. "He's upset, naturally. He said he'd call the substitute teacher back who's been in your room since you've been off."

"Thank you." She paused. "I have a—a pretty weird request."

Amber cocked her head. "Under the circumstances, you have total dispensation from 'weird.' Nothing you say or do will be held against you."

"I was hoping for a little less courtroom and more church. Like you did with Skylar the other day."

"Huh? You mean when I listened to her confession?"

"Yes. I need to say this out loud and I can't tell my mom. It'd hurt her so much. And Danny—well, he's just got enough on his plate right now. Amber, I saw you with Skylar. You're the only person who might understand. Please don't hate me."

"I could never hate you, Jenna, no matter what." Amber took one of her hands and held it tightly between hers. "Go ahead. I'm listening."

"I-I . . ." *Oh, God, help.* She gulped a deep breath. "I slept with Cade."

Amber's eyes grew large. She didn't move a muscle. She seemed to stop breathing.

"The night after the funeral. I just couldn't handle being scared and alone anymore."

Two big tears spilled from Amber's eyes and slid slowly down her cheeks. "Oh, Jenna."

"Don't hold it against Cade. I pressured him into it."

Amber winced.

"Amber, did God hurt Kevin to punish me?"

"No, Jenna. Oh, no. He doesn't treat us that way."

She wasn't convinced but continued to unload her pent-up fears. "How can I bring Kevin home to this? He'll hate me. It's the worst thing I could have done to him. I know I did it in part to get back at him for leaving me, for going to that awful place. I'm not making excuses, but that's the truth."

"He'll forgive you, Jenna."

"What if he doesn't? Why would he?"

Amber squeezed her hand. "Shh. Let's take care of first things first. Make your confession to God—"

"To God! Why would He listen to me? I am so ashamed."

"Jenna, He's always listening because He loves us just as we are. I bet Kevin doesn't love you any less first thing in the morning than when you're all gussied up for a date night. God's like that. He's not going to turn us away because our lives are a mess."

"But how can He ever forgive me?"

"He already did, when Jesus died. Talk to Him. Tell Him what you're telling me."

Jenna closed her eyes to shut out Amber's tearful face. How many times had she heard similar teaching from her grandmother? For thirty years Nana's words had fallen on deaf ears and a stone-cold heart.

But now—having committed the emotional equivalent of murdering her husband—she could suddenly hear. Her heart ached so badly she thought it might literally break apart.

"Lord, I am so sorry. Please, please forgive me f-for . . ." She swallowed.

"Name it," Amber whispered.

"It's so awful." She expelled a loud breath. "Forgive me for committing adultery. Please keep Kevin safe right now, in surgery or on the plane or wherever he is. And please, please, please let him be able to forgive me."

Silent moments passed. Jenna felt nothing. And then . . . a subtle lessening of the ache, a faint light in the blackness that had filled her soul. Hope stirred within her. Whatever her daily pleas had been, they had not been confession. They had not been this true acknowledgment of sin before the living and holy God.

Amber said, "Father, thank You for hearing the cries of Your child. Fill her up with Your mercy. Let her know she is forgiven."

A distinct sense of release settled over Jenna. Yes indeed, God had heard her cries at last and He had answered.

Finally, she began to cry.

Sixty-three

Monday morning Claire sat with Indio and Skylar in the hacienda kitchen, sipping coffee. Plates and the remains of breakfast littered the table. Nobody moved to clear it.

Skylar said, "Well, thanks for the last meal, ladies."

Indio smacked her forearm with a teaspoon. "Enough with the gallows humor. You're just going away for a little while."

"You have God's word on that?"

"Yes, I do, as a matter of fact. He told me the moment you said 'last meal.' Receive it, child." Skylar smiled. "Okay."

Claire sniffed and smashed a napkin to her face. Jenna and Danny were on their way to Germany to be with Kevin. Rosie was due any minute now to pick up Skylar. Their police friend had somehow convinced the FBI that she would escort Skylar to the airport for them.

Too much letting go all at once.

They sat in silence. The clock ticked and tocked. It was a sunny day.

Lexi and Tuyen had already said their good-byes to Skylar earlier in the morning before they left for work. Now, Ben and Max waited outside for Rosie.

All too soon they ushered in Rosie. Erik, surprisingly, followed. Lately his consulting work with a production company had kept him busy.

They said their good-byes in the kitchen. One by one hugs were

315

exchanged. Indio prayed softly as she hugged Skylar. Claire waited to embrace her last.

"We will visit you, Skylar," she whispered into her hair. "I promise you that. You are like a daughter to me. I love you very much."

Skylar nodded.

And then she was gone.

No one moved or said anything.

Erik broke the silence. "Did you notice, no handcuffs? Rosie said she wouldn't put them on until she has to at the airport."

Claire's stomach turned, grateful that Rosie said it would be best if they parted at the house. It would have humiliated Skylar further to do so in public.

She said, "Your Rosie takes good care of us."

"Yes, she does. Speaking of Rosie, my video camera is in the car." He waggled his brows at Claire, Max, Indio, and Ben. "Ta-da! It's interview time. I figured you'd all need a diversion right about now."

Ben harrumphed and strode toward the door. "I got horses to tend to. Just lost my best helper."

"I'll catch you out there, Papa."

Max followed his father. "I'll be somewhere."

"Chicken."

Indio moved toward the couch. "I really need a nap. Later, maybe."

"Night-night." Erik turned to Claire. "Mom. Puh-lease don't run out on me."

"What is this project all about?"

"I told you I'd teased Rosie, not long after we met, about turning her life into a movie. Well, I got started with Nathan's help. At first it was a documentary about this amazing policewoman, but then it turned into something else. Which is still a secret from her and everyone. Are you game?"

Claire looked around the kitchen and sighed, already missing Skylar. "Sure."

"Meet me in the sala in three." He rushed out the door.

This is my mother, Claire Beaumont." Seated on the couch beside her, Erik spoke toward the video camera he'd set up on a tripod. He used his so-called professional voice, which wasn't much different from his everyday one, perhaps a touch smoother. He always did have an ease with speech and sounds that inspired others to listen.

"Erik, you really are gifted in front of a camera."

"Mom." He moved his head in a circle. "Later."

"Oh. Sorry."

"No worries. I'll edit this stuff out." He sat unblinking, statue still. When he spoke again, he was back in character. "Claire and my father raised four children and now, in their latter years, have taken over my grandparents' Hacienda Hideaway, a retreat center near Santa Reina, California. They—"

"'Latter years?' I can't even see sixty on the horizon."

He blinked. "When do latter years begin?"

"I don't know. Not yet, though. Do they?"

"I'd say postfifty, fifty-five."

"That's because you're hardly postthirty. Just you wait. Fifty is young. Fifty-five is prime time, nowhere near the downward side of life."

He blinked again. "Tell you what, Mom. I'll record this intro part later. Let me move over here." He went to a chair beside the camera. "And you just talk to me. Tell me about the first time you met Rosie Delgado."

"Should I look at that red light on the camera?"

"Whatever you're most comfortable with. Me, the camera, the ceiling."

"I'd look pretty silly talking to the ceiling."

His composed, handsome face revealed nothing. The growl revealed a lot.

"Erik, maybe now is not a good time. I'm a little on edge. As a matter of fact, I think I may now understand how you felt that night you went on the air after drinking because you were upset over Felicia. You had to go on. You had a job to do. You did some stupid things, but sometimes life can push us so hard we behave irrationally.

"Like the second time I met Rosie. You were in the hospital because of what she had done to you and there I was, sitting at her father's restaurant, waiting to meet her. I was curious what kind of woman could do a thing like that. Lexi had told me she was special, though, in a good way. But naturally I harbored some ill will toward her. I mean, after all, she did shoot you.

"Then she walked up. She didn't look anything like a cop in her flouncy blouse and skirt. And, oh! Her expression was pure anguish. The first thing she said was how sorry she was. Her only concern was for your well-being. What could I do but hug her? Now I love her like a daughter."

She paused, overcome with a sense of *motherhood*. It was a dance of complex steps, but there was a rhythm to it, a consistent beat. It must have begun with her first pregnancy: Hold them close, let them go. Hold them close, let them go. Shelter them in the womb, present them to the world.

Now others had joined in the dance. Claire stubbed her toe time and again following the unfamiliar steps. *Is Kevin the right one for Jenna? Rosie's world can never mesh with Erik's. Nathan better not hurt Lexi. Skylar can't possibly be Danny's match.*

But her mama's heart stretched and they all fit into place. Her feet learned the new pattern.

She said, "I love Skylar like a daughter too. I love Kevin like a son. Nathan is taking up residence in my heart right next to him. With my own four in there, it's getting to be a crowded place. My prayers grow longer. Every single day I have to let each and every one of you go.

'Lord, they're Yours.' This letting-go business is harder than I ever imagined. Good grief, if I had grandkids, I'd never get off my knees."

The room came back into focus. She didn't know what she'd been facing as she talked but now she searched Erik's eyes. "But this video is about Rosie. Well, all I have to say is, Erik, she's the best thing that's ever happened to you. If you don't marry her, that would be really dumb." She exhaled. "Now, if I may be excused, I'm going to take a long, hot bath and a longer nap. Was that MIT?"

"MIT?"

"You know, too much information?"

He gave her a slow smile. "No. Not TMI at all, Mom." He pushed a button on the camera. "And that's a wrap."

Claire only hoped the day was a wrap.

And it wasn't even noon.

Sixty-four

*D*_{*éjà vu.*}

It was all Jenna could think. She had already lived the scene two months before. Why was she in it again?

There was that all-encompassing aura of *hospital.* Antiseptic odors. Soft beeps and hisses. The squish of rubber soles against linoleum. Harsh lights. Muted voices.

ICU.

There were differences, though.

Kevin waited on the other side of those doors, not Amber.

Jenna was family, no fudge factor necessary.

Danny sat beside her, not her parents.

Outside the walls lay Germany, not her hometown. She'd never visited the country, had never intended to. The November day was frigid and overcast.

The nurse Sammie said, "You don't know yet?" She wore her black hair in a tight bun. Compassion poured from eyes of liquid gold. Her posture had military written all over it. Insignia lined her blouse.

Jenna shook her head. No, they didn't know any details about Kevin yet except that he was alive and on the other side of those doors.

Danny said, "We feel like we've been given the runaround."

"I'm sorry. It can seem like that at times. Overall, your husband is doing very well. I talked with him, and his attitude is fantastic. He wanted to stay awake until you got here, but the pain got pretty intense, so we upped his medication."

A shudder went through Jenna. Kevin didn't do meds. For him there was no such thing as intense pain.

Sammie said, "He's heavily sedated at the moment, but you'll be talking to him in no time. Technically, he's in stable condition, but we want to keep a close eye on him tonight. His trip here on top of everything . . ." Her voice trailed off.

Jenna leaned against Danny. He wrapped an arm around her shoulders. Gone was the Tigger-like kid of their youth. He was a solid rock for her, guiding them steadily through a maze of airports, planes, a strange city, a military base . . . It seemed that with each passing mile they had both matured.

Danny said, "Technically, what exactly is 'everything'?"

Sammie took a breath. "Kevin lost a leg in the blast."

A whimper sounded from Jenna's inmost being.

The nurse went on. "The left one. It was severed at the time of impact just below the knee. The doctors in Baghdad amputated at midthigh. Mrs. Mason, he will walk again with a prosthetic. He will run and play ball and do everything again."

The woman faded from view as images of her big, strong, muscular, athletic Kevin filled her mind, a gangly piece of plastic hanging from his thigh. How could he ever do the same things? Be the same man?

Danny said, "What are his other injuries?"

Other? Dear God.

Sammie said, "There was no trauma to the brain, which is a major blessing. His left side received shrapnel. His arm sustained third-degree burns. These are all wounds that will heal."

Jenna moaned. "His left arm?"

"Yes."

"His tattoos."

"Ma'am?"

"His tattoos. Are they still there?"

"I-I'm sorry, ma'am. I haven't seen beneath the dressing."

She cried softly. Kevin loved his tats. The USMC one had already been in place when she first met him. A more recent, small one engraved near it was in memory of a young man killed in the war. She had fussed like a crazed woman over its addition.

Danny said to the nurse, "What about his back?" He stretched an arm to the back of his shoulder. "His shoulders. Any injuries there?"

"No."

Danny laid his chin atop Jenna's head. "Then he's still got the one, Jen," he whispered. "The one he would say is the most important."

Danny referred to the "JEN" across Kevin's shoulders in large calligraphy. When Kevin had it done without her knowledge, they had argued hotly over it . . . over the definition of art . . . over the expression of love.

What a stupid thing to argue about. What an idiotic thing to harbor ill will toward.

She sobbed.

The nurse led them into Kevin's room.

Jenna held tightly to Danny's hand and entered.

Tubes. Wires. Bags. Monitors. Machines. Hissing. Beeping.

She was on Kevin's right side. She moved nearer the bed, Danny next to her, their hands entwined.

Kevin's body dwarfed the bed. His arms lay atop a white blanket, the left wrapped, the right with IV tubes taped into place. A short-sleeved hospital gown covered his neck and chest.

He wore his troubled expression, the space between his brows creased into a vertical line. He'd had a haircut recently. The buzzed blond hair was nearly invisible. It was evident in his face that he had lost weight. His skin was dark and shiny against the white pillow cover.

How had he described the desert conditions? *"It's a freaking spa here, Jen,"* he wrote once in an e-mail. *"You're going to love my new look—120 degrees and sandblasting wind have done wonders. Got a tan to die for, no trace of love handles, and the free microdermabrasion treat-ments are bee-utifying my complexion."* She still remembered the smiley faces he'd added.

She studied his form outlined under the blanket. Chest, torso . . . right thigh, right knee, right calf, right foot. A thick bulge on his left side.

Jenna let go of Danny's hand and walked around the bed.

She touched the emptiness below Kevin's left thigh. She bent over and pressed her lips to what remained of his leg, hoping the kiss would penetrate through the hard cast. "Love you, Kev," she whispered.

She walked back around to his other side and touched the bed. The narrow lane between him and the edge would be enough. She turned halfway and scooted her hip onto it.

"Ma'am—"

"I'm lying down with my husband."

"Ma'am, I'm sorry, you can't—"

"I am lying down with my husband."

Danny said, "Nurse, please?" His face was wet with tears. "For a moment?"

Jenna stopped listening. She climbed onto the bed, careful of the tubes in his arm. She settled on her side against him, tucking one arm beneath herself, carefully laying the other across his stomach.

Someone stood behind her, steady against her back. It would be Danny, propping her up, keeping her from falling.

She whispered, "I'm here, Kevin. We're going to be all right. We're going to be just fine."

She continued to talk, telling him about the trip with Danny, about the whole family, about Skylar, about Miranda and the other wives. She teased him about wanting a medal, about the idiotic way he chose to get an early out.

He could hear her, she knew.

She would keep on talking until she saw his gorgeous sky-at-dusk blue eyes twinkle at her . . . until she heard him call her "pretty lady."

Sixty-five

Danny's head ached but if he unclenched his jaw, the weeping would start and progress quickly to wailing. Totally undudelike.

He blamed the doctor seated across the table from him and Jenna. A little less compassion from the MD would have helped. But no. The guy swam in an ocean of it, riding its wave on into the room where they had met him a few minutes before.

Dr. Adams removed his black-rimmed glasses and pinched the bridge of his nose. When he looked again at them, his eyes glistened. "The good news is you've already heard the bad news. From here on out it'll be only hopeful or challenging news. I can already tell that Kevin is totally on board with this way of thinking."

Jenna nodded. His sister vacillated between catatonic responses and a take-charge demeanor. Every last vestige of a whiny princess had been blasted from her attitude.

Adams said, "He's not going to sit around feeling sorry for himself. His main concern is you, Mrs. Mason."

"Me?"

"He asked me to pray for you to have the strength to hang in there."

Danny watched thoughts parade across Jenna's face as clearly as if she spoke them. Any caring person would not want to see his loved ones suffer over his distress, but Kevin's concern stemmed from his wife's "princess" status. He not only teased her over it, he often encouraged it in the way he catered to her.

Jenna's face relaxed. She flashed a smile. "Ooh-rah."

Dr. Adams grinned. "Ooh-rah." His expression softened again beneath a halo of neatly trimmed silver hair. "You can take him home soon, perhaps by Saturday. We want to wean him off the IV drugs. I'm guessing his pain tolerance level is high. We also have to wait for the swelling to go down in the residual limb."

Danny mentally translated that reference to mean what was left of Kevin's leg. He wondered if this was hopeful or challenging news.

"Home?" Jenna said.

"Home to the States, to San Diego."

"To the Wounded Warrior facility."

He nodded. "He's part of the C5 program."

Danny shut his eyes briefly. Hopeful or challenging news? Kevin had visited the facility, had met amputees during their rehab. Now he'd be one of them.

The doctor said, "They have state-of-the art everything. They'll take care of him and you, Mrs. Mason, from here on out."

"Call me Jenna."

He nodded. "They offer everything from counseling to climbing walls and obstacle courses to expertise in prosthetics. Okay?"

"Okay, as long as it's not me doing the climbing."

He smiled.

"How long are we talking, Doctor?"

"Above-the-knee amputees need at least, on average, twelve months of rehab. When the knee is intact, the use of a prosthesis comes more easily."

"But we're talking about Kevin."

"Right. Scratch half of what I say."

"Already have. He's going to be an outpatient in no time."

Danny wondered who the woman was living inside his sister's body.

Dr. Adams said, "Kevin will experience phantom pains that over time will become more of a sensation. His brain thinks the limb is still there. I've heard bizarre stories of what it feels like. You and Kevin and the therapists will figure out how best to live with it."

"That's what this all comes down to, doesn't it? Figuring out how best to live with these changes. Hey, Danny." She looked at him. "Don't you think Kevin's going to be really glad not to have to hike up two flights of stairs to an apartment?"

"He's going to love the house, Jen. Great foresight."

"Foresight? Danny, get a grip. God was taking care of things. As Nana would say, He is good."

Definite alien in place.

Too keyed to sleep, Danny and Jenna sat in the hospital cafeteria, drank coffee, and waited for Kevin to waken.

"Jen, Kevin's going to be proud of his princess."

"I doubt that. I only quit being a royal pain in the neck the night we heard he'd been injured. I think that was just last night?"

"Depends on what continent you're on."

"Anyway, we're talking seven months of unhinged and at least two of making really dumb mistakes."

"The war is the really dumb mistake."

"Danny, come on. I'm not going to blame circumstances. What's happened has happened. We have a long row to hoe. We're going to need marriage counseling on top of everything else. No doubt I'll cry some more, but guess what? Whining isn't going to put Kevin's body back together."

"Wow, what has happened to you?"

"What do you mean?"

He widened his eyes at her.

She shrugged. "Well, I just realized what you've been telling me all along. That God loves me. And . . . and forgives me. Call me slow to catch on, but there it is."

"Hmm."

"I was actually living my dream life, you know. I was married to a bona fide hottie. I was a teacher thinking about the day I could quit and have a baby."

"Was there something wrong with that?"

"It was all about me. About me being comfortable and looking good. Suddenly that's not my priority. I was praying on the airplane over here for Kevin, of course, and Miranda and those other wives and kids, especially poor Evie. And our whole family and Skylar and Rosie and Nathan, Tuyen and Hawk. Then I got going on the doctors and nurses helping Kevin. Then I ran out of words. I had no words but I felt like I was groaning inside for others. Where is all this coming from, Danny?"

"God's Spirit."

"Really?"

"Jenna, you've heard this stuff your whole life from Nana."

"Obviously I wasn't listening." She tossed her hair over her shoulder. "I know what your problem is with Skylar."

He stared at her.

"It's so all about you, Danny. It's about you being hurt by Faith Simmons eons ago. It's about you being hurt by Skylar. It's about you looking like a horse's rear end because your girlfriend is in prison. You really need to quit wallowing in self-pity and get over yourself."

"Yeah, yeah. I admit it."

"Good." She abruptly pushed back her chair. "Kevin's awake."

"Huh? How do you know he's awake?"

"The Holy Spirit?" She shrugged and hurried toward the exit.

He followed at a slower pace. The new Jenna had taken the old Jenna's bossiness to another level. It was as if the princess had grown into queen and understood how to exercise her increased power to its fullest extent. She would be all right on her own.

He wondered how soon he could get on a plane.

Like a fly on the wall, Danny watched Jenna and Kevin's reunion. He had hesitated but she had insisted he be that near.

He loved Kevin like a brother. He was a guy's kind of guy. Athletic, funny, loyal. Danny had never understood how the man could fall for his sister until now. Maybe he had sensed the emergent woman beneath the pouting royal pain in the neck, the woman who would eventually stand by him through thick and thin.

Jenna practically melted into Kevin. "Hey, Kev."

"Hey." His voice rasped. "You really here?"

"Yeah." She kissed him full on the mouth for an embarrassingly long time.

"Oh, man." He chuckled. "My hallucinations never hit me like that." His eyes strayed over her shoulder. "Danny?"

"Yeah. Hey."

"Hey. Now I know this is for real 'cause you sure never showed up in my dreams."

"I'm glad to hear that, buddy."

Kevin struggled to move his arm, giving Jenna more space to scoot in close. "How you doing, pretty lady?"

"Good, Kev, I'm good. Now that I can see your blue eyes. We're going to be all right."

He touched her face. "I screwed up big-time."

"Yeah, you did. But I love you more than ever."

The scene blurred. Danny excused himself and went in search of a phone to call the airlines.

Sixty-six

Within forty-eight hours of grasping his brother-in-law's hand in a hospital in Germany, Danny was sitting on Bells Beach in southern Australia. A chill went through him as he studied awesome waves that bore little resemblance to San Diego's typical surf.

Was he insane?

All things being equal, he had no doubt he could handle the challenge of the swells before him. He'd practically grown up on a board. He'd won local contests through the years. He'd surfed the monsters in Hawaii.

But things weren't exactly equal these days.

He'd lost his first love. Not Faith Simmons. Not Skylar. No. It was the God he'd known since as far back as he could remember.

The surf pounded in his chest. Its roar filled his head.

He had left Jenna in a good space. Unlike ever before, his sister was running on all cylinders. She felt absolutely no trepidation about getting Kevin home. Her biggest concern was how to handle his mother, who would visit from Indiana. She was a difficult personality even Nana avoided.

Danny had flown to Melbourne, rented a car, driven to Torquay on the coast, purchased a surfboard, checked into a motel, and called Lexi. The only unmarked item on his agenda was to use the board. If Jenna was right, his wallow in self-pity had just swung into high gear. It was party time for the ego.

With his mind he understood that he had bought into his grand-parents' faith with few questions asked. Christ was real to them; He was real to Danny. They talked to Him in an ongoing conversation; he talked to Him in an ongoing conversation. They went to church; he went to church. The whole world should follow suit.

He'd always said the right words because he knew them, because he saw them work in Papa and Nana and in his own life. But his rational mind went into overdrive, especially—*yeah, yeah, okay*. Especially around the time Faith Simmons exited the scene. He needed to take the legalistic path, needed a way that provided an answer for everything and bypassed the heart.

But he'd experienced heart connections with the almighty God. He had . . .

As a tyke . . . Papa put him on a boogie board and told him in his booming voice to ride with the Holy One, the Creator of the wind and the seas, the One who put the curl in the wave just so, the perfect place for Danny to meld into the Father's embrace.

As a kid . . . his dad signed him up for surf camps.

As a twelve-year-old . . . Nana slipped him money to buy his first board.

As a thirteen-year-old . . . he entered his first surfing contest.

As a seventeen-year-old . . . he floated on a glassy sea, mentally connecting the dots for a Web site design that led him into a career he cared for passionately.

The connections always involved the surf and his grandfather's words. *Ride with the Holy One.*

The echo of Papa's voice had faded. Just as well. Danny needed to hear another voice and meld again with Him. If there was a way back to his first love, it would happen on the water.

Sixty-seven

You all must be praying up a storm, right?" Skylar's green eyes shone beneath her short auburn hair. "I mean, I'm surrounded by angels. The guards are polite and the inmates seem normal." She laughed. "Normal to me, anyway, and you know how that goes."

Max chuckled with her and Claire smiled. The girl's attitude amazed her to no end.

"And you two. I can't believe you flew up here for a twenty-minute visit through Plexiglas." She touched the barrier between them as she spoke into the phone, their only audible connection.

Claire winked. "Max owed me a trip to San Francisco."

He bumped her shoulder and spoke into the receiver they shared. "We would've come anyway."

Skylar's smile was sad. Claire fumed to herself. Marlie and David Rockwell, residents of the city, had not yet visited their daughter. Their excuse? The narrow window of opportunity to make it to the jail did not work for them. They would be at her hearing, however.

Skylar said, "Is Kevin on his way home?"

They had spoken on the phone since Jenna's arrival in Germany, so she already knew the specifics of Kevin's injury.

Max said, "Yes. They're scheduled to arrive late tonight. We hope to see him Monday or Tuesday."

Claire added, "Jenna sounds upbeat. She's officially on leave for the remainder of the school year to be with him. If it works out in the spring, she can sub in schools on the base. She's already an expert on amputees." Claire felt a jolt of disbelief whenever she said that word. "Kevin's mother arrived. She's staying at the hacienda."

Skylar chuckled. "Indio told me stories about the woman."

Max said, "All true. I had to make my mother promise to be on her best behavior."

"I can't wait for Indio to try out her best behavior with my mom." Skylar wrinkled her nose. "What about Danny?"

Claire waited for Max to respond, but he nudged her to do it. "Danny's in Australia, surfing." She shrugged. "He talked to Lexi and said he'd keep us posted on his whereabouts but not to expect him home anytime soon. I'm sure Lexi held back some of their conversation. They've always done that."

Max said, "The bottom line is he needs time alone to sort through whatever. Jenna says he's either having a late adolescent identity crisis or an early midlife crisis."

"Max." Claire admonished with her tone. He and Jenna could strip an oak clean of its leaves by the force of their sarcasm.

Skylar said, "He's hurting. But he'll be okay. He's got you two for parents."

Max chuckled. "You really don't have to make points with us, Skylar. We'll come visit again."

"I'm serious. He has healthy roots in you and Ben and Indio. You've learned the balance of holding close and letting go."

Claire still wondered about that. She supposed she had a better grip on it than Skylar's parents, who never held their youngest close. Or Kevin's mother, who held her son too close because his father had left the family.

Max said, "Is the lawyer working out?"

"Hector is great. He's got *Law and Order* written all over him. Thank you again."

"You're welcome. Where do things stand?"

"The plea bargain negotiations are almost done. The FBI interviewed me. I have information they need to convict Fin and some others." She blew out a breath. "In exchange they'll reduce my sentence."

"To what?" Max asked.

She shrugged. "Depends on the judge."

"If it's not enough, we'll appeal—"

"Max." Skylar smiled. "Chill. It's in God's hands. It's only by His grace I don't have to serve the maximum sentence. I am just so happy I get to plead guilty."

Max shook his head. "You are nuttier than a fruitcake."

She laughed. "Be serious now for a minute. I have a question. There's a chance they could send me to a federal center near Los Angeles."

Claire gasped. "Skylar, you'd be close to us! We can come visit!"

Tears glistened in Skylar's eyes.

Max said, "What's the question?"

It took her a moment to respond. "Claire answered it. I was hoping it was all right if we asked for that. Visitors can come on weekends and actually sit in a room together. Hugs are even allowed. I wouldn't want you to feel obligated to come or anything, but . . ." Her voice trailed off.

Claire dug in her pocket for a tissue.

Max said, "Skylar, you know us better by now, right? You know we love you."

She nodded. "It's unconditional, isn't it?"

"Yep," he said. "Totally."

Sixty-eight

Seated beside her attorney Hector, aka Perry Mason, listening to the swish of the judge's robes and muffled coughs of spectators behind her, Skylar could have sworn she was on a movie set. The scent of old polished wood reminded her, however, that the situation was for real.

Her parents had opted to visit her the previous evening and skip today's high-profile public hearing. No big deal.

She sighed to herself. Yes, it was a big deal. Hector had told her it was a big deal. Claire and Max had told her with their expressive eyes that it was a big deal. Her heart told her that it was a big deal.

God, are You here?

She slowed her breathing and imagined Jesus standing behind them, one forearm on Hector's shoulder, the other on hers, speaking softly about how He had everything under control.

The big deal lay not so much in her mom and dad's absence, but in her recognition that they had indeed hurt her beyond measure most of her life.

At the jail last night they had been allowed to sit with her for a short while. Their hugs had been stiff, their teasing silly, their sage advice even sillier.

"Annie," her dad said, "you got a good one. Hector Laredo has a solid reputation. You're cooperating with the FBI, right?"

"Completely."

"That's the sensible thing to do. You understand why we can't be here tomorrow? I do a lot of work with the city."

She had nodded. "Maybe I can change my last name before things get started. Again. Officially this time."

"It's already in the papers." That was her mother's astute observation.

Talk about a disconnect. Their conversation never made it beyond that level of skimming the surface. But then why should it after all these years?

Skylar began to see them as two hurting souls. They had aged. The years of alcohol abuse and pot smoking had caught up to them. A sadness settled into her heart. Indio would probably clap with glee and tell her she might as well start praying for her parents now. It was going to happen eventually.

She didn't. Not yet. Maybe after the hearing.

In the courtroom now she strained her ears to hear what Jesus was saying. Maybe that He loved her?

She glanced at the profile of the solid man beside her . . . at the wise-looking, silver-haired woman judge . . . at the federal prosecutor's smooth face . . . at the FBI agent's teddy-bear appearance . . .

She most definitely was not on a movie set. Too much kindness pervaded the place. Too much tilted in her favor.

Mercy. Yes, that's what it was. Mercy, sweet and thick as molasses, protecting her soul. No matter what they all decided was her future, nothing could take that away.

Sixty-nine

The day they buried Uncle BJ's remains in the military cemetery in Pt. Loma, Jenna attended the memorial service by herself. As much progress as her strong husband had made in five weeks, the long day and rough terrain would have been too much for Kevin.

Except for Skylar, he had caught up with the family. Erik took Rosie to meet him; Lexi took Nathan; Papa and Indio took Tuyen. He'd always loved the Beaumonts and thought the new additions perfect. He seemed more than ever able to receive the love they poured onto him. His first visit from the hospital would be the hacienda. Her mother already promised to cook his favorite meal.

A clear, blue December sky and a tangible sense of release mitigated the sadness of the occasion. The Navy did their whole bit with the missing man flyover for a fallen pilot.

Tuyen stood proudly and received the flag that had draped the coffin. Papa had one arm around his Vietnamese granddaughter and one around Nana. Max and Claire cried through it all. Beth Russell was there with her husband, who seemed like a really nice guy. Danny was still in Australia. Lexi and Erik were there with Nathan and Rosie, both all but members of the Beaumont family. Skylar, of course, couldn't come, but Lexi had been to see her, and she'd sent her prayers.

Everyone was talking about prayers.

After the ceremony people lingered. It was a beautiful setting overlooking San Diego Bay and the downtown area. Jenna had driven herself in order to return to Kevin as soon as possible, but she needed a private moment with Beth Russell, the enigma who had tried to tell her how to make it.

They walked along the narrow road.

"Jenna, dear heart." Like before, the petite woman oozed compassion. "Tell me how you're doing."

"Better than the last time we talked."

Beth's eyebrows rose. "Despite all that's happened." It was a statement, not a question. "Then God has been drawing you to Himself."

"He has." Jenna shut her eyes briefly. Publicly recognizing God's hand in her life felt less and less awkward the more she did it. Still, though, she had to fight down brief attacks of embarrassment. "I have a friend, Amber, who helps me see how God works in my life. Kevin and I have a counselor who is a believer. Kevin, like me, was always more on the independent side."

"You had a nodding acquaintance with faith?"

"Exactly. Interesting how a trauma can kick-start you in a whole different direction."

"I believe God lets us walk paths that are best suited to our own personalities. He knows what will sharpen our hearing to better hear Him."

"He's given us hearing aids, too, then." *Thank You, Lord, for that.* "We've been through . . . Beth, I didn't do it your way. I failed miserably. I-I cheated on Kevin."

Wordlessly, Beth took her hand and held it as they continued strolling.

"I confessed it to Kevin." The horror and pain of that moment haunted her.

"How is he?"

"Okay. The counselor wasn't sure of the timing. How much more could my poor husband take after losing a limb? But our marriage is a major part of our learning to live in Kevin's new reality. It had to come out. He cried. He's angry. That's lessening slowly. He's struggling to understand forgiveness. He has moments of wanting to beat up the guy. He's had extra sessions with the counselor. But he loves me. I don't know why, but he does. He refuses to quit on us."

Beth squeezed her hand. "He won't quit. You won't quit. And God won't quit. You'll get through it."

Jenna nodded.

"Have you forgiven him?"

"For-for what?"

"For leaving you vulnerable. For getting injured."

"I hadn't thought about it that way."

"You will now. Trust God to give you the strength to let it all go. Do you remember the sycamore tree in your grandparents' courtyard? The one with the black streak and the new growth?"

"Yes."

"You have been scorched, but the new growth has already sprouted. May I come meet your Kevin before I leave town?"

"Really? I would love for him to meet you."

Beth smiled. "I like to meet people I've been praying for."

Prayers again.

Jenna didn't want to consider where she'd be without them.

Seventy

Indio set her teacup on the table beside her rocker with a decided thump. "We've got BJ home, and Kevin. Now we need to get Danny and Skylar back."

Claire sipped her tea and gazed out the window at the rain. Christmas was in six days. She had turned down guest requests to spend the holidays at the Hideaway. Not this year, she had told them. She wanted it quiet for her son-in-law, who'd been injured in the war. And besides that, she thought to herself, she was doing a little gathering. Danny and Skylar had used up all her surrendering energies for the year. She was reserving enough guest rooms for everyone to have a place to sleep overnight, including Rosie's father.

She sighed "Indio, I was doing just fine until you said that. I miss Danny and Skylar something awful. But there's no way Skylar can leave prison. I haven't even prayed for Danny's return because he needs this time away. I can give that to him. Just let me enjoy the ones who will be here."

Indio chuckled. "Hit a nerve, did I?"

"Yes, I guess you did. Why does that make you giddy?"

Indio laughed out loud. "Because it means God is at work!"

Claire rolled her eyes. "Let's just slow it down for a bit, shall we?"

"What?"

"Nothing."

"Listen, I've been praying since Thanksgiving about our couples. I asked God to bring Danny home for Christmas, to shorten Skylar's stay, and to give Jenna and Kevin a baby. Did you know they can have babies? That Kevin is, you know, functioning in that way?"

"You asked?"

"Didn't you?"

Claire gaped at her mother-in-law.

"And I prayed oodles of blessings on the other couples. They're all just so right for each other. Even that odd boy Hawk with Tuyen."

"Amen. Can I get you some more tea or anything?"

"You're changing the subject, dear. Now, pay attention. If God wants to send an earthquake to the detention center and break Skylar out of it, He will."

"Indio! You didn't ask Him to—"

"No, not specifically. I'm only thinking of what He could do. If He wants to upset the entire penal system so the paperwork releases her this week, He will."

"Skylar is adamant about serving her time."

Indio swatted the air. "She has a thing or two to learn about grace. The point is, are you with me?"

"In believing God can do anything? Sure." *Whatever. Just hit the brakes and end this crazy ride.*

"Good." Indio rocked, an expression of smugness on her face. "Let's just sit here and expect God to do something."

"Close enough to hitting the brakes," Claire muttered to herself and went over to the oven to check on a batch of cookies. When the phone rang she froze, the cookie sheet in her hand.

Indio clapped. "That didn't take long."

Claire set down the pan and picked up the phone, surprised at a twinge of anxiety. The caller ID read *Private*.

"Hello?"

"Mom, it's me." Danny.

Claire pulled out the desk chair and sank onto it. "Hi!" A giggle started somewhere deep in her chest. She held it in.

"Surprise! I'm in L.A."

She grinned. "No way."

"Yeah. I'll be there late tomorrow night. I'm staying over here so I can . . . so I can visit Skylar tomorrow. They have Sunday visiting hours, don't they?"

"Yes, yes they do. That's great, Danny. I'm glad to hear that." They chatted for a few minutes about mundane things. Claire said a silent prayer of thanks that Skylar had already—in faith—put Danny's name on her approved visitors list.

She told her son good-bye and turned to Indio.

Her mother-in-law laughed and clapped her hands again. "All you had to do was ask Him."

Seventy-one

The security rigmarole at the prison far surpassed any airport's.

Understandable, Danny thought, but it threw him for a loop. What was he getting himself into besides the room for visitors?

At first glance, he didn't quite recognize Skylar. Because the woman's vibes struck him as familiar, though, he took a second look.

Her hair was short, its natural auburn color grown out to the very ends, which may have been three inches from her scalp. Her freckles were more pronounced, as if they'd come out to see for themselves the unusual surroundings.

"Hi." Her smile wouldn't stay put.

He felt his own slip likewise. "Hi."

"Gotta ask something right off. Are you here to tell me to get lost?"

He shook his head. Odd choice of words.

"Do you think our conversation will lead to a hug?"

"I-it might."

"Two are allowed per visit. One right now, one when you leave. I wouldn't want to waste a hug."

"Skylar." He stepped to her and wrapped his arms around her. She felt smaller to him, but so solid. So blessedly solid. "Okay if I still call you that?"

She nodded. "I prefer it."

Other people around them greeted one another, people in street clothes and women in blue denim. Hugs. Murmured words. Boisterous hellos. Children subdued.

Skylar took his hand and led him to a bench on a patio. Beyond it was a small playground where mommies in blue denim took the kids to play.

His time with Skylar would be short, less than thirty minutes. He didn't want to waste one by looking around or asking her unnecessary questions.

They sat.

"Sky, I brought you a couple of books. They confiscated them. Said you would get them eventually."

"Thanks."

"They're about Australia."

She nodded, her clear green eyes never leaving his. Her hand still held his. Evidently hand-holding was permitted.

"I can't believe you're here, Danny. I made myself believe you would never come. That way I wouldn't be so disappointed."

"It was time. I should have written, but . . . I'm sorry I ran out on you."

She huffed a noise of disbelief. "You didn't owe me anything."

"Except love. That's all we're to owe each other."

"I should know what book that's in."

He smiled. "New Testament somewhere."

"I'll look it up." She smiled back at him.

"Please forgive me."

"Already done, dude."

They used up several moments just looking at each other.

"How are you?" he asked.

"Great. Food is . . . mediocre. Guards are surprisingly cordial for the most part. I have a few new friends. I told your parents that their prayers have put angels in place. My experience is not like an ugly prison movie."

Thank God. Thank You, God.

"The hard part," she went on, "is . . ."

"What?"

"Being locked up." She shrugged. "'Course that's the whole point, isn't it?"

"I guess."

"I miss trees and rocks. I miss cooking. I miss your family. I miss you, Wally Cleaver, something awful."

He rubbed his thumb across the back of her hand. She used her other to brush tears from her cheeks. He wasn't sure how to sit and watch her cry and do nothing.

He took a deep breath. "I miss you too."

She eyed him as if she didn't quite believe that.

"I didn't want to, but I do, Sky. I do."

She sniffed.

He pressed on. "Jenna told me I needed to get over myself. She was right. I'm so arrogant. I really don't know why you ever hung out with me. So I went surfing. I told God I wanted to hear His voice, but for a long time I did all the talking. I told Him I couldn't love you. Man, what would my friends think? When we got married, what would people we meet think? How would we tell the kids their mom was a felon? Of course we might be fifty years old by the time you get out, then I wouldn't have to worry about that part.

"The real question was how could God do this to me? Set me up with the likes of a radical who changed her name and was arrested by the feds? Such an obvious black-and-white issue for the likes of cocky me. Dump the chick. She's bad news."

She gazed at him as if mesmerized.

"Waves in Australia are awesome. I got knocked around a lot. Got some of the hubris knocked out of me. Especially the time some other guys had to get me to shore."

"Are you okay?" The concern in her voice was nice.

He touched his head. "Bruise has gone down. I was only out for a few minutes."

"Danny!"

"No worries. I'm here, aren't I? Eventually I reached a quiet space and started listening. I saw Him in the waves, in the sky, the coastline. I began to know like never before that He loves me. That I'm to keep focused on him, not the guy next to me. Or the girl."

She waited.

"The girl next to me makes me laugh. She challenges me to do better, to think more, to give more. And now life seems pretty much boring and pointless unless I can share it with her."

"You've lost your mind."

"Nah. Just my heart. So, here's my plan. I'm moving up here—"

"Danny, no. Don't change your life for me."

"Didn't you hear a word I just said? I love you, Skylar. I want to be near you. For now that means visiting on the weekends. I'd rather not drive two hundred miles every weekend and stay in a motel."

"'For now' means six years. Six, Danny! You can't live your life around weekends, hours away from the ocean you love—"

"It's not several hours, and why not?"

She didn't reply.

"Laue, the guy working for me, is doing great. I did work some long-distance. I'll keep doing that from up here. His percent of the profit has grown by leaps and bounds, but he deserves it. The only reason why I wouldn't move is if you wouldn't let me visit. If you wouldn't receive the love I'm offering you. Why wouldn't you receive it?"

She blinked quickly, but tears still fell. "I can't take your life from you."

"You're not. I'm giving it."

She took a ragged breath.

"So what do you say, Sky?"

"I say I love you," she whispered.

He closed his eyes and his heart beat loudly in his ears.

"But."

He looked at her.

"You have to promise me that when you need to surf, you'll surf. When you need to see old friends, you'll go. When you—"

"Yeah, yeah. I get the picture. Now promise me something."

"Okay."

"You won't leave without telling me."

A slow smile spread across her face. Her eyes sparkled in the old way. "I promise."

He squeezed her hand. "What's the kissing rule?"

"When you come and when you leave."

"Next week we won't waste that either."

Seventy-two

Max, what is this?" Claire towel-dried her hair and eyed the tray he carried into the master suite. She saw her coffee mug, a toasted bagel spread with cream cheese, a linen napkin—and a ring-sized box wrapped in red foil and gold ribbon.

"You're still wary about my gifts?" He smiled.

"I guess I am." She put the towel on the floor, tightened her robe belt, and sat on the love seat. After thirty years of receiving gifts based on his guilt, it was difficult not to default to skepticism when she saw a jewelry box from him.

He set the tray on a table and sat beside her. "Just remember the gift I gave you a year ago Thanksgiving."

It had been a note inside a small box. "You asked me to remarry you." She smiled. "That was a good one."

"And last Valentine's Day?"

"Cruise tickets for our honeymoon. That was good too."

"So get over it already. We are in healed territory when it comes to my gift giving. I am not working out any guilt via a gift." He leaned over and kissed the tip of her nose. "Merry Christmas, sweetheart."

"I don't need anything, Max."

"What do you want?"

"Skylar home and a grandchild."

He laughed.

She had seen gift boxes from Max for her under the tree in the sala. Most likely they contained a pretty sweater—winter at the hacienda was colder than where they used to live near the coast—and a novel she would have mentioned to him in passing at one time. Perhaps a skirt. He had been paying very close attention lately.

He gave her the small box. "Not to rush you, but Rosie and her dad are already in the kitchen. Jenna and Kevin are on their way."

"Rosie and Esteban are here? It's only eight o'clock!"

"Potluck to him means working in your kitchen."

She chuckled. The chef and owner of a Mexican restaurant adored her state-of-the-art kitchen. "Is this his coffee?"

"Yes."

Christmas could wait. She reached for the mug and savored her first sip. The schedule called for the closest family members to gather for brunch midmorning. They would then open gifts, play games, and relax. Others would join them for dinner, including Hawk and Amber Ames. Some would spend the night in guest rooms.

"Oh, Max." She gushed. "We are so blessed. I can't imagine anything I want—"

"Just open the box," he growled and took the mug from her.

She laughed and began unwrapping. Inside the first box was a ring box and inside that lay two neatly folded papers. Curious, she opened the one that looked like a receipt and grinned. "Season tickets to the symphony. *Two* of them?" She looked at him.

"I'll be going with you."

"You hate the symphony."

His brown eyes twinkled. "That was the old Max. I'm ready to learn how to appreciate it. I want to."

"Thank you."

"You are welcome."

She unfolded the other paper. He had written a note. "Our new home lacks two things: a grandbaby and a baby grand. I can only give you one."

Claire gasped. They had sold their old upright piano with the house. There had been just too much to put in order at the hacienda.

Some parts of her life went by the wayside. Except for occasionally pulling out her violin, music was one of them.

Max said, "It'll be delivered tomorrow. I've got your old music group lined up to play here next week."

"Oh, Max!" She scooted across the cushion and threw her arms around his neck. "Thank you."

"It was a good one?" He kissed her neck.

"It was a good one."

Later that day, Claire fell silent often just to feast her eyes on the scene before her. Norman Rockwell couldn't have portrayed a more evocative family Christmas gathering.

They had it all, from decorated tree to toasty fire to a mess of opened boxes and wrappings. From grandparents to the orphaned grandchild from Vietnam to those few friends who might one day become family. From the wounded war veteran to his wife setting his crutches on the floor beside his chair. And the one sorely missed—the one out of town who could not be with them—waited on the other end of the phone line.

Max had answered the phone, accepted the collect-call charges, and immediately held it out to Danny. "It's Skylar."

Danny planned to see her the next day during visiting hours. He tore across the room now and caught Max's toss of the phone midair. "H'lo! Skylar!" The rest of them pretended not to eavesdrop.

They didn't have to do so for long. Danny whooped loud enough for the horses to hear.

He turned to them, a grin stretched across his face. "Her sentence got reduced!" He spoke again into the phone. "Yeah. Okay. Yeah. That's great. I will. I love you, too, Sky."

Indio was clapping and shouting. "Woo-hoo!"

Max said, "What happened, Danny?"

"Well." He paused, obviously struggling to pull himself together.

"God happened. They arrested Fin Harrod and a couple others in Nevada. One thing led to another. Skylar's attorney and the judge got involved. Her time was reduced to three and a half years."

Claire didn't know how her heart could leap and sink at the same time, but it did. Three and a half years was, of course, less than six years. Maybe the good behavior aspect would make an impact, too, and she would get early parole. Still . . . Skylar wasn't coming home tomorrow. Or not even next month.

Indio caught her eye. "Merry Christmas from the Father."

Claire nodded.

Cut!" Erik shouted. "Cut!"

Everyone stopped in their work of cleaning up the sala to look at him.

He was on his hands and knees, pulling something out from under the couch. "We are not finished with this scene. It's another gift. To . . . let's see . . ." He peered closely at the slender box. "To Rosie! From no name!" Grinning, he gave it to her.

Claire smiled to herself. She was perfectly content to have Erik not living with them. His dramatic tendencies had worn on her as a young mom. It was right for those days to be over.

Rosie looked at Erik suspiciously. "You just happened to find this under the couch? This very minute?"

"Yes, Officer," he said in his deepest, most sarcastic, voice.

She laughed. "Okay, okay. I will put the cop to rest."

"Attention, everyone! Rosie is opening a gift. Let's show her due respect here. Come on, come on. Have a seat."

Amid laughter and protests, Rosie sat back down and opened the gift. As a DVD inside a plastic case came into view, Claire wondered if this was, at long last, the mysterious video Erik and Nathan had been working on.

Rosie stared at it. "It's a disk without a label."

Erik huffed. "You promised to put the cop to rest."

She laughed.

Danny said, "Rosie, you have got to quit encouraging his tedious witticisms."

"Well, I kind of like them." She walked over to the television cabinet and opened its doors. While she set things up, Erik directed the others to hush.

Within moments background music played and the television screen displayed opening credits. *Rosa Maria Delgado: A Tribute. Created and produced by Erik Beaumont, with all my heart and some help from Nathan Warner.*

Rosie said, "Did I die?"

Her father harrumphed. He was a large man and did it well. "Rosita!" he snapped. "Have some respect for this gringo."

She smiled.

The video continued. There was a biography complete with old photographs of Rosie as a little girl with her now-deceased mother. Esteban talked through much of it. Family friends were interviewed. Then the Beaumont interviews began. Along with Claire's rambling—Erik had not cut a word of it—the others spoke about meeting Rosie. While Claire had reminisced about her time with Rosie after the shooting, Max and his parents described the incredible moment she brought Tuyen into their home for the first time. Danny and Lexi remembered Rosie as a kind policewoman who offered to help them in spite of the fact she had arrested their brother.

Like Claire, they all revealed a profound fondness for her. Danny stated solemnly that although she revealed a serious lack of judgment by dating Erik, he was grateful for the attention she gave the hopeless, troubled man.

Esteban took center stage again. He faced the camera, his native Mexican features drawn together in a somber pose. "Rosita, the following message has been approved of and paid for by me, your father."

"Not paid for." Erik's voice was in the background.

"But the words flow well, don't you think?" He grinned.

The scene was replaced by Erik seated on the same couch. He wore a dark suit and red tie from his TV anchorman days and smiled the killer smile that accounted for his 80-percent female audience.

"Rosie," he said. The camera followed him as he slid onto one knee on the floor. "I love you dearly. Will you marry me, please?" He held out a ring. The camera focused in on a diamond sparkle, and then the screen darkened, the music faded.

The group was hushed. Claire glanced around through her tears and saw Lexi, Jenna, Tuyen, and Indio wiping their own. Nathan, Kevin, and Danny grinned. Ben looked as smug as if he'd thought the whole thing up himself. Max took her hand.

Erik dug into his jeans pocket and knelt before Rosie. Like on the video, he held out a diamond.

Rosie appeared to be in a state of shock. "You wanted witnesses, didn't you?"

He shook his head. "Backup. We all love you."

"I suppose if I marry you, I get the whole family?"

He grinned. "Yeah."

"Then yes." A smile lit up her face. She sniffed, cried, and giggled.

A collective "Aww" went round the room and then pandemonium erupted with cheers, hugs, and a much-admired diamond sliding onto Rosie's finger.

Claire melted into Max's embrace and whispered a prayer of thanks. Erik had really taken the step she feared he might never have found strength to take. And Rosie was ready to meet him in it.

Would Nathan and Lexi get to that place? And Tuyen? Hawk was a comfort to her. Could he settle into marriage?

Kevin's physical healing set records. He would get his prostheses in a couple weeks. Skin grafting would be done on his left arm and make the burns less obvious. Emotionally, though, would he and Jenna ever be ready for a child?

And Danny and Skylar. Could any more bricks have been thrown onto their path?

Max kissed the top of her head. "You're thinking too much."

"What?"

"I can hear the gears clicking and clacking from here."

She smiled. He knew her too well.

How did Indio do it? Steer the tandem, serve as matriarch, cover them all with consistent prayer—and yet not be always tied up in knots?

She watched her mother-in-law hugging Rosie, struck again with the woman's peace in the midst of chaos and uncertainty. "God is good" would be pouring from her lips into Rosie's ear.

God was indeed good. And He was the One who steered the tandem from up front.

Claire hugged Max and consciously took her foot off the imaginary brake. She wasn't in charge.

Epilogue

Seven months later

Few things unhinged Jenna Beaumont Mason. She could do cool, calm, and collected. She could do serene. She could go with the flow. She could chill.

Honestly, she was married to a Marine.

But try as she might, she could not talk around the lump in her throat.

Kevin smiled down at her, his eyes laughing beneath the bill of a Padres cap. They sat on bleachers in the Shamu stadium at Sea World on a hot summer day with thousands of other people. Far below, in the clear pools, enormous orcas swam gracefully.

He said, "You'll be fine."

"I'll cry. I am crying."

"That's okay." He waggled his brows. "You're not worried I'll fall flat on my face?"

She shook her head. Kevin moved with amazing agility with his prostheses. Artificial limbs. Plural. He needed three of them to make a thigh, a knee, a calf, an ankle, a foot.

"You're not embarrassed about the way I look, I know that."

People stared at his prosthetic leg whenever he wore shorts. They stared at his left arm's odd color and texture whenever he wore short

Reading Group Guide

In keeping with the other titles in the Safe Harbor series, *A Time to Surrender* references concepts found in Ecclesiastes 3. There is a time to uproot, to throw away, to lose, to give up. These all speak of surrendering.

1. Discuss what the characters give up in this story. It may be material things, attitudes, strongholds, or something else.

   - What does Claire as a mother surrender?
   - Jenna as a young wife?
   - Danny as a confident-in-his-viewpoint believer?
   - Skylar as a keeper of secrets?
   - Ben as the father of an MIA son whose fate has been learned?

2. In all their surrendering, in putting off their old selves, the characters move into the reality of the theme verse taken from Ephesians 4:22–24 "You were taught . . . to put off your old self . . . to be made new . . . to put on the new self."

   - By the end of the book, what is the new Jenna like?
   - Danny?
   - Skylar?

3. What sorts of things have you surrendered, given up, or thrown away in your own life?

4. How were you changed by that action?

5. Is there something you sense you need to surrender, to hand over to God in order for Him to clothe you in something new?

6. What do you think about Claire's statement that a "safe harbor" is not a landlocked body of water but an open area where people are free to come and go? How might that describe the "safe harbor" God is always offering to us in His presence?

Reader comments are always welcome.
Please write to us in care of Thomas Nelson publishers,
by e-mail to sallyjohnbook@aol.com,
or visit www.sally-john.com.

About the Authors

Sally John is the author of more than ten books, including the popular Other Way Home series and In a Heartbeat series. Illinois natives, Sally and her husband, Tim, live in Southern California. The Johns have two grown children, a daughter-in-law, and two granddaughters.

D_r. Gary Smalley, one of the foremost experts on family relationships, has written or cowritten more than fifty books, based on more than thirty-five years of experience as a teacher and counselor. A best-selling and award-winning author, Smalley has appeared on hundreds of local radio and television shows, including Oprah, Larry King Live, Fox & Friends, and NBC's Today. He and his wife, Norma, have been married forty-two years.